DEATH
on
WINDMILL
WAY

DEATH
on
WINDMILL
WAY

A Hamptons Murder Mystery

By
CARRIE DOYLE

DUNEMERE
Books

New York
San Francisco

PUBLISHED BY DUNEMERE BOOKS

Copyright © 2016 by Caroline M. Doyle
Cover illustration © 2016 by Jill De Haan
Book and cover design by Jenny Kelly

The characters and events portrayed in this book are fictitious.
Any similarity to real persons, living or dead, is coincidental
and not intended by the author.

ISBN: 978-0-9972701-4-3

DEATH
on
WINDMILL
WAY

Prologue

DECEMBER

"Oh, it's you," said Gordon Haslett, his voice tinged with its usual irritation. "You're always sneaking up on me. Drives me nuts. You just appear like a ghost. Trying to scare the hell out of me?"

Gordon propped the rake against the tree and wiped the sweat off his brow with the back of his hand, leaving a smear of dirt along his face. This small dose of physical labor had intensified his breathing, causing his chest to rise and fall dramatically under his vest. After taking a few gulps from a bottle of water, he examined his visitor critically. "So are you going to help me or what? Don't just stand there watching me. We both know this isn't *my* damn job."

He turned and resumed raking the stack of wet leaves that were blocking the door to the garden shed. They were soggy from the rain and stacked together in sad little clumps. The air smelled moldy, of musty earth. Gordon had apparently been out there for a while, as the brick path leading upward to the shed had already been cleared. He turned gruffly when he felt a tap on his shoulder.

"What?" he barked.

His visitor held out a handkerchief, and motioned towards the beading sweat on Gordon's forehead. Gordon grabbed the cloth.

"Thanks."

He pressed the handkerchief firmly to his head and aggressively wiped his entire face.

"What the hell?" yelped Gordon, suddenly dropping the handkerchief and taking a step back. "Damn, something stung me!"

Gordon began furiously slapping his face, then stopped and glanced around in confusion. He held one index finger to the side of his face. His skin was burning hot. Suddenly his entire face began to swell, and his eyes were enveloped in clouds of puffiness.

"What the . . ." He couldn't finish his sentence. Instead, Gordon clutched his throat and dropped to his knees.

"Go get help," he whispered.

His visitor nodded. And then turned and walked as slowly as possible back to the inn, and waited.

1

OCTOBER
(Ten months later)

It was a glorious fall night in East Hampton. The sky was inky black with thin clouds racing past a full moon, and the ancient trees along the village streets cast long shadows in the silver moonlight. In the distance, the ocean waves murmured, providing a romantic background soundtrack. The air outside was crisp, not too chilly, but with just enough kick to necessitate roaring fires in the Windmill Inn's public rooms. It was a cozy Friday evening; just how innkeeper Antonia Bingham had imagined it would be when she dreamed of her move to the East Coast from California. Combined with the medley of delicious smells wafting from the kitchen, the weather and atmosphere gave Antonia a sense of great satisfaction.

The dining room of the Windmill Inn was by no means filled to capacity, but for the first time in the six weeks since Antonia had opened the restaurant, half of the tables were occupied. She had heard, of course, that it takes a while for new restaurants to gain momentum, particularly when they are replacing old restaurants that had reputations for terrible service and inedible food. But still, those first few nights when the seats remained empty she had felt completely disheartened. Not to mention embarrassed: the sound of every ice cube clinking in a glass seemed magnified and the busboys were too eager to replace half-eaten rolls, just to have something to do. But gradually—very gradually—reservations had picked up, with locals and weekenders popping by, eager to try a new place, and more guests booking rooms at the inn and venturing down to try Antonia's home-cooked meals.

Finally, in Antonia's mind, the future was beginning to look a little brighter. She hoped she wasn't delusional; she was by nature an optimist who chose to look at the bright side of things. However, Antonia's optimism made her prone to bad judgment calls, resulting in infrequent but spectacular failures. "Older and wiser" was one of her mottos, and with her recent purchase of the inn, Antonia was hoping that she could put some of the knowledge and experience that she had acquired in her thirty-five years (twelve years of catering!) to good use. She just needed to avoid past mistakes.

Now, as Antonia roamed the sleek navy and white dining room, she surveyed it critically. It was a large space that seated sixty-five diners and the décor was comfortable, while also streamlined and uncluttered. Whereas Antonia had chosen to make the rest of the inn feel cozy-formal with antiques, lots of prints and colored fabrics, she had given the restaurant a bright and crisp interior. The walls were painted eggshell white and held large canvases of modern art, mostly bright abstracts, but a few small, individually lit oil paintings as well. The floors had been stained a dark walnut wood, brushed smoothly and evenly. In the front of the room, by the maître d' station, was a dark azure lacquered bar. Its eight barstools had button-tufted backs and sides studded with pewter nail head trim. Beyond that were a dozen freestanding tables set formally with starched white linens, white china and blue Murano goblets.

When she was decorating the inn, Antonia had sat on dozens of chairs in an effort to find the most comfortable; one that would encourage diners to linger and order more courses. The winners were softly rounded and upholstered in blue, with gently sloping arms and maple-stained legs. In the back of the room, beyond the swinging door to the kitchen was a nook housing four booths, their banquettes covered in in cobalt vinyl with white piping. Antonia had debated whether or not the booths made the place feel too casual, but tonight they had allowed her to successfully accommodate a last minute party of seven. Smiling benevolently at the happy group, Antonia knew she had made the right decision in adding the booths. They made the restaurant feel complete.

Tonight Antonia was clad in her best black satin dress, replete with a plunging neckline to both accentuate her ample breast and move everyone's eyes away from her widening girth. (*Ah, the havoc that working with food wreaks on your waistline,* Antonia often despaired.) She had on the lowest high heels that she could find, as anything even a half an inch higher caused major wobbling in the manner of a drunken streetwalker. It was the last thing Antonia would have liked to have been wearing—sweats, elastic waisted ruffled skirts, soft cardigans and Crocs were more her speed—but her manager had told her that she needed to "sex it up and work the room" in order to encourage first-time customers to become repeat customers. She hardly thought that her looking all dolled up would entice diners, especially in this small town, but with all of her money on the line with the restaurant and inn, she agreed to do whatever had to be done for the bottom line. As a result, Antonia had pulled out all the stops tonight, blowing dry her glossy black hair until it fell in cascading waves down to her shoulders and even applying makeup. Her cupid's bow lips were deep red, her porcelain cheeks blushed pink and her already thick lashes fluttered darkly around her bright blue eyes.

"Another wonderful dinner, Antonia, thank you," said Joseph Fowler as he signed his check and flipped the leather-bound cardholder closed. He placed it on the table next to the small pumpkin centerpiece. After finishing the last sip of his sherry, he dabbed his mouth with the cloth napkin.

"Thank you, Joseph. You always make my day!" Antonia beamed at her favorite dinner guest.

Joseph was a renowned writer of historical fiction. He had been recently widowed when his wife of thirty-plus years died after a long bout with cancer. Joseph was Antonia's first customer at the restaurant, and for that she was eternally grateful, especially as he had turned out to be a tremendous cheerleader for her. An elegant man, with refined features (aquiline nose, arched eyebrows, chiseled cheekbones, impeccably combed silver hair) he always dressed in custom-fitted monogrammed dress shirts and a bowtie, cords or khakis (depending on the weather), and a beautiful tweed blazer. As he was still only in his early sixties, Antonia fervently hoped he would find romance again. It was too soon for her to play matchmaker but she had already targeted some of the ladies who came to tea at the inn as potential suitors. Should she mind her own business? Probably. But that wasn't really her style.

"Joseph, I'd love your feedback, what did you think of the truffled polenta with Gorgonzola? It's a new recipe I'm trying out. You can tell me honestly."

He smiled. "It was exquisite."

"I'm not fishing for compliments, are you sure?"

He patted her hand. "My dear, I would have it every night if I could."

"You know how to make a lady happy," she said, wagging her finger at him. "I'll take your word for it, but I still think it needs some tweaking—maybe a different herb. It says rosemary but I have to be honest, I'm not the biggest rosemary fan. It sort of tastes like shampoo, don't you think? I much prefer tarragon or sage. Even chervil. Thyme could work, but it's kind of wimpy. Well, we'll see . . ."

"My advice to you is don't over-think it. The best thing about your food is that you cook from the heart. And it shows."

"Well, I try."

Antonia motioned for Glen, the maitre d', to assist Joseph into his scooter. Joseph had suffered a bout of polio as a child and although he could walk with the assistance of crutches, in recent years he had primarily used a scooter to get around.

"There ya go, Mr. Fowler," said Glen in his strong Long Island accent. "I tell you, I could use one of these things to escape from the ladies."

Glen was attractive but in an unctuous, hair-gelled way, like Guido the Killer Pimp. A failed actor with an inflated ego, he was a high-maintenance employee but very good at charming women and making customers feel at home.

Joseph chuckled. "Well, I don't exactly have that problem."

"All in good time."

"Have a great night," said Antonia cheerily.

Joseph winked. "You too, my lady."

Antonia moved around the room to greet other guests and to solicit any suggestions they might have about the food. She enjoyed meeting people as much as she enjoyed cooking, and it was always an internal debate as to where she should spend more time. It was fun for her to find out where guests were from, and what their story was, but at the same time, she also adored her time in the kitchen, concocting her latest culinary adventure, darting about, plating dishes. If she could slice herself in half and do both she certainly wouldn't hesitate.

After sending off a cute couple that was visiting from New York City (house-hunting) she stopped off at Len and Sylvia Powers' table. Len headed up security at the Dune Club, a very fancy country club on the ocean, and his wife was a teacher. Tonight they had brought their son in to celebrate his twenty-fifth birthday.

"You've done an amazing job, Antonia, I tell you, just amazing. The inn looks gorgeous and the food is fabulous," said Sylvia Powers, her big cerulean eyes twinkling. She patted her mouth with her napkin, leaving a stain of the hot pink lipstick that was her trademark, then patted her stomach appreciatively. "I tell you, it is so wonderful that you brought this place back to life. And so quickly, what was it, only six months?" She didn't wait for an answer but continued, "I can't tell you how sad it was to see it fall into disrepair all the years Gordon Haslett owned it. What a mean guy! And that made the place mean. We stopped coming here long ago, didn't we Len?"

"Well you didn't really have a choice, Mom," said Matt, giving her a sly smile.

She frowned. "Nonsense. We had a choice. That business was all settled. Right, Len?"

Len Powers glanced up from his apple cheddar crisp, and looked around, dazed by the interruption. He was a large man, with a belly that arrived in a room ten seconds before he did. Everything about him was big and fleshy, from his bulbous nose to his ruddy cheeks and giant ears. "I can't talk! I don't want to tear myself away from this incredible dessert."

Sylvia laughed. "I already inhaled my dessert. I tell you, that chocolate caramel cake with the little dots of sea salt was majestic. This is our third time here and every time I sample some new yummies."

"Thank you," Antonia beamed.

"This may seem like a back-handed compliment but you

cook in a very homey style. The way I like to think I can cook, but actually can't. I like that it's not all that fancy new wave stuff—foams and edible flowers. That just sounds disgusting to me. Some of those cooking shows, I think, yuck! Fois Gras ice cream? Come on. When I have ice cream, I don't want meat in it. But I'm not a food snob. I just prefer food that tastes how it's supposed to. Don't mess with what ain't broke."

"Well, I'm so glad you liked it," replied Antonia. "And thank you for your kind words. I say to everyone I know that the biggest compliment they can give me is to spread the news around. I want everyone to know that there's a new sheriff in town, and the Windmill Inn is back in business."

"Oh everyone knows that already, Antonia," said Sylvia, chattering on. "East Hampton is a small town. Especially when the summer people are gone. Ah, the summer people! Did you know we call the season '100 days of hell'? Oh, they're not all bad, I'm joking. But it's nice to have the town back to ourselves, where we can get up in everybody's business! Ha, I'm joking again. But of course everyone knows that the inn changed hands when Gordon Haslett died. In fact, Matt was there—he's a paramedic." Sylvia gestured proudly at her son.

Antonia was having a hard time following Sylvia's dramatic stream-of-consciousness rambling. She looked to Matt for clarification.

Matt put down his fork and nodded. He had a pretty boy face composed of dainty features: a small straight nose, plump red lips, and thickly lashed eyes. There was also something morose and gloomy about his temperament that Antonia was certain thrilled girls who were attracted to the dark, broody types. Looking at his jolly, big-boned parents, it was hard to tell where Matt had come from.

"Yes, I was the first responder to the scene," he said solemnly and with an air of authority. "I arrived less than oh-five minutes after the call. But there was nothing I could do, he was already D.O.A."

"Well, I've no doubt you would have done everything you could have," said Antonia sympathetically. She patted his shoulder warmly. "But obviously there's not a whole lot you *can* do when someone suffers a massive heart attack and dies before you get there."

"Right," said Matt, nodding, his face oddly empty of emotion.

"*If* it was a heart attack," said Sylvia. She nudged her spoon into her husband's crisp and took a huge bite for herself.

"Mom," warned Matt, rolling his eyes. "Let's not go there."

Sylvia shrugged and put her hand to her lips to block the view of food while she talked with her mouth full. "Didn't you say, sweetie, that you thought he died of a bee sting?"

Matt squirmed uncomfortably. "Official cause of death was a heart attack."

"Yes, but one that was brought on by a bee sting," prompted Sylvia. She dove into her husband's dessert for another bite.

"Yes, I did suspect that," said Matt officiously. "He had a red welt on his cheek at the two o'clock position, and his face was inflamed concurrent with an allergic reaction. But that idea wasn't pursued."

"Why not?" asked Antonia, vaguely intrigued by this new information, gossip or not. She motioned for a busboy to refill the Powers' water glasses.

Matt rolled his eyes. "The family didn't want to. Didn't want an autopsy. But it was December, and who gets stung by a bee in December?" He was indignant.

Antonia nodded. "I guess that is strange."

"They thought I was an alarmist, being swayed by the whole reputation of the inn . . ." he continued.

"Um, Matthew . . ." his mother interrupted. She widened her eyes and shook her head.

Admonished, Matt abruptly stopped speaking. Sylvia shifted uncomfortably in her chair, and Len shoved a large bite of crisp into his mouth. Antonia glanced at each of them quizzically.

"What is the reputation of the inn?" she asked finally.

Matt looked past her at the wall. "Um, nothing, just an old superstition."

"What's the superstition?" pressed Antonia.

Sylvia sighed. "It's nothing, just a silly thing. And we all know that old stories like that are nothing more than stories. Someone wanted to concoct a ghost story and that's all it was."

"But what was it?" asked Antonia again.

"I wouldn't worry about it, dear," said Sylvia in a cool, reassuring voice (one that she probably used on her third graders at the John Marshall School). "I tell you, it's nothing."

"You can't leave me hanging!" Antonia said in a light voice, although underneath, her heart was racing. "Come on, now, help me out. I bought this place sight unseen eight months ago on the advice of my friend Genevieve. I moved all the way from Petaluma to East Hampton, a town that I had never stepped foot in. Then I poured every last penny I could to get it up and running. I have eight guestrooms and a restaurant, and a dozen full time employees. I need to know every facet of the inn's reputation so I know what I'm up against."

Antonia blinked her long lashes several times and smiled brightly, in an effort to alleviate the panic she was feeling. Ever since she'd bought the inn she had been experiencing moments of extreme nervousness and self-doubt, basically questioning her impulsivity. Had she made a mistake? Perhaps she should have been more suspicious of how quickly the sister of the deceased had accepted her low-ball offer. She had congratulated herself on a steal, but maybe she had been the one who was swindled? She wished she would have done more research, but she always became completely restless whenever she was in front of a computer. Honestly, she found the Internet to be a colossal waste of time in regards to everything excluding searching for recipes or antiques. But perhaps if she had taken time to Google Gordon Haslett's death she wouldn't be having this conversation.

The Powers family all glanced at each other uneasily. Finally Len spoke. He held his fork in the air, indicating he would be brief so that he could return to his dessert.

"The story about the Windmill Inn is that the owners die under suspicious circumstances. Now, it's just a story, makes the place more dramatic."

"I actually think one of the previous owners conjured it up just to attract some business," added Sylvia quickly. "I mean, I taught some of the kids of one of the owners, there was nothing there, oh dear, now wait . . ."

She stopped speaking, as if remembering something.

"Well is it true?" Antonia asked. "I mean, before Gordon Haslett, did the other owners die of suspicious circumstances?"

Sylvia and Len exchanged a look. "Well," began Sylvia. But she didn't finish her sentence.

Len cocked his head to the side, as if he was thinking, and finally shrugged.

"It's kind of true," said Matt finally.

"Kind of?" asked Antonia. "What does that mean?"

"I guess it means yes. Some of the owners of the inn have died under suspicious circumstances."

"Great," said Antonia weakly. She needed a drink.

2

The Windmill Inn was finally quiet at midnight. The diners had almost all left by ten-thirty, except for a last lingering couple who, judging from their body language, appeared to be on their third or fourth date. They stayed until eleven, after working out whether or not they would be retreating to their own homes or having a sleepover. Only three of the guest rooms at the inn were occupied and when Connie, the front desk receptionist, confirmed that everyone had retired for the evening, Antonia had locked all of the doors to the inn with the exception of the two in the kitchen.

It was Glen's responsibility to shut down the restaurant for the night but Antonia usually helped him out, since it was still early days. It was important for her to establish a hands-on approach from the get-go so the staff would know that she was firmly in control. And it was always important to keep track of the money. Other restaurateurs had told her that it was crucial to watch out for skimming, no matter how much you trusted your employees. They advised her to get a sense of how much was coming in so that she could sense if anything was going out that should not be.

Antonia and Glen went over the books, locked up the bar, and looked at the reservations for the following evening. While he ducked in to the office to print out the next day's menu, Antonia went into the kitchen. Juan and Albert, the busboy/dishwashers, were just finishing up when Antonia went into the staff changing room to switch out of her high heels and into her Crocs. When she returned they were leaving and she shut the back door behind them, pressing firmly to confirm the click of the latch. The staff had been having trouble with that door closing all the way; it was still warped from the summer heat. Often it would blow wide open and bang loudly against the wall, startling anyone who was standing next to it.

When Antonia went back to the dining room, Glen had returned with a stack of printed menus, which he placed on the maître d' stand. He turned off the lights and shrugged into his soft leather jacket. She walked with him back into the kitchen so he could exit from the side door. When he opened the door a gust of wind came flooding in.

"Wow, it's picking up out there," said Antonia.

"Yeah. You're lucky you don't have anywhere to drive to get to your bed."

"I know. Living at work does have its plusses."

"Oh, I forgot to mention, Antonia. This guy from a local

microbrewery came by tonight. I told him to come during the day since we don't order during dinner hour."

"Good idea. I'll let Marty handle it. Goodnight, now."

Marty was Antonia's sous chef and he was a lot tougher than she; she liked to let him deal with the vendors. Antonia firmly shut the door behind Glen and twisted the lock. She turned and glanced around the kitchen to make sure everything was in place. The glasses were drying on racks on the counter and all of the prep stations were wiped down. The pots and pans were hung neatly on their pegs. It was difficult to believe that just an hour ago this place had been buzzing. Antonia flicked off the big overhead lights and walked towards the pantry to do the same. It was quiet now, with only the hum of the two industrial dishwashers making a fuss. Antonia heard Glen start his car, then watched as his headlights flicked across the darkened ceiling when he exited.

Antonia walked back through the dimmed dining room for one last proprietary glance. She thought of all of the people who had come through the door of the inn over the last hundred and fifty years. Throughout much of the nineteenth century the Windmill Inn had housed a tannery in the barn out back; guests stayed in the main building while their saddles were treated. Were any of their ghosts lurking there now? Antonia shuddered; all she needed was a headless horseman! She glanced around at the shadowed tables. Antonia had always thought that empty restaurants looked a little eerie, as if the ghosts of the people who had just dined there somehow dissipated into thin air. She wondered if she was particularly on edge tonight having just heard the news that Gordon Haslett's death was somehow suspicious. Had previous innkeepers really met untimely fates? She pushed the thought out of her mind.

Instead of heading straight across to the small staff hallway that led to her apartment, Antonia made a right and walked towards the front door. While she had taken special care to sand down the floors in the dining room, the floors in the rest of the inn had been left more or less in their original state. Over the years they had buckled under the extreme seasonal oscillation between temperatures, and were squeaky and uneven. Antonia had placed a few Oriental carpet runners along the way, but they did nothing to contain the noise and tonight it seemed as if the floorboards creaked particularly loudly under her feet. The chandelier in the front hall was lit but dimly. Its light was the only one that seeped through the other public rooms.

Antonia turned left into the parlor to make sure that the staff had straightened up before they departed. A few glowing embers amidst the ashes were all that was left of the fire that had been roaring earlier. Her eyes darted around the room, straining to identify objects in the shadows. Although she knew that there was a seating arrangement with a sofa and two club chairs in the forefront of the room, they looked different in the darkness. Antonia walked over to the backgammon table against the wall and clicked on the bouillotte lamp. There was no need to completely shut down all of the light in the building. What if a guest was restless and came down to read? These things had to be thought through! Being a novice inn owner was challenging and Antonia was going on instinct. She just hoped that she would do a good enough job that the guests would return and would recommend the inn to friends. That was one reason she always solicited advice and impressions from her guests. She pulled the cord to light the bright bulb and all of the furniture in the room came into clear focus. *There*, she thought. *Much better.*

Antonia moved towards the chairs and picked up various pillows to re-fluff them. They didn't really need it, but something was compelling her to remain in the room. She noticed that a book on Hamptons style had been left on the coffee table so she returned it to its place, sliding it into the shelf next to the fireplace. Antonia then straightened the side chairs that leaned against the wall and bent down to touch the soil in the potted plant to make sure that it was damp. They were all minor adjustments, ones that no one but a perfectionist would notice, but that's what made Antonia a natural innkeeper.

Suddenly Antonia stiffened. What was that noise? She thought she heard something scratching. She paused and listened. There it was again! It sounded like fingernails scraping a blackboard. She strained her ear to find which direction it was coming from and waited. Her head jerked towards the back of the room, from where the sound was emanating. Taking a deep breath, she proceeded to the back, where there was another cluster of upholstered furniture with plush cushions that you could sink into underneath the bay windows. Antonia hesitated for a moment when she reached it, her knees bumping into the low coffee table. She glanced around apprehensively. She waited for the sound. Once again, there was the noise.

Antonia paused. An image of swarming bees attacking flashed in her mind. Her stomach turned with nervous anticipation. She slowly turned her head, but to her relief, she realized that the noise she was hearing was only the wind slapping a branch from the birch tree against the window. She exhaled, suddenly realizing that she had been holding her breath.

This was so silly, she told herself. *Why am I psyching myself up?* Last night, before she had heard the suspicious deaths rumor, she had been fine. In fact, she had been sleeping in this inn for six months and never felt frightened. She wasn't a scaredy cat; that wasn't her thing. Hell, she had survived an ex-husband who'd used all of his energy to scare and harass her for years. So why was she freaking herself out *now?* Just because the Powers family had told her that the previous innkeepers had died suspiciously? It was absurd.

Antonia stood up straight and strode firmly out of the parlor. This was her inn. She was the boss! She walked towards reception and gave it a cursory once over, and also glanced briskly inside the deserted library. No one was awake in the inn. There was nothing to give her pause. She made her way back down the hall towards her apartment, refusing to be disturbed by the shadows along the wall. She walked past the small antique elevator that was used to transport luggage or guests who needed assistance and peered through the glass. No one was hiding there. Antonia promised herself that she would not let this ghost story about the inn haunt her. She would not succumb to hysteria.

3

SATURDAY

East Hampton, renowned for its award-winning beaches, picturesque villages, and the ethereal light that had inspired some of the greatest American painters, is nestled on the tip of Long Island's south shore, bordered by the Atlantic Ocean on one side and various bays on the other. Everything about the town is profoundly quaint; from the acres of farmland bursting with abundant crops to the shaded streets lined with windmills, shingled houses and churches that actually look like churches. The center of the village is comprised of two streets—Main Street and Newtown Lane—that meet in an L-shape, and are home to neatly kept and freshly painted one- to two-story storefronts. Since the end of the 19th century when the Hamptons became a resort community, summers have attracted the rich and famous, not to mention a chaotic amount of tourists. But for all the glitz and fanfare, most of the time East Hampton feels like any other small town in America.

Antonia Bingham had never thought she would leave California. She was born and raised in Petaluma, and had assumed she would stay there forever. Why wouldn't she? But Antonia hadn't counted on the relentless abuse of her ex-husband, Philip. During their marriage she had been a virtual prisoner, and after she finally mustered up the nerve to leave him, Philip embarked on a tyranny of terror that made her life a living hell. Her pleas to the police went unheard. And of course that would be the case: Philip was one of them, a sergeant in the force beloved by his brothers in arms. Restraining orders, calls to 911, and reason didn't matter. No one believed her and eventually, no one listened. Until one fateful day when Philip showed up at Antonia's house and her frail father tried to intervene on her behalf. A kick to the stomach from Philip sent her father to the hospital where he died two weeks later from complications. Philip escaped jail time with an Academy Award winning, teary-eyed and remorseful performance in criminal court, but she won a restraining order and settlement against him in civil court. It was that money that she had used to purchase the inn, and the inheritance from her parents that she used to maintain it.

Her friend Genevieve, who had worked for Antonia's catering business as a waitress after a relationship with a vintner in Sonoma went sour, sold Antonia on East Hampton, the town where Genevieve's family had rented a house every August. She talked of lush seasons, a town as charming as any Norman Rockwell painting, unspoiled vistas, sandy dunes rolling down to the edge of the blue Atlantic, and Antonia was sold. It was impulsive, but something drastic had to be done. She said goodbye to her parents who were buried side-by-side in the Calvary Cemetery, and made the opposite trip that her ancestors had made one hundred years ago when they set out for California. But in both cases, the Binghams were searching for the "promised land."

* * * * *

"You're a die-hard, too!"

Antonia turned around and then nearly gasped out loud. She couldn't believe her eyes! It was Nick Darrow, the movie star, talking to her, Antonia Bingham, civilian. She knew he lived in East Hampton but she had not seen him until just now. And here he was, standing in front of her at Main Beach in all his handsomeness, two yellow labs frolicking at his heels, talking to *her*. And she was struck dumb.

"Excuse me?" she murmured, at least she thought she murmured, because she was too busy trying to control the blush that she was certain was creeping up over her pale white cheeks. Damn her English skin! When she was embarrassed it was as if she paraded it on her face like a scarlet letter.

"I said you're a die-hard. Not many people are out on the beach at six-thirty in the morning in late October. And I know this is not a one-off because I've seen you here the past three weeks."

"You have?" she squeaked.

"Yes. Sorry that sounds creepy. I'm not a stalker. I'm Nick," he said, thrusting out his hand.

Of course he was, she knew *exactly* who he was, but *she* also didn't want to appear like a stalker. His handshake was firm, and his hands surprisingly warm on this brisk morning.

"I'm Antonia."

He wore a barely perceptible smile on his face, and yet his expression warmly conveyed a feeling that they were both in on the same joke. It was an intimate gaze, one that wholly embraced a person and created a cozy space for just the two of them. Antonia knew intellectually that it was just Nick Darrow's innate charisma, but he had it on a much higher level than most people. *That's why he's so famous,* thought Antonia. *He just has a spectacular, glowing energy.*

Whatever it was, Antonia was totally star-struck. She couldn't believe this was happening; it was surreal. And it was all so casual, as if he were just some guy on the beach. But he wasn't; he was Nick *Friggin'* Darrow! And although Nick was now in his late forties and definitely not the gorgeous poster boy that he once was, age totally agreed with him—he was more smoldering than ever. He still had very thick dark hair, albeit now graying at the temples, a strong jaw, blue eyes, which were amped up by the orange Patagonia that he was wearing, and plump lips. *Kissable lips*, Antonia thought. Yes, everything about Nick Darrow was sexy, including the zesty aftershave that she could slightly smell from a few feet away and the way his faded jeans hugged his muscular legs.

"So, are you on vacation? Some people would say you picked the wrong time of year, but I'd say you picked the very best time to be in East Hampton," said Nick with a smile. "I love it when the town clears out."

He bent down and picked up a ball and threw it near the breaking waves. Both of his dogs took off in furious pursuit.

"No, I actually moved here a few months ago."

"And you waited for the worst possible days to take up walking on the beach?"

He motioned to the barren sand around them. The sun had barely peeked out, and the breeze was ripping through the dunes as if getting the hell out of dodge. Even the waves appeared grumpy, lazily smacking the shore like a teenager dragged out of bed too early. The air was chilly, though the weatherman had promised temperatures in the high fifties.

Antonia laughed. "No. I used to walk later in the day. But now for work it's better for me to leave early so I can be there when the guests wake up."

"Where do you work?"

"I bought the Windmill Inn on Main Street."

"Oh that's *you*."

He said it in such a way that made Antonia feel self-conscious. Had he heard about *her*? Was this a practical joke? Antonia peeked around to see if some camera crew would pop out of the bushes. Maybe he was a Nick Darrow impersonator? She studied him with squinted eyes. No, it was definitely him.

"Yes, I bought the inn. I did indeed," said Antonia. *I did indeed?* She didn't really talk like that. What was she, eighty? She wished she could say something really cool right now but all she could think of adding was, "and I'm the chef at our restaurant."

"*Really?*" he said in a drawn out, interested manner. "What kind of food?"

"I guess you'd call it American. Just sort of home cooking. Things people like to eat. Or at least, things I like to eat."

He smiled. "And what do you like to eat?"

"Oh, you know, well, to be honest, my favorite food is bread. I could eat that all day long. And I don't discriminate: it can be sourdough, raisin nut, olive, pretzel rolls, you name it . . ." she realized she was rambling, and about gluten, too. "But as I can't serve bread exclusively, I also have things like roast chicken with crispy skin, baked stuffed lobster with bourbon-spiked butter, grilled pork loin, hash browns cooked in duck fat. Butterscotch pudding with whipped cream."

"Wow! Sounds great! You're making me hungry."

"You'll have to come by. I mean . . . if you're around. Come by. No pressure," she was embarrassed she was so forward so she quickly added "You know where the inn is, right?" She felt herself become redder.

"Of course. Everyone knows."

"Yes, it's been there for over a hundred and fifty years."

"I know."

"You do?"

"Sure. It's a small town."

"Right."

Antonia wasn't sure what to add to that. One of Nick's dogs returned and dropped the slobbery tennis ball at his feet and he in turn picked it up and hurled it across the sand. Antonia could sense the strength of his muscles even through his fleece. The dog took off again, bounding across the sand to retrieve it, with Nick watching him. Antonia realized that she was watching Nick watch the dog and instantly felt foolish. Was she supposed to linger or should she keep walking? The uncertainty made her blush deeper. To her relief, Nick returned his attention to her.

"So you're not worried about the curse?"

"The curse?"

"Sure, you have to have heard about it before you bought the inn."

"You mean that the innkeepers there die under suspicious circumstances?"

"Yes, that one."

Whatever red was hovering in Antonia's cheeks now drained. "Well, no one told me before I bought it. In fact, the first time I heard anything about it was last night. Now you're the second person to alert me. So what's the deal? Am I like, the biggest moron in town? Did I make the biggest mistake of my life? Which by the way, by all accounts, now sounds like it will end shortly."

Nick Darrow laughed. He had a big, booming, hearty laugh that made the people who made him laugh feel intensely gratified.

"I don't know; I'm sure it's just local legend. I mean, there was nothing suspicious about the last guy who died, I think it was a heart attack."

"I've heard it might have been a bee sting."

"Bee sting, whatever. A bee sting isn't suspicious, actually."

"A bee sting in August isn't suspicious," replied Antonia. "But a bee sting in December is."

Nick smiled. "True."

"What about the guy before that guy?"

"I don't really know, I just heard maybe he poisoned himself or something and they weren't sure what happened."

"Poisoned himself?" asked Antonia, her voice rising. "Great, just great. How many months do you give me?"

Nick put his hand firmly on Antonia's shoulder. The warmth from his palm trickled down all the way to her toes.

"I have total faith that you'll break the curse."

She looked deep into his eyes and wished desperately that she was another type of woman; they type who could now reel off a coy, flirty little response, but instead she blurted, "I have bad luck."

"You do?"

Antonia instantly began to backtrack. There was nothing tackier than someone unloading all his or her problems on a total stranger. Especially total strangers who happened to be movie stars. "I mean, just kidding. Anyway, how does everyone seem to know about this curse? Is there a library book I could take out to get to the bottom of it?"

"I don't think anyone has written a book about it just yet," said Nick.

"Okay, then how am I going to prepare myself to stave off my potential suspicious death? I need to be ready in case I accidentally pick something poisonous from my garden and make a soup out of it."

"You know what you can do? I've got a friend at *The East Hampton Star*. Larry Lipper, covers the crime beat. His office is on Main Street. Just stop by and tell him I sent you."

"The *crime* beat?"

Nick laughed again. "Yeah, I know. He mostly writes about DUIs or reports on those 911 calls that people make where they think they heard something but it turned out to be a neighbor. But doesn't matter. If there was anything to the inn story, Larry will know."

* * * * *

Antonia was oscillating between two extremes as she made her way back to the inn. On the one hand, she felt extreme elation at the fact that she had just had an entire conversation with *Nick Darrow*. He was handsome, he was nice, and he acted totally normal. It was literally as casual as talking to the guy at the hardware store, total chitchat. And yet this was a guy who had been voted *People Magazine's* "Sexiest Man Alive"! But all of that excitement was tempered by the confirmation that the inn had a curse, and if lore proved true, her untimely demise was imminent. Antonia smacked her steering wheel as she headed along Ocean Avenue. Damn, had it been a totally stupid move buying the place? What had Genevieve talked her into? She had wanted a new start, a new adventure, but one that ended in homicide wasn't exactly what she had in mind. She felt duped. Should she call her broker and give him a piece of her mind? Demand her money back? The inn had already given her a fair share of problems in the six months she had owned it.

For one, the rambling three-story Georgian revival building was built in the late 1840s and required constant maintenance. It was so run down when Antonia purchased it that it had taken a solid five months to update the rooms and bathrooms and renovate the kitchen to a professional chef's kitchen that would accommodate the restaurant. She had totally missed the summer season and had to delay her opening, which was a major loss of potential income. And when one upgrade was finished something else always needed to be done: the exterior had to be repainted white, the shutters needed a fresh coat of green, the front yard had to be nuked and new sod lain and the brick path needed to be fixed before someone fell down and broke their neck. The to-do list was endless, and the fact that she was a bit of a control freak/ perfectionist didn't help. The one thing Antonia had on her side was naiveté, because if she had known what she was getting into, she never would have done it.

But now, to be honest, Antonia was glad that she had been ignorant. She loved her inn. She loved the antiques that she had chosen for the parlor and the crooked floors in the entryway and the unpredictable twists and turns of the hallways. And she loved East Hampton. The fluidity of the place appealed to her; she appreciated the way that population ebbed and flowed, just like the tides at Georgica beach. And now she loved everything a bit more because she had just met Nick Darrow and although it was silly, it was so cool that he had even heard of her. Or well, not her, but that he had heard that someone had bought the inn, and that was her. Did that even make sense, she wondered?

The interaction had put a spring in her step and even made her a little flaky. She was usually good with names but upon returning to the inn, when she went to greet the couple from Rhode Island who were staying in Room Two, their names escaped her. And later, when the farmer came from Pike's to take her order for next week's vegetables, she completely blanked that she needed potatoes, which would require a phone call to amend. In fact she was so distracted all morning that she didn't even notice when Lucy Corning, the manager of the inn, came to find her in the kitchen. Antonia had been stirring the mix for ricotta doughnuts, dreamily fantasizing about kissing Nick by the dunes on the beach when she felt a tap on her shoulder.

"Antonia, are you okay?"

"Huh?" Antonia jumped, startled back into reality. She blinked several times before realizing where she was, and unfortunately, where she wasn't. "Sorry, I didn't hear you."

"I was calling your name, but you looked like you were a million miles away."

Antonia blushed. "I was just thinking about something."

A slight smile crept across Lucy's face as if she knew *exactly* what Antonia was thinking about, but she immediately dismissed it and got down to business.

"I didn't mean to interrupt you. But we have a situation."

Antonia sighed. She glanced at the small mousy woman in front of her. Lucy was probably in her early-to-mid-forties, waif-thin, with one of those nondescript hair colors (is it brown? Is it dirty blond?) and one of those nondescript hair styles (bob? Shoulder length?) She was neither unattractive nor attractive—somehow just neutral. And clearly somewhere along the line, Lucy had been encouraged to go with an eclectic, vintage look because she insisted on wearing quirky black framed glasses, and either her trademark cashmere sweater set and retro A-line skirts, or dresses that made her look like an aging 1950s schoolgirl. Come to think of it, Lucy had even mentioned once that she worked at a vintage clothing store and found her style there. Antonia had raised her eyebrows, but kept mum.

Antonia didn't mean to be judgmental because Lucy had proven to be a competent employee—so competent, in fact, that Antonia had promoted her to manager from her previous position of bookkeeper. Lucy was amazingly prudent in helping keep Antonia in line with a strict budget. It was like having an in-house system of checks and balances. And it was a bonus that she had been working for the inn under Gordon, because she had the technical hospitality background that Antonia didn't possess yet. Antonia had high hopes for her, except she did notice that Lucy seemed to appear gleeful every time she had to report bad news, like a cancellation or a broken toilet.

"What's up?" Antonia finally asked.

"It's not good," said Lucy gravely.

* * * * *

"Ladies, ladies, be quiet! It's Saturday morning, many of my guests are sleeping in. Please stop, oh geez, stop!"

There was so much yelling that Antonia's voice fell on deaf ears.

After working her way around the bottom of the staircase, with Lucy hot on her heels, Antonia swiftly inserted herself into the middle of the two women who were loudly fighting in the front hall of the inn. On one side was a voluptuous blond woman around the age of forty-five, who wore a jean jacket over a scoop-neck spandex floral dress. On the other side a wiry, pencil-thin brunette of about sixty, clad in a white zippered windbreaker over blue slacks. Both women were shrieking obscenities at each other, with the brunette desperately trying to seize hold of the small cardboard box that the blonde was clutching in her arms.

"Stop this right now!" bellowed Antonia at the top of her lungs.

They momentarily fell silent. From the doorway, Lucy gave Antonia a decisive nod of approval.

"Now, I don't know what is going on, but I know that this is *my* inn, and you ladies can't act like this here. Now tell me, what the heck *is* going on?"

They instantly spoke at once, their words accusing and angry, and the tone rapidly rose from normal speaking voices to a shouting match. Antonia put her thumb and index finger to her mouth and blew a whistle. (She was so proud that she knew how to do that; the lifeguard at the YWCA pool had taught her when she was fourteen.)

"Let's try this again. I'll start with you, Naomi. What is this about?"

The brunette—Naomi Haslett—shook her head with exaggerated dismay. She was the late Gordon Haslett's sister, and had been the co-owner of the inn along with him. Her hair was pitch black—the color of shoe polish—and cut bluntly into a Louise Brooks bob, with razor straight bangs slicing across her wrinkled forehead. Her face was pale and craggy, and Antonia couldn't help but think that her hair color actually aged her. Naomi would do much better with a softer look across the board, especially since every interaction Antonia had had with Naomi proved that her character was as sharp as her haircut.

Naomi pointed at the other woman, the sexy blonde whose name fittingly happened to be Barbie, and who was Gordon's girlfriend at the time of his death. "Antonia, I think you should call the police. She is *trespassing* on your property."

This was interrupted by Barbie's furious rebuttal. "I am not! It's my stuff!"

"Barbie, you will have a chance to talk," said Antonia, silencing her. "Naomi, continue."

Naomi gave Antonia a slight smile while Barbie glowered. "Like I said, Barbie is *stealing*. That box in her hands? It's yours . . ."

" . . . Is not! It's mine!"

"Barbie!"

"Listen, Antonia," said Naomi, "When I sold you the inn, I sold it lock stock and barrel. Everything from the doors to the hinges, right?"

"Yes," concurred Antonia.

"Well, according to our agreement, that included the boxes

that were in the storage areas. And now this woman has snuck into your inn and is taking *your* box!"

"It's mine!" protested Barbie.

Antonia turned to Barbie. "Now let's hear from you."

Barbie Fawcett pressed the box firmly to her chest, smashing her ample bosom in the process. "You said, Antonia, that I could take any of my belongings out of the inn. I had forgotten about this box, so I came here to retrieve it." Her voice was flustered and husky, and in the tussle with Naomi bits of mascara had flaked off her lashes and landed in black dots on her rouged cheeks like measles.

"It's not your box," snapped Naomi.

"Yes, Naomi, it is mine."

"May I ask, what is in the box?" asked Antonia.

From behind Antonia, Lucy spoke. "It's nothing, some old notebooks that Gordon used to jot down to-do lists and things like that."

"Lucy, stay the hell out of it," snapped Barbie, craning her long swan neck in Lucy's direction.

"Barbie, that's not necessary . . ." said Antonia.

"Does she really need to be here for this?" asked Barbie impatiently. "I'm just wondering when that woman will disappear forever. She's like a tick that just keeps hanging on. Doesn't know when to leave. Lucy, it's over. Go home."

Lucy reddened. "Say what you want, Barbie. But I ran Gordon's office. I went through everything when he died. I'm not sure what you're looking for, but it's just a bunch of office notes."

Barbie tapped her foot impatiently and rolled her eyes to the ceiling. "Is this how you'll get your revenge?"

"I'm telling you the facts," insisted Lucy.

"See, Barbie? You're not going to find anything that you claim is here because it doesn't exist," said Naomi impatiently.

"I'm lost here. What is Barbie looking for in the first place?" asked Antonia.

Naomi shook her head with irritation. "She claims my brother had another will in which she stands to inherit the inn," said Naomi. "But it's all a lie. An exasperating lie. We just came from court where she is still trying to obtain a piece of my inheritance. But Gordon would have never left this . . . this . . . person . . . anything. I'm positive."

"Naomi you're forgetting that your brother and I lived together for *five* years. I'm not some one-night stand. We were in a committed relationship. I was his common-law-wife . . ."

Naomi scoffed. "Concubine."

"I helped with the inn, day in and day out. It would not look like this if not for me," Barbie said waving her arms around at the polished mahogany staircase, the gleaming wood floors carpeted in Oriental rugs and the brightly shined brass sconces. Antonia wanted to correct her and tell her it would not look like this if not for *me* and hundreds of thousands of my dollars, but she bit her tongue.

"What a joke," scoffed Naomi. She turned to Antonia. "You can ask anyone, my brother was done with her. He was trying desperately to shake her. There are people who will vouch for that."

"I know who you're referring to, and Ronald Meter is

hardly a reliable witness," replied Barbie before turning to Antonia. "That guy is a disgruntled former employee who Gordon fired when I told him that he was stealing money from the inn. He's vindictive."

"And so were you," muttered Naomi.

Barbie narrowed her eyes to slits. "You know, Naomi, you were always jealous of me because you knew that Gordon would leave me his share. There is no way he would have left you anything! He thought you were a money-grubbing user who let him do all the work and tried to drain him of any profits. You always undermined him, since you were children."

"I gave him the money to buy the place!" sneered Naomi with exasperation.

"And he paid you back in turn. But you never stopped. You were always shaking him down for money! That's why he quit taking your calls. And that's why he made sure that I would get his share. He showed me the will! I just need to find it."

"You'll never find it because it didn't exist!" Naomi bellowed.

"Yes it does!"

"Oh, no it doesn't! And now do you realize that it was a mistake to kill my brother?"

Antonia's head shot around. "What did you say?"

"You heard me. This witch killed Gordon!" Naomi's eyes were feverish, and her fists were balled up, ready to pounce.

Barbie snorted with disdain. She turned her head away and looked down. "You're delusional. I wasn't even at the inn when he died."

"Am I? Am I?"

Antonia was beginning to feel dizzy. "Wait, wait. Time out, now. Gordon died of a heart attack, did he not?"

"Yes," said Barbie firmly.

Naomi glared at her.

"Naomi, didn't Gordon die of a heart attack?" prompted Antonia.

"Yeah, right, whatever." Naomi rolled her eyes.

Antonia was exasperated. "No, *not* 'yeah, right, whatever.' Did he or did he not die of a heart attack?"

"Yes," said Lucy from behind. "Heart attack."

Antonia didn't shift her gaze from Naomi's face. "Isn't that so, Naomi?"

Naomi looked down at her tennis sneakers. They were very clean white Reeboks that she had worn every time Antonia had met with her. She took some time to answer, after taking several deep, relaxing breaths that looked more appropriate for a yoga class.

"The official cause of death was . . . a heart attack," she said at last, glaring at Barbie, who still wouldn't meet her eye.

Antonia felt her heart race. "What was the unofficial cause of death?"

Naomi finally glanced in Antonia's direction. She gave her a small smile, her lips curling enough so that her thin top lip disappeared into the bottom. The look reminded Antonia of a defiant child forced to lie to a teacher.

"Heart attack," Naomi repeated before adding, "but I'd bet my bottom dollar that this tramp here figured out a way to cause it."

Barbie snorted. "Like I said, I wasn't even here when he died. How could I cause a heart attack?"

Antonia kept her eyes on Naomi. "Why didn't you tell the police if you suspected it?" asked Antonia.

Naomi rolled her eyes. "I wanted to make sure I could sell the inn. No one would have bought this place if they thought Gordon was murdered. That's my official story and I'm sticking to it."

4

The only way Antonia could persuade Naomi and Barbie to leave was to confiscate the cardboard box that they had been fighting over and promise to review the contents herself. After ascertaining to whom it rightfully belonged, she would personally deliver the box to her. It appeared to temporarily appease both ladies.

"What do you think?" Antonia asked Lucy, as they sat in her cramped office to regroup. Antonia immediately poured herself a cup of Earl Grey tea, which Lucy refused, and brought out a plate of coconut macaroons that were fresh out of the oven. As Antonia popped the third cookie in her mouth, she noticed Lucy watching her with a somewhat disdainful look. She slid the plate in Lucy's direction but received a vehement shake of the head.

"Sorry, but I totally believe in comfort food," said Antonia, wiping her fingers on her napkin before she took a big gulp of her milky tea. She grimaced slightly at the bitterness and spooned another large scoop of honey into her mug. "Anything bad or unpleasant and I dive for the pantry. Break my heart, pass the banana bread. Steal my money, serve me some buttered noodles!"

Antonia smiled but when Lucy did not, she became serious again.

"So, back to business. Can you tell me a little bit more about the personal history here? Because I am totally confused."

Lucy smoothed her skirt and took a moment to gather her thoughts before answering. Antonia had noticed that she was always very precise. That and she had excellent posture. Even now while Antonia sat flopped in her chair, Lucy was on the edge of her seat, sitting erect. It made Antonia straighten up a little and reminded her of her mother who always used to admonish, "Sit up straight, shoulders back, head up, stomach in!"

"Well, as I'm sure you can tell there was never any love lost between Naomi and Barbie."

Antonia waited, but when Lucy didn't continue, she probed further. "Okay, so maybe they hate each other. But why would Naomi accuse Barbie of murder?"

"I'm not really sure."

"But was there a suspicion that Gordon had been murdered?"

"I never heard that," said Lucy, stifling a yawn. "Naomi is just being dramatic."

"But she seemed to believe it."

"People can believe what they want if they so choose. I

could walk out of this room and say you punched me and even though there was no proof, many people would believe it."

"True," conceded Antonia, momentarily wondering if such a thought had actually crossed Lucy's mind. "Do you think it's because of the whole mythology of the inn?"

Lucy paused. "I only recently heard about that."

"Really? But you've lived in this town your whole life, haven't you?"

"Well, not really. I've been in East Hampton on and off my entire life; we moved away for a while. But yes, I consider myself a native. And I don't really believe in all that gobbeldy-gook. I have better things to worry about."

"That's reassuring," said Antonia. She took another sip of her tea while Lucy waited. She could tell Lucy was eager to return to work and was only humoring her boss, but Antonia wasn't done.

"What do you think is in there?" Antonia motioned towards the disputed box, now sitting on the edge of her desk.

"Like I said to Barbie, nothing. I packed all those boxes myself. It was just scraps of paper that Gordon jotted things down on, flyers, junk mail. I went through absolutely everything twice and I know there was no will in there. I should have dumped it way back when. I'll go through it again this afternoon. But it really should just be thrown out."

"That's okay, I can do it."

"Are you sure? It's no problem."

Antonia shook her head. "I got it. I don't understand, why was Barbie so hostile to you?"

With a tilt of her head, Lucy paused to consider this. "We got along fine when Gordon was alive, pretty much had minimal contact. I think she's just bitter that I'm still working here and she's out on the street."

Antonia thought there must be more to it than that. "But those were some fighting words she threw at you."

Lucy's face quivered slightly, and Antonia thought she might be embarrassed. "Perhaps I wasn't as discreet as I should have been. I clearly came down on the side of Team Naomi whenever there were these kerfuffles."

"Got it. So, what was Gordon like?"

Lucy shrugged. "Well, I knew him for a long time. Gordon was not a popular man. He alienated vendors, he would impulsively fire staff . . . One could say he was rude, mercurial and selfish."

"Geez, doesn't sound like the right personality to run an inn! This is a service business after all."

"I know. It didn't suit him. But *sometimes* he could be wonderful and fun. There was something oddly charismatic about him that made people want to please him. Almost mesmerizing."

"Really? That doesn't jibe with everything I've heard about him."

"Well, no one is one-dimensional. I assume there were many layers to Gordon. But I wouldn't really know, I kept my head down and did my work."

"What was his relationship like with Barbie?"

"I tried not to get involved, I'm just an employee, and I do like to keep things professional . . ." Antonia felt this last remark was pointed at her and this line of questioning. Once again Antonia didn't let her off the hook.

"But . . ."

"It *was* hard to avoid it sometimes. They fought like cats and dogs, always screaming at each other, breaking up, making up. Very toxic."

"Bad relationship but nothing out of the ordinary, then?"

"Not really."

"You dealt with the finances, the books. Do you think Gordon was going to leave his share to Barbie?"

Lucy hesitated a beat too long. "I don't know . . ."

Antonia pounced on the opening. "Come on, Lucy. I feel like you're holding back . . ."

Lucy glanced around the room, avoiding eye contact. Antonia could tell she was wrestling with some sort of internal debate as to whether she would spill what she knew. Antonia was certain she could break her.

Finally, Lucy sighed deeply. Her face was troubled, her eyes distant. "I would prefer to let sleeping dogs lie, Antonia."

"Ah, but they are not asleep. What do you know, Lucy?"

Lucy was quiet for an entire minute, perhaps waiting for an out, but Antonia didn't bite. When she grasped that she was cornered, Lucy conceded defeat.

"I overheard a conversation Gordon had on the telephone. I don't know who was on the other end. But he said that he *was* changing his will. And he wanted to make sure Barbie got nothing. It sounded like he had originally planned to give her everything, but he was so angry at her that he was cutting her out."

"Why was he angry at her?"

She shrugged. "I don't know for sure."

"And *not* for sure?" Antonia prompted.

Antonia could practically see the wheels in Lucy's brain turning. "I think she had another guy on the side."

"Why?"

"I saw her around town a few times in odd places at odd hours with another man."

"Who?"

"I think he may work at a liquor store. I vaguely remember that because of his shirt, I can't remember what it said exactly, but I was left with that impression. Physically, he's tall, handsome. Married."

"Married?" asked Antonia, raising her eyebrows. "How do you know?"

"Gordon. Those last few months, he was trashing her. Said something about the man being married and that she'd end up with nothing if she pursued it.'"

This reminded Antonia of something. She almost mentioned it to Lucy, but decided to keep it to herself for now. Instead, she shifted directions.

"So you think he'd have left his share to Naomi?"

Lucy met her eyes and leaned in, as if she was revealing something she shouldn't. "What Barbie said was true. Gordon was furious at Naomi. Claimed she was stealing money from him. If I told him she was on the phone, he'd slam it down. He even threw her out of the inn a week before he died."

"So, he was feuding with both women."

Lucy's head bobbed in agreement. "Yes."

"Then they both had motives," announced Antonia with a shiver. "And this so-called tale of innkeepers' untimely deaths might be true after all. I'm doomed."

"I wouldn't go that far."

* * * * *

Antonia had been tempted to drive, but figuring that was *very California* of her, especially since it was only about three blocks, she opted instead to slip out of her Crocs, don her Uggs and amble east down Main Street, also known as Route 27. To be honest, Antonia found any sort of physical activity repellant in general, but since the extra ten pounds she had been carrying around on her 5'5" frame had now morphed into an extra eighteen pounds, she vowed to make walking her thing. She was half Italian (from her mother) and half English (from her father). But instead of inheriting her mother's beautiful and smooth caramel complexion, she had her father's white skin (she'd call it pasty, others referred to it as "peaches and cream"), and instead of her father's slight, skinny frame, she had her mother's wide hips. Oh well.

Although Antonia's state of mind was frazzled and concerned, it was a glorious fall day and *that* she could appreciate. The leaves on the ubiquitous plane trees were the color of flames, pumpkins and gold, and when the wind blew, the leaves cascaded to the sidewalk like fireworks. The October sun dappled the various houses along the far side of the road, and Town Pond shimmered in the orangey light. Antonia was

almost regaining her high spirits until she glanced at the cemetery, which prominently held court in the center of the village
green. She couldn't help but feel as if it were mocking her. *No
way, you won't get me now,* thought Antonia as she determinedly
swung open the front door of the two-story, gambrel roofed
shingled building that housed *The East Hampton Star. I will not
go down because of some stupid curse!*

The Star was a weekly paper that had existed for over a
hundred years. Like most small town papers, it covered local
politics, commerce news, business transactions, current events
and sports. A large part of the newspaper was classifieds and
real estate advertisements. The editorials were opinionated and
often incurred spirited "letters to the Editor" and the sports
coverage was a bit reverential, because all the stars were home-
grown. Fortunately, the reviews of local restaurants were usually
laudatory, and Antonia had already been featured in a glowing
piece. Since then it was the only newspaper she read.

She was directed to a small office in the back, next door
to the restroom that appeared to double for both men and
women. After knocking briskly and being invited to enter, Antonia found herself in a disorderly mess of a room with framed
posters of Bob Dylan adorning the walls and a random assortment of globes. At first they appeared to have been collected
for a decorative effect but now looked more like a cluttered
afterthought.

Larry Lipper had a chiseled jaw, a full head of salt and
pepper hair that matched the two days worth of stubble on his
cheeks, and thickly lashed, piercing grey eyes. He would have

been considered remarkably handsome except for the fact that he was profoundly diminutive. Small in stature, with eyes bordering on beady, and small hands, small ears, and a small nose, Antonia found herself wondering if the old adage was true . . . but then stopped herself.

"Hello," he said, giving her the up and down. His voice was remarkably deep for such a little man. "To what do I owe the honor?"

"Hi, is this a bad time?"

"No . . ."

She didn't need further encouragement but continued on. "You don't know me at all, but Nick Darrow referred me to you. I'm Antonia Bingham; I just bought the Windmill Inn down the street. Can I sit down? I am sorry to bother you, but I really need your help."

"Whoa, hang on a second. Hang on. Did you just come from the city? You are talking way too fast for this town," he said, leaning back in his desk chair and folding his arms behind his head. He threw her a bemused look. "You've got to slow down."

"Sorry. I'm just a little worked up. I'm not from the city. Believe it or not, I've only been there twice, but maybe those three cups of caffeinated tea that I just had didn't help."

"What's going on, Antonia Bingham?" he said in a sing-songy voice. "You do seem like a lady who needs a drink."

"That could be true, although I don't like to think of myself as a daytime drinker. I would never refuse if Bailey's found itself into my afternoon espresso, but I don't actively seek out booze in daylight."

He glanced around the room and eyed a half finished bottle of whiskey on his window shelf. Next to it were two shot glasses that appeared sticky and used. He reached for the bottle but Antonia stopped him.

"No, really, that's okay. I don't need anything."

"You sound like you do."

"Really, I'm fine. I mean, alcohol-wise."

He gave her a skeptical glance but put the bottle back in its place.

"Take a load off and tell me what gives."

Antonia sat down but just as quickly rose and removed the spiral notebook that she had inadvertently sat on, and after glancing around at the mounds of books and stacks of papers on his desk, decided to place it on a bookshelf next to a Yankees mug and a Bart Simpson bobble head.

"I'll just put this over here," she said.

"Yeah, sorry about that. My work is pretty complicated, and I need a lot of books to keep it all accurate."

"I'm sure."

"So what about you? What can I do you for?"

"Well, as I said, I just bought the Windmill Inn. And now I'm hearing all these stories about it. Scary stuff. So, Nick Darrow suggested that I talk to you, that maybe you would have some ideas?"

"Nick Darrow suggested me?"

"Yes, he thought you could help."

"Huh," he said, scratching his chin idly. "What's going on?"

"Well, you know Gordon Haslett, the previous owner? Was

there any sort of 'cloud of suspicion' about his death, as they say? Because his girlfriend and sister were just at my inn and they were pretty angry. One even accused the other of murdering him, and I have reason to believe they both have motive. And, as they were fighting, I remembered something that I found when I first moved into the inn. I didn't think much of it at the time, but now it is haunting me. Here, look at this."

Antonia pulled out a crumpled piece of paper from her pocket and unfolded it. When she had spoken to Lucy earlier it had reminded her of something, a note she had found. She was so happy that she had kept it and now presented it to Larry. He took it from her, scanned it, and then glanced up.

"I don't get it."

"No, of course, let me explain. I had an industrial cleaning service do a *very* thorough cleaning of the inn. But a few weeks ago I was opening the window, which is one of those old windows—very hard to open, gets stuck all the time. So I was exerting an inordinate amount of energy trying to get it open . . ."

"Maybe you should work out."

"Thanks, yes, perhaps. And you should read Emily Post, but anyway, all of my pushing and heaving of the window caused the cross to fall off my necklace behind the radiator. When I reached down to retrieve it, I found this sheet of paper. I was distracted so I just glanced at it and tossed it into my bottom drawer. It is written in what I now know from other documents to be Gordon's handwriting. See what it says? '*I swear to god that B is trying to kill me.*' B trying to kill me! Gordon's girlfriend is named Barbie. So he might have been referring to her! But then the weird thing is he said '*that* B' not just 'B.' So he might have been referring to someone else and meant, 'that B' like the word that rhymes with witch, possibly referring to his sister. It seems like both women had something to gain from his death. So there is possible proof that Gordon Haslett knew that someone wanted him dead. So what do you think? I know, I'm rambling, but do you have any thoughts? Should I go to the police? I do try to avoid them at all costs."

Larry leaned back further in his chair and put his feet on his desk so that now Antonia had worn, dirty black soles staring her in the face. He kept his gaze on her, studying her face as if he were registering her story. Finally he spoke.

"How do you know Nicky?" he asked.

"Excuse me?"

"Nicky Darrow. You said he sent you to me. How do you know him?"

That was his takeaway from my entire story? Antonia thought. *He wants to know how I know Nick Darrow?* "I don't know him actually. I briefly met him today."

Nick put his feet down and shifted in his chair.

"He's a great guy. You should really get to know him."

"I'm sure a lot of people would love to get to know him, as he is one of the most recognizable actors in the world. But I seriously doubt he's on the lookout for new friends."

"We're pretty tight."

"That's great."

"Yeah, Nicky and I have done some serious damage in this

town. That guy can out drink me and you won't find many people who can do that."

"Really," said Antonia flatly.

"Yeah, but it's not all party-party. Did he tell you how we met?"

Antonia shook her head.

"It was intense. He was doing a film where he played a reporter. He wanted it to be authentic, and you know, he was playing someone who covered the grittier stories. Not a big city reporter, that's been done a zillion times. But someone like me who has to straddle being a member of a community that he has to report on when the people in it do bad things. So Nick followed me around for a week when he was researching the part. Did I tell you who his co-star was?"

"No, you didn't mention it."

Again Larry brought his feet back up to the table and nestled in for a chat. Antonia watched as his eyes drifted back down memory lane.

"Kate Winslet. That is one ballsy lady. But you know, she has kids and is busy being a mom when she's not working, so it was really Nicky and I hanging hard . . ."

Antonia listened impatiently as Larry droned on about his contribution to Nick's acting career. He began describing in detail how his incredible reporting skills were an inspiration for Nick, and how Nick even had some of the script rewritten to include actual anecdotes from Larry's life. Antonia fervently hoped Nick had won an Oscar for the role, because having to tolerate this homunculus was going above and beyond his duty to his craft. Larry Lipper was an arrogant, boastful, self-aggran-dizing person and she couldn't wait to depart from his pres-ence. She finally had to cut short his discourse.

"I'm so sorry to interrupt and I would totally love to hear more about this, but I actually have to return to my inn to start dinner service. I'm gathering from your subsequent rambling that you were not impressed by my story about the note from Gordon about people who wanted to kill him and then the fact that he died. That's fine. But I had hoped that perhaps there was something you might know about Gordon Haslett, or really any of the previous owners, I would be most grateful. But if not, I won't waste your time any more."

Larry gave her an unctuous smile. "What? You don't have time for a little get to know you, Bingham?"

Antonia gritted her teeth. "I would like to chat with you, but right now I'm in a rush. I don't mean to be rude, but just hoped you might have some quick information."

Larry abruptly pulled his feet off the desk and landed them with a thud on the floor. He leaned in towards Antonia, once again his eyes glued to her chest. "You're attractive."

Antonia reddened. "Thank you."

"So what's your damage?"

"My damage?"

"Your damage!" he said again in his singsong voice, spread-ing out his arms at the same time. "How did you end up in East Hampton? Everyone who moves here has a history."

"I'd argue that everyone has a history."

"Very funny. You know what I mean. A divorce, a layoff, an

alcohol problem, financial problems, something that made you move here to get away from it all. Because this place is paradise for *everyone* three months of the year. And everyone else who sticks around beyond that is searching for a year-round paradise that doesn't exist. So, what was your deal?"

"My deal is that I like to keep my so-called history to myself, thank you."

Larry gave a gleeful smirk and banged his fist on the table. "I knew it, divorce!"

Antonia stood up. "I'm sorry if I wasted your time. Thank you for listening."

"You didn't waste my time. And you didn't waste your time either. Because in . . ." he glanced at the watch clasped around his hairy forearm, "five hours you can seat me in the best table at your restaurant, buy me dinner and a nice bottle of wine, and I will give you all the information you need."

Antonia gave him a curious glance. "What are you talking about?"

"I mean, I can help you. I'll get you information."

She wasn't sure how to respond. "Okay . . ."

"Don't look so serious, Antonia! I can tell we're going to be good friends."

Antonia didn't have the heart to tell him that she was absolutely sure that would not be the case.

5

Saturday afternoon tea was being served in the parlor and Antonia did a quick detour to check in before she headed to her office. Quite a few tables were full and Antonia greeted several guests, including Ruth Thompson and Penny Halsey, two older local ladies who had become a fixture every day at three PM. Antonia couldn't help but feel proud as she surveyed the well-appointed room, which looked much less foreboding in the daylight than it had the night before. In her fantasies, this was exactly how she had imagined her snug inn would be. There was a roaring fire at one end, a smattering of antique tables, and plush seating that ladies of a certain age could sink into as they tucked into their scones with jam, served on real English china. At least aesthetically, it was a success. She did notice, with chagrin, that one of the bulbs needed replacing in the recessed light above the bay window, but if any of the guests detected it, they didn't say anything. She made a mental note to replace it later.

When Antonia reached reception Connie told her that she had a friend waiting for her across the hall in the library. Antonia found Genevieve deep in an armchair flipping through the latest issue of *Cosmopolitan*. Of course, the shelves behind her were lined with the classics from Shakespeare to Faulkner and every masterpiece that Antonia could think of when she compiled it, but that was of little interest to Genevieve. As usual, she was dressed to the nines, appearing as if she was straight out of a Ralph Lauren advertisement, which in a sense she was, as she managed the Ralph Lauren store in East Hampton and exclusively wore his label. Today, she had on a camel colored cashmere poncho over a cream cashmere turtleneck, and brown suede skintight pants tucked into chocolate leather boots. A few Native American style necklaces in silver and turquoise were draped around her neck, and she wore a very large aquamarine ring that engulfed her entire middle finger. At first blush, Genevieve was absolutely striking; she had olive skin; long, silky chestnut hair; enormous round green eyes, and was what one would call "a stick"— very tall and very thin. But upon closer examination, her features didn't entirely mesh; the eyes were too close together, her forehead too broad; it was as if the spacing was off. She was, however, inherently sexy, which offset her physical shortcomings. Her immaturity was another unfortunate problem.

"So, what gives? I thought you were chained to your inn. All those excuses that you can't do anything, but then I show up on my lunch break to keep you company and find out you're gallivanting around town," said Genevieve, loudly flipping the page. "Ooh, I love these shoes," she added, casting a disparaging glance at Antonia's Uggs.

"I'm sorry. I should be chained to my inn, in fact, I should be in the kitchen right now working on the loin of pork with the green peppercorns, but I have totally abandoned Marty and Kendra for a wild goose chase."

Antonia sunk into the chair opposite Genevieve. She promised herself she would relax for five minutes, and only five minutes, before returning to work.

"Who the hell are Marty and Kendra?"

"My sous chef and station chef? You've met them ten times."

"Oh yeah," said Genevieve. She blew a large bubble with her gum before popping it loudly and flipping the page of the magazine. "So, where were you?"

Antonia filled her in on Naomi and Barbie and the curse and the trip to Larry Lipper. She chose not to mention Nick Darrow, knowing that it would lead to an entirely different conversation where she would have to field twenty questions just about his outfit.

"The point is this is so not me, running around worried about a curse, or trying to find out if this guy Gordon was murdered. What do I care?"

"Well, it is *kind of* you, but that's not the point."

"What do you mean?"

Genevieve rolled her eyes. She dropped *Cosmo* on the coffee table and picked up *Vogue*. "You're kind of nosy. I mean, didn't your parents nickname you Snoopy because you were always snooping around?"

"I never should have told you that . . ."

"Don't get offended, it's not a bad thing. I never would have known Steve was cheating on me if you hadn't followed him to the bar that day."

"Sorry about that. But I knew the guy was a cad."

"You saved me years of heartache."

"Years?"

"Okay, months."

"More like weeks, judging from your romantic history."

"Hey, watch it."

"How can I watch it when you are calling me nosy?"

"It's not a bad thing. What I mean is that you like to figure stuff out. I remember you used to be obsessed with your ex-husband's cases. You were more of a detective than he was."

"I was better at it than he was. Nothing wrong with that," sniffed Antonia.

"Most of the time, no. But it's not so great when you think that you are the only one who can do everything."

"I do not."

Genevieve cocked her head and raised an eyebrow. "Take the inn. You decorated it all by yourself; you're the innkeeper, the head chef. A cushion rips, you sew it yourself. I've seen you with tools trying to fix the toilet, and pulling weeds out of the flowerbeds."

"Someone has to take responsibility."

"Okay, but what about trying to be superwoman? You do your own taxes. You try to play local matchmaker. You're lobbying the town of East Hampton to reduce noise from the airport . . ."

"I just . . ." Antonia began to protest but then stopped. It was true. "I guess you're right."

"I know I'm right."

"Are you saying it's a bad thing?"

"No. I'm just saying that you're thirty-five years old. Time to know who you are."

Antonia bit her lip. She could say the same thing to Genevieve. "I think I know who I am."

"Great. Then you know that you're the type of person who will absolutely positively uncover a crime if there was one."

Antonia conceded that it was true. She was about to offer some explanation for it and psychoanalyze herself but as usual Genevieve's attention was fleeting and she had already grown bored of the topic. Genevieve turned *Vogue* towards Antonia and held up a picture of an anorexic model leaping across a stream whilst clad in an absurd metallic jumpsuit. "Hey, would this look good on me?"

"Everything looks good on you, it's just a little ridiculous."

"I'm too fancy for this town."

"True. The same cannot be said of me," said Antonia, glancing down at her prairie skirt.

"That's for sure. But you never listen to me. You just insulate yourself in all those damn layers of clothes. I promise you, if you made yourself sexy, you could find a man. You have great boobs."

"Please. Why do you always want to give me a makeover? I'm happy the way I am."

"What about Larry Lipper? Was he hot?"

"God, no! A vile man. And tiny."

"I met the hottest guy the other day. Okay, early twenties so I know that's like, robbing the cradle for me, but he was so cute . . ."

Antonia stared out the window as Genevieve droned on. She watched Hector, the gardener, winding the hose by the front porch. It then dawned on her she should ask him about Gordon Haslett. He had been the one that found him, slumped on the ground by the barn. Dead.

"You're not listening," said Genevieve accusingly.

"Huh?" said Antonia, jerking her head back towards her.

Genevieve sighed dramatically. "Are you really so upset about this guy possibly being offed? See? That's why I didn't tell you."

"You knew?"

"Everyone knew. But deep down no one really believes the story because it's totally manufactured. All that bull about the gardener killing him because Gordon had fired his wife for stealing . . ."

"Wait, what?"

"Yes, it was the old, 'the gardener did it in the solarium with the hoe'."

"I never heard the gardener mentioned."

"Yeah, I don't know. Apparently, his wife worked at the inn as a maid and Gordon fired her for stealing a few weeks before he died."

"Really?"

"Supposedly. Who knows?"

Antonia turned and glanced again at Hector. He was small in stature, compact, but muscular and she knew for a fact, very strong. She watched as his muscles rippled through his shirt when he bent down. He wore his black hair in a short-cropped buzz cut and was always tidy and meticulously dressed, even when he had been working outside. From the first time they met, Antonia sized him up as hardworking and competent, and to date he had proven reliable and honest. He was a family man, proud and devoted to his wife and small children. Very proud. Would he have murdered someone to defend her honor? She didn't think so. But maybe she didn't know.

"It's just racial profiling," said Genevieve dismissively. "Don't worry about it. And anyway, if someone killed Gordon Haslett, I would like to personally thank him or her. He was a jerk and his dying brought you to East Hampton, so we're all much better off!"

*　*　*　*　*

An hour after Genevieve left, an odd incident occurred that unnerved Antonia and once again gave her pause about her own mortality. She wasn't sure if she was psyching herself up, but she was definitely flustered. She realized that perhaps there was something to the whole notion that innkeepers at the Windmill Inn were an endangered species.

After the completion of tea service, Antonia had grabbed a stepladder and gone into the parlor to replace the bulb that was out above the window. It had been bothering her for an hour. The afternoon sun was drooping and the south-facing room was growing dark. Outside, the yard was already in deep shadow. Antonia had unfolded the ladder and pushed it against the window seat. It was rickety and when she pressed down on the first step, it heaved under her weight. She felt wobbly as she ascended; it was time for a new ladder. She climbed gingerly to the top and reached up to remove the old bulb. The ceilings were high in this room and Antonia had to rise on her tiptoes to unscrew the bulb. She wasn't afraid of heights but it did feel precarious balancing on the narrow step while she reached sky-ward. It was a small exercise but it definitely reminded Antonia again how out of shape she was. Her arms felt as heavy as lead as they extended straight up to untwist the bulb. She made a mental note to buy some weights to work on her biceps.

Antonia slowly worked her fingers around the edge of the bulb, turning and turning until the bulb was loose. She pulled it out but with such gusto that she almost lost her balance and the bulb flew up in the air. Fortunately, her quick reflexes worked to her advantage and she caught it with both hands before it smashed to the ground. Antonia's heart was thumping with the near miss and the exertion she had to use in order to complete the small task. She stepped off the ladder and put the bulb down on the console table. She glanced up. Perhaps it might be better if she stood on the window seat instead of the rickety ladder, she decided.

Antonia removed her shoes and wiggled her stockinged toes. She took a new bulb out of its sleeve. Holding it in one hand she used the other to hoist herself on top of the uphol-stered window bench. She stared upwards towards the light.

No, this would not do. The distance was too far and she would have to hold her body up at a ninety-five degree angle in order to replace it. It was physically impossible. She sighed deeply. Genevieve was right; she was such a control freak. She should cut her losses and ask Hector to come in with his large ladder and do it. But then she felt silly, what, she couldn't even change a light bulb? It was like a joke, how many innkeepers does it take to replace a light bulb?

She had an idea. The curtain rods were strong, she knew that. They were thick-brushed brass and when they were installed she had asked the contractor to make sure they were doubly secured because she was hanging very heavy damask curtains on them. She would step on the ladder and hang on to the rod while she replaced the bulb. Easy peezy.

Antonia held the bulb in her hand and mounted the ladder. She grabbed on to the curtain rod and then hooked her arm underneath it so that she was basically hanging on it. She was aware she would look ridiculous to anyone who entered, but she didn't care. She was focused on getting this done. Antonia had the bulb and she rapelled her weight away from the window so she was horizontal to the floor and began screwing it in. Her foot was beginning to slip off the ladder but it didn't matter because she was so intent on the task at hand. She slowly twisted the bulb. Her back now was to the room, facing out the window. She heard someone come in, but she didn't want to glance around for fear she would lose her balance.

"Hello? Just putting in a bulb," Antonia said.

Silence. She must have been wrong; there was no one there.

Beads of sweat were forming on Antonia's brow as she finished twisting. Her underarm hurt from the rod pressing into her armpit. She hoped she wouldn't bruise, that would really be an inane injury. She leaned further, slipping her foot off the top shelf of the ladder completely so that now the only thing holding her was the curtain rod. It would just take a second, she told herself. But she had put it in at an angle so she had to start over. She turned the bulb again, slower now, confirming it was set in place. With the final twist, the light bulb illuminated and Antonia flinched from the blazing brightness that shone directly into her eye. She blinked several times, but all she could see were burning spots. She paused, waiting for the flashes of light to disappear from her retinas.

Keeping her eyes clenched shut, she pointed out her toe in an effort to locate the stepladder. She couldn't find it. She swung her leg back and forth, searching for it with her toe. It was absurd, her fumbling around. Her arm was hurting but she realized she was flailing around for no reason. She took a deep breath and again tried to locate the ladder with her toe. Still, she was unable to locate it. She waited again until her eyes finally cleared. When she was not blind anymore, she glanced down. The ladder wasn't there. Antonia blinked several times to make sure her eyes weren't playing a trick on her. But there was no ladder.

Had it fallen down? She craned her neck as far as she could without falling. No she couldn't see it anywhere from her angle. And besides, wouldn't she have heard it if it had fallen? Antonia's heart raced. Her arm was on fire; it hurt so much from pressing into the rod.

She took a deep breath. She had no choice. She slowly wiggled her arm out from under the rod. That meant that she had to push one hand against the wall to hoist herself up so that she could remove the arm. She counted to three then did so. She quickly grasped the rod with her hand and found herself hanging onto the curtain rod. She felt totally ridiculous, but it was only for a split second because her sweaty hands could no longer hang on to the rod and she slipped off and fell to the floor with a thud.

She froze. She was alive. She wiggled her feet and arms. She could move. Embarrassed, Antonia sat up. She was lucky; she was okay for the most part. Her butt was another story, and she could feel it already turning purple and bruised: a lovely image. She dusted herself off and turned and scanned the room. Fortunately no one had seen. It was a relief that she was alone. But then suddenly Antonia's eyes locked on something and the blood drained from her face. She felt chills. The ladder was there behind her. But the strange thing was that it was folded and propped against the wall five feet away. It could not have done that itself. Was someone intentionally messing with her?

6

That evening during dinner prep, Antonia asked around about the ladder. Had it been a prank? Had someone thought it was funny to move it? She asked around but no one copped to it. And who *would* think that was funny? She could have landed wrong and really hurt herself, and then who would run the inn? After her questions were met with odd looks and sympathetic clucks, she decided to put the ladder out of her mind. It had just been a fluke. Luckily tonight was a whirlwind of activity, so she didn't even have time to think once dinner service got under way. She kept her head down in the kitchen and focused entirely on the food.

They had never been this busy in the dining room, and as a result were a bit understaffed and unprepared. Things were tense. For the first time, the timing was a bit off, and surges of orders seemed to arrive at the same time, which made everyone scramble. They actually ran out of salmon, which was completely embarrassing and they had to make last minute adjustments. A busboy dropped a tray in the kitchen, unleashing a string of obscenities from Glen, who was already cranky from the unpredictable arrival of several walk-ins, messing up the seating chart that he had spent way too much time on.

Marty, the sous chef, had been manning the grill all night, whining commands at everyone in his nasal voice as the flames danced in front of him. He oversaw the kitchen but was primarily in charge of entrees. With his wiry frame, limp gray ponytail, and pock-marked skin he was an aging hippie, his appearance better suited for someone selling pot at a Phish concert than cooking fine food. But that was where looks can be deceiving; there was nothing laid back or hippie about Marty's personality. A type-A cantankerous perfectionist, he was one hell of a chef. Alternatively, Kendra, Antonia's line cook, appeared as if perhaps like she had spent *too* much time in the kitchen. With the exception of her ginger hair and a random assortment of tattoos, everything about her was pale and dense, like a ball of bread dough. She moved slowly and precisely, and had an intuitive approach to food that Antonia appreciated, always seeming to unearth the missing ingredient that would pull a dish together. Kendra was in charge of salads and desserts and spent most of the night composing them, assisted by Liz, the eighteen year-old intern. (Antonia was attempting to mentor Liz, despite some grumbling from the kitchen staff.)

The activity in the kitchen was relentless from opening until ten o'clock, when things abruptly died down. Marty and Kendra bolted out to have a cigarette. Antonia gave Liz a tutorial on how to plate rare steak without all of the juices dripping into the mashed potatoes. When Marty returned, Antonia took the opportunity to make her way through the dining room to see what remained of her guests.

Antonia was tired, and the stress from the kitchen as well as the day's unpleasant developments suddenly seemed to catch up with her. She felt exhausted. But she brightened when she saw her friend.

"Joseph! How was everything tonight?"

She was happy to see him there for his second night in a row, in his cute little green bowtie. As she stared at him tonight, he reminded her so much of her father, with his calm, thoughtful demeanor and the way his eyes shone behind his glasses. She suddenly felt a pang of sorrow and a crushing sense of loss. She missed her parents. They were wonderful people. And it was obvious Joseph missed his wife as well.

"It was delicious, Antonia. Just fantastic. You're doing a great job. Treasure it. Enjoy these moments. Beginnings are wonderful."

Again, it was something that her father would have said and as soon as the words were out of his mouth, tears filled Antonia's eyes. She was mortified and feigned a coughing fit in order to account for them.

"Excuse me, I had something stuck in my throat."

Joseph raised his eyebrows as if he knew she was not being truthful and invited her to sit with him for a nightcap. Although she felt she had to make the rounds, she accepted.

"How is everything with you?" he inquired.

Once again her eyes filled with tears. What was going on? This was crazy! Antonia glanced around the dining room to make sure no one else could spot her, but the remaining guests were all engrossed in their own conversations. She was profoundly grateful that she had insisted on low-wattage and mostly candlelight to illuminate the dining room or else she would have been discovered.

Joseph put his hand on top of Antonia's and smiled. They sat like that for a minute, Antonia fighting tears, and dabbing her eyes with a napkin. They both waited until she was able to speak.

"I'm so embarrassed, Joseph. You just remind me so much of my father and it hit me like a ton of bricks."

"Don't worry, my dear. I understand."

This made her want to cry harder. There was nothing that makes you cry more than when someone is nice to you when you are crying. She finally exhaled. "Sorry."

"Don't be," said Joseph. "You know, my father died when I was twenty-one and I remember at his wake a friend of my mother's said to me that her father had been dead for twenty years and it didn't seem like a day had gone by since he died. I couldn't fathom it at the time, but now I understand what she means. And there is something oddly reassuring about it. It's nice to think that you feel the loss as much today as when it happened. It's wonderful to love that much."

Antonia nodded. "I like looking at it that way . . . I didn't know you were twenty-one when your dad died. I was ten when my mom died."

"I'm sorry to hear that."

"Thanks. It was strange because she was much younger than my father, almost twenty years younger. And they'd always joke how he'd die first and she'd remarry some handsome guy her own age. Then she got cancer and died within six weeks of her diagnosis. My dad never got over it, he was completely heartbroken. Life is strange."

Joseph patted her hand and waited before speaking again. "It must be tough taking on this whole inn and restaurant by yourself. But you wouldn't know it by watching you. It's so nice to see your smiling face and taste your delicious food. I had the truffled macaroni and cheese tonight with a side of sautéed broccoli rabe. My doctor would be apoplectic but I loved every minute of it."

Antonia laughed. "There's a lot of butter in those two dishes!"

"Bring it on, as they say!" he chortled. He took a sip of his sherry and watched Antonia intently.

"I'm sorry for everything, Joseph. I haven't been myself all day. I heard something yesterday that set me off."

Antonia filled him in on all of the talk about the previous innkeepers dying suspicious deaths, including the new revelation about the possible bee sting. She added that it was making her a nervous nelly, and she replayed the stepladder scene from that afternoon, lamenting that she may be next in line.

Joseph looked excited. "No, don't worry! Biddy Robertson is still alive. She only briefly owned the inn before Gordon, way back when, but that still counts!"

"Really?"

"Sure. Lives in a condo near Springy Banks Road."

"Are you friends with her?"

"Not socially. But my wife Margaret ran the Ladies Village Improvement Society Fair one summer and worked with Biddy on that. I think Biddy still volunteers at their thrift shop."

"Well, that's reassuring!"

"Quite."

"What about the owner before her?"

Joseph removed his glasses and wiped the lenses with his handkerchief. "Well . . . I'm afraid that's *not* such a good story."

"Ugh! Okay, now you have to tell me."

"Greg McKenna was his name. He was a nice man, very energetic, some might say a touch too enthusiastic, but he meant well. He had all sorts of plans. In fact, he was the one who originally put the restaurant in the inn. Before that there was just a hot plate and a coffee maker for guests to self-serve."

"Then I bow to him," smiled Antonia.

"Yes, but his kitchen was nothing like yours. He was big on ideas but short on execution."

"Did he live here alone?"

"No. He owned it with his wife Charmaine; they'd met in college in Florida. She had some family money, I believe, that was used to purchase the inn, but he was the real self-starter who made it happen."

"So, what went wrong?"

"Well, it's all rumor and conjecture . . . but, there was talk around town that Greg was having an affair with his wife's sister, Lois. Lois actually lived here at the inn with Greg and Charmaine, and was one of those gay divorcees who cut a dangerous figure. By all reports she was extremely selfish; only out for number one. Apparently, Charmaine had been trying to force Lois to move out for months, calling her a leech and a mooch, but she refused, and Greg kept leaping to her defense, which caused a tremendous amount of conflict between him and his wife. In fact, some people thought he and Lois were lovers and I am sure Charmaine suspected that. Well, one night they had a family dinner and Charmaine made a carrot cake for dessert. She knew carrot cake was her sister's favorite dessert. And she knew that Greg hated carrot cake. Well, that night it was strange, because Lois refused to eat the cake—said she was on a diet. But Greg decided it looked so good that he would have some. According to Lois, Charmaine tried to talk him out of it, but perhaps he felt bad that no one wanted it, so he tucked in to a large piece. Ate every last bite. Next thing you know, he's violently ill, throwing up all over the place. Charmaine, who also had some, was sick also; too sick to help him. Greg went to bed, and into cardiac arrest and he died in the night. His daughter discovered him on the floor of the bathroom. The kid found Charmaine in time and called 911. She was saved, but not her husband. They found arsenic in the cake, which Charmaine swore must have gotten in there by accident. She had picked some thyme from the garden to add to the cake and must have mistakenly included it, she claimed. But the theory always was that Charmaine meant to kill her sister and dispose of her. Ate just enough of the cake to not be a suspect, and ended up killing her husband."

He paused, his eyes shining, and awaited Antonia's response.

"Wow." She shivered.

"Yes. Terrible story."

"What ever happened to Charmaine and Lois?"

Joseph paused and shifted in his seat. "Lois became even nuttier. She knew what Charmaine had done and accused her, but as she was a bit of a drunk who'd had a few skirmishes with the law—stole some money from ex-boyfriends and the like—and the police didn't believe her. I think she left town, no one really knows where she went, but I fear it did not end well."

"And Charmaine?"

"Not six months later Charmaine married her high school sweetheart and was living back in Winter Park, Florida in one of those mini-mansions, raising her kids with her new husband as if Greg had never existed. Sold the inn to Biddy and never looked back."

"It's an incredible story . . ."

Before Antonia could finish her sentence, someone behind her interrupted her.

"I made it. I'm sure you were beginning to lose hope, but hell, if you knew the kind of night I had, you would freak out, so make sure you show me some gratitude. I'm friggin' starving. Is this the best table in the house?"

Larry Lipper plopped down on the chair between Joseph and Antonia and dropped his brown leather satchel on the floor next to him. He pulled Antonia's glass of sherry towards him and downed it, before wiping the back of his mouth with his hand. There were bags under his eyes and he was markedly wearier than he had been earlier in the day. All trace of handsomeness was replaced by a worn and weary façade.

"Joseph Fowler." Joseph put out his hand to shake but Larry ignored it.

"Larry Lipper. Can I get a menu? What's good?" asked Larry.

"Well, the kitchen is just about closed . . ."

"Don't screw with me. I wouldn't have come if you hadn't promised me a great dinner."

Antonia wanted to protest but decided it was futile. This Larry Lipper clearly lived in an alternate reality.

Antonia asked Glen to bring over a menu and she watched Larry pore over it with intensity. He made clucking noises, voicing his disapproval over various items, and seemed at a loss as to what to order. Joseph gave Antonia a quizzical look but she just shook her head in resignation.

"What the hell is this, smoked pork sausage and sweet corn custard? What is corn custard? A pile of mush?"

"I can assure you it's delicious," said Joseph defensively. Antonia loved that he was protecting her.

"Yeah, whatever, give me the flank steak," he said, handing his menu to Glen. "Easy on the onions, and extra shoestring potatoes. I like them crispy, not greasy. And forget the mixed greens that accompany it, I gave that crap up long ago."

Glen threw Antonia a look of disgust and recoiled. She could only imagine the conversation in the kitchen when Marty received the order.

The busboy came and placed a large basket of fresh baked bread in front of Larry and he dove for the sourdough. He smeared a large slab of butter on his piece before shaking on enough salt to cause a heart attack. He shoved it into his mouth with relish.

"God I need this!" he said with his mouth full.

Antonia summoned all of the niceness in her body to interact with Larry. "So, what happened tonight that kept you? Because I was really waiting with bated breath."

"I knew you were, Antonia. You were like a dog in heat this afternoon."

That was too much for Joseph. He started to protest, but Antonia stopped him.

"I couldn't get any of the information you begged me for today about the former owners of this joint. As soon as you left I heard a call on my scanner about a possible crime and so I had to cover it."

"Oh, really? What happened?" asked Antonia, hoping to erase the sound of *dog in heat* that was still ringing in her ears.

"It was a total waste of time at the end," Larry said, a large slab of white bread bobbing around his tongue. "But you know how it is here. Someone dies, and if it's not straightforward like they were dying for months, it's as if its first time that anyone has ever died in this town and it gets the 'suspicious' treatment. The police get called, I get called. You know, because I'm the press and they always want the press there."

"Who died?" asked Joseph.

"This old lady," he glanced at Joseph and gave him the up

and down. "You know, in her seventies. She doesn't show up for breakfast with her friend at John Pappas Diner, the friend is worried, goes over to her house, sees the lady slumped on the floor. Lo and behold the woman was dead."

"What really happened?" asked Antonia.

"They think it was late at night, the woman went to make herself a cup of tea. Turned on the gas, it didn't go on all the way, you know, old range, woman was tired, forgot and went to bed. The windows were all shut—you know how old people like it super hot—and then she inhaled all that carbon monoxide and croaked."

"How awful!" said Antonia.

Joseph's eyebrows furrowed with concern. "Who was this 'old broad' as you call her?"

"I don't know. Some woman named Elizabeth Robertson."

Joseph's mouth dropped. Antonia gave him a curious look.

"What is it Joseph?"

Antonia could see his Adam's apple bob as he gulped. He took a sip of water and finally spoke. "You mean, *Biddy* Robertson?"

"Yeah, that's the one."

Antonia felt the blood drain from her face. She and Joseph exchanged shocked glances.

"Another innkeeper," whispered Antonia.

"Poor Biddy," said Joseph.

7

Antonia had retreated as soon as she could to her tiny ground-floor apartment and changed into the soft flannel pajamas that had been with her since college. Her apartment was snug and cozy, consisting only of a bedroom, a living room with a kitchenette, and a bathroom. It suited her perfectly as it was low-maintenance and compact and faced the back, which afforded a pretty view of the gardens. She had thrown her heart and soul into decorating the inn—scouring East Hampton and all the neighboring towns for antiques, spending hours on the Internet searching for the few things that she didn't find at Ruby Beets, Mecox Gardens, Hildreth's or Rumrunner—but her own rooms were decorated with less vision, erring more on the side of comfort than style.

The living room consisted of a white, plush, squishy, over-sized sofa with matching armchairs, the type that an elderly person might sink so deeply into that they'd need the Jaws of

Life to escape. There was an upholstered ottoman that served as a coffee table, a sideboard cluttered with pictures of her parents, grandparents, and since she was an only child, some snaps of her cousins and their children, with close friends thrown in for good measure. A wall of built-in bookshelves were stocked with a variety of tomes as well as miscellaneous objects like a set of crystal candlesticks that had belonged to her parents; a ceramic lion; two floral cachepots that held dried boxwood plants; board games (Scrabble, Clue and Trivial Pursuit circa 1990) and a box of tissues. The books were an eclectic assortment based on Antonia's whims. She was a phase reader—for a few months she'd read nothing but mysteries, followed by a few months of self-help, then cooking, and then books on angels and near-death experiences. This was all reflected in her personal library. She had also managed to hang onto all of her dog-eared copies of *Saveur, Food & Wine,* and *Gourmet* magazines, which held court at the top of the shelves.

The walls of the apartment were all painted a uniform petal pink, Antonia's favorite color, and featured framed posters of Matisse and Van Gogh paintings from the Met and Pushkin Museum, as well as a few watercolors of East Hampton that she had bought the previous summer at the Clothesline Art Show at Guild Hall. (She'd waited on line patiently a full hour before it opened.) A thick, creamy white wall-to-wall carpet ran from the living room into Antonia's bedroom, which was also a testament to comfort: its giant king-sized sleigh bed was adorned with an enormous white comforter and a surplus of pillows. Antonia loathed spending money on herself but she had two vices: expensive sheets and beauty products. Expensive sheets not because they were expensive, but because she adored the buttery softness that accompanied high thread count Egyptian sheets. Whatever those Egyptians were doing, she was incredibly grateful. And beauty products because she couldn't resist any cream or solution that promised her less wrinkles, eradication of cellulite, softer skin or any simple solution to battle the signs of aging. Her bathroom cabinets were bursting with jars and bottles of every size, shape and fragrance.

When she had first purchased the inn, this space had, of course, been where Gordon and Barbie were living. The walls had been dark; leather furniture had been the dominant theme and the kitchen appliances and bathroom fixtures were broken. It was as if Gordon stubbornly resisted making this anything other than a functioning bachelor pad. There was no whisper that a woman had lived here with him. Now that lack of compromise on Gordon's part resonated with Antonia. Had he been done with Barbie?

Antonia had the TV on with the sound muted and was busy sifting through all of the papers in the disputed cardboard box. She was drinking a glass of cabernet and nibbling on pecan toffee squares that her intern Liz had made that afternoon. Antonia was notably impressed with Liz, who had appeared on her doorstep four weeks prior, begging to work her ass off if Antonia taught her the trade. She had reminded Antonia of herself when she was young, possessing that naïve dogged determination that makes you bold. Marty thought it was a waste of time and space letting Liz help out, but even he had recently muttered that she was "doing good," which was high praise for him.

Antonia knew it was late and she should retire to bed, but she was absolutely jolted by Larry's revelation about Biddy Robertson. *Dead.* The only other living Windmill Inn inn-keeper was now out of the picture, and under suspicious circumstances to say the least! With everything that was recently revealed about Gordon, this had to be somehow linked. Joseph had reluctantly concurred with her, although Larry was not convinced. He had been insistent that he was on the scene of the crime, and being the Cracker Jack reporter that he was, would have been able to suss out if there had been any foul play at work. And despite Antonia's protestations that it was too coincidental, especially as all this speculation about Gordon's death was arising this week, Larry held firmly to his belief that there was no motive and therefore no crime.

Antonia focused on the cardboard box, hoping that there might be some answers there. She leafed through a variety of menus for local East Hampton restaurants, a pamphlet for bike rentals, and a few postcards from satisfied guests, who promised to return to the Windmill Inn in the near future. There were some old Post-Its with a few phone numbers jotted down, but nothing that piqued Antonia's interest. Lucy was correct, it appeared to be just a pile of random papers that Gordon had shoved into a box rather than thrown away. The only promising thing seemed to be a spiral bound note-book, the kind that every middle schooler receives, in which Gordon had jotted some notes on an inconsistent basis. If this was where Barbie was hoping to find the will, she would be disappointed.

Antonia flipped through page after page and felt as if she was gathering more information into what sort of person Gordon was and why his inn had not been very successful. He kept a sporadic account of things that he needed to order for the inn that were very neatly detailed, as well as lengthy, delineating everything from toilet paper to light bulbs to candles. But on each list there were only one or two essentials crossed off, implying that the other desired items were still outstanding. It was the same with his "to do" lists. He'd written about his plan to fix the leg of a chair in the parlor, or to repair the ripped headboard in Room 3, but once again very few of those things had checkmarks against them. It was totally consistent with everything she had heard about Gordon. He was capable of large bursts of activity and enthusiasm but after an initial bold effort, he failed at follow-up.

It wasn't until Antonia reached the last page of the notebook that she felt a rush. There, in Gordon's unmistakable handwriting, was written in all capitals:

LUCY—HAVE RONALD METER'S SEVERANCE PACKAGE READY. I AM FIRING THAT BEAST TODAY.

Antonia ran over to her hall table and picked up the scrap of paper that she had retrieved earlier. She held it up. *I swear to god that B is trying to kill me.* That B. That beast.

Antonia paused, her eyes gliding from one to the other. Finally she slid the scrap of paper into the notebook and slapped it shut, before replacing it in the cardboard box.

Ronald Meter was the former manager who Gordon had fired. Why had he fired him? She couldn't remember. But things were starting to piece together. It was time to visit Ronald Meter. Her alter ego Snoopy had reared his ugly head. It was time to investigate.

*   *   *   *   *

Sunday

Nick Darrow was on the beach as usual on Sunday morning but this time he was in conversation with a young couple, so Antonia merely waved. Disappointed, she cut her walk short and had ample time to make breakfast before setting out to Ronald Meter's house, which was situated at the end of a cul de sac near Accabonac Harbor in Springs, one of East Hampton's many hamlets. Springs was renowned for the Jackson Pollack-Lee Krasner Museum, which was located in their former house, and where they had spent many years painting. The sign that led into Springs said, "The Springs" and as it had become a trendy part of town in recent years—its proximity to the bay and picturesque clammers and fishing boats were a big draw—and it had attracted all sorts of hipster New Yorkers who referred to it as "The Springs." But that made the locals snicker. To them it was Springs; no fancy "The" preceding it. The school was Springs School, not "The" Springs School, they'd point out. But it was one more way to differentiate the locals from the interlopers.

Antonia felt somewhat presumptuous dropping in on Ronald Meter unannounced, but her fear of imminent death by a psychopath who hated innkeepers spurred her on. When she pulled into Meter's gravel driveway she took note of the large "For Sale" sign stuck in the grass. Hmmm, Antonia wondered. Was there a reason Ronald was moving? Fleeing town, maybe? She filed away the thought as she exited her car. Antonia was quick to assess that Ronald Meter had done the best job possible with what was an ordinary run-of-the-mill one-story shingled house. The shutters were painted a dark pearl gray and the front door was a cherry red, with a shiny brass knocker centered on it like a smiley face. A row of neatly manicured boxwoods lined the sides of the house, and there was a well-maintained slate path leading up to the entrance. Beyond the house, she could see the bay in the distance, and the salt marshes, which were the most exquisite mosaic of purples, reds and greens at this time of the year. It was by far the best-tended house that she had seen in the neighborhood. She glanced around to steal another glimpse of the neighbors' houses and realized with disappointment that theirs were obstructed from view by the large thicket of trees. Unfortunately, Antonia realized that in the event that Ronald Meter did turn out to be a killer who enjoyed killing owners of the Windmill Inn, she was royally screwed. No one would see a thing. She patted herself down, fumbling through the pockets of her barn jacket for something to use as a weapon. Nothing but balled up Kleenexes and the keys to her trusty Saab were available to her. She clasped the keys in the palm of her hand and tried to visualize stabbing someone in the eye with them. It wasn't ideal. But hopefully it wouldn't come to that.

When she creaked up the front steps, she heard a TV and through the window could make out a shadowy figure seated on the couch next to the door. This was it, Antonia thought. No backing out now. She took a deep breath of the brisk morning air. She was feeling that antsy lack of exercise gnawing at her. She couldn't believe she actually missed exercising. Although was a walk on the beach really exercise? And maybe what she was really missing was the chance to run into Nick Darrow again.

As soon as Antonia rang the doorbell, a dog started barking, and the figure rose and chastened him, before swinging open the screen door. Ronald Meter was a very tall man, at least 6'4", with reddish gray hair and a matching goatee. His face was broad and expressive, but also friendly. Antonia put him in about his mid-fifties. It appeared to her as if he was either wearing someone else's clothes or had recently lost weight. His ill-fitting khaki pants seemed to bunch up around his crotch area as if the brown braided belt he wore double looped around his waist was strangling them. He had on a light blue button-down shirt, with a darker blue undershirt peeking through, and wore black leather sneakers. There was something awkward about him and his bulk, and rather than emitting an intimidating aura, he seemed more like a big oaf. Not unlike the dopey-looking golden retriever that sidled up next to him.

Antonia watched him size her up with curiosity, before giving her a warm smile.

"Are you here to look at the house?" he asked brightly. She detected a slight southern lilt to his accent.

"Um, no, actually. Sorry. I'm Antonia Bingham, I own the Windmill Inn. I'm sorry to barge in on you on a Sunday but I was hoping I could talk to you for a minute?"

He seemed momentarily deflated but then he recovered quickly. He started to say something, and Antonia could see the wheels turning but then he abruptly stopped.

"So you're the one who bought the inn," he said neutrally, but it still made Antonia pause. It was the second time in two days that someone had seemed to know more about her than she knew about them. It was a bit disconcerting.

"Yup, that's me. Some may say the 'crazy one who bought the inn.'"

Ronald laughed heartily. "Aw, I wouldn't say that."

He politely invited her inside, with a few disclaimers about how he was watching his morning cooking shows and apologies for the mess. He flicked off the plasma television (Rachel Ray was rolling chicken breasts in panko crumbs) that hung over the mantel and carefully placed the remote next to it.

She accepted his offer of a glass of water, if only to give herself time to assess his living quarters while he retreated to the kitchen. After discovering that everything was immaculate, she wondered what he would think of her apartment if this was his idea of a mess. Sure, there was a newspaper strewn on the waterfall Lucite coffee table, but other than that, everything was in order. His décor was sophisticated and modern. He had two leather armchairs in the style of that famous Swedish furniture designer whose name was always a clue in crossword puzzles, but Antonia could never remember. The chairs faced a contemporary beige sofa that was flanked by two white lacquered side tables holding red gourd lamps. Two built-in bookcases bordered the mantel and Antonia could see that they held an abundance of expensive coffee table books, the over-sized glossy kind that people often give as presents but rarely read.

Antonia took the opportunity to tiptoe over to the dining room to get a better look. It was also tastefully decorated. There was an open laptop on the dining table next to a pile of mail. Antonia glanced at the mail, which appeared to be mostly bills. The computer screen was in sleep mode and Antonia was just debating whether or not to "accidentally" press a button to see what Ronald was working on, when her snoop was interrupted.

"Here you go," said Ronald, handing her a tumbler of water with a slice of lemon in it.

Antonia was startled. She turned around abruptly.

"You didn't have to go to so much trouble," said Antonia.

"It's no trouble."

He didn't appear to notice her snooping and invited her to sit down in the living room. He set out two coasters on the coffee table before placing his own glass down. If he was interested in why Antonia was there, his polite manners restrained him from revealing anything. In fact, his graciousness and ease made Antonia feel as if she was an invited guest just over for a cup of tea. She could see why someone had tapped him to be manager of an inn. He was definitely a pro at hospitality.

They engaged in brief pleasantries about the weather before moving towards the topic of the inn. Antonia confided the trials and tribulations of redoing the place and getting it up and running and Ronald commiserated. He sighed deeply when she delineated the construction woes and nodded encouragement. The fact was, Antonia found him totally pleasant and as mild as a pussycat despite his big size. There was daintiness to his hand gestures, and this coupled with the languid tone of his southern accent relaxed Antonia. She wondered if she was insane to think he might be a killer. She also wondered if she was totally insane to have put herself alone in his house if indeed he was a killer.

"Well, I suppose you're wondering what I am doing here?" Antonia asked finally, after they had exhausted all chitchat.

"I'm happy to talk to you about the inn, but yes, I am curious as to what brings you to my doorstep," Ronald said politely.

"Look, I'll be honest. I know that things ended badly between you and Gordon. But I also have gleaned from everything I've heard that he was a difficult man."

"To say the least."

"I'm trying to piece together what went wrong, so that I won't make the same mistakes." Antonia had just thought of that pretense, and was pleased with herself for thinking on her feet. The truth was, she didn't really have any idea what she was going to ask him. She was hoping that if he was somehow guilty he would confess, but that seemed both unlikely and absurd.

"Well, it's not that simple, I suppose. You see, Gordon was unstable. I'm not a psychiatrist but I really believe he was bipolar. He would have these fits of manic energy that could last anywhere from a day to a month, during which time he would take on all sorts of projects, and renovations, and be totally enthusiastic and joyful to be around. Then he would abruptly change and become angry, rude and totally incompetent."

"That seems to jibe with his notes that I found. All these to do lists that were never completed."

"Exactly. It was maddening."

"So why did he fire you?"

Gordon glanced at his water as if it held the answer before taking a sip. He recrossed his legs and looked at Antonia. "It was very challenging for me to deal with all of his mood swings, but I am proud that I hung in there for as long as I did. And as I said, he could be very abusive and destructive. When he was manic, he did bad things, that's all I'll say. But then when he came down, after he slept off all of his manic energy, he really didn't seem to remember them. And you felt sorry for him, because he had really no idea what he had done."

"Like what had he done?"

Ronald shifted. "I don't feel comfortable talking about it."

Antonia was surprised. Was he actually protecting Gordon? Even after Gordon fired him? She decided to press.

"Did you know that Barbie was cheating on him?"

Ronald put up his hands as if stopping her. "All of this

drama is water under the bridge for me. Look, I just tried to do my best to manage the inn and not make everything go to hell. I was furious that Gordon fired me, and even more furious that he told everyone it was because I was stealing. But I know that all came from Barbie . . ."

He stopped himself.

"Because you knew Barbie was cheating?"

Ronald sighed deeply. "You got it. Why are you asking me if you know?"

"Because I don't know everything. Please tell me."

Ronald raised his shoulders. "Yes. I saw Barbie. She was all over some guy at Rowdy Hall. I stupidly told Gordon and next thing I know, he's accusing me of stealing, they're back together all lovey-dovey, and I'm fired."

"You must have been furious at Gordon?" prompted Antonia.

"I was more furious at Barbie. I knew she manufactured this whole lie."

"But Gordon was the one who fired you."

"Yes, but as I said, he was all over the place. And he was vulnerable. And for all his faults, he did have a skill at making people he betrayed stick around and feel the need to defend him, as you know. But Barbie is bad news, that cheap bottle-blonde prom queen. Sorry, she just gets my goat. Point is, I wouldn't trust her as far as I could throw her."

"Really? Do you think she was using Gordon?"

"I think she has big plans for herself. Gordon was a stepping-stone. And frankly, I think she stole the money that she accused *me* of stealing. It's her nest egg and she's hidden it somewhere."

Antonia nodded. She believed that Ronald was telling her the truth. He didn't seem to have a grudge against Gordon, just Barbie, and as far as Antonia knew, she was still alive.

"Did you know Gordon was allergic to bees?"

"Bees? Why would you ask about bees?"

"Someone had mentioned that to me."

Ronald gave her a quizzical look before he spoke. "I don't know about bees . . . I knew he had all sorts of allergies and afflictions. But no, I never discussed that with him. Why?"

"I was just wondering if people knew. Wouldn't someone have warned him if there were a hive in the yard?"

"I don't remember ever seeing a hive in the yard. That seems odd. But you'd have to ask Hector."

"Yes, I definitely need to talk to him. He'll be in later, after church."

"May I ask why all the interest in Gordon and bees? I know you said you don't want to make the same mistakes, but it seems we're talking more about his personal life."

Antonia had to think fast. "True. Well, Naomi and Barbie just showed up and were battling over some of his belongings. I just want to know what I'm getting into in the future with those two. I want to be prepared if they somehow drag me into it."

Ronald nodded as if that answered his question. He took a sip of his water before replacing it on his coaster. "Naomi is a tough one."

"Really?"

Ronald nodded. "Mean as a snake. She'd double cross her own mother."

"I didn't realize that."

"Fortunately, she liked me for some reason. Not sure why. Well, I suppose in general she prefers men to women. She's the type who's threatened by all women. I think I remember hearing she was once married and her husband ran off with her friend."

"That's awful. But I guess that explains it. Do you think she really hated Gordon?"

Ronald cocked his head from side to side as if he were weighing pros and cons. "No. Despite her meanness, she had a soft spot for him. I think he was her baby brother and she loved him. Sure, they fought like cats and dogs but I think there was love there."

"So, you don't think she would kill him?" asked Antonia in a light tone as if she were joking.

"A lot of people wanted that man dead but no, I don't think his sister was one of them."

Antonia took a second to process that. Was he trying to tell her something? She took a sip of her water and watched him over the rim of her glass. He was sitting on the edge of his seat staring at her. His gaze was unblinking, his face stony. The pleasantness had drained from his façade. She decided it wasn't a good idea to proceed with this line of questioning. Sometimes you've got to cut your losses.

"Right. So, where are you moving to?" Antonia asked, changing the topic.

Ronald smiled, breaking the stern demeanor that had seized him. "I'm going back home, South Carolina. There's a small inn there that has the oldest landscaped garden in America. Horticulture is really my true love."

"I noticed your beautiful flower arrangement."

"Thank you. I have a garden out back. I love wild flowers. And it will be nice to start over. I've already planned some big landscaping projects. I've been doing my homework."

He motioned towards the bookshelf. Antonia's eyes zeroed in on the glossy coffee table books. She rose and went over to examine them. Her eyes flicked across tomes entitled *Southern Style Gardening, British Gardens, Private Newport Gardens,* and *Charleston Gardens.*

"Wow, these are beautiful," she said, sliding out a copy of *The Gardens of Versailles* and flipping through it.

"I know. I adore them all. I spend hours literally poring over them. I cannot wait to sell this place and head down South and get started!"

A thought occurred to Antonia. "These are very expensive books."

"I know," sighed Ronald. "Thank God for the L.V.I.S. thrift shop. I purchase all of my books there. You wouldn't believe the things people give away! Whenever one of those big old estates is sold, they send everything to thrift! Half of my house is decorated with furniture from there. And you should see the boxes of books that people have donated. No one seems to want books anymore! But I must be a Luddite because I cannot stand to read things on the Internet. Oh, I love this one."

He pulled a copy of *Gardens of Eden* out and started flipping through it. "The roses in here are just gorgeous."

Antonia paused. She closed the book in her hands slowly and turned to face Ronald. "The L.V.I.S.?"

He glanced up at her. "Yes, I'm sure you know it? Right on Main Street in the old Gardiner Brown Mansion, down the road from you. The thrift shop is called the Bargain Box. It's a great resource. For everything."

He returned to examine his book.

Antonia felt her pulse quickening. "Biddy Robertson worked there."

She stared at Ronald to watch his reaction. He kept his eyes downward, focused on a close-up of a sunflower that from Antonia's upside down view, looked a little phallic. "I know Biddy, of course."

"Do you know she died yesterday?" asked Antonia. She felt as if she had a frog in her voice so the question barely squeaked out.

Ronald kept his eyes on the picture a beat too long in Antonia's opinion. He glanced up. "Sorry, what did you say? I become so carried away when I read these."

"I said Biddy died last night," she repeated, eyeing him carefully.

Ronald's eyebrows shot up. "Oh, dear, how awful. She didn't seem that old."

"She wasn't. She left the stove on and died of carbon monoxide poisoning."

"Oh how sad," said Ronald. His face remained expressionless.

Antonia watched him carefully. "Did you know her when she owned the inn?"

"That was before my time."

"Oh yes, of course." Antonia closed the book she was looking at and lifted it back to its place on the shelf. "Well, I should be going. Thank you for taking the time."

"My pleasure. I'll try to stop by the inn for dinner before I go. I'd love to see all the changes you made."

"Anytime."

Antonia could feel him walking behind her as she made her way to the door. If he planned on sticking an axe in her back, the time was now. She abruptly stopped and turned around. Ronald didn't appear to be harboring any sinister plans because he smiled. Antonia stuck out her hand.

"It was nice meeting you," she said.

He took her hand into his large paw and shook it firmly. "You too."

She was about to turn for the front door, when something caught her eye. Straight ahead she could see through the kitchen to the backyard. There was a large vegetable patch and the flower garden that he had spoken of, but also something else. Antonia squinted.

"Is that a beehive?" asked Antonia.

Ronald looked flustered. "No . . ."

Antonia wanted to take a step forward, but she would have had to push Ronald aside. He was staring at her, his chin raised almost defiantly.

Antonia backpedaled. "Sorry, I just thought it was."

"No," said Ronald, quickly opening the door for her. "Thanks so much for coming by!"

Antonia walked back to her car with confusion. She didn't know much about bees, but she was pretty sure that was a beehive she had seen in the back yard. Why would he deny it? Only if he had something to hide, she concluded. As Antonia got into her car, she could swear she saw Ronald watching her through the window. She shuddered slightly. Was he really 'a beast' as Gordon had referred to him? And was he 'that B' that Gordon thought was out to get him?

8

The glazed sticky buns had come out so beautifully that Antonia was mentally high-fiving herself as she pulled the sheet out of the oven and slammed the door closed with her foot. She held them close to her nose and breathed in the fragrant aroma of cinnamon and cooked sugar that never failed to disappoint. She felt no greater joy than when she had baked something scrumptious. Call her simple, but that was what the true meaning of life was all about; sticking your teeth into a chewy slab of sweet bread with icing and having it swirl around your mouth.

She called over her intern and impressed upon her the importance of indulgences.

"Liz, let me give you a word of advice. If you master two dishes in your life, sticky buns should be one of them. See how gooey they are? No one can resist them."

"They smell delicious."

"They are. And what I am trying to revolutionize is that they are not just for breakfast anymore. No siree, sticky buns can be eaten all day. That's why we will serve them for afternoon tea today. They are one of life's most precious gifts."

"I hear you. What's the other dish I should master?"

"Learn how to make a good roast chicken. Always a crowd pleaser. I'll teach you next weekend."

"Thanks, Chef."

Antonia smiled at her apprentice with maternal pride. Liz was mature for her age, but still looked like the seventeen year-old that she was. She wore her brown hair shoulder length with bangs, and had big chocolate eyes that didn't miss a trick. She had not yet opted to pluck her eyebrows and Antonia hoped that she never would because there was something so cool and Brooke Shields like about the look of her dark thick eyebrows. She was definitely striking. And despite her lack of formal training in the kitchen, the girl was proving herself.

"How are the tea sandwiches going?" asked Antonia.

"Very well. I've finished the egg salad, cut off all the crusts, and now working on the tomato."

"Don't forget the mayonnaise on the tomato. That's key."

"I definitely won't."

"Good girl. And cover them with a damp tea towel as you go so they stay moist."

Antonia helped Liz plate and prepare for afternoon tea. Marty and Kendra only worked dinner service, so it was really up to Antonia to organize everything for the three o'clock crowd. So far, afternoon tea was not a moneymaking venture.

It was actually a money-losing venture. But Antonia liked the idea that she was bringing more people into the inn, and she also thought it was important for the visiting guests who were staying at the inn to have somewhere to go during the late hours of the day when they needed a little pick-me-up.

"Antonia, we have a problem."

It was Lucy, wearing a sour face. Today, her skirt was pea green with such a wide A-line that it appeared she had a hula hoop underneath.

"What's up?"

"*Barbie* is here again," retorted Lucy, shaking her head. "Refused to even talk to me when I asked her to leave."

"It's okay," said Antonia, wiping her hands on a dishtowel. "I invited her."

A flicker of surprise passed over Lucy's face and she stood up straighter. "Oh . . ."

"Yes, I just wanted to talk to her about this box and everything so that we can avoid another scene."

Lucy nodded. "Okay. Shall I accompany you?"

"No, I'll be okay. Thanks."

* * * * *

Barbie stood under the chandelier in the entrance, staring at the large nineteenth century map of Long Island that Antonia had found at an antique store in Quogue. It had been hidden behind a stack of botanical prints and had a thick layer of dust and a tear in the corner, but Antonia had it cleaned up and had it reframed. It was her goal to collect as many antique maps of the region as possible to decorate the various rooms of the inn. She'd also recently purchased a set of architectural plans of early East Hampton homes that she had mounted in frames and hung in the powder room.

Barbie appeared much less frantic today than she had been yesterday. She was wearing tight blue jeans tucked into high-heeled boots and a long black cardigan that went all the way down to her knees. Underneath, she had on a flouncy black and orange paisley blouse, the type that was fashionable but could double for maternity wear, especially with breasts as ample as Barbie's. Her hair, as usual, was styled in cascading curls that ended just above her shoulders, her makeup appeared perfect and her nails were long and painted red.

She was one of those women who fit the bill for classic American beauty: tall, blonde, blue-eyed and buxom. In Antonia's opinion there was no doubt that she was pretty, but she just wasn't *special*. She'd probably been homecoming queen, Antonia thought, and no doubt a cheerleader, and a popular sorority gal, too. But there was just something generic about her face, a vagueness that left you cold, which had nothing to do with the fact that she was now in her mid-forties.

Antonia led her into the parlor, and after briefly waving and saying hellos to guests, they sat down at a table by the window that afforded a view of the side yard. The afternoon wind had picked up and was dragging leaves across the grass, causing them to dance in whirling circles. A lone guest was outside, lounging on a patio chaise underneath a burning heat lamp, idly flipping through a chunky paperback. But the rest of the outdoor tables and chairs were empty. The slanting rays of the sun were spotlighting a patch of grass in front of the white iron bench that stood in the corner of the yard.

The waitress came by, and greeted Barbie with familiarity. Barbie was pleasant in return, but a bit standoffish. Antonia ordered a full tea service and watched Barbie while she scanned the menu. She noticed for the first time how much makeup Barbie wore; an entire coat of base topped with powder, blush, bronzer, eye shadow, liner, mascara and lipstick. It was a thick layer of cosmetics for daytime, in Antonia's opinion, as if suggesting that Barbie had once had bad skin that she got in the habit of covering up. The sides of Barbie's forehead by her temples were full of deep wrinkles but surprisingly the center was smooth as a baby's bottom. Antonia wondered if she had begun a poorly administered course of Botox.

"This place looks great," said Barbie in her husky voice. She glanced around the room. "I love the walls."

"Thanks. I lacquered them green. I like shiny."

"You really went fancy."

"I suppose," admitted Antonia. "I had a clear image of what sort of inn I wanted. I liked the idea of antiques—English Regency and Biedermeir furniture, oil paintings, chandeliers, but I wanted to mix in modern fabrics on all the upholstery, which is why I chose a lot of Ikat and stripes. I feel like stripes are always in style."

"I was always trying to get Gordon to do stuff to spruce this place up. He wouldn't take advice from anyone," said Barbie.

"Yes, I heard he was quite headstrong."

"To say the least. Whenever I tried to urge him to do something, he'd always say, 'Barbie, baby, you do your thing, I do mine,' in that raspy tone of his. Drew out the my name so that it was ten syllables long."

"Is Barbie short for Barbara?" asked Antonia.

"No. Carol."

As Antonia was pondering that, the waitress brought the tea and they waited in silence until she had set up the table. Antonia wasn't exactly sure what she wanted from Barbie, or how she should try and interrogate her (because really that's what she was doing) so she decided the best way would be to let Barbie do all the talking. Her mother had told her once to say as little as possible, particularly in a job interview, because people actually want to hear themselves talk more than they want to hear you. Antonia always found it tough to heed her mother's advice on this one (a chatterbox by nature; she couldn't help herself) but on the rare occasions she did, it always proved true. She found that if you stayed silent, people would keep going on and on and "get themselves in soup," as her mom used to say.

Barbie poured two packets of Equal into her tea and swirled it with a spoon. Antonia noticed the ropy veins on her hands and understood that was the one thing that truly gave away Barbie's age. She slipped her long red nails around her teacup and raised it towards her mouth to blow. Antonia watched as her bright red lips puckered causing the dark liquid to ripple like a pond on a windy day. Barbie took a sip, leaving a faint trace of her lipstick on the rim, before putting it down with a clink on the saucer.

"Did you get a look at the box?" she asked, taking a sticky bun off the caddy and putting it on her plate. She licked off the trace of icing that had stuck to her index finger before picking up a butter knife and cutting the bun in half.

"I did. And I didn't see anything that resembled a will at all. Lucy was right; it was just some notes."

Barbie smiled and cut her sticky bun into quarters. "I knew you would say that. Of course."

"Why of course?" asked Antonia before selecting a soft egg salad sandwich that folded completely into her mouth in one bite.

"Because why would you tell me if you found it? It would only cause complications for you, legal issues, et cetera."

"Barbie, if I had found something, I would have told you. Trust me, I'm not out to break the law."

Barbie laughed and shook her head with condescending disbelief. She stabbed a piece of the sticky bun with her fork. "Oh, Antonia. I know you have this whole wide-eyed, good girl from out-of-town thing going. That little, 'Aw, shucks, who me?' But you're a businesswoman. You're shrewd. Hell, you fired most of the staff that had been here for years. Why would I assume that you would be on my side?"

Antonia felt herself becoming mad, but even worse, defensive. It was not how she liked to play things.

"First of all, Barbie, in regard to the staff. Yes, there were several whom I chose not to invite back. And that was because I was not impressed with their work ethic, or frankly the condition of the inn when I purchased it. I invited many of the busboys and wait-staff to return, but as the inn was closed for six months while I refurbished it, understandably, many had to seek other employment and couldn't wait for us to finish.

"I am not sure why you accuse me of playing some sort of 'aw shucks' role, because I am certainly not trying to pretend to be anything that I am not. And as for being on your side, I am not on anyone's side. I have no vested interest in what happens to Gordon's estate. But you, on the other hand, seem determined to benefit from his death."

Barbie put down her fork. "I resent that. I'm not trying to *benefit* from Gordon's death. But I was his common-law wife for five years. I helped him with every aspect of the inn. And for that, I deserve something!" She waved her arms up in the air. "This was my *home*. Without me, this place would have been a dump. I deserve something. I put up with Gordon and all of his craziness. I shouldn't be thrown out on the street like yesterday's trash."

Antonia watched her as she wallowed in self-pity. Her eyes filled with tears as she looked dramatically around the room. She took deep breaths, as if she was trying to stop herself from crying. It was all very moving . . . and yet, Antonia felt there was something totally inauthentic about it. Especially since she knew that Barbie had been having a relationship on the side with another man.

"I'm sorry that you lost both your boyfriend and your home," replied Antonia, trying another tack. "You are always welcome here."

"Thank you for saying that," said Barbie with satisfaction. She resumed ripping apart the sticky bun, balling up little pieces between her fingers and leaving shreds on the plate. "It's all Naomi's fault. She is *evil*."

"I'm glad you brought her up," said Antonia. "I was wondering why she said that you had murdered Gordon."

Barbie snorted before taking a sip of her tea. More lipstick found itself onto the rim of the teacup. "She's delusional. Quite honestly, Antonia, you know what I think?"

She leaned in conspiratorially. Antonia did as well. "What?"

"I think *she* killed Gordon."

With that, Barbie raised her eyebrows and sat back in her chair with the smugness of a cat.

"Why do you think that?"

"Money."

"Huh," said Antonia. "I admit money is a powerful motive. But he was her brother. The inn wasn't doing well. There's been nothing to prove she was homicidal."

"I found a secret account in her name. She had been stealing from the inn. Gordon was so mad he was going to tell the police!"

Before Antonia could respond Barbie continued.

"And," said Barbie, leaning in again. "I know for a fact that Naomi has had problems with her temper. She could get just as angry and crazed as Gordon, I'm sure you saw that the other day. She once got a summons for threatening her neighbor with a baseball bat. She smashed the neighbor's car windows while she was sitting in the car!"

"Really?" asked Antonia with surprise. Naomi was tough

but she was so thin and wiry she couldn't imagine her doing that. But you never know.

Barbie nodded. "Maybe she just snapped one day with Gordon."

"But how did she kill him?" asked Antonia. "He died of a heart attack."

"So they say," said Barbie. She smoothed the tablecloth with her fingers. "If it were me, for instance, maybe I'd give him some poison somehow. Like, slip rat poison into his coffee."

Antonia eyed her. Barbie glanced out the window, possibly daydreaming about murder.

"Don't you think the police would have found that?"

"Remember, *Naomi* didn't want the autopsy. She was the one who said no way."

"True," agreed Antonia. "Then why would she have even brought it up yesterday? If she had committed murder and gotten away with it clean, why would she even suggest it?"

"To deflect attention from herself."

"Aha. But still. No one was on to her. No one had been talking about murder."

"You see?"

"No, not really. See what?"

"It's part of her plan," said Barbie, raising her eyebrows. She cut into her sticky bun.

"What is the plan?"

"To trip people up. Make them think I murdered him."

Antonia became conscious that they were talking in circles. She took the opportunity to inhale another sandwich, this time cucumber. Ah, when butter meets vegetables, it is so lovely, she thought, a marriage made in culinary heaven! She swallowed gently as if reluctant to release the sandwich from her tastebuds to her stomach.

She resumed her interrogation. "What about the bee sting?"

"What bee sting?" asked Barbie.

"I heard that some people think Gordon was stung by a bee and that's how he died."

Antonia slid a piece of sticky bun onto her plate. Now that she had gotten through her vegetables and protein, it was time for sweets.

"I never heard that," said Barbie. She bent down over her plate so that Antonia couldn't read her expression, and speared another piece of sticky bun with her fork. "Why would that matter, anyway?"

"He was allergic to bees, wasn't he?" asked Antonia with confusion. Shouldn't Barbie know this? "A sting could have sent him into anaphylactic shock and killed him."

"Oh."

Something in her tone alerted Antonia. She furrowed her brows. "You did know he was allergic to bees, didn't you?"

Barbie shrugged. "I don't know."

"You don't know? But you lived with him for five years."

She waved her hands. "Gordon had a *lot* of ailments. A lot of allergies, too, so sure, maybe I knew. Or maybe not."

Antonia decided to let it pass. She moved forward with another question. "Who do you think, besides Naomi, would have wanted Gordon dead?"

Barbie chortled. "The list is kind of endless."

"Throw me some names. Anyone who pops into your head."

"Well, Naomi."

"We covered her."

"And Ronald Meter. That beast."

"Uh huh."

"He's really a terrible person."

"I know you didn't get along."

"Oh, you don't believe me? I could tell you stories about how bad that guy was . . . he robbed us blind. He set up a secret account."

Antonia listened as Barbie delineated all of the offenses that Ronald enacted against her and Gordon, but with an air of skepticism. She didn't really want to waste time on Ronald Meter right now. Although she hadn't ruled him out as a possible suspect, Antonia was aware that Barbie's information would be biased based on personal slights. And for sure she thought that Barbie was an unreliable narrator when it came to Ronald.

When she had finished rehashing everything about Ronald—which was just as Antonia thought it would be, petty offenses along with the supposed theft of the money—Barbie paused.

"Anyone else who hated Gordon?" Antonia asked.

Barbie cocked her head to the side. "There were all sorts of former employees whom he fired . . ."

"Right." Antonia thought about Hector, the gardener whose wife had been fired. She had to remember to talk to him.

"I mean, the list is long. Gordon was mad at a lot of people and they in turn hated him. Some of the vendors that he fought with probably hated his guts. The guy at the bank who managed the mortgage. Gordon screamed at him one time, made a huge scene. There was the building inspector who cited the inn for all these infractions. Gordon thought they were imaginary and the guy was just trying to get him to comp him dinners here."

"Wow, popular guy," said Antonia.

"He was tough. Lots of people loved him. Lots hated him. Oh, and Biddy Robertson."

Antonia replaced her teacup on its saucer with surprise.

"Biddy Robertson?"

"Yeah, the woman who owned the inn before Gordon. He bought it in foreclosure for a really cheap price and pushed her out. She was furious, said she was literally on her way to the bank with the money when he pulled a fast one on her. She was always writing him terrible letters, badmouthing him around town. Very vindictive."

Antonia put down her sticky bun. "Biddy Robertson died last night."

Barbie stared into Antonia's eyes. A small smile crept across her face. "Pity."

Antonia waited for her to say more but she didn't. The waitress came to ask if everything was all right and that moved the conversation to a different topic, which prevented Antonia from continuing to review Biddy's death. She wasn't sure she would draw more out of Barbie anyway, as Barbie's cell phone started buzzing and then Barbie was tapping away at a response with a silly smile on her face. Shortly, Barbie begged off saying that she had to meet a friend. Antonia was pretty sure her "friend" was her boyfriend. On her way out, Barbie made one last plea for the cardboard box but Antonia resisted and she didn't press. Perhaps she believed Antonia that nothing in it would be of help to her.

After Barbie left, Antonia sat at the table for a few more minutes to process everything. Her head was spinning and she felt as if her quest was leading her in so many different directions. Was it even worth pursuing? Maybe it all just was a coincidence. She wanted to think that, but that was the easy way to look at it. "There are no coincidences," her mother would say.

She sat back in her chair and took one last gulp of her now lukewarm tea. She glanced over at Barbie's plate, and noticed for the first time that after all that cutting, picking and forking, Barbie had not eaten one bite of the sticky bun. *Oh well,* thought Antonia. *Her loss.*

9

Antonia's shoes crunched along the leafy path as she wended her way through the back yard: a wide expanse of sprawling grass enclosed by a privet hedge and a deer fence. Thickets of trees lined the back edge of the property as well as dozens of bushes that flowered various times of the year. On the right side of the lawn there was a long fenced patch of vegetable garden, which was currently dominated by cauliflower, spinach and squash. The other side held wildflowers and a large magnolia tree. The garden shed that had once been used as the tannery was backed against the most recessed part of the yard, in the shadows of some pine trees.

Antonia loved the smell of the East Coast autumn air, which was a revelation for her after all those years in California. The fresh breeze contained a combination of earth, fireplace smoke, musty leaves and pumpkins. It was hard to explain but she wished one of her vintner friends back in California could bottle it all into a cabernet that she would enjoy with a thick slice of Vermont cheddar and some soppressetta. With such a lively and happy aroma, it was strange to think that autumn is the season of death—where all of nature is falling to the ground and dying. Including Biddy Robertson.

Antonia found Hector towards the edge of the yard, planting bulbs in the bare spots between the perennials. Gardening and flowers and plants were all things that Antonia appreciated but had known very little about until recently. In California, she had lived in a town house and paid dues to have others maintain the grounds. It was a relief to have someone else trim bushes into perfect cones and meticulously color-coordinate flower boxes so that everything was as neatly manicured as Disneyland. But now that she owned an inn with a giant yard, she felt it was crucial for her to learn more. For instance, Hector had just told her that spring and summer flowers need to be planted six weeks before the ground freezes in the fall. So they had spent an afternoon flipping through a catalogue, selecting hyacinths, Dutch Master daffodils and Spanish bluebells to be planted. And now here he was, bent down, pushing them into the earth. He was so focused on his digging, that he didn't hear Antonia approach. Although it was chilly, he had taken off his jacket and laid it on the ground next to his tools. The back of his green shirt had sweat marks, which clung to his back while the rest of his shirt rippled in the wind. He wore Carhartt pants and brown work boots, the standard gardener uniform. When Antonia called out his name he stiffened, before turning around.

"Yes, Mrs. Antonia?"

"Hi Hector, sorry to interrupt. Do you have a second?"

"Sure."

He wiped sweat off his brow with the back of his hand and put down his shovel. He looked up at Antonia with an earnest, eager look, and she at once dismissed the idea that he killed Gordon. This was not that type of person. If there was one thing Antonia trusted, it was her gut. This guy didn't read killer. Now there might be some people who questioned her gut when it came to bad decisions like marrying her ex-husband. But if she were truly honest with herself, she would recall that she knew from the beginning that the darkness in Philip's eyes was not a brooding intensity but rather a menacing rage. She was too young to distill the depth of his anger, and optimistically thought she would be able to shake any darkness out of him, like in those romantic comedies where the nice well-intentioned girl changes the badass thug into a charming suitor (see *Grease)*. How wrong she was.

She momentarily lost her nerve. Instead of asking Hector anything about Gordon, she immediately peppered him with questions about the bulbs and what his plans were for their ailing birch tree. He then showed her a hole in the back fence where the deer had broken through, and she gave him permission to buy more wire. Deer were a huge problem in East Hampton; the town was overrun with them. Beside the fact that they ate all of her plants and flowers like candy (she was particularly bitter about the row of yews that used to line the side of the driveway that would now basically be considered a pile of firewood) deer were dangerous. They carried diseases, not just Lyme, which was particularly debilitating, but many others. And they would run out in the road at top speed at dusk and a driver could slam right into them, totaling a car. Ask most people in East Hampton what they thought about deer and you would not receive a response that was warm and fuzzy like Bambi. Deer were vermin.

After exhausting all of the deer conversation, as well as re-iterating all of Hector's plans for the grounds, Antonia had run out of dialogue. She could tell Hector was waiting to return to work, but was politely humoring her. She finally had to make a move.

"How is your wife, Hector?"

He nodded and answered in his thick Guatemalan accent. "She's good. She has a new job, only part time, she stays home with the kids a lot."

Antonia nodded. "That's great. Nice people?"

Hector shrugged. "Yeah, nice."

Antonia nodded again. "Well, so, did she like working here at the inn?"

A brief flicker of anxiety flashed across Hector's face. "Yes, she like. But then, you know, Mr. Gordon was not so . . . well, it didn't work out."

"I heard what happened, Hector. But I also heard that your wife said it wasn't true. What was her side of the story?"

Hector's eyes darted around and he hesitated. Antonia could see the wheels turning in his mind. She wanted him to trust her, because she could just instinctively tell that he was an honest and decent man, the way she could tell a ripe peach from a mealy one.

"Soyla, that's my wife, she work hard for Mr. Gordon. That's okay. She do the sheets, the bedrooms, the bathrooms, and the living rooms. She work from seven in the morning until eight at night for three years. Then one day a guest say that she missing gold hoop earrings. She say Soyla take them. Soyla didn't take them, I promise you, Mrs. Antonia. We are Christians, we go to church every Sunday, we no drink, no smoke, no drugs. Soyla never took the earrings. But they missing . . ."

"Gordon accused her of stealing them and fired her?"

He nodded. "Yes."

"Were you mad?" asked Antonia.

Hector blew air out of his mouth in a deep sigh. "Yes, but I no quit because I need this job, Mrs. Antonia. It's a good job, I work all year here, not just summer."

"Did you ask him to hire her back?"

"I tried talk to Mr. Gordon but he no listen."

"Did you try to talk to anyone else?"

"Well, Mr. Ronald was already fired, so it was just Barbie who help Mr. Gordon, and she no care."

"She didn't try to help you?"

He shook his head. "She said she would talk to him, but I don't think so. And I didn't want to ask her again."

"Was Barbie nice to you?"

"She fine," he said in a tight voice. Antonia could tell he was holding something back.

"Did she do something to you?"

− 114 −

Hector glanced longingly at his shovel and Antonia could tell he wished he were not having this conversation. She wanted to reassure him, tell him everything would be okay, but of course after a man like Gordon treated you and your wife like that, it was wise to be hesitant.

"I don't know. Maybe she . . ."

"She what?" prodded Antonia.

"Someone say, maybe *she* took the earrings. After the guest leave, maybe one week later, Barbie wore new gold earrings. She said she got them for her birthday but, I don't know. The woman who lost them say they were gold with little blue stones on the bottom. These were the same."

Pieces were beginning to fall into place for Antonia. She shook her head. "That's bad."

"Yes. And she also . . . well, I heard she said *she* had some things stolen from her room, and the hotel. She blamed Soyla for that also."

"Barbie did?"

"Yes."

"Like what?"

"She said she no find a red scarf and some shoes, oh and she was mad about a pair of small dishes she couldn't find. They had seashells on them, and they were in the parlor."

"She was missing all that?"

"She say."

"Do you think she was telling the truth?"

"I don't think so."

"Do you think she killed Gordon?"

Hector gave her an astonished look. "What? No, Mr. Gordon had a heart attack. I found him over there . . ." he pointed to the other side of the lawn.

"But maybe it wasn't a heart attack."

Hector was again amazed. "I think it was heart attack."

Antonia didn't want to press it. Instead she changed the subject. "Hector, have Soyla come talk to me. Maybe we can find her a position at the inn again."

Hector's face brightened. "I will, Mrs. Antonia. Thank you!"

This Barbie is tricky, Antonia thought to herself as she made her way back to the inn to prepare for dinner service. Definitely more to her than meets the eye.

10

MONDAY

Antonia was in a grumpy mood when she pulled her weather-beaten Saab into the small parking lot that abutted the L.V.I.S. It was her own darn fault; she had psyched herself up and inevitably was disappointed. This morning she had risen early, a skip in her step, and dressed carefully. She wore a long red and blue paisley Ralph Lauren skirt that she had bought using Genevieve's discount, her emerald green turtleneck sweater and silver earrings that she'd purchased in New Mexico. Her one nod to comfort was her beloved Uggs. Despite the early hour, she'd put on some makeup and taken time to brush her long dark hair. She looked good, maybe too fancy for a walk on the beach, but not inappropriate.

And of course, all for naught, because Nick Darrow was nowhere to be seen on the desolate beach. Antonia felt silly to have expected him; what were the chances? But nonetheless, she had been fantasizing about another exchange with him.

She had even planned to invite him to her restaurant if it came up naturally. When she interacted with attractive men she had a habit of blurting out non-sequitors. She once met a guy in a bar who told her he was an accountant and she immediately asked him if he liked crab cakes. It was as if she couldn't control herself, like Tourette's of the heart. But with Nick, she'd secretly rehearsed a few possible conversations with him in her mind, just so she wouldn't appear needy, celeb-crazed, or talk about how she had bad luck and loved bread. She would stay away from politics, gossip, and murder (so she wouldn't get worked up) and thought a safe topic would be dogs, since he had two and clearly loved them. She had never owned a dog, but she thought they were cute. She had a cat growing up and liked cats, but she refused to have a cat now that she was single and middle-aged. It was just too cliché. Even Genevieve said it would be slamming the door on a future of romance. Not that she was searching for romance exactly, but she didn't want to slam any doors.

So after pacing up and down the beach for half an hour, being humped by an over-eager bull dog whose owner was too distracted by her large Starbucks Venti Latte and iPhone to drag him away, and watching two brave surfers take on the roaring waves, Antonia had called it a day and left. She stopped back at the inn to help with the morning service, but when she found herself barking orders at her line cooks, she decided it was better to remove herself from the situation. She wolfed down a chocolate banana muffin and a mug of milky coffee and set off. And now here she was at the L.V.I.S. and she had no idea why but she felt like she needed to learn more about Biddy Robertson.

The Gardiner Brown House, home of the Ladies Village Improvement Society, was built circa 1740 and is now listed on the National Registry of Historic Places. It is a large two-story shingled house (plus attic) with white trim, framed by well-manicured bushes along the front. A giant American flag flutters in the breeze atop the enormous flagpole in the front yard. The L.V.I.S. is the oldest organization in East Hampton and began in 1895 when twenty-one housewives came together to water down the dusty streets and clean up the railroad station. Since then, the group, comprised of volunteers, have maintained and preserved historic landmarks, parks, ponds, greens and trees as well as done community outreach to better the town. Without these ladies, East Hampton could have ended up looking like the Jersey Shore boardwalks.

Antonia zigzagged up the wheelchair ramp on the side entrance and entered the Bargain Box. She was instantly confronted with the distinct musty smell of old books, worn clothes and antiques that may have sat in an attic for several decades before someone got hip to the fact that they could receive a tax write-off by donating them. The thrift store was located in a series of small rooms that fed into each other. The ceilings were low, with large rectangular overhead lights emitting unflattering brightness, and the walls were mostly white, with the exception of a few that were the color of faded sunshine. An inordinate amount of windows made the place feel less claustrophobic than it could have. The store was extremely well organized, and every attempt was made to market the donations in a user-friendly way. Antonia couldn't help but thinking of the old adage, 'one man's trash is another man's treasure.'

After walking by shelves filled with a variety of vases, porcelain figurines, Venetian goblets and decorative china plates Antonia hooked left into the main room where the register was located. Two women stood behind the counter in front of a bulletin board that reminded people not to talk on their cell phones and gave them all sorts of information about the guidelines to donating. The women were conversing in hushed tones. The first was in her early sixties, with thin white-blonde hair that curled in an upwards flip above her shoulders. She had pale skin with the faintest hint of rouged cheeks, and thinly arched light eyebrows. She dressed demurely and had on a pearl choker, pearl earrings and a white button down blouse under a black cardigan, over which she wore a green apron, as did her companion. She was a classic faded beauty who, Antonia could tell, had been very pretty as a younger woman. The nametag on her apron said LINDA. The second lady, whose nametag said ANNEMARIE, was older and wore her white hair in an unstyled pixie cut. She had the husky voice of a smoker and the yellow stained teeth to confirm it. The green apron fit snugly over her Easter egg blue sweater and her low-hanging ample breasts were making an effort to burst out of the front but instead were flopping out to the sides. She had on gold dangling earrings that softened her somewhat harsh, bird-like features. Antonia walked closer and pretended to be perusing the basket of leather gloves that were by the register. She had a feeling from the solemnity of their voices that they might be talking about Biddy, and bingo, she was right.

"It's just odd how one minute you can be discussing sangria recipes and the next minute the person is dead. I mean, I know life is like that, but it is still odd," said Linda.

Annemarie nodded. "I know. There are lots of people where you see it coming, but not with Biddy! Heck, I know she was seventy, but she was a *young* seventy. She swam in the ocean every day this summer."

"And she was sharp as a tack. That's why the whole leaving the kettle on seems strange to me."

Annemarie sighed. "I agree. I didn't even *know* she drank tea. She always had a cup of coffee in her hand. Maybe she drank tea at night? I like an occasional cup of chamomile to put me to bed."

"I suppose."

When they paused, Antonia moved over to another section so as not to incur suspicion. She had noticed other customers when she entered, but it appeared they had filtered into the neighboring rooms.

"Biddy's son is coming down from Boston to make the arrangements."

"He's a wonderful boy. She adored him."

They paused.

"Those are darling, aren't they?"

Antonia was so busy eavesdropping on their conversation that she didn't even realize they had stopped and directed their attention to her. She was holding a pair of brown suede high heels in her hand that she would never have even thought to buy, but as the shoes were close to the desk where the ladies were gabbing, she had pretended to be totally enamored of them.

"Yes, very nice," she said, turning around and facing the ladies. "I love them in theory, but unfortunately I think I'd fall down flat on my face if I were to wear them."

Linda laughed diffidently. "They do take practice."

"You're still young, you should take advantage," said Annemarie. "Hell, if I didn't have varicose veins all over my legs, I would still be wearing my mini-skirts. I loved my mini-skirts. Believe it or not, Linda, I had great legs."

"Oh, I believe it, Annemarie. You still have great legs."

Annemarie turned back to Antonia. "Honey, take my advice. Wear what you can, while you can. It doesn't get any better."

She laughed heartily, one of those guttural, contagious laughs, and soon Antonia and Linda had chimed in. And then for no reason at all, they all laughed harder, and couldn't stop.

"Sorry," said Annemarie. "I apologize. We're a little discombobulated here today. One of our colleagues, a friend, died two nights ago."

Linda wiped the tears of laughter that had formed in the corners of her eyes and nodded her head. "Yes, I think Annemarie and I are just in shock. You know that wide range of emotions that has you going from one extreme to the other."

"I understand," said Antonia gently. "I have honestly found myself laughing at funerals. It sounds horrible but it's just so stressful and emotional, you can have a hard time processing it."

"I guess that's why," agreed Linda. "I don't know quite what it is, but since Biddy died, I have felt completely frantic."

Antonia nodded sympathetically. Here was her opening. "You were friends with Biddy Robertson?"

"Yes, did you know her?" asked Linda.

"Not personally. But I actually own the Windmill Inn now. How rude of me, I'm Antonia Bingham."

The women made their introductions and briefly questioned Antonia about how her move to East Hampton was going and what the progress of the inn was. She answered in detail, hoping to make them feel comfortable and cozy with her so that she could eventually pepper them with uncomfortable and uncozy questions. After stretching out the conversation as much as possible and inviting them to dine at the inn, she wiggled the conversation back to Biddy.

"I have to be honest with you, and please don't take this the wrong way because I am very sympathetic to your loss, but I'm a little nervous since all I've heard about for the past few days was how the previous owners of the inn died under suspicious circumstances."

Both women looked at her with astonishment. Antonia reddened, instantly regretting that she had even mentioned the topic. Here they were mourning their friend and she was telling them how she was sad about it because of how it affected *her*. It was very tacky and very rude.

"I'm sorry, I just . . ."

But Annemarie cut her off before she could finish. "No, it's not you. It's absolutely strange! I had . . . I forgot all about that. I had heard that long ago and didn't remember until you said it. What are the chances?"

Linda gave Antonia a worried look. "If that was true, I *would* think you would be concerned right now . . ."

"Well, to be honest, I am," confided Antonia. "I mean, I know that it's just an old rumor, I don't even know what you would call it, folk tale? Lore? Myth? But whatever it is, it seems *awfully* coincidental."

"Wait a second," said Linda. "Biddy's death was an accident. She died of carbon monoxide poisoning. So when you say 'suspicious' circumstances, you just mean accidents and things that aren't natural causes, right?"

"Right. I'm not implying anything sinister." Antonia didn't want to bring up murder.

"How did the last owner die?" asked Linda. She was twisting her pearl earring nervously. "I don't remember hearing that was suspicious."

"No, you're right," said Annemarie. "He died of a heart attack, I think."

"Wasn't he Naomi Haslett's brother?" asked Linda.

"Yes," interjected Antonia. "Do you know Naomi?"

"Not very well," admitted Linda. "But we've run across each other's paths at ARF events. We're both dog lovers, and we both had Westies."

"I see."

"Linda has the cutest little Westie I ever saw," said Annemarie. "Teddy. Just a doll."

"My baby. I don't know what I would do without him! He is just so wonderful. Sadly, Naomi's dog Jack passed. I felt bad for her; she adored her baby as much as I adored mine. She was distraught. And then her brother died. . . ." Her voice trailed off.

"Yes, that's tough . . . do they think his death is suspicious because he was so young? I think he was early fifties," asked Annemarie.

"Yes, exactly," said Antonia quickly. She wasn't ready to lay down the whole murder theory with total strangers. "He was so young."

Annemarie nodded. "Just a kid to someone my age."

"Right. That's why some people are thinking that his death was strange."

Antonia watched as both women absorbed the idea. Finally Linda broke the silence. "Well, I hope it was truly Biddy's time to go. I hate to think that just because she briefly owned the inn, she died earlier than she should have."

Annemarie nodded firmly in agreement. "That's the important fact. She didn't own the inn when she died, so it's just a coincidence."

"Agreed," said Antonia.

Linda continued twisting her earring, staring off into space until Antonia finally saw her eyes focus. "You know what? It's good that you're here. There is actually a box here that is marked for the Windmill Inn."

"Really?" asked Antonia with surprise.

"Oh, you're right," said Annemarie. "In the back."

"Yes, I'll go fetch it," said Linda.

She disappeared into the back room. Annemarie gave her a warm smile. "Don't worry about all this nonsense about the inn. It's just drama."

"I hope you're right."

Linda returned with an old box that had previously held seltzer, judging from the labels around the edge of it. It looked worn and musty and had probably been used to transport some kitchen items, thought Antonia, as it had stains embedded into its sides. Linda placed it down on the counter and before Antonia could glance inside, Annemarie peered down deep into it, sinking her bird-like nose as if she were a pelican grabbing a fish out of the water.

"I'm not sure what it is exactly, Biddy put it together, but she told us that it had to go back to the Windmill Inn," said Linda.

"Go back? To whom?" muffled Annemarie from inside the box.

"I don't know."

When Annemarie emerged, Antonia moved towards the box. She glanced inside and suddenly felt a chill. The contents included a red scarf, a pair of black chunky platform boots with worn gold buckles, and two little dishes with seashells on them. Exactly the items that had gone missing, according to Hector.

"Where did she obtain these?" asked Antonia.

"I'm sorry, but I really don't remember. I know she said someone dropped them off but then she realized there must be some mistake and those things belonged to the Windmill Inn."

"Did she say who dropped them off?" asked Antonia. She could tell both Annemarie and Linda were becoming disconcerted with her rising alarm. She had to play it cool.

"No. I don't recall . . ." said Linda.

"Why? What are you thinking?" asked Annemarie.

"Oh, nothing. It's just . . . well someone told me that they thought these items had been . . ." Antonia didn't want to say stolen. Then the police would become involved and it would turn into a bigger thing. "Missing. Someone misplaced these items, they were meant for storage and they were taken, I suppose, here, by mistake."

"Well, I guess Biddy knew that, so that's why she gathered them together," said Linda.

Annemarie gave her a quizzical look. "Who was missing them?"

Antonia took a deep breath. She couldn't lie. "Barbie Fawcett. Gordon Haslett's girlfriend."

"Oh, I know her," said Annemarie in a tone that suggested that she knew her but didn't like her.

"Perhaps it was Ronald Meter who took them by accident," said Linda.

"He comes here a lot, doesn't he?" asked Antonia.

"Yes, now and then. He buys books. He's dropped off things to sell."

"What sort of things?" asked Antonia.

Linda looked down uncomfortably. "Sorry, but I'm not sure we are supposed to disclose . . ."

"Oh, I'm sorry for asking. I just know he has a great . . .

candlestick collection. I was wondering if he ever let any of those go."

Annemarie gave a disapproving look to Linda. Then Linda responded, abashed. "No, not candlesticks."

"Oh."

There was an uncomfortable silence. Antonia definitely didn't want to end on an awkward note. "Well, thank you for this box. I'll bring it back to the inn and call Barbie."

"Great," said Linda brightly. "Oh and tell Hector Gonzalez that we have a new shipment of children's clothes, please."

Antonia paused. So Hector was a customer also? "Hector?"

"Yes, isn't he still the gardener?"

"Yes, yes, he is. Okay, will do."

The door closed with a soft bang behind her and Antonia trotted down the steps to her car. It was so hard to narrow down the list of suspects in a small town, where everyone knew everyone and small dislikes could grow and fester! She placed the box in the back seat of her car and wondered what she would do with it.

11

Instead of heading back to the inn, Antonia decided to zip over to one of her favorite stores in East Hampton. Dorothy's Cupboard, situated on North Main Street, was the quintessential artisanal cheese shop. Located in a low-slung building that had formerly housed a barbershop, Dorothy had kept the barber pole and painted it a festive red, yellow and white. Three brick steps led up to red double-doors and inside, the interior walls were also painted a matching bright yellow, with white shelves.

Antonia was feverishly in love with cheese shops. One of her fondest childhood memories was going to town with her father and stopping in the local cheese shop. She remembered perfectly the smell of all the cheese varieties mingling together; the sawdust on the floor; and the little ceramic dishes filled with samples that you just had to stab with a toothpick and pop in your mouth. She always tried the samples, and adored how the cheese monger would take his slicer from his apron and cut ribbons of buttery and tangy cheese for her to try. They would burst on her tongue and then melt in her mouth. And buying fancy cheese always meant that they were preparing for a party, so to this day, she felt that sense of hopeful expectancy, like something fun is about to happen, whenever she stepped into a cheese store.

Antonia took her time tasting the various new cheeses while she chatted with Dorothy. There were some new luscious triple creams from Northern California, and a nice, sharp, semi-firm Gouda. All of those went well with some apricot and almond biscuits from the North Fork. There was a bluefish spread produced from fish caught of the coast in Montauk that Antonia smeared on an onion cracker. And of course there was new smoked soppressetta with the faintest hint of truffle that just burst with flavor. Antonia was becoming very content.

Antonia took the time to peruse the other various items on display, and found herself loading up on spicy red pepper jam, oatmeal shortbread cookies and mango jalapeño chutney. She was a total sucker for artisanal pantry items and could never have enough. How great was it when she was tired after a long day to just boil some pasta and coat it with a jar of Parmesan artichoke puree? Voila, instant dinner! As she lifted a packet of caramelized walnuts out of the case, a flash of blonde outside the window caught her eye. When she glanced up to take a better look she realized that it was Barbie.

Barbie pointed her key at her white Toyota Prius and pressed a button to lock it. She slid the keychain into her pocketbook—one of those over-sized satchels, made up of calf-hair and pebbled leather, with all sorts of gold zippers and buckles everywhere and the designer's initials prominently displayed in the center, just in case you missed the memo that it was expensive and fashionable. Today, Barbie had on black leggings tucked into low boots, and wore some sort of gray fur vest over a light pink sweater. She strode confidently across the street towards the I.G.A. paying little heed to the traffic, which had the light and the right of way. Just before Barbie disappeared through the electric door into the store, a tall man in a dark blue windbreaker came up behind her and put his hand right on her ass.

Antonia's every sense jolted with excitement. *This must be the boyfriend!*, she thought. She watched as they entered the store and then vanished out of sight and into the aisles. Were they already so intimate that they were shopping for toilet paper and detergent together? And if this dude was married, wasn't he acting very boldly by hitting a grocery store with his mistress in the middle of the day? These were things Antonia needed to know. She quickly paid Dorothy for her provisions and beelined across the street.

Antonia made a sharp turn past the eggs into the produce section. She figured she'd go aisle by aisle until she found them. She had a hunch that they wouldn't be stocking up on vegetables, but you never knew what turned people on. This time, her hunch was correct. The only people perusing fruits and vegetables were an older lady in a purple velour sweat suit, who was squeezing lemons, and a small hunched man who was loading an inordinate amount of green peppers into his cart. Antonia walked down the aisle and took a sharp left into the dairy section. Blasts of cold air immediately smacked her in the face. She wished, once again, that they would distribute sweaters on loan in the refrigeration section so that she wouldn't have to sprint down the aisle into the warmth of canned goods.

Finally she spotted her prey. They were arm in arm, making a left into beverages. Their backs were to her so they hadn't seen her yet. Even if they had been facing her, their body language was telling Antonia that they were probably too preoccupied to notice her. She was about to approach them when she abruptly stopped by the rack of pretzels. She had no plan. Should she just go say hello? The fact of the matter was, if they were out and about like this, then they had nothing to hide. Was she going to bust them for shopping?

She peeked behind the rack and watched as the guy put a six- pack of Heineken into his basket. It would make sense that he was after booze, thought Antonia. Didn't he work at a liquor store? For the first time, she had a visual of him. He was handsome, in a bland everyday way. Very tall, broad-shouldered with a full head of brown hair and a face as round as a moon, her only slight criticism would be that his head appeared to be a bit too small for his body, and he stooped slightly as if he had never become comfortable with his height. He looked to be in his mid-thirties, definitely younger than Barbie, and that fact was illuminated when she snaked her wrinkled veiny hands around his waist. Barbie was a cougar! Antonia should have smelled that a mile away. They laughed at some inside joke and then walked over to the tortilla chip section, adding a bag and some salsa into their basket. *Oh, they have fun planned for tonight*, thought Antonia. As they continued down the aisle, Antonia leaned a bit forward to watch them. Would they stop by the freezer and snag some ice cream? That would really determine the state of their relationship. Scarfing down ice cream in front of a man meant that he had seen you naked. Just as they opened the door and were reaching Antonia felt a poke in her ribs. She jumped as if a snake had bitten her.

"Ah!" yelled Antonia. She whipped around.

"Scared ya!" laughed Larry Lipper, mischievously.

Antonia thought she would throw up. Her heart was literally in her throat (okay, not literally in the *literally* sense, but literally in the sense how people over-use that word to make strong points.) This little rodent had scared the dickens out of her and now he stood there gleefully smirking, his tiny body in his tiny jeans shaking with mirth, and she wanted to strangle him.

"Larry, you shouldn't sneak up on people."

"How could I resist? You were ripe for the picking."

Antonia took a deep breath and vowed she would not throttle him. "Okay, you got me."

"Damn straight. What were you doing? It looked like you were spying on someone." Larry walked around her and stood in the beverage aisle, attempting to bust her. Antonia momentarily held her breath but was relieved to find that fortunately, Barbie and her man had moved on. The aisle was empty with the exception of a young mom pushing a cart while her toddler daughter pushed a mini-cart next to her.

"I was just trying to figure out which pretzels to buy," said Antonia, grabbing two bags from the rack. "Reading the ingredients."

Larry gave her a suspicious look. He wagged his finger at her. "I don't know, I think you were up to something."

Antonia felt herself reddening. She motioned towards the basket he was holding. "I didn't know you had kids."

"What?" he said, and held up his basket as if seeing it for the first time. Inside were two boxes of Kraft macaroni and cheese, a box of Lucky Charms, a small quart of whole milk and a pack of Jell-O pudding.

"Oh, no," he shrugged. "I just like kid food."

For a second, Antonia could swear he was embarrassed, and she was secretly glad. Let him squirm.

"I can't believe you eat all that garbage. It's really bad for you. All those preservatives . . ."

"I know, I know. I'm glad you care."

"I don't care," blurted Antonia.

"Yes, you do!"

"Larry, I'm just trying . . ."

He interrupted her. "Whatever. Listen, I found out a hot tip that you might be interested in."

"Changing the subject, fine. What is it?" asked Antonia.

Larry smiled obnoxiously. "What will you do for me if I tell you?"

"You're kidding me, right?"

"Come on, this is hot stuff."

"I won't do anything. If you want to tell me you will."

"You drive a hard bargain, lady."

"I'm not driving any bargain. I really don't care either way."

What was it about this man that made Antonia behave as if she were in kindergarten? Really, if she had acted this way with anyone else she would have been mortified. But he brought out this bratty, childish toddler inside of her. She had to seize control of herself.

"Alright, since you are so critical of my eating habits, you can make me dinner."

"Larry . . ."

"Trust me! This is worth it."

Antonia took a deep breath. "Okay, what is it?"

He looked like a kid at the candy store. "Well, as you know I have friends in law enforcement . . ."

He paused for Antonia to make suitably impressed exclamations, but she remained silent so he continued. "They tell me that they are actually going to look into Biddy Robertson's death as a possible homicide."

Antonia's heart leapt. "What? Are you kidding me?"

"I knew you'd freak out."

"What changed? Why do they suddenly think something happened?"

Larry shrugged. "I'm not sure. My buddy just said they were taking and I quote, a 'renewed interest.'"

"That's all?"

"The rest you can read about in my column this week."

Antonia felt the blood boil in her veins. She grabbed Larry's arm and pushed him into the rack of pretzels. If she had to crush every bag of snack food to elicit more information from him, she would do it. "Are you crazy? Larry, I'm not waiting until later this week to read your column! What else did he say?"

"Antonia, I didn't realize you liked to play it rough."

"Larry, come on," said Antonia, flinging his hand down. "Don't do this. What would Nicky Darrow say?"

Larry's lips widened into a large grin. "Oh, you're going to celebrity name drop."

"I'll do what I have to."

He cocked his head to the side and stared at her breasts. "Okay, I'll tell you, but only you."

"Thank you."

She folded her arms and waited.

"Biddy has a nosy neighbor. She's actually the one who called the police when she smelled the gas. Lives in the adjoining town house, condo, whatever you call it. She heard someone leave Biddy's house at about nine o'clock that evening. Heard the door shut and Biddy say goodbye and then a car door shut and drive away."

"So? Maybe Biddy had a friend over."

Larry nodded. "But then two hours later, she heard the car return. Heard the same footsteps, the person walked to the door and quietly let herself in."

"Well did this neighbor have a look at the person?"

"She's blind."

"She's blind?"

"Yeah, that's why she has such good hearing. My buddy

said they gave her a few tests and it was uncanny how she could tell all sorts of differences between footsteps and everything. She has ears like a hawk."

"Isn't it eyes like a hawk?"

"Antonia, she's blind!"

She let that one slide. "So that's enough for them to think it's a homicide?"

"I'm thinking there must be other reasons, but that's the only one they told me. Probably because this blind neighbor is going to be running her mouth off around town about the mystery guest. Talk to anyone who will listen. I'm heading over to interview her right now."

"I'm coming."

Larry gave her a quizzical look but then smiled again. "I knew you were hot for me. Can't stay away."

12

Larry had wanted Antonia to accompany him in his car and drive over to the neighbor's together but the thought of spending time with him in a confined space made Antonia sick to her stomach so she refused. Not without a battle, though. Forcing him to impart Biddy's address took epic strength. For someone so diminutive he had an enormously inflated sense of self. Antonia had to wonder about his parents. Maybe since they knew he would be vertically challenged they indoctrinated him with messianic beliefs that he was the second coming. She sincerely didn't think that it was a defense mechanism and that he acted out of insecurity. He definitely thought he was God's gift to women and this earth.

After a search for directions on her phone, Antonia found the location of Biddy's condo. As Antonia drove there, she sifted through all of the recent revelations in her mind. The whole situation reminded her of when she would go on camping trips in high school with her friends. One person would inevitably rise in the night to retrieve water from the stream, and they would see or hear something suspicious. Then the next day, others would add in things—mysterious sounds they'd heard, items that they swore had been moved, shadows that they had definitely seen lingering over their tents in the moonlight. They would all psych themselves up so they were appropriately terrified, and return home from their adventure with a tale to tell. Everything that Antonia had heard about Gordon's death could be examined through this filter. Maybe he had been stung by a bee; that was very rare for December but not absolutely impossible, especially if the weather had been mild enough.

Gordon had several enemies (and friends) who would want him dead: his sister Naomi, because she needed money and wanted to sell the inn; his girlfriend Barbie, because she had a lover and was also possibly pilfering things from guests; Hector, the gardener, who was angry that his wife was fired; Ronald Meter, the former manager, who was angry that he was fired; Biddy Robertson, who was angry that Gordon bought the inn right out from under her. The fact was, they all had motive, but motive was flimsy. You had to have exhibited homicidal tendencies, too, didn't you? This would have to have been an incredibly well thought out plan: to procure a bee, smuggle it to the inn, then have it sting Gordon. Were any of these people furious or psychotic enough to do it? Antonia wasn't sure.

And now there was Biddy Robertson. If it turned out that she had indeed been murdered, the only reason to suspect that her death was linked to Gordon's was because they both owned the inn at one point, and there was that strange 'curse' on the Windmill Inn owners. There was also the box that Biddy had put aside to return to the inn. Could that be the reason she was killed? It seemed absurd. All of this information just seemed like a miscellaneous collection of facts that couldn't support any theory.

And yet . . . there had to be something to it all. Why would the police now think Biddy was murdered? Obviously, they had information. Antonia had to agree with Larry and bet her booties that it wasn't just what the blind lady thought she might have heard. And there was something odd about Gordon's death, some sort of fuzziness that she couldn't pinpoint. People who knew him were acting strangely.

Antonia turned right into Treetop Lane and drove down the bumpy road. A scattering of leaves still held firmly green, but the tupelos had turned a fiery red and the swamp maples were an orange-y maroon. The contrast between them and the yellow leaves of the hickories was dazzling. Some of the most impressive species of trees were in this area, with colors that matched those in the Appalachians. The trees were so thick that immediately everything darkened as if someone had turned off the light switch. Only cracked fragments of sun were able to make it through the heavy leaves. Antonia was not a fan of the woods; they made her claustrophobic. Besides, they were filled with roaming wildlife that made life unpleasant for humans. She would be happy to let the ticks have the woods, if she could have the streets, the farmland and the manicured lawns. It was a fair trade, wasn't it?

When she pulled into number seventeen, she found Larry Lipper leaning against his blue BMW, with a smug look on his face. The condo structure was comprised of attached units and painted mustard yellow, with brown roofs, brown doors and brown trim around the wide un-paned windows. Antonia wondered about the thought process of the person who chose these Howard Johnson colors. When has anyone ever purposely chosen mustard yellow for anything? Something about it said 'reject color.' And to combine it with brown? She instantly thought of a uniform that a sad diner waitress might wear, in the middle of nowheresville, taking orders from sexist truck drivers. Yes, it was a stereotype.

"That's your car?" Larry sputtered. "You kidding me?"

Antonia glanced back at her beloved blue Saab. "Yes, why?"

"It's a piece of junk. They don't even make them anymore."

"It's a good car."

"No, it's not. If it were a good car, they would still make it. This is a good car," he said, pointing to his own.

"Whatever."

"Do you know how they marketed Saabs? They called them 'near luxuries.' Come buy this 'near luxury.' That's why they are out of business. Who the hell wants to buy 'near' luxury? You want to feel good about your car, like you're getting the best thing out there. Not *nearly* the best. It was idiotic."

"Well, clearly I fell for it."

"We'll need to talk about that," said Larry, trying to put his arm around Antonia. She wiggled away. "I think you have low self-esteem."

She changed the subject. "So this is Biddy's?"

There was a small unobtrusive sliver of yellow police tape blocking off the doorway. Other than that, there would be no reason to suspect possible foul play had occurred there.

"Yeah. The neighbor lives there, let's go."

"Hold on, I just want to peek in for a second."

"What are you going to see?" asked Larry with exasperation.

"I don't know, but I just need a sense."

The white curtains were drawn shut on the large picture window at the front. Antonia cupped her hands around her eyes and pressed her face to the glass. She was unable to make out anything but shadowy pieces of furniture. She walked off the deck and around to another set of windows, but again, the curtains were shut. Oh well, so much for her sleuthing. She was hardly expecting to find a note from a murderer, but at least she thought she would try.

* * * * *

Sharon Getz was in her mid-fifties, heavy-set with short brown hair and a neck full of wrinkles that splayed out across her chest like chains. Her eyes were big and brown and blinking, and if Antonia and Larry hadn't known she was blind, they would have never guessed. Larry immediately pointed out this fact.

"You don't look blind," he told Sharon as she led them into her living room. She moved with ease and the same confidence that any seeing person might have.

Sharon laughed. "I know. I'm legally blind, not totally blind."

"What does that mean?" asked Larry.

"It means I have no peripheral vision but can see a small pin-prick size amount. Shadows, colors, but not anything clearly."

"Have you always been blind?"

"Yes, I was born this way. Please, sit down."

Antonia and Larry sat down on a large white sectional couch in the cavernous living room. The ceiling was extremely high, with a massive skylight cutting through the center. Antonia instantly thought of what a pain in the neck it would be to clean it, and she could see from the filmy layer of dirt that it had been awhile. There were large screen doors along one wall that overlooked a terrace where a table and chairs stood, behind which was a brief strip of yard that led into woods. The living room spilled into a dining area, which then opened into a kitchenette with an island and two stools. The walls were all painted taupe, and the floors were a very blonde wood that matched most of Sharon's furniture. It looked to Antonia as if she had bought everything in an Ethan Allen showroom, in one go, as it all seemed to be part of a set. There was very little in the décor that revealed Sharon's personality, which Antonia supposed was understandable seeing as she was blind. There were no books, no framed pictures, and the only artwork was a Van Gogh poster. In the corner on top of a cabinet a television was perched, one of the older ones that had a giant screen but was big and clunky, not like the newer thin plasma or high definition models that everyone seemed to have nowadays. Next to it stood a violin on a music stand.

After they politely refused her offer of water or coffee, Sharon sat down across from them, sinking into the swollen armchair. She wore black crepe pants and an oversized shiny red button-down shirt that flounced over the edge of her seat. Around her shoulders was a colorful scarf, more decorative than warm. Round gold hoops swung from her ear lobes, and she had several thick gold rings with various semi-precious stones on her fingers.

"Are you married?" asked Larry, glancing around.

"Divorced," said Sharon.

"Really?" exclaimed Larry.

"Yes, why?" asked Sharon with alarm.

Antonia threw him a look. "Yes, why, Larry?"

"It's just odd for me to think blind people get divorced. I would think, you know, you need all the help you can get."

"Larry!" admonished Antonia. She turned to Sharon. "I'm so sorry."

Fortunately, Sharon was a good sport. "I know what you mean. I may turn a blind eye to some faults, but when a man cheats on me, I can't turn a blind eye to that!"

"Good one!" said Larry.

Sharon turned to Antonia and winked. Or at least Antonia thought she did, how could she be sure? Maybe it was a blind twitch.

"See, even blind people have a sense of humor," said Sharon.

"And even short people can be rude," said Antonia before Larry could answer.

"Touché," said Sharon.

"Okay, down to business," said Larry. He whipped out a small brown leather notebook, the type Antonia had seen reporters and detectives use in movies and not in real life.

"Don't you have a digital recorder or something? It is the twenty-first century after all," asked Antonia.

"I'm old school, Bingham."

"Right."

He ignored her and instead turned to Sharon. "Tell me what you heard the night Biddy Robertson died."

Sharon proceeded to tell them the same story that Larry had repeated earlier. The only embellishments were a few complaints about a dog that lived two units down and barked incessantly, and several gripes about the management company's inability to clear the paths and fix the streetlight that stood in front of her condo, which had been out for several weeks now, and was causing problems for Sharon's guests. Larry was incredibly thorough in his questioning and Antonia was impressed, but the story remained the same. Sharon had heard goodbyes, footsteps, a car, then car, footsteps and a car again. She was friendly with Biddy but not very close, more like pleasant neighbors. Biddy rarely had company, except when her son from Boston was visiting with his children. She was also divorced, but she had an active social life that kept her away from home most evenings. She was a zealous volunteer, an avid bridge player, a film enthusiast, a fan of prix fixe dinners and a Guild Hall theater regular, according to Sharon.

"How could she afford all that?" asked Larry. "She lost the inn in foreclosure."

Sharon nodded. "Yes, but then her son started doing very well in his work, some sort of finance. He supported her."

After Larry had exhausted all of his questions as to whether Biddy had any enemies (not that Sharon knew of); had been acting suspiciously (not to Sharon); had been unduly stressed (not to Sharon's knowledge); or had been threatened (again, not to Sharon's knowledge), Larry closed his little notebook.

"Why do you think this visitor might have killed her?" he asked finally.

"I can't tell you exactly," confessed Sharon. "It was just something about the footsteps. They didn't seem natural . . ."

"Could it be that the person was trying to be quiet so as not to wake every in the complex?" asked Antonia.

Sharon shook her head. "No. It was almost as if someone was wearing shoes that didn't fit. They were trying to be quiet but having a hard time walking."

"But don't you think it could have been an accident?" asked Larry. "Say a friend comes over, they have tea, friend leaves, Biddy forgets to turn off the stove, friend comes back because they forgot something. . . ."

"But why didn't the friend ring the doorbell?" asked Sharon.

"Or maybe it was someone else entirely. You said the street-light was out in the front yard. It's not that easy to see the unit numbers, and probably very difficult in the dark. Maybe some-one unfamiliar with the complex was trying to go to another house and went to Biddy's by accident. When they saw her number, they left," said Antonia. She was proud of herself for this one, it was totally probable.

"Could be," agreed Larry.

"But . . ." said Antonia. She could tell Sharon wasn't convinced.

"It was the same footsteps. Trust me."

"And then the next morning you woke up and smelled gas?" asked Larry.

Sharon nodded. "Yes. I have a good sense of smell."

"That's a nice consolation from the gods," said Larry.

"Larry," reprimanded Antonia.

Sharon smiled. "That's okay. I'm a big girl. I know this one is a tease. How long have you been together?"

"Oh, we're not together," protested Antonia. "No way, no how."

"Sorry, I just assumed," said Sharon.

"It's okay." Antonia wanted to add that maybe if Sharon could see she would know that Antonia would never go for Larry, but she knew that would be rude.

"Although you are right to pick up on the sexual tension," added Larry. "I can't keep this one away."

Antonia rolled her eyes, but declined to engage. "Sharon, is there anything else you can think of that may be important to us? Anything that Biddy had done or said lately that stands out? Any divergence from her usual routine?"

"Hmmm . . ." began Sharon. "I'm straining to think of anything at all. She had started swimming at the rec center . . ."

"Uh huh, anything else?" asked Antonia.

Larry swirled his finger around in a motion that meant Antonia should wrap it up but she pressed on.

"I was watering my flower boxes one day and she said she was heading off to Indian Wells for lunch with a former partner."

"Partner? Who?" prompted Antonia.

Sharon shrugged. "I don't know and I didn't ask."

"That's all she said about it?"

Sharon furrowed her brow. "She said something that they'd worked together and I don't know, I got the impression that it didn't work out because when I told her to have a good time she said, 'It will be interesting.'"

"*It will be interesting?*" repeated Antonia.

"Yes."

"What do you think that means?" asked Antonia.

"It means it would be interesting, Bingham, Geez, do we need to waste time on this?" interjected Larry.

Antonia shot him a dirty look. "I think it could be something."

"Like what?" asked Larry.

"Like, I don't know. Who was this person she had lunch with?"

"I couldn't say," answered Sharon.

"Can we move on?" asked Larry impatiently.

"Fine, anything else of importance?"

"I know she recently bought planters for the back patio."

"Can we go now?" Larry whined.

Antonia glared at him. How could he call himself a reporter when he had so little interest in cultivating sources? Unfortunately, she could see it was futile to continue with him around. "Fine."

After they said their goodbyes to Sharon, Antonia and Larry drove their cars to the end of the complex driveway and waited until they were far enough down the road to exit their cars for recon.

"Why did you rush me?" demanded Antonia.

"We were getting nowhere," snapped Larry.

"How do you know? Maybe she would remember something. What do you think of what she said?" asked Antonia.

"I think Bored Blind Lady."

"Larry, you are the least politically correct person I know."

"Thank you."

"That's not a compliment."

"To me, it is."

"Why do you think she's bored?"

"I don't know. Look, I want a murder as much as anyone. I'm dying for it; do you know how awesome that would be for my byline? I already have the exclusive; it would just be a money machine for me. I'm talking book deals, and more! I could join forces with Nicky Darrow and do a movie. He'd play me, you understand. But this whole footstep thing is flimsy."

"I guess. She did seem convinced though."

"I'm convinced I make great coffee, doesn't mean it's true."

"Why Larry, that's the first time I've heard you say anything self-deprecating!"

Larry ignored her. "The fact is, there has to be something that's making the police sniff around. But I don't think it's coming from Sharon."

13

Antonia went to her apartment to drop off her groceries from Dorothy's Cupboard and the box of rejected items from the L.V.I.S. Bargain Box there. She placed all of her new condiments in her personal kitchenette cabinets, where they joined about one hundred other jars. One day she would have to host some sort of tasting party, appetizers and hors d'oeuvres only, where she could set out the plethora of chutneys, jams and mustards she had been collecting and open up some crackers and biscuits to sample them. She slid four cheeses out of the bag and noticed that the two triple creams were drooping from being left out of a refrigerator. Ripe cheese, slightly oozing, was like the last temptation of Christ for Antonia, so she unwrapped them and opened a box of Carr's crackers and quickly dug in. Majestic. Cheese and crackers were definitely on her Last Supper menu.

After taking a few nibbles of the harder cheese, she reluctantly rewrapped them all and placed them in her refrigerator. She washed her snack down with a glass of apple cider from the Milk Pail and wiped her hands with a dishtowel. Even though Antonia's apartment was in the inn, she actually spent very little time there, choosing instead to retreat to her office when she had a spare moment. For that reason, there was something decidedly unfinished about Antonia's apartment, a little neglected. She glanced at the two potted plants on her windowsill with dismay. It never mattered that she followed the florist's instructions to a T, she always killed plants. It was a personal failure in her opinion. She filled up a glass of water from the tap and poured it into the pots, and just as she did so, three dead leaves fell to the counter in protest. Antonia sighed. What was she doing wrong? Sunlight, check. Water twice a week, check. Loving glances from afar, check. It was not good to kill plants. Antonia believed in Feng Shui and it was crucial to have plants in your home. They symbolized life, and now she was killing them. She tried not to think of the larger implications, in the whole scheme of things.

Antonia went to her bathroom to freshen up her makeup. She wore little but felt it was necessary to at least maintain what she had on. She carefully reapplied mascara and put on a little blush. Her hands were beginning to crack from the cold so she squirted a shea butter cream into her palms and rubbed her hands together. The smell was pure divinity. She had just picked up the lotion at White's Pharmacy along with a new container of bath salts that she planned on soaking herself in as soon as she returned home from work. On her way out of the bathroom, Antonia caught a view of her profile in the full-length mirror and paused. She was instantly depressed. There was a definite thickening around her thighs, no doubt about it. And that little wheel of fat that she referred to as her 'bread belt' was growing like an inflatable inner tube.

She turned to eye herself critically. The positives (and she always tried to focus on those) were that her hair was still a shiny, lustrous black. Not a gray had appeared (she hoped it never would) and her mane was thick and wavy. She did have some wrinkles on her face, but so far those were really more character-revealing and not something that should send her to a dermatologist's chair. Her eyes were still a bright blue (her vision still perfect) and her teeth were remaining white due to the Crest White Strips that she faithfully applied (she had to battle the coffee and tea stains). Her breasts had not yet drooped, her upper arms didn't have that hanging flab that women incur (no matter how fit) and she had no varicose veins.

But the sad truth was that she was overweight. And at the rate she kept binging on everything bad for her, it was only going to get worse. She sighed and went to her room and sat on the edge of her bed. Yet another full-length mirror on the opposite side of the door didn't allow her to escape her image (why did she have so many mirrors?) She watched as her tummy popped out over her elastic waist. Muffin top, bread belt, cheese gut, whatever you wanted to call it, she had it. Antonia had tried diets from time to time. But they really only lasted a week at most. And forget juicing, that was absurd! She needed to crunch her way through her day and exercise her pituitary gland or else she wouldn't survive. Okay, perhaps she would survive, but the fact was, what fun was life without food? It was her main source of joy. She loved eating it, shopping for it, preparing it, and feeding people. It was her whole life. Her relationship to it was unhealthy, but doesn't everyone have a vice?

Yes, she would like to be ten to fifteen pounds thinner. But she did not want to make sacrifices to do so. And if this hampered the possibility of a romantic life, so be it. Antonia had tried that before and it hadn't worked. She'd had a boyfriend in high school whom she had worshipped, and that had ended on a bad note. And then she had married Philip, and he had turned out to be a monster. She just wasn't good at love. It wasn't her thing. But she *was* good at food. So let that be her thing. It only took a few minutes for Antonia to convince herself of it. Deep down she knew she was taking the easy way out, but she believed that sometimes that was the way you had to take to protect yourself.

After running a brush through her hair and changing into a clean denim shirt, she went back to her kitchenette. The box from the L.V.I.S. was still sitting on the corner, its miscellaneous contents enticing her like a giant question mark. She had to think through what to do with them. If they were indeed Barbie's, had she just donated them to the thrift store and then accused Soyla of stealing them in order to have her fired? If that were the case, why? She probably could have just told Gordon that she thought Soyla was a bad cleaner. Why would she have to ruin her reputation? Or perhaps someone else like Ronald had stolen the goods and donated them to the L.V.I.S.? But then what was the point? There were too many outstanding questions that would have to wait, because right now her services were needed in the inn's kitchen.

But instead of heading straight there, Antonia decided to pass through reception to pick up her messages and swing by her office to make sure everything was running smoothly. The buzz of activity gave her some much-needed adrenaline. When she had first looked at the inn, Antonia had been dismayed by the reception area. She had pictured an old fashioned nook at the base of the grand staircase, with a wooden counter where a pleasant person would greet guests and offer them tea while their rooms were being set up. She wanted old England, comfortable and inviting. Instead, Gordon had ripped out the original built-ins (and ripped out Antonia's heart when she found out that they had been there for over a hundred years before he did so—did he have no shame?) and put in a modern white Formica desk with sleek silver stools. When she asked the realtor what in the world he had been thinking, he said Gordon had tried to modernize the inn. But since when did "modernize" meant "tacky-ize"? Needless to say, those were the first to go. Antonia had scoured the Internet and found the contents of an old inn in the Cotswolds that were on sale. She had the glossy walnut reception desk shipped over and then she tucked it in neatly under the staircase, where it fit snugly. Atop it she put a burnished forest green leather blotter and a silver cachepot filled with black felt tip pens and two brass lamps with green silk shades. There was always a basket of seasonal flowers next to the silver bell that guests would press for service. Today an orange vase held cherry brandy bi-colored roses, burgundy mini-carnations, butterscotch daisies and red asiatic lilies. Next to them, Antonia had placed some small pumpkins and gourds to celebrate the season.

Behind the desk, Antonia had an antique postman's cubby that she individually marked for each room. Guests generally didn't stay long enough to receive mail, but she would have Lucy type up any of the day's activities around town, weather information and the dinner menu and place copies in each guest's box every morning so that they felt like they had some correspondence. Above the desk, Antonia hung a wooden sign that spelled out in white cursive, "Enquiries," and above that was a vintage brass clock that needed to be constantly wound. Fortunately, ten feet away, Antonia placed a large Grandfather's clock that ticked grandly and loudly and kept beautiful time.

Connie was chatting away with a middle-aged couple who had arrived two nights prior from Maryland. Sometimes Antonia worried that the loquacious front desk manager spent a little too much time gabbing with guests, but she hadn't had any complaints. And this couple were very relaxed—they were repeat customers who had been guests at a wedding in East Hampton a decade earlier and had fallen in love with the town enough to make an annual pilgrimage. Antonia had been gratified when they told her that they could not believe the remarkable renovations that she had made, and Antonia was giddy with excitement watching their genuine amazement as she toured them around the public rooms. They had noticed every detail, and complimented her on all of her success.

"Hello, Mr. and Mrs. Winslow, how is everything with you?" asked Antonia.

They were a thin, energetic couple who both had the trim sporty physique of long distance runners. She wore her brown hair in a ponytail and his was short and sparse, but they were youthful and bursting with energy.

"Super, thank you, Antonia," said Mrs. Winslow. "We had a fantastic day. We picked up some goodies from Round Swamp and went out to the lighthouse in Montauk and had a picnic."

"I LOVE Round Swamp," exclaimed Antonia. "It takes every single ounce of strength I have to not go there every day! I would weigh four hundred pounds if I did!"

"The cinnamon buns are pretty incredible!" said Mr. Winslow.

"Incredible? They are a narcotic for the soul. I love cinnamon buns. But everything is good there. The peach raspberry pies? The mini berry muffins that you can just pop in your mouth? And the chocolate fudge cake is divine," said Antonia, her mouth beginning to water.

"We love the baked goods but the main courses are pretty super also," said Mrs. Winslow. "I love their grilled shrimp kabobs. We picked up some of those and had some of their pesto pasta with peas and roasted brussels sprouts. It was so tasty."

"I'm jealous! But have you had their Mexican layer dip?" Antonia asked, raising her eyebrows.

"Oh, I've had that," interjected Connie from behind the counter. "That is dangerous."

"We haven't tried that yet," said Mr. Winslow.

"My gosh, you are missing out," said Antonia. "Now I'm not sure if it's five layer dip or seven layer dip, but whatever it is—it's a whole new level. There's cheese, sour cream, beans, guacamole, salsa . . . yum. It's a creamy, gooey mess. You just heat it up so the cheese is all melted and find one of those sturdy tortilla chips—not one of those pale white corn ones that crumble when you try and scoop up some salsa—but one of those thick ones that won't break and can act like a spoon— and you just scoop up the hot dip. It has a little bit of spice, but it all melds so wonderfully together. I tell you, *nirvana*. You have not lived until you tried that!"

Mr. Winslow turned to his wife. "We're trying that tomorrow!"

"For sure!" she agreed. "Wow, Antonia, you should be a food writer! I just ate an hour ago and I'm already hungry."

Antonia laughed. "I'm always hungry!"

They chatted a bit more about food and Antonia reminded them that they could not possibly leave town without trying Pasquale's homemade mozzarella at Red Horse Market, which was fortunately on their way out of town. "Like candy" is how Antonia described it.

Before Mrs. Winslow headed up to her room, she stopped Antonia. "Oh, and I just want to say it's so nice to see Gordon's girlfriend is still here."

Antonia was momentarily confused. "His girlfriend?"

"Yes, I bumped into her yesterday."

Antonia realized she must mean Barbie. She was just happy that it hadn't been the day prior when Barbie was tussling with Naomi. "Oh, right . . ."

"I'm glad she's still around, I mean, it doesn't surprise me, because she once told me that her lifelong dream was to own an inn."

Antonia smiled brightly. She did not want to bad-mouth Barbie in front of a guest so she gritted her teeth. "Yes, well, we had tea yesterday."

Mrs. Winslow nodded. "Well, I was worried when I heard the inn was sold that she wouldn't be here, so I'm glad to see her. She was very helpful. Last time I was here, I lost a pair of earrings, I put them down somewhere when I was talking on my phone and I couldn't for the life of me find them. I was so distraught, searched everywhere, and at last she found them in the parlor and brought them to me. I'm so grateful."

"How wonderful," said Antonia.

As she made her way into her office, Antonia's mind was filled with Barbie. Was she just a garden-variety kleptomaniac? She had probably stolen Mrs. Winslow's earrings herself and planned on selling them or wearing them but when Mrs. Winslow caused such a scene, she aborted her mission and tried to play the hero, Antonia conjectured. It was all so bizarre. But it was interesting that she had revealed it was her 'lifelong dream' to own an inn. To what end would she have gone to fulfill such a dream?

Antonia was planning on sitting down at her computer

and "Googling" everyone from Barbie and Gordon Haslett to Larry Lipper but she noticed with dismay that her in-box was overflowing and demanded immediate attention. She lifted up the pile, flipped through and was disappointed to see it mostly consisted of bills. It sometimes felt as if her in-box self-generated bills. She'd pay a round of them and then more would magically appear, as if someone had sprinkled a fairy dust that just serviced creditors. Antonia was trying to figure out how the electric company could be demanding so much money from her when Lucy entered her office.

"Ah, finally. I need you to sign off on those so I can pay them," Lucy said, a twinge of reprimand in her voice.

Lucy remained in the threshold of the door, her arms folded. She was wearing a black and white mini-polka dot dress with a cherry red cardigan on top; she was one red, tied neck scarf away from doing the bunny hop. She wore very peculiar pointy black shoes that made Antonia think if she clicked them together Lucy may end up in Kansas or some far off Midwestern state.

"Yes, I suppose I've been avoiding them," sighed Antonia. "Why does it seem like the bills keep coming?"

"I have to pay them if we want to keep things moving along here."

Antonia leaned back in her chair, the foam inside the cushion flattening under her weight. "I know. Ugh, I just hate dealing with this part of it."

"Antonia, can I be frank with you?"

"Of course."

"The inn is losing money."

"What do you mean?"

"I think perhaps, you don't understand the extent of things. I don't mean to speak out of place but as your bookkeeper, and now manager, I feel it is necessary to warn you that you are in a precarious financial situation. The inn has not yet been fully booked. Yes we are steadily making progress, but we've never even had guests stay in the upstairs suite—and the restaurant is hemorrhaging money."

"I can't understand how that is happening. I know we're new, we've only been up and running for six weeks, but I thought that we had a bigger cushion than this."

"Your renovation costs were hefty. You had to carry all of your utility costs during that period, and pay the small group of employees that you chose to continue working here. The furniture and décor you chose were most definitely extravagant, as you are well aware. You insist on having the best of everything—soaps, towels, shampoos, food . . ."

"If I want to be a high end boutique hotel, I have certain standards that I need to adhere to . . ."

"I don't disagree. But how will it help you to be that certain type of hotel if you are bankrupt?"

Antonia opened her mouth to protest but snapped it shut. As her mother always said, 'don't kill the messenger.' It was perhaps a conversation that she needed to have. She knew deep down that she had been coasting and trying to avoid the entire financial component of running an inn and restaurant. Ultimately, she had to face the facts. The income from the stocks that her father had left her when he died generated a nice income for her, but it wouldn't last forever if she kept selling them off to make payroll. She would have to figure something out.

"So what are you proposing?" she said finally.

"If we were prudent we would shut down the restaurant," Lucy said firmly.

Antonia thought she would be sick to her stomach. A wave of nausea came over her. "You're kidding."

Lucy pressed her glasses up closer to her eyes. "I'm not."

Antonia sat in stunned silence. Lucy shifted her weight in the door.

"But . . . that's my favorite part . . ." Antonia said weakly.

"I think you need to make some hard decisions."

It would be a total heartbreak for Antonia to have to close her restaurant. During her darkest days, when she was suffering from the tyranny of her ex-husband, she used to imagine owning her own restaurant. It didn't need to be ambitious or fancy, she just wanted to serve homey comfort food, all of her favorite things that she loved. It was the good dream, the dream that kept her going. If she had to shut down the restaurant, it would mean more to Antonia than just a failure. It meant that Philip, her ex, would have won. The money she received from him would be gone; all lost in the failed inn, and all that she would have is the nagging sense of failure. Cooking was the one thing that made Antonia happy. Feeding people. She had always loved it. And now, to close it down?

"There has to be another option. We're just gaining traction with the restaurant."

Antonia gave Lucy an imploring look. She could tell there was one side of Lucy that was sincerely enjoying this masochistic exercise. Lucy was probably one of those people who enjoyed breaking bad news to people. She'd hide behind her numbers, or statistics or whatever, but she would wear that secret smirk that she was wearing now. She should have been an emergency room doctor next to a racecar track.

"I knew you wouldn't want to take this step just yet so I have a temporary solution. We are heading into winter, and everything will start slowing down. I don't think you should keep the restaurant open seven days a week anymore. Starting next week we should move to winter hours. Only Thursday through Saturday night. This will save on food costs. We can't offer tea service every day . . ."

"No!" the word leapt out of Antonia's mouth. Lucy gave her a stern look and continued.

"For now. Only offer it a few days a week. And I have comprised a list of alternative vendors we can use for produce, sundries and laundry. We have to reduce the fresh flowers around the inn, scale back on our wait staff and find more partnerships with local businesses who can bring more people into the inn."

She handed Antonia a spreadsheet. Antonia glanced at it with dismay.

"Really?"

"Antonia, I'm sorry but this all has to be done. Again, I don't mean to overstep, but you don't have experience running an inn. I've been in this business longer than you and I know what the costs are. We are struggling."

Antonia stared at the spreadsheet. It was like watching a horror movie; she saw how all of her money was drifting away. "Okay," she said finally.

She knew Lucy was right. It stank, but maybe if they did all this they could generate some money and stay afloat.

"Is that all?" asked Antonia.

"For now."

14

Antonia was morose as she prepped for dinner service and everyone in the kitchen could sense it. Marty and Kendra made an effort to keep their bickering in check, and Liz assisted Antonia in silence. It was Monday night, and Antonia had instigated a 'Fun Monday' prix-fixe three course meal, where everyone in the kitchen (including busboys and waiters) could submit an idea for an appetizer, an entrée and a dessert and the zaniest would make the menu, and that usually led to a rowdier atmosphere in the kitchen, but tonight was subdued.

"Liz, why don't you make the special dessert," said Antonia. She poured a measuring cup of maple syrup over a baked ham and started spreading it evenly with her brush.

"Me?" sputtered Liz.

"Sure. You came up with it."

"But . . . I'm just an intern."

"That's okay, I think you're up to the task. You probably have some idea how to make Captain Crunch cakes with bacon and candy corn ice cream or else you wouldn't have suggested it."

Liz smiled. "I did make it once at home."

"Go on, I'll help you if you need anything."

Liz gleefully went over to the pantry to gather provisions. Antonia couldn't help but crack a smile. Liz reminded her so much of herself it was crazy! There was something so liberating about just purely cooking the food you love. Maybe Lucy was right and she should just cut her losses. But instead of the inn, just do the restaurant. Here she was in her happy place, and she was unable to enjoy it because she was worried about money. It seemed absurd!

For the rest of the afternoon, Antonia took on the more laborious and less rewarding tasks like filleting the fish, butchering the meat and peeling the shrimp. She knew she was being a little masochistic but it felt good to get down and dirty and stab things. By the time dinner service commenced, Antonia's hands felt as if they would fall off. If she had to ladle one more scoop of gravy onto the roast chicken and mashed potatoes she thought she would scream. So it was a relief when Glen came in the kitchen and told her she had a friend who was asking for her. Marty and Kendra were only too eager to have her leave the kitchen, so she realized that her bad mood was rubbing off on everyone. She had to make a note to try and contain her problems and not let them affect everyone around her. That was no way to run a business.

"Hey girlfriend! So glad you came out. Please come sit with us for a bit!"

Even though she had seen her yesterday, Antonia felt a rush of joy at seeing Genevieve. No one could cheer her up like her old friend. She wasn't sure what made them click, but there was something about Genevieve that was so light-hearted and fun, and just amused Antonia to death. Gen had been there in her darkest days with Philip and was always a source of beaming light. Maybe it was because she was the polar opposite of Antonia, so irresponsible, kind of crazy and scattered, that the friendship worked.

Tonight, Genevieve was, as usual, dressed to the nines. She had on a glittery gray sequined blouse underneath a black velvet dinner jacket. Her dark hair was slicked back into a tight ponytail and she wore dramatic eye makeup that quite honestly, looked a little crazy in Antonia's opinion. Antonia never went for that intense eye-liner-ed look that was so popular in fashion magazines. It looked absurd on her. But some people could pull it off. Just like the approximately seven thousand gold bangles running up and down both of Genevieve's arms that reminded Antonia of Egyptian mummies. She worked them as well as she worked the large gold necklace so tightly coiled around her neck that looked to Antonia as if it could strangle her.

Genevieve was seated in the banquette next to a very young looking blonde man (teenager?) who was wildly underdressed in a blue v-neck t-shirt and jeans. His baby face was tanned but smooth, not a wrinkle to be found, and he seemed so young that at first Antonia wondered if Genevieve was babysitting, but when she saw her put her hand on his knee, she prayed that wasn't the case or else Genevieve was headed to the clink. It was all very Lifetime movie, in Antonia's opinion.

"Antonia, this is Ty, please meet."

Antonia held out her hand to shake but Ty gave her the peace sign instead.

"What's up?" he asked. His teeth were white but a bit crooked and he had the slightest, tiniest, hint of blonde mustache under his lip but nothing on his chin. His jawline was weak, which was a shame, because it was as if God himself had sculpted the top of his head but then got tired and quit in the middle, rendering him gorgeous at first blush but then kind of average and pinched when you studied him.

"Nothing, just work."

Antonia sat down across from them. Genevieve gave her one of her 'I can't believe how lucky I am' looks and Antonia rolled her eyes.

"Dinner was awesome," said Genevieve. "We had the fun menu. I totally loved the potato chip fried chicken with peas n' cheese mash. That was so yummy."

"I'm glad you liked it. Kendra created that dish."

"Who's Kendra?" asked Genevieve, taking a sip of her Cosmopolitan.

"For the umpteenth time, she's my sous chef!"

"Oh, right. Well, she's talented."

"I know."

"That cereal dessert was rocking," said Ty in his slow surfer drawl. He drained the contents of his beer mug. "I could have eaten that all night."

"Thanks," said Antonia. She folded her hands in front of her and tried not to be judgmental. This guy was too easy of a target. "So, Ty, what do you do?"

He swept a piece of blonde hair off the side of his face and gave her an earnest look. "What's my job or what's my passion?"

"Both, I guess," said Antonia. She refused to look at Genevieve because she knew Genevieve would be sending her imploring glances.

"Yeah, well, I work in the pool industry in the summer, through the season really."

"Swimming or billiard?" interjected Antonia.

"Swimming," said Ty, nodding his head solemnly. "You know, opening at the beginning of the season, cleaning throughout, closing at the end."

"And how's that for you?"

"Mellow. I can rock it with my head phones on, so it's like, no prob. Pretty straightforward, I would say."

"Ever find anything interesting or unexpected in a pool?"

"Naw, usual crap. Leaves, toys, mice, bugs, nothing sexy."

"Got it. No floating bodies," joked Antonia.

"Naw, not yet," Ty answered with all seriousness.

Antonia smiled. "And in the off-season? What do you do then?"

She could see Genevieve fidgeting out of the corner of her eyes, squirming. Genevieve did not like to engage in any sort of intense exchanges with the men she dated. She preferred to take them all at face value. Ty didn't seem to care; he gave Antonia the smile of a Cheshire cat.

"That's when I live out my passion. I follow the waves."

Of course, thought Antonia. "Where do you follow them to?"

"Wherever they take me. Where the ride is the most badass. Hawaii, South America, wherever."

"That sounds nice."

Antonia wanted to proceed with her line of questioning but Genevieve interrupted. "Okay, enough third degree. Ty and I are here to have fun. Any update on the murder sitch? Shall I be planning your funeral?"

"Ha ha, very funny," said Antonia. She felt the stress creeping back into her body. "Nothing to report."

Genevieve squinted and studied Antonia's face.

"I'm glad. And I hope you dropped it. You have to stop looking for trouble. You're like a pig sniffing for truffles. Life is great, you're happy but you feel the need to bring problems to yourself. Let it go," advised Genevieve.

"I'll try."

"Don't try. Succeed."

Genevieve definitely had her mantras that Antonia suspected came from feminine hygiene commercials and the like, but actually tended to be prudent. She *should* succeed in making herself happy. Why the heck was she snooping around trying to solve murders that may not really be murders?

"Dude, what murders?" asked Ty.

"Antonia thinks the previous innkeeper was offed."

"Seriously?"

"No, no, Genevieve is just teasing you," insisted Antonia.

The last thing she wanted was to perpetuate the inn's reputation as a place of death.

"I never thought of East Hampton as dangerous as South Central but dude, this place is seriously sketchy these days."

"What are you talking about?" asked Genevieve incredulously. "There's basically no crime here."

Ty wiped a piece of hair out of his eyes. "Don't you remember that someone stole my phone off the beach when I was riding the w's?"

"Okay, but you were practically asking for it. You left it on a rock on the jetty. Someone probably thought it was lost."

"Yeah, well, if they'd have looked out in the ocean they would have seen me."

"Whatever."

Ty bristled at being blown off. "Okay, and then like, the other night, my sister heard this bang in her backyard. Someone was climbing over her garbage cans."

"And?" asked Genevieve.

"She yelled out and said she had a gun; saved her own life. The intruder ran away."

Genevieve and Antonia exchanged skeptical looks.

"Maybe it was an animal?" asked Antonia finally. "Where does she live?"

"Northwest Woods. And no, it wasn't an animal because she saw someone running away, and then get in a car and drive off."

"Did she call the police?" asked Genevieve.

"Naw. She's kind of the type who likes to take the law into her own hands. She's waiting for them to come back."

"What did she think they were after?"

"She collects vintage birdhouses. They're super valuable."

Antonia nodded. "Were any stolen?"

"Naw," said Tyler.

"She was lucky," said Antonia. Only Genevieve detected the amusement in her eyes.

"Totally."

Soon Ty grew bored of the inquisition and started to make sounds about going home, which made Genevieve nervous, so Antonia took her leave. She found Joseph finishing up his dinner and went over to join him.

"You weren't here yesterday, I was worried," said Antonia light-heartedly. She sat down across from him and motioned for the waiter to bring her a glass of wine. Time to relax.

Joseph dabbed his chin with his napkin and didn't meet her eye. "Yes, I couldn't make it yesterday."

"I'm just teasing you. Of course you don't have to come every night. I know there are other restaurants out there. I'm not jealous!"

Joseph reached down into a worn brown leather satchel and carefully pulled out a manila folder that he held in his knotted hands. He placed it on the table and slid it towards Antonia.

"What's this?" asked Antonia, flipping it open.

"After we heard about Biddy Robertson, I couldn't shake her from my mind. I was in the library yesterday and decided to do some research."

Antonia scanned the article from *The East Hampton Star* that Joseph had printed out for her. It was the police blotter from six years prior. Underneath an item about a Friday report of youths smoking in the Waldbaum's parking lot there was the following mention:

> *The owner of 15 Treetop Lane, Elizabeth Robertson, accused her neighbor Naomi Haslett of placing a dead raccoon on her doormat. Haslett denied the allegations, and as there was no proof, no arrests were made. Police advised the two women to stay away from each other and call them if there were more problems.*

"Wait, Naomi and Biddy are neighbors?" asked Antonia with astonishment.

"Were neighbors," Joseph corrected. "According to the "Recorded Deeds' section of a later issue of the *Star* it says that Naomi sold her condo four years ago."

"Wow. Was there anything else about this raccoon?"

He shook his head. "No more mentions of their conflict."

"Obviously they hated each other if Biddy would think that Naomi put a dead raccoon on her doormat."

"Agreed."

"That's also pretty disgusting. You'd definitely have to be a certain type of person to use road kill as an act of retaliation."

"Absolutely," said Joseph. He took a sip of his sherry.

"Oh, Joseph, what to do now?" lamented Antonia. "I spent the entire afternoon and evening thinking that I had to stop focusing on this ridiculous theory and return my attention back to my inn and restaurant that are clearly struggling! And just when I want to get out, you pull me back in!"

"I'm sorry, my dear, I did not mean to distract you. I thought it necessary to provide you with all the information I had at hand, but it doesn't mean you have to do anything about it. Remember, the police are already looking into Biddy Robertson's death as a possible homicide. So I am certain that they found this information and are interviewing Naomi Haslett."

"I guess, but for some reason I feel responsible. At least to look into the possible Gordon murder side of things. Clues and weird coincidences keep popping out at me."

Antonia filled him in on all of the recent revelations. There was her discovery of Gordon's note that referred to 'firing that B'; her meeting with Ronald Meter and the possible beehive in his backyard; the sighting of Barbie and her boyfriend; the box of stolen inn items that she reclaimed at the L.V.I.S., her interview of Sharon. Did it all add up to something or was it a whole lot of nothing?

"There are definitely a lot of unanswered questions," conceded Joseph.

"That's for sure. But I think at this point, I realize I'm way out of my league. I'm of the mind set, 'don't quit your day job,'"

Antonia sighed deeply and drained her wine glass. Joseph paused and pensively played with the edge of his spoon.

"I also read up on bees yesterday. Fascinating creatures. I didn't know much about them other than what a nuisance they can be when you want to have a beach picnic in early September. But then, I'm not having many of those in my current invalid state."

"Oh, please."

"It's true, dear. But yes, bees are interesting. Did you know there are nearly 20,000 species of bees? And that's just of the known variety; the actual number is probably higher. Bees are found on every continent in the world except Antarctica."

"That makes sense. Where there are plants, there are bees."

"True. It's actually amazing how much humans rely on them. It's estimated that one third of the human food supply depends on insect pollination, most of which is accomplished by bees, especially the domesticated European Honey Bee. What is frightening is that over the past four decades we have seen a rapid reduction in the number of bees, especially in the United States."

"Why?"

"It's an accumulation of many different factors. The winter generally knocks off about twenty-five percent of them to begin with. There was a DNA based virus that scientists discovered in 2010 that when coupled with a particular fungus proved one hundred percent fatal to thousands of colonies. Pesticides have played a great role in their eradication, as well as mites and the reduction of commercial beekeepers. In addition, urbanization is a problem. As we expand, wildflowers decrease and thus eliminate the food bees need to survive."

"Leave it to the humans to mess things up. A pity on so many levels, but especially since I truly appreciate a community where the queen is the bigwig."

"Agreed, my dear. And bees are revered in most societies. In ancient Egypt, the bee symbolized the lands of Lower Egypt, and the Pharaoh was referred to as 'He of Sedge and Bee.'"

"But they are considered pests to a certain extent," added Antonia.

"Well, actually that's sort of a misnomer. It's yellowjackets and hornets that are the ones that mostly bother us. And they are misidentified as bees. In fact, virtually all bee species are non-aggressive if undisturbed and many cannot sting at all. Unless you are allergic to bees, in which case a sting is fatal, it is actually humans who are more dangerous to bee than the other way around."

Joseph paused to sip his drink. Antonia furrowed her brows.

"Would there be any way to know if Gordon was stung? And how would that have happened?"

"If we are proceeding with the theory that someone with knowledge of Gordon's allergy procured a bee to sting him, than I conjecture that it would have been a honeybee. Someone could purchase—or steal—one from many of the commercial hives in the area, or purchase one on the Internet, as they are the most popular and easiest to obtain. Or breed them, like that man you mentioned?"

"Ronald Meter."

"Yes. The fact is, a honeybee rarely stings away from her hive, unless mishandled and treated roughly. If the murderer brought one to the garden, aggravated it, then somehow set it on Gordon, it would sting him. And a honeybee leaves a stinger inside the victim."

Antonia considered this. "Then if that's what happened to Gordon, the stinger may still be inside him?"

"I'm not sure what happens when the body begins to decompose."

"Hmmm, there's only one way to know. What do you think, we try and exhume the body?"

"Oh dear, I hope it won't come to that."

"Me too," laughed Antonia. "Plus, no one would allow us to do that just on a gut feeling. Especially if one of our major suspects includes the next of kin. Too bad. But how are we going to find out who killed him?"

Joseph took off his glasses and wiped them with his handkerchief. "I think you need to focus on Detective work 101."

"And what's that?" asked Antonia.

"Who has the most to gain from Gordon being killed?"

15

TUESDAY

The winter birds had arrived. The ospreys and the cormorants headed south, but the southern terns, the western kingbird and the dickcissel had landed to set up residence. Despite the approaching winter months, and the promise of cold to come, the trees and dunes were still bursting with feathered life.

The morning air was brisk. Antonia had set out early for her walk in an effort to clear her head. The waves had thumped the shore violently overnight, and the tide had driven the water all the way up towards the edge of the dunes. The sand was wet and compact, and with every step Antonia took she cracked a piece of it underneath her.

The mansions that lined the coast were weather-beaten but defiant. Most of them had withstood numerous hurricanes, eroding dunes, infestation of the Piping Plovers, but they remained sturdy and grand, like true Yankee stock. She loved the dichotomy of an old shingled house with a gambrel roof and a wrap-around porch that was perched next to a stark white modern Charles Gwathmey-style masterpiece with walls of windows and irregular angles. Each had its own personality. Celebrity maps weren't sold in East Hampton but Antonia wished they were because it would be nice to have an idea of whom they belonged to. She knew the CEO of Starbucks lived in one house, and a newspaper magnate lived in another. President Clinton rented one every summer, too, and there was one supposedly in trust for a sixteen year-old orphan. There were countless billionaires who had their homes on the beach, but others belonged to old East Hampton families whose bank accounts had been depleted and were now house-poor. What they all had in common was this majestic view of the Atlantic Ocean and instant access to one of the most pristine beaches in the country.

"There you are!" boomed Nick Darrow as he trundled toward her. He wore jeans and a black zippered fleece and his hair was damp, as if he had just showered. He carried a white paper bag in one hand and his dogs were heavily in pursuit.

At first Antonia thought there must be someone standing right behind her but when she remembered the beach was fairly empty she turned a crimson red and realized he must be talking to her. "Hi," she said shyly.

"I thought you came every day?"

"Me?"

"Yes, you, who do you think I'm talking to, Antonia?" He glanced around dramatically to look for other people. Antonia felt a rush inside her. He remembered her name.

"Yes, I do. I was here yesterday."

"Oh, I had a thing yesterday. But I didn't see you the day before. I thought you said you were always here?"

"Right. I had something also. A thing . . ."

"Got it. I guess we both have these elusively named things that sometimes keep us away," he said. Then he winked at her. "So I brought us some donuts this morning. From Dreesen's."

He held out the bag and offered her one. Antonia was totally and completely touched. He had brought her something? He had thought of her? She was on his radar even? Wow. No matter that she had already wolfed down a pumpkin muffin—nothing was going to stop her from partaking in one of these amazing confections. She chose a cinnamon over a powdered sugar (for fear the powdered sugar would end up all over her face) and she bit into the warm, sugary sweet.

"Delicious, thank you."

"I love Dreesen's donuts. I used to buy them when I was a kid. Back when there was still an actual Dreesen's and they weren't sold by Scoop du Jour."

"The town has changed a lot from what I understand."

He shrugged as if it was an old argument. "Look, yes. Some things for worse, a lot worse. But I choose to focus on the positive transformation. East Hampton is now a town that offers everything, all year 'round—there's a great art scene, wonderful beaches, fantastic restaurants, as you well know . . ."

"You sound like you're running for mayor."

Nick laughed. "No, maybe someday though." He shook his head. "But the comparisons to the past get old."

"It seems to me that it's the summer people that are the most nostalgic about the way it's changed."

He ran his hand through his thick hair. "True. Because it used to be this fantastic secret and there were wide open potato fields and no big gates and hedges. And it was easy to do everything. You could park right on Main Street in town on a rainy summer day and go to the movies. Nowadays, good luck trying to find a parking space anywhere in August, even on a sunny day! Everyone has discovered this town and the population has exploded. There's more congestion, more noise, and more attitude. People pay a lot of money to come out here for a short period of time so the expectations and demands are high. And they can be rude about it."

"I know. Then what are the benefits to this?" asked Antonia with a smile.

"There's more going on during the off-season. It doesn't feel like a ghost town when the summer ends."

"So you live here all year?"

"Yes, except when I'm on location. My son is in school here."

"You have a son?" asked Antonia with her mouth full. She was genuinely surprised.

"Yes, Finn. He's seven."

"I had no idea."

Nick gave her a sideways glance but didn't say anything. Antonia realized he was probably not used to meeting people who didn't know everything about him. But she had purposely avoided Googling him on the Internet. She knew if she did, and was ever lucky enough to talk with him again, that she would slip up and mention something that she had read about him and would appear stalker-ish. It was starting to become a big fear of hers that she would come off as a stalker.

Nick's dogs came bounding up towards him. One held a slimy wet ball in his mouth. He dropped it with a thud on the sand in front of Nick. "Oh, you want to play?" asked Nick, before hurling the ball down the beach. The dogs ran after in hot pursuit.

Antonia finished her donut and rubbed her hands together in an attempt to rid them of the sugar. She was tempted to rinse them in the water, but then she'd have the salt stuck to her fingers and that was no better. Her hands felt sticky. She tried to discreetly wipe the sugar on the back of her thighs and hope the sugar speckles would not be illuminated on the legs of her dark pants. How did women eat donuts elegantly? She supposed that was an oxymoron. Elegant women most certainly did not eat donuts.

Antonia and Nick walked down the beach, and he continued his game of throwing the ball to his dogs while they retrieved it. She was dying to ask more about his son but felt as if the topic was too personal. And all of a sudden something dawned on her. If Nick had a son, the son must have a mother and did that mean that Nick Darrow was married? Antonia didn't like that idea at all.

"So are you shooting a movie now?" Antonia asked. She had to break the silence somehow.

"No, not until December. I'll be gone for several months so I made sure I'm around now for Finn."

"Oh." So he didn't say, for Finn and my wife, thought Antonia. That was a plus. Maybe a wife wasn't in the picture.

She tried to think of another question, but Nick announced he should probably head back so they turned around to walk back towards the parking lot and her opportunity for clarification was gone.

* * * * *

Antonia steered her car into the inn's small parking lot and squeezed it between Lucy's red Mini and the Winslows' blue Audi with white Maryland plates. She turned off her ignition. The radio, that had been warbling a new tune by an aging female country star who had crossed over to pop, went silent, and the hum of the engine clicked off. Antonia was instantly enveloped in silence. She made no motion to move, feeling very content sitting completely still in her warm leather seat staring at the leaves scattering around the backyard through her windshield. She had this strange calmness wash over her as she reflected on her talk with Nick Darrow. She was excited about it, but didn't want to be. But hell, it was hard not to be excited and flattered when a movie star remembers your name, brings you a donut and asks why you missed walking with him the other day! That definitely doesn't happen everyday. That happens in fantasies. She wondered again whether he had a wife. If he had a wife, then he was just a friendly guy. But if he didn't have a wife. . . .

A flash of movement across the yard interrupted Antonia's musings. She squinted to see if she could make out anything. Her eyes scanned the cluster of oak and sassafras trees that stood in front of the back privet hedge that bordered the property. The only motion was branches swaying in the breeze. With a deep sigh, Antonia reluctantly pulled the handle of her car door. As she hoisted herself out of her seat, once again something caught her eye. She halted and stared once again, waiting. It had just been a flicker, but it was enough to give her pause. Her eyes danced back and forth until finally settling on the rhododendron bush. She waited, certain that there was something behind it. It could possibly be a deer, there were always tons of them, but they blended so much into the East Hampton landscape that she would doubt a deer would even have garnered a second look from her.

Antonia briefly hesitated before crunching over the pebble driveway to the brilliant green of the still-young sod. It held the morning dew and she could feel the suede on her Uggs becoming damp. She wiggled her toes inside, letting the fur nestle between them. She loved her Uggs. There was a cigarette butt on the ground next to the white wrought iron bench and when Antonia bent down to pick it up, she saw a white streak run from behind the rhododendron bush to the safety of the azalea bush.

"Hello?" yelled Antonia.

There was no response. If it was a guest, then what were they hiding? She wondered. Antonia moved quickly to the bush.

"Hello?" she repeated.

Antonia pushed aside some branches and rounded the

corner, to the mulch clearing that stood between the trees and the back fence. She saw a figure in white running the other direction.

"Naomi?" Antonia bellowed.

The figure stopped and froze, then slowly turned around. It was Naomi Haslett. She was once again in her white jogging pants and sneakers and this time she had a white windbreaker over which she wore a hot pink down vest. Her hair hung straight in limp clumps, giving the impression that she hadn't washed it lately, and her wrinkled face was contorted into a frown. She took a deep breath, as if Antonia's interruption was a huge inconvenience.

"Hi Antonia." Her voice was weary and neutral, as if they were acquaintances who saw one another often, but really had nothing to say to each other.

"Naomi, what in the world are you doing?" Antonia put her hands on her hips and tried to appear authoritarian.

Naomi met her gaze evenly and stood up straighter. "I was jogging."

"Jogging?"

Naomi raised her eyebrows defiantly. "Yes."

"Come on, Naomi, I find that hard to believe."

"It's true," interrupted Naomi.

"Then why in the world were you 'jogging' in my back-yard?"

"I was jogging down Windmill Way. Then I saw a cardinal and I decided to follow it. It happened to fly into your yard."

Antonia gave her a skeptical look but to humor her, glanced

around the bushes. The clearing was dark from the tangled branches hanging overhead, and clotted with leaves. There was no wildlife in evidence, least of all a cardinal.

"I don't see one."

"Flew away," said Naomi.

They stared at one another in silence. Antonia felt as if she was in *West Side Story*; it was a total stand off. If Naomi was embarrassed or remorseful for 'jogging' in the backyard of the inn, she did a sensational job hiding it.

"Why are you really here?" asked Antonia.

"I told you. I saw a bird."

Antonia sighed. She decided to change tack. "You're always welcome here, Naomi. You don't have to sneak around the back yard."

Naomi appeared surprised. "Thank you."

"I'm sure this place means something to you."

"There will always be part of my heart buried here."

Antonia nodded. There was a pause and she couldn't resist taking the opportunity. "On another note, did you hear Biddy Robertson died?"

Naomi's rolled her eyes back slightly. "Yes."

"I suppose you're not shedding any tears."

"She was a lunatic."

"How so?"

"You know, we were neighbors. Our condos were next door to each other. We were friendly. Not friends, but polite. I had no idea that she owned the Windmill Inn, nor did I suggest to my brother that he buy it in foreclosure. I agreed to lend him the money and become his partner, but as you can see I had very little involvement other than the initial financial backing. It was all his idea. Then one day, Biddy shows up banging and screaming at my door and accuses me of stealing the inn out from under her. I had no idea what she was talking about. I tell her to get the hell off my property. She was a raging storm. And then the next thing I know the police arrived and she accused me of throwing some dead animal on her doormat!"

"Why did they think it was you?"

"Hell if I know! The woman was crazy. I didn't see it coming. She thought I was doing all this plotting against her. It was ludicrous. And she never got over it. I finally had to move away."

"What about now? Did the police question you? I heard they think she was murdered."

Naomi's lower eyelid quivered but the rest of her face remained emotionless. "I'm really not at liberty to say. And besides, I don't think it's any of your business."

"True," conceded Antonia. "But come on, Naomi. How does it look to me? After your little tiff with Barbie last week and all those accusations of murder, I'm a wee bit suspicious, don't you think that's fair?"

"Don't think twice about Barbie. We've almost finished all the legal issues surrounding Gordon's estate and she will be high-tailing it out of town, penniless and with her tail between her legs. Trust me on this one."

"Okay," Antonia replied.

"Gordon had his flaws, but the primary one was his taste in women. He always went for the crazy girls. And they flocked to him like bees in honey. Pardon the expression." Naomi pulled the zipper on her vest all the way to the top so that it strangled her veiny neck. "I'm going to finish my jog now."

"Alright," said Antonia.

With that, Naomi turned on her heels and took off. Antonia watched her odd slow gait and thought to herself if that could be considered a jog, then when Antonia raised a spoon to her mouth it could be considered weight-lifting.

Once Naomi was definitively out of sight, Antonia glimpsed around the clearing. What was Naomi really doing back here? She trudged through the damp mulch, stepping over dead wet leaves, clearing them with her foot. She kicked something with her toe, but when she bent down she saw that it was only a large rock propped in the ground. She peered high and low, but there were no markers, no signs of recent digging or removal of anything. It was very odd.

16

Antonia entered by the back door that led into the sunroom. It was empty, but there were signs that a guest or two had recently chosen it as a spot for breakfast. A discarded copy of *The New York Times* lay on the coffee table, with the business section folded on top. Alongside it was an emptied coffee mug and a plate with mixed berry scone crumbs. Antonia picked them both up and walked them into the pantry area. She handed them to the dishwasher before working her way back towards the front hall.

It was only about eight-thirty but the inn was coming to life. The cleaners had arrived and were currently sweeping out the fireplace. Antonia spotted a few guests having breakfast and reading the paper in the parlor. Connie was talking on the phone, while Lucy stood next to her, leafing through the guest registry. Today Lucy wore a bright orange skirt made of a heavy wool and a cream silk blouse with one of those loopy bows that were popular with businesswomen in the eighties. She glanced up and began to say something to Antonia, but Antonia had already started with her Naomi story.

"You cannot believe who I just found in our backyard! Naomi Haslett. I have no idea what she was doing but it was very strange. She was hiding by the back bushes and she tried to run away from me when I saw her! Do you have any idea what's behind there?"

Lucy was surprised. "No, that's so odd. Antonia . . ."

"She always was a nut," said a male voice behind Antonia.

Antonia turned and was face to face (well, more like, face to belt buckle) with Ronald Meter. Today he wore a tweed blazer over baggy khakis (that he must shop at a Big & Tall store, Antonia thought) and brown loafers. His goatee was neatly trimmed but his face was a bit flushed as if he had just done some strenuous physical activity, or had gotten wind-whipped from sticking it out a car window like a dog.

"Mr. Meter, nice to see you again," said Antonia.

"Thank you," he drawled. "I was hoping for a quick chat if you have a minute."

"Certainly, let's go into my office," said Antonia.

She exchanged glances with Lucy, who gave her a look as if to say, 'I was about to tell you' before leading him away. Antonia noticed that Lucy gave Ronald a look of disdain as he passed. Clearly no love lost between those two, thought Antonia.

Ronald hunkered uncomfortably into the captain's chair that sat across from Antonia's desk. It was definitely not made for men of tall stature. Ronald looked like toothpaste squeezing out of a tube. He accepted her offer of tea but declined pastry. Antonia ignored his refusal for food, believing that no one could turn down her baked goods once confronted with them, and rang for a waitress in the kitchen to bring them a full breakfast service. "All the bells and whistles," she had instructed, hoping that the kitchen would understand what she meant.

"You really shouldn't go to trouble," Ronald said.

"No problem at all."

He admired the way she had set up her office, even though Antonia knew he was being polite. The roll top desk was about to snap in half with all of the paperwork piled on top of it. Her bookshelves were a messy display of someone who does not operate an organized system of organization. It looked as if someone on acid had just shoved all the paperwork between every book and hoped it would go unnoticed. But now all the loose pieces of paper were spilling out. Ripped envelopes and mounds of junk mail lay in messy heaps that Antonia had abandoned. A sloppy collection of miscellaneous rubber bands was piled on the radiator for no apparent reason.

Oh well, yes, it was a disaster zone, Antonia thought, but at least she had her strong suits. The artwork was nice; Antonia had framed local watercolors of the beach in a beautiful blush gold-painted wood that she felt was both subtle and classy. And her desk chair was an antique that she had painted white and outfitted with a cushion upholstered in a pretty blue batik from Quadrille. On the far wall she had hung a beautiful calendar that featured famous still lifes from MOMA that would be exceptionally classy if it was turned to the correct month (it was currently opened to July.)

The waitress arrived with a tray and Antonia glanced at it and was pleased to find that they had indeed understood what 'bells and whistles' meant. She pulled out a tray table that was leaning collapsed by the door and opened it next to Ronald. (No use even attempting to clear off her desk to make room for it.) The waitress placed the tray on top and offered to serve but Antonia declined. When she had left, Antonia moved over to sit in the other guest chair next to Ronald. She poured the steaming tea into the flowered china and glanced up at him.

"Milk or sugar?"

"Just milk, thank you."

Antonia gave him a generous portion before reaching for the other dish on the tray. "Would you like some honey?"

Ronald hesitated. His eyes met Antonia's. "No thank you."

"There are some mini-muffins in the basket as well."

"I'm all set."

She handed him his cup and gave him a curious look. "I love a good pot of tea. Actually, I also love a good mug of coffee. I'm an equal opportunity caffeine drinker."

"Oh, me too."

"I will take it in virtually any form. I try to lay off the soda, but I've been known to imbibe. It's impossible to go to a movie and eat popcorn without soda. Ditto a slice of pizza. Although red wine will work with that. But soda is better. The only thing I really steer clear of is Red Bull. I've never even tried it; it just sounds disgusting to me. I suppose I have my standards. It's the same with wine. I love wine, but would never drink it out of a box. I think we all know deep down when we have to control our addictions."

Ronald had been holding his cup to his mouth, blowing softly as she spoke. He took a sip and firmly placed it back down in the saucer. It made a clanking noise.

"I apologize," he said.

"No worries."

Ronald twisted uncomfortably in his chair and Antonia made a mental note to entertain tall visitors in the sunroom or parlor.

"Antonia, I came here today because I wasn't truthful with you the other day."

Antonia arched her eyebrows and gave him a quizzical look. He glanced down, as if very uncomfortable with what he was about to confess, and sighed deeply.

"As you were leaving, you asked me if I had a beehive in the backyard."

He peered up at her and waited. She held her breath. Was this going to be a confession? She wished she had one of those buttons underneath her desk that she could press and record everything. She had never assumed she would need one, seeing as this wasn't the Oval Office, but of course you never knew. Now that she was involved in a possible murder case, she was way behind the eight ball. She wondered if one day she'd have to put a little room behind a mirror so that police could watch from the other side, undetected. . . .

"Yes, I did," she prompted.

"Well, I'm sorry I wasn't truthful. The fact is, it *is* a bee-hive." His eyes gave her an imploring gaze.

"Oh? Well, I'm not sure why you would hide that?" she said, playing dumb.

"I know, it seems silly. They are legal, for Lord's sake. But you see, well, you didn't know me before . . ."

He trailed off. Antonia stepped in. "No, we just met."

"Right. Well, I used to be a large man. I mean, I am a large man now, but I used to weigh a lot more. I'm not sure if any of the gang here told you, but I lost one hundred and eighty pounds."

"NO!"

"It's true. I'm the 'Biggest Loser' at my church. Although, I hate that title. Problem was, I always had a sweet tooth, and I ate all the time. I gobbled up everything! I'm from the South and we liked it fried, breaded and sugarcoated. But then I found out I had diabetes, and I had to cut back. My doctor warned me, my pastor warned me. So I did. I cut out all sugar and the like. Began to exercise, which is a hoot!"

He paused, evidently conjuring up the image of him exercising in his brain. It didn't seem so absurd to Antonia, but then she didn't know him before. He continued. "Well, then. I do have a vice. I adore honey. Lord, how I adore it. I didn't set out to have a beehive, it just sort of happened. I kind of inherited it. And they make the most delicious honey in the world! I promise you, it is my one vice. I just can't quit it. And sitting here, staring at that sweet little dish of honey that you have on that tray is making me, well, all of my self-control is holding me back from drinking it. So there, that's my dirty little secret. And I am sorry I lied."

He stared at her with a guilty look, more apt for someone who had skinned her cat than someone who told a fib about owning a beehive. Hey, whatever floats your boat, thought Antonia.

"Ronald, I appreciate your honesty. Thank you for telling me the truth. But I just wonder why . . . You didn't lie about anything major. You don't have to answer to me, so why come tell me this?"

He nodded as if he had known she would ask him that. "I mentioned my pastor to you. I've gone through things in recent years, had some issues, and I have turned to my faith more and more. And this was burning on my conscience so I talked to my pastor who advised me to speak to you. I just want honesty in my life. Clarity. Sobriety. I'm trying to be a good person, not to succumb to any vices or temptations."

"Wow, I think that's great. I should take a page out of your book. Everyone should."

"Oh, I hope I'm not preaching. Different things work for different people, that's what my mama always says."

"She sounds smart. I quote my mom also."

"Mother knows best to this day," laughed Ronald.

Antonia removed the dish of honey as well as the mini muffin basket and asked Connie to dispose of them somewhere far away. Antonia and Ronald finished their tea without any temptations, and had a pleasant chat about a variety of topical issues. Her impression of him was that he was a nice man, but attempting to live his life in a way that might not be organic to who he was. It was almost as if he had been subjected to an intense amount of therapy recently, the type that started off being very beneficial but then became a little bizarre and self-indulgent. In addition, his pastor seemed to be very influential on him. At least it sounded like he was pushing him towards goodness. It did make Antonia wonder how dark it had been for Ronald before this pastor. Was this religious inclination new, say, post-murder? Had Ronald been an angry enough person to kill Gordon?

After tea, Antonia toured Ronald around the downstairs of the inn. He was suitably impressed with the changes, and extremely flattering. Antonia was such a sucker for that, especially since she had poured so much time and effort (not to mention money) into every change and upgrade. He particularly appreciated how she had restored the original millwork, most of which had been stripped out. Antonia had scanned through all of the photos and archives of the inn to ascertain what it had originally looked like. She spent hours at the East Hampton Library searching for anything that would be helpful. Then she had worked with an architect to recreate the crown moldings on the ceilings, the wainscoting along the walls in the front hall and public rooms, and to reproduce mantels that resembled the originals. Ronald was the first person to articulate how much of an effort it had been.

They were in the sunroom when Liz came to find her. She wore an apron over her white chef's pants, and had her hair back in a ponytail, which made her look younger than her years.

"Sorry to bother you, Antonia, but the vegetable delivery is in and Marty wants me to confirm the mushroom order with you."

"Okay, sure." She turned to Ronald who spoke before her.

"Oh, don't worry about me. I'm on my way anyway. Just will pop out and say hello to Hector. I'm so glad you kept him on."

"Yes, he does a wonderful job."

"Well, thank you so much for the tea and company. You've done beautiful things with the inn."

"Thank you," said Antonia.

They shook hands.

17

WEDNESDAY

It rained all day Wednesday. Not just rained, but teemed. When Antonia's morning alarm sounded she reached for it with excitement, ready to bound out of bed and prepare for her beach walk with (hopefully) Nick Darrow. But she was dismayed to see the wet drops furiously pounding against the glass panes, forming streams of water that rushed down to the ground. She rose and surveyed the yard from the window, but it was futile. Pools of water had already formed on the lawn and the walkways were slick. No one in his or her right mind would be walking the beach that morning.

With dismay, Antonia returned to her bed and curled up in her cozy comforter. As she stared at her ceiling she thought to herself that this must be the first time in her entire life that she was disappointed to forgo exercise and remain in bed. Geez, what men can do to you! And of course, once again she had to remind herself that she was being silly. Nick Darrow was probably just a friendly guy who had no interest in her other than in a neighborly fashion. He probably was nice to every one, perhaps to sell movie tickets. Maybe he took that "one ticket at a time" approach.

After breakfast service, there were enough tasks, chores and concerns to keep Antonia busy for the next few hours. These days she felt as if she always needed to be in three different places at once. She knew she had to put in some time for clerical duties, but there was so much to be done in the kitchen with deliveries arriving and prep work to be done. She wished she could hire an extra person to help either in the office or in the kitchen but after Lucy's stern dressing down about costs, she realized it was not possible. She was also going to have to let the current staff know that starting the first of November, the restaurant would only be open four nights a week. Oh, she dreaded these management duties! If only she could just do the fun parts of owning an inn and a restaurant.

At eleven thirty, Antonia made herself a little lunch and escaped to her office with a tray. She bit into one of her all time favorite sandwiches—St. Andre cheese on a crusty baguette with sliced cornichons, cherry tomatoes and Dijon mustard. The cheese had to be soft enough to be gooey and spread evenly on the bread, and the cherry tomatoes had to be chopped so they didn't squirt everywhere when you bit into them. The sandwich also demanded lots of pepper and a hefty sprinkle of truffle salt. A slice of lemon in seltzer along with some vinegar potato chips accompanied it. Antonia was in heaven, practically moaning with satisfaction when her telephone rang. Reluctantly she answered.

"Bingham, it's Lipper."

The hunk of bread dropped down her throat like a ball of lead. If there was anyone who could ruin the moment it was Larry Lipper.

"Hi, Larry," said Antonia in her fakest cheery voice. "How are you?"

"Put November twelfth on your calendar," he barked on the other end of the phone.

"What's November twelfth?"

"There's a Ross School benefit at Wolffer Vineyards. Billy Joel is headlining. I know you love him, so you'll go with me."

"Wait, I do love him, but how did you know?"

"You're the type."

"Huh. Well, I'm not sure that date will work for me. It's a Saturday night and the restaurant is open . . ."

"My boss got a table. It's free. You'll be with me."

"Yes, see, it's not really a great time . . ."

"I thought you loved kids. Don't you want to support them?"

Antonia did not recall having any sort of conversation about children with Larry Lipper. "I do support kids, and I like kids, it's not that . . ."

"Blah, blah, blah. Look, enough with playing hard to get. You and I both know where this is going . . ."

"Excuse me?" bristled Antonia.

"We can play this dance, or we can cut to the chase. I like to cut to the chase . . ."

"Larry, what are you even implying? Contrary to what you

may think, I am not trying to facilitate a romantic relationship with you."

"Who said anything about romance?"

Antonia was instantly embarrassed. "Oh, I thought . . ."

"I'm thinking *sexual* relationship," said Larry.

"I'm hanging up now."

"I wouldn't do that."

"Why?" asked Antonia. She took a large bite of her sandwich and waited for him to continue his clumsy courtship.

"Because I have more scoop about Biddy Robertson's death."

Antonia tried to speak but her mouth was so full of bread and cheese and pickles that it all came out in a muffled bumble.

"What the hell are you saying, Antonia? Did you swallow your sock?"

Antonia put up her finger as if instructing him to wait, but comprehended that it was useless, as he couldn't see her, so she chewed as quickly as possible and washed down her bite with some seltzer. She drank the seltzer so quickly that the bubbles burned the back of her throat and she proceeded to have a coughing fit.

"Jesus, Bingham. You really turn on all the charm when a man tries to ask you out. I'm loving all the sounds you're making," complained Larry.

"Tell me about Biddy," Antonia garbled as soon as she could speak again.

"Say you will go to the benefit with me."

"Biddy first."

"Benefit first."

It was a standoff. Antonia kicked herself because she knew she would lose. Curiosity always trumped self-respect in her book.

"Alright," she conceded in her most defeated and dejected tone. "I'll go. Now tell me about Biddy."

"And promise you'll wear something hot. Show off your tits."

"Larry!"

"Come on!"

"I promise to dress appropriately. Now tell me about Biddy. And it better be good or else I won't go."

"Fine. My buddy on the force told me that at first, when they went to her house it all seemed pretty status quo, just like a bad accident. She forgot to turn off the stove."

"Old news," interjected Antonia.

"Bingham, let me finish!"

"Sorry."

"Then my buddy noticed something in the kitchen. There was an outlet by the floor against the wall. Nothing was plugged in. Didn't appear as if anything had been there. But then the sun started pouring in and he realized—this guy is good—that there was a dust outline along the wall as if something *had* been plugged in there. Something the shape of a carbon monoxide detector."

"Interesting. But how could they know for sure?"

"This is where it gets good. Biddy had some photos attached to her fridge. Her grandson had taken them; they were shots of Christmas last year. The family cooking in the kitchen—all that irritating junk people do together around holidays before everyone drinks too much and the backstabbing begins."

"You paint a lovely image of the holidays."

"I'm a realist. So sure enough, in one of those photos, Biddy is standing next to the refrigerator, and you can clearly see the outlet and the carbon monoxide detector plugged in. Someone removed it."

Antonia was stunned silent, which didn't happen often. "Wow."

"Yeah. They got confirmation from the son that the old lady was really diligent about that crap. Had all sorts of alarms and everything ready."

"Do the police have any suspects yet?"

"Not that they're telling me about. But it will all come out soon."

"Larry, let me ask you this. Did you mention to your buddy anything about the inn or Gordon Haslett's death? Did they think there was a connection?"

"I sorta threw it out there but he laughed at me. And anyway, I agree, it's a waste of time. But if you're scared of going to bed at night for fear you'll be the next one whacked, I can tell you my bed is warm and I got satin sheets."

"Why do you always have to make these references?"

"You love them! Gotta go."

Antonia resumed munching on her sandwich and thought about what Larry had told her. Why would someone want to kill Biddy Robertson? From all accounts she was just an average, run of the mill woman. The only motive that Antonia could think of was that she had once owned the inn. If the police didn't take the connection seriously then it was up to Antonia to figure out why someone would want every owner of the inn dead, or else she would be next! She picked up her phone and dialed Lucy's extension, but there was no answer and she remembered that Lucy said she was running to the bank to deposit some checks. It was time to compile a list of all the employees who had worked for both Gordon and Biddy. Maybe that was the connection? Antonia jotted down a few names that she could think of, but after getting nowhere she pulled out an old issue of *Cooks Illustrated* to read as she finished her lunch. Then there was a knock on the door.

Hector was standing on the threshold and next to him stood a petite woman that Antonia knew at once must be his wife Soyla. She was approximately early thirties, thin and neatly dressed in a jean skirt and a red and blue striped long sleeved shirt with a v-neck. She wore small pearl earrings and a gold cross on a chain. Her black hair was pulled back neatly into a bun, and her eyes were big and prominent on her thin face. She appeared nervous, her hands fidgeting with the brown leather pocketbook that she wore over her shoulder.

After apologizing profusely for interrupting her, Hector asked if it was a good time for Antonia to talk to his wife Soyla. Antonia did her best to be effusively positive but despite that, Hector and Soyla still exchanged worried glances when he left the office to allow Antonia to talk to her in private.

"Your husband does a wonderful job with the gardens here," said Antonia. She smiled brightly.

Soyla nodded. "Thank you."

Her voice was but a whisper. She sat upright on the edge of the chair that Antonia had offered her with her hands still clasped around her pocketbook as if someone might burst in and try and rip it from her arms.

"I understand you worked at the inn."

Soyla nodded.

"Did you know Biddy Robertson?"

Soyla looked confused. "No."

"How long did you work at the inn?"

"We worked here five years."

"Oh," said Antonia, who made a mental note to scratch Soyla and Hector off the list of crossovers who worked for both Biddy and Gordon. She returned her attention to Soyla.

"From what I have heard from various sources, you were a good worker. Now I know that Gordon Haslett was a tough boss. And I know there were some accusations. But I would like to hear from you what happened exactly."

Soyla began her story. Her English was much better than Hector's but she spoke so softly that Antonia had to crane her neck to hear her. She told how she worked at the inn for three years without problem, but then one day a guest had lost some earrings and accused Soyla of stealing them. Gordon ended up firing her. It was all information that Antonia had heard, but she wanted to watch Soyla carefully as she told it.

"I would never take anything, Mrs. Antonia. I promise you. I am not like that. I saw many things in the rooms that I could have taken. But I would never. It is not me. It is not my religion. I just can't believe Mr. Gordon thought that I took it!"

Antonia could see tears welling in the corners of Soyla's eyes. She handed her a tissue. Soyla wiped her eyes fiercely, as if angry that they had betrayed her, and shook her head. "Most of all I feel shame."

"I'm sorry about that. And I just want you to know, I do believe you."

"Thank you."

"But do you have an idea of who you think *did* steal the earrings?"

Soyla hesitated. She glanced at the door and then quickly back to Antonia. "I don't know . . ."

Antonia sat up straight. "Please, Soyla. It's important to me. I need to know."

Soyla looked down at her pocketbook as if it held the answer. Antonia waited. *Let her do the talking, don't speak.* Antonia used all of her self-control to pipe down. She knew the only way to prompt Soyla to talk was to be patient. Not one of Antonia's strong suits, but she had to try. Finally, Soyla broke the silence.

"Some people thought it was Barbie . . . but . . ."

"But?"

"One day we were looking for a pair of cufflinks. A guest said they were missing. They were blue with pink whales on them. I was looking; the ladies I work with were looking. Ronald, Mr. Gordon, everyone. And I found them . . ."

"Where?" asked Antonia breathless.

Soyla spoke very softly. "They were in Ronald's office. In

his drawer. I didn't go there to check but Mr. Gordon needed the stamp for the inn and he asked me to go get it in Ronald's office. I opened his desk drawer and the cufflinks were there."

Antonia sighed deeply. She had sort of hoped to rule Ronald out as a thief and now his name was back in the ring. Ugh, would she ever find out the truth?

"Did you ask him about them?"

Soyla shook her head. "I went to Mr. Gordon and I asked him to come with me, I said I wasn't sure which stamp he wanted. He was not happy but he came. When I opened the drawer, he saw the cufflinks."

"What did he say?"

"He just looked at me, and said thank you. We both understood."

"And what happened after that?"

"I went home so I don't know."

"Was that when Ronald was fired?"

"No, because I was fired first. Maybe he gave Ronald one more chance, I don't know."

Antonia twisted a piece of hair between her fingers. Something wasn't adding up. "It's possible that someone else put the cufflinks in Ronald's drawer."

Soyla nodded. "Yes."

"Did you ever suspect Ronald of stealing from guests?"

"I don't think so," said Soyla, shaking her head. "He was always so busy. And also, it was mostly ladies stuff that was stolen, except for the cufflinks. Why would he want that?"

"True."

They sat in silence as Antonia considered everything. Did Barbie frame Ronald? This question seemed to keep popping up. The answer was, she didn't know. If only she had a time machine and could zap herself back to see what really happened.

Eventually Antonia changed the conversation and returned to the topic of Soyla's employment.

"As you know, we currently have a cleaning staff."

"Yes, my cousins Rosita and Angela."

"I didn't realize that! Yes, they do a great job."

"Yes, they are very good."

"The thing is, the inn is struggling right now, to be honest. And I just had a discussion with Lucy, who is now our manager, about ways to cut cost. The sad fact is, I'm not really in the position to hire anyone right now."

"I understand."

Antonia felt horrible. She hated to disappoint everyone. And it made her sad to think that Soyla had gotten all dressed up only to experience rejection. It was awful. "Where are you working now?"

"I'm working at the South Fork Farm. Only part time."

"What do you do there?"

"I do everything. I help with the food stand, I help clean, I help with the beehives . . ."

"Excuse me?" asked Antonia.

Soyla gave her an alarmed look, clearly terrified by Antonia's new intensity. "I work with the bees . . ."

"They have a bee farm?"

"Yes," said Soyla, not understanding Antonia's wild interest. "They make honey."

Antonia's mind was racing. Here was another link to bees. Soyla worked at a bee farm, Hector was her husband, his boss was stung by a bee, was there a connection? Did she have to consider Hector a suspect again? "Soyla do you know who Biddy Robertson is, or was?"

Soyla shook her head. "No."

"Are you sure?"

She nodded. "Sorry, is it important?"

Antonia shrugged. "No, not important. Don't worry."

"Okay."

Antonia took a deep breath. It was time to conclude the meeting. Soyla got the hint and stood up. "Thank you for taking the time to meet me."

"Thank you," said Antonia. "And if something changes I will definitely call you."

"Yes."

As she was leaving, Antonia watched Soyla eye the issue of *Cooks Illustrated* on her desk. Something about it gave her pause.

"Do you cook?"

Soyla smiled, for the first time she appeared relaxed. "Yes, I like to cook."

"Are you good?"

"I've never had training, but my family says I'm good. I cook for everyone, I love to cook."

"What do you cook?"

Soyla smiled shyly. "I make my native dishes, but I also make pies and cakes."

Antonia sat back down as Soyla continued. Finally, Soyla resumed sitting, and for the next twenty minutes they compared recipes and cooking notes. She told Antonia her trick of roasting mushrooms before frying them to dry them out so they were not so watery. Antonia asked her what she made out of tomatillos, as Antonia had never had much luck with them. As they continued talking, their mutual excitement grew. Until finally Antonia wrapped up the conversation with the following question:

"Soyla, how'd you like to help me out in the kitchen?"

Soyla beamed. And all Antonia could think was how Lucy was going to kill her.

18

After Soyla left, panic set in. Antonia wanted to kick herself. She had acted totally impulsively. One minute, she's regarding Soyla as a potential suspect or at the very least the wife of a potential suspect. Someone who has motive for murder and whom she learns over the course of the interview has access to beehives. Antonia is building the case in her mind, picturing Soyla handing off a purloined bee to Hector who in turn lures Gordon into the back yard and smashes it into his face (okay, the picture was a little fuzzy) and the next minute Antonia *hires* Soyla for a job the woman has zero experience doing, not to mention that Antonia is supposed to be cost cutting not adding to the overhead she has to carry. Was she insane? Why not double the order for expensive linen napkins while she's at it? Why not narrow the margins on alcohol?

And yet. Antonia trusted her instincts about people. She had a good vibe about Soyla. She didn't truly think she was homicidal, or that her husband was. The motive was way too flimsy. People didn't kill just because they were fired, did they? And Hector probably appreciated his job; there would be no reason for him to put it in jeopardy, because if he killed Gordon, there was no job security. And the fact was, Antonia did need more hands in the kitchen. This would be a trial run; she had only hired Soyla for a probation period, so there was always an out. Antonia did not want to work herself up into a lather. She decided to focus on the positive.

Liz was slicing lemons in the rear of the kitchen when Antonia entered. Lemons were an expensive luxury. People didn't know how much lemons cost, and would toss aside the slices that adorned their diet cokes or their hot tea. That always killed Antonia, even more so now that she was counting every penny. Sometimes she just wanted to yell and say, 'people, lemons are not free!' But that would be inane.

"How's everything today?" asked Antonia.

Liz gave her a brief rundown on what was happening. Marty was outside accepting deliveries, his little scale in hand, and no doubt haggling over every gram of fish and meat. The executive chef was usually the one who negotiated with vendors, but Antonia needed someone tough and no nonsense to make sure that no one was ripping them off and Marty was better at that than her. The margins are tight at any restaurant. Every ounce of meat counts, because that's where the money comes from. She had been told that it was important early on to be tough with the vendors so they wouldn't cheat her. And because she didn't exactly have a tough personality, she had nominated Marty for the job. He adored arguing, complaining and grumbling so he was very well fit for the task.

"You should have heard Marty yelling at the fishmonger," laughed Liz.

"Uh oh, what'd he do now?"

"He was blasting him about the striped bass. Said he'd get better quality at Petco."

"Oh, dear."

"Yes, and he refused the bluefish. Said it was garbage."

"What is he talking about? I can make a nice smoked dip out of the bluefish and serve it with a little crudité, yum."

"You better tell Marty before he scares them back to Montauk."

"Geez, what have I done?"

"Actually, I wouldn't worry, Antonia. I think that they respect him for it," said Liz.

"See, that's why he is perfect for that job. I can be tough for a minute but then I buckle."

"Yeah, but they probably wouldn't try to cheat you. You're too nice."

"I don't know about that."

Antonia went and peeked out the window at Marty. He was talking to the fishmonger, but another man was standing next to him, a grin on his face.

"Who's that other guy?"

Liz peered over Antonia's shoulder. "That's the guy from the local micro-brewery. The one that wants us to sell his Summer Honey Ale."

The guy was in his mid-thirties with scruffy facial hair and greasy dark hair. He had on an army jacket and blue jeans. He was not bad looking but it occurred to Antonia that he might need to be boiled in a hot bath to disinfect. She wondered if Genevieve had caught a glimpse of this guy yet.

"Is Marty giving him a hard time?"

"Not yet."

"He *is* persistent. Maybe we should give him a shot."

"You're a good person."

"I try to give everyone a chance."

Liz smiled. "I meant to mention it to you, Antonia, but friends of my parents are searching for someone to look after their house. It's not a full time job, but they live in the city and just want someone to open it up when there are deliveries, and basically make sure no one is robbing it. I thought you might know someone who was looking for that sort of work," said Liz.

"Hmm, let me think about that. Where is their house?"

"Lily Pond Lane," said Liz, sheepishly.

Lily Pond Lane was the fanciest street in East Hampton, home to billionaires, rock and movie stars and an entertainment lifestyle maven who did time in prison. The road, shaded by a promenade of Pollard Plane trees, ran between Georgica and Main Beaches, and half of the houses teetered on the dunes of the ocean. Sweeping lawns, manicured landscapes and refined mansions were the norm. To Antonia, it was elegance at its greatest.

"Oh, I love Lily Pond Lane," said Antonia. "So gorgeous. Wow, it must be a beautiful house."

"It is," said Liz. "And they're really a nice family. The kids are teenagers, one in his twenties, and the parents—their names are Joan and Robert Masterson—aren't out here as much as they want so they need someone to make sure everything is ok. They used to have a caretaker, but he retired to Florida."

Antonia felt the bristle of an idea. "It's not a full time thing, is it? I mean, could someone like me do it?"

Liz brightened. "I think so. They just want someone to make sure it's still standing. I don't see why not."

"Hmm . . . Maybe I could talk to them?"

"Of course. I'll set it up."

"Great."

If Antonia was able to supplement her income by looking after houses, she could reduce her current salary from the inn and use the money to pay for Soyla. Then Lucy couldn't complain and everyone would be happy! The more she thought about it, the more excited Antonia became. The fact was, she walked Georgica Beach every morning anyway, so how hard could it be to pop in and check on a house after her walk? And it would be good motivation for her, in the dead of winter when she really had no desire to hit the beach, to force her to make the effort. Yes, this could be a jolly situation all around!

On her break, Antonia practically skipped to the front of the inn to find Lucy. She was perhaps a bit premature in assuming that the friends of Liz's parents would hire her to watch their house and pay her enough money to make even a dent, but she preferred to think positively. Wishful thinking, perhaps, but her mother had always told her to look at the bright side.

While Antonia's office was located behind the reception area, keeping her in the loop on arriving and departing guests, Lucy's was situated across the hall on the other side of the grand staircase. It had been her office since she was the bookkeeper, and although there was another office next to Antonia's that was designated for the manager, Lucy had preferred to remain where she was and Antonia acceded. She'd use the other office for printers and some storage, until she needed it. Lucy's door was usually kept tightly closed, as it was now, so Antonia was never quite sure if Lucy was in or not. Antonia knocked and was greeted by Lucy's invitation to enter.

If one of those shelter magazines decided to do a "before" and "after" shoot of what an office in an inn should look like, Antonia's would certainly be chosen for the before picture and Lucy's for the after. Where Antonia's was bursting with papers, mail, books, magazines, files and jumbled coffee mugs, all smashed together in a cozy mess on top of her antique desk, Lucy's was absolutely pristine. First off, the entire room was white—including all furniture, shelves and desk accessories. It reminded Antonia of a science lab in a highly classified bio-tech company. Not that she had ever been to one, but she had certainly seen them depicted on CBS crime shows. Secondly, there was not an errant paper to be found. One wall had draw-ers of filing cabinets (all white) that had swallowed every scrap of paper that Lucy had chosen to retain after processing her in box. And speaking of the 'in' box, Antonia wasn't sure it could ever be referred to as that because she had never ever seen any-thing 'in' it, as if Lucy had a pathological need to immediately remove the 'in' to 'out.' Another thing that amazed Antonia was the fact that Lucy's desk had no drawers. True, Lucy had a wall of filing cabinets, but even if Antonia had three walls of filing cabinets, she would need desk drawers. Where else would she stuff rubber bands, hole punchers, paper clips, old birthday cards from her mother and father, mailing labels, Chapstick, dental floss, stamps, earrings that she took off when she was on the phone and forgot about, instructions on how to use her camera, fabric samples, extension cords, knobs that had fallen off her antique desk, old key chains with old keys, deposit slips, blank Christmas cards, Pottery Barn catalogues and Paul Simon and Carly Simon cds that she wanted to download on to her iPod? A desk without drawers was . . . a table. (Unless, Antonia supposed, you were an architect. But even their workspace was called a drafting *table* not a drafting *desk*.)

However it obviously worked well for Lucy, who was Antonia's most efficient employee. Antonia was thankful for her because she allowed Antonia to run around and do the fun stuff. That's what teamwork was.

Antonia found Lucy seated in her modern swivel chair, staring at her desktop, where an Excel spreadsheet was pulled up on screen. She gave Antonia a terse smile but behind her kooky glasses Antonia could see a flicker of irritation in her eyes, as if she disapproved of being interrupted.

"Lucy, I just wanted to let you know that I am working on a plan that may allow me to reduce my salary."

When Lucy didn't respond, Antonia continued. "Well, it's not definite yet, but I may get another job, just a small job, and anyway, that could supplement my income and I could put more money back into the inn."

Lucy pressed her hands down on her pleated wool skirt. "How much would you reduce?"

"Well, I'm not sure yet . . ."

Antonia realized she had jumped the gun a bit, by already disclosing this news to Lucy. She hadn't even met Liz's friends yet. What was she thinking? What if it was only an hourly rate, like $20 an hour? That really wouldn't help her very much. So she checked on the house twice a week, two hours, that's . . . $40? And why did she suddenly feel like she was a lowly kindergartener being called into the principal's office. Wasn't *she* the boss? All of her inflated ideas about teamwork drifted away.

"Okay, just let me know when you will be sure," said Lucy. "Otherwise, I am currently examining more cost cutting ways. Perhaps we switch to paper napkins in the restaurant."

"Paper napkins?" Antonia wanted to faint. "No, no, no. We can't do that."

"We have to examine all of our options. The money is flying out the door, Antonia. And not coming in."

Antonia felt nauseous. She decided she had to change the subject. "Lucy, on another note, can you tell me who worked here when Biddy Robertson owned the inn?"

Lucy squinted, again with disapproval. Antonia had a feeling Lucy enjoyed needling her about cutbacks. Bookkeepers could be so humorless. "You want a list of every employee?"

"No, only those employees who worked here for both Biddy and Gordon."

Lucy jumped up with such vigor that Antonia was startled. She hadn't expected that response. Lucy went over to the file cabinets and bent down to the ground so that her entire skirt pooled around her on the floor as if she were a dancer in a Broadway musical. She pulled open a drawer and flicked through various files with mechanical precision. Finally, she pulled out a folder that had one of the longest labels Antonia had ever seen—all broken into subdivisions based on year, month, employee list, etc—and handed it to Antonia.

"This should help you. It's the list of employees that remained with the inn the first year after Gordon purchased it from Biddy."

Antonia took it and opened it. "Wow, thanks. So thorough."

Lucy gave her a look as if to say, what did you expect? "I believe the only person who is still here is Samuel, the dishwasher."

"Ronald Meter worked for both of them," said Antonia, pointing to the list.

"Yes, he did."

Antonia scanned the rest of the spreadsheet. That was the only name that stood out to her. Samuel, the dishwasher, was for all intents and purposes, deaf and made little effort to interact with the rest of the staff, so she could hardly imagine him having any reason to murder anyone.

"Antonia, may I ask, what you are looking for exactly?"

"I have no idea. I just think there has to be a connection. Someone who worked for both Biddy and Gordon killed them."

"Why?"

"I haven't gotten there yet," confessed Antonia.

Lucy gave her a puzzled look. "You are just conjecturing."

"You could say that."

Lucy glanced down but Antonia could still see the amusement in her eyes. She clearly thought Antonia was on an insane bender, wasting her time. *Well,* thought Antonia, *you may be right; but without the creative thinkers in this world, all that would be left would be the number crunchers like you. Take that!* Antonia wanted to snap, but restrained herself. She knew deep down she was being defensive.

"I do have some proof that something happened, but I can't disclose it right now," said Antonia.

Lucy nodded, but again Antonia could decipher skepticism. Antonia realized she was being childish. She didn't have anything to prove to Lucy. Who even cared if Lucy thought she was on a wild goose chase? It was *her* wild goose chase.

"I hope you can figure it out," said Lucy. She reached across her desk and made sure the two sheets of papers on her desk were perfectly aligned. Antonia glanced at one and saw that it was a mortgage form from Bridgehampton National Bank.

"That's not for us, is it?" asked Antonia.

Lucy glanced down at the paper as if seeing it for the first time. "No, they just constantly solicit the inn. Gordon was their best customer. He had it leveraged to the max."

"I guess I'm realizing just how much a money pit an inn is."

Lucy gave her a thin smile.

"Okay, well, time to start dinner service."

"Alright now," said Lucy, making no sign that she regretted Antonia taking her leave. She took out a sheet of white paper from under her desk and placed it on top of the letter from the bank. Antonia wondered if her OCD made her hate to look at anything offensive.

*   *   *   *   *

Later that evening, another unsettling occurrence transpired. Glen—who was already in one of his moods—came into the kitchen to complain that not only had they run out of bev napkins, but also his key to the storage closet wasn't working. Although he was always prone to histrionics, tonight he was especially dramatic and worked up, due to the fact that he had two last minute cancellations. Rather than deal with his prima donna behavior, Antonia took off her apron and left the kitchen to retrieve the napkins herself. Glen "protested" a bit, but she had little interest in engaging in a longer dialogue so she ignored him and brushed by him and out the door.

The storage closet was located off the hallway under the staircase. It was actually quite a large walk-in closet that had been used as a waiting area for footmen back in the day. Antonia went into her office first to retrieve her keychain and then backtracked to return to the closet. Her key turned the lock with no problem. She left her key in the lock so that she could secure it easily when she was done and pulled the light cord to illuminate the room. Although early efforts had been made to keep the storage area organized and neat, in the haste to open the inn, items had been thrown inside with little regard to system. Stacks of paper towels, extra blankets, light bulbs, miscellaneous tools, towels, toilet paper, cleaning supplies, copy paper, printing cartridges, and DVDs were stacked up in a jumble. Antonia waded her way forward to the racks by the back, certain that was where she had last seen the napkins.

With a look of dismay at all the clutter, Antonia promised herself that she would make it a priority to neaten up the place. Perhaps she should put Lucy on it. Judging by her office, she knew how to deal with clutter. Antonia saw the napkins on the bottom shelf of a rack in the corner. They were obstructed by three twenty-packs of Bounty paper towels. Antonia heaved the paper towels to the side and then moved deeper into the closet to retrieve the bev napkins. She bent over and grabbed three large packets. Just as she did so, the overhead light went out. Quickly, Antonia popped up and hit her head on the corner of the shelf.

"Ouch," she said, rubbing her head.

The room was now completely black. Great. Antonia moved back towards the door, knocking down random boxes as she did so. She fumbled in the blackness. Her eyes finally adjusted and she could see strips of light from the side of the door. She instantly thought of Sharon Getz and became more sympathetic to her plight. It was unnerving not being able to see, to say the least.

When Antonia finally reached the door, she groped around for the handle, sliding her hands up and down. At last her fingers grasped it. She turned the knob and pressed. The door wouldn't open. Antonia twisted again. But the door would not budge.

Antonia felt a wave of panic. She was not good with small spaces. Nor was she good with small spaces that were pitch black. She instantly felt claustrophobic. Antonia tried the knob again and again, pressing against the door and pulling it towards her, but it would not budge. It was as if it was locked.

Antonia reached up and tried to find the cord for the light, but she couldn't see it in the darkness. She turned back towards the door and began banging on it, smacking it with one hand while trying it with the other.

"Hello? Hello? Anyone out there?"

Antonia was met with no response. She increased her yells, her voice become more shrill and desperate.

"Hello? Anyone!"

She banged and banged the door and began kicking it. Then she took a step back and lunged at it, hoping it would unstick. Nothing happened.

Antonia paused. She was sweating. She felt panicky. She had to calm down, as she was starting to hyperventilate. She thought she heard footsteps.

"Hello? Help! I'm locked in the closet!"

But there was no response. Antonia told herself to calm down. She would try again. Someone had to come along. Antonia banged on the door again. Then she took one more step back and did a small run towards the door. Just as she did so, the door opened, and Connie was standing on the threshold. Antonia almost knocked straight into her.

"Antonia! Are you okay?"

Antonia was jubilant to have been released. "The door locked! I thought I was stuck."

"Oh, that's awful," said Connie. "I just turned the key. It must have stuck."

Antonia looked at the knob. Her key was still in there. "I don't even remember closing the door."

"Maybe the wind blew it shut?"

"Maybe."

But Antonia was skeptical. How would the wind blow it shut? She turned around and pulled on the light cord. The light instantly went on. Why had it gone off before? Had someone pulled it off?

"Connie, did you see anyone around here?"

"Like who?"

"I don't know . . . anyone who would lock me in?"

Connie's face fell in astonishment. "No . . ."

"Sorry, probably nothing. I just got a little crazy in there."

"Yeah, it's scary to be locked in the dark."

"You're telling me."

Antonia was disturbed for the rest of the night. Was there a ghost at the inn? A mean ghost who folded up her ladder when she changed light bulbs and locked her in the storage closet? Or was it someone else? Could it be someone who liked to kill innkeepers? Antonia shuddered each time she thought about it.

19

THURSDAY

Although the weather had cleared Wednesday afternoon and the sun had peeked out, the following morning the sky was a uniform bluish gray. There wasn't any rain, but it appeared as if a shower was imminent. The air was heavy but still, biding time before it opened up to dump its contents out on the streets, like a balloon about to be pricked with a needle. The birds seemed to have gotten the memo, because there were thick packs of them flying west, squawking en route. Squirrels were dashing into thickets of trees, heading for cover.

Antonia's slumber had been restless. She had nightmares about killers and ghosts and found herself waking up every other hour worried that she had heard something. She finally took her cell phone and pulled it under the covers with her so that she would have a shot at calling the police if someone appeared. As a result of her bad night's sleep, she overslept the next morning and by the time she arrived at the beach, Nick was loading his dogs into his SUV, his walk finished. They had a brief chat over the weather before he politely begged off for a meeting. Antonia's disappointment was so immense that she was tempted to turn around and get back into her car and forego the walk. Curling back up in her bed to catch up on her sleep was a nice temptation. But a glance down at her thighs propelled her onwards. She was here; she might as well get some exercise. With her hands thrust into the pockets of her jacket and her jaw locked in defiance, she set out like a reluctant child being dragged by her mother to do something abhorrent. Antonia forced herself to march down to the jetty and then did an abrupt turnaround and marched back. That was sufficient for the day.

When Antonia walked from her car to the back entrance of the inn she noted with dismay that there was a hole in the fence by the side yard. It couldn't have been done during yesterday's rainstorm and that meant only one thing: deer had breached the fence. She was irritated until she decided her revenge: she would put venison on the menu next week. Served with braised radicchio and red wine sauce, it would be delicious.

She walked out towards the back yard in search of Hector, in order to alert him about the fence in case he hadn't seen it. She hadn't yet had a chance to discuss Soyla's new employment with him, either, although by now he probably knew.

She found Hector standing in the back towards the fence, staring at something he held in his hand. He had dropped his rake next to him, and there were garbage bags full of leaves stacked in a neat row.

"Hey, Hector. Well, the bad news is the deer got in again, as I am sure you know. But I think the good news is that Soyla's going to be joining us here at the inn again!"

Hector glanced up, distracted, his face confused. Finally he smiled. "Thank you, Mrs. Antonia. Soyla came out to tell me. She's very excited."

"I think it will work out."

As Antonia approached, she peered into his hands. "What have you got there?"

Hector furrowed his brow and glanced down. "I don't know. I was raking in the back and I found it buried under the pile of leaves."

Antonia peered closely. It was a small enamel box, white with a swirling blue font that spelled out monogrammed initials: ERV. Antonia scrutinized it carefully.

"What's this?"

Hector motioned behind him. "I found it over there. I'm not sure how it get there, the fence is so tall. I don't think someone would throw it over."

"Have you seen it before?"

He shook his head. "No. I raked here before the storm and I didn't see it."

"May I?"

Antonia took the box into her hands and studied it. The 'R' was bigger than the 'E' and the 'V', which meant that it was the last name.

"Hmm . . . I wonder . . ." but then Antonia stopped herself. She didn't have to wonder. Things were beginning to click into place. "Was it lying on top of the ground or buried?"

"It had a lot of leaves on top of it, but not buried into the ground."

"Like someone put it there who wanted it to be found. Maybe not right away, but soon."

Hector looked confused. "But why? It's a nice box."

"It *is* a nice box."

And Antonia was 99% sure that it was a nice box that had belonged to Biddy Robertson.

"Who would put it there?" Hector asked.

Antonia looked at him. She did not want to tell Hector that she now knew for sure what Naomi Haslett had been doing, lurking around in her backyard the other day. *Bird watching, my ass. Disposing of evidence was more like it,* thought Antonia. *Actually, planting evidence was more like it.*

"I don't know. But do you mind if I hang on to it?"

Antonia returned inside and went to the mudroom off the pantry where the staff changed into their chef's clothes. She put the box down on the bench and stared at it briefly. What was the significance of it? She had to think. Of course, she would have to turn it over to the police. And she'd have to tell them about Naomi. But did she have to do that immediately? No. As of now, there was no proof that it was anything other than a discarded item. She had no legal obligation to report something found on her property. There was no proof it was anything. Right?

Antonia tucked her Uggs underneath the bench where other assorted pairs of dirty shoes stood. She retrieved her

Crocs as well as a clean apron from her cubby and sat down to put on the shoes. She stood and looped the apron around her neck before firmly tying the belt around her waist. Finally, she slid the box into the pocket of her apron and debated her next move.

No, she would not tell the police, she decided firmly. They were, in fact, the last people Antonia wanted to deal with at all. Not the East Hampton police (yet) but police in general. When her ex-husband, the cop, was making her life hell, his colleagues did nothing to help her. It had been scary how they all joined together and made her seem like a crazy woman. It was only when that final drastic series of events happened that a woman on the force finally took Antonia seriously. But by then it was too late. So what would propel her to enlist their help now?

It was odd to Antonia that she had been put in this position. She had always thought of herself as a reasonable, law-abiding person, who was not a hysteric by any means. But the contempt of the Petaluma cops had left a bad taste in her mouth, and now she was wary of any interaction with the police. She often found herself driving the exact speed limit so she there would be no reason to be pulled over. She would avoid jaywalking or any other sort of minor infraction that could put her onto their radar. She followed the letter of the law. And yet now, she found herself hunting down a possible killer, working in parallel to the police. She sighed to herself and supposed it made sense. She didn't trust them to do their work, so she'd have to do it *for* them.

*   *   *   *   *

That night, dinner service was smooth except for two eventful occurrences: Barbie showed up and made a scene, and Joseph didn't show up at all. Although initially it appeared to Antonia that the Barbie situation was more distressing, it was only later that she revised her opinion. The night itself would have been a total disaster if the restaurant had not made more money than any other evening so far.

The kitchen was busy, frantic really, producing food as fast as possible. But unlike the previous night, where staff grumblings abounded, tonight they were excited. They were finally hitting their stride, the restaurant was gaining momentum and clientele, and they were really getting the hang of it. Even Marty kept his bitching to a minimum, perhaps distracted by how many entrees he had to put out, but his commentary was definitely more of a background noise than a disruptive rant. Kendra was excited about the mushrooms they had procured, and had concocted a variety of salads to showcase them, dishes that were met with enthusiasm by the customers who couldn't order them fast enough. And Liz was pleased with the added responsibility—tonight she was actually plating and cooking vegetables—more than a typical intern.

Glen was back and forth from the dining room, providing a running dialogue about who was there and sitting where, and describing in detail the many challenges maitre d's face on busy nights. At nine-thirty he swung through the kitchen door, flushed and agitated, and announced dramatically to Antonia that a very intoxicated Barbie had shown up with a girlfriend to sit at the bar.

"How drunk do you mean?" asked Antonia, who was placing a sprig of parsley on the striped bass lightly sauced with lemon caper butter.

"Three sheets to the wind," said Glen with obvious disapproval. "And loud as all get out. So is her friend, who laughs like a hyena. They came in and didn't even wait for me to seat them, but proceeded to the bar as if they owned the place and then sat at the stools. I had been saving the stools for the Felds, who had called earlier and very graciously asked me to reserve them. They were going to a play at Guild Hall first, and would be late. So when I asked Barbie to move, she refused, which her girlfriend found hilarious. Now what shall I do with the Felds? They're good people. I don't want to piss them off."

The Felds were lovely people, Antonia agreed. She had met them the previous summer at a wine tasting at Morrell's and they had hit it off. They promised to be her first customers when she opened the restaurant and they lived up to their word. They'd been very supportive to her ever since, sending business her way. She knew that was why Glen liked them, but in addition, she knew they tipped him heavily.

"Let me see what I can do about it," said Antonia. She wiped her hands on a dishrag and took off her apron.

"Look, I can get rid of them myself, I just don't want to cause a scene. I already have a taxi waiting outside."

"No, it's okay. I can do it."

The restaurant was full. Every table was busy, with a small

group waiting to be seated. Through the throng at the bar, Antonia spotted Barbie and her friend swilling glasses of Chardonnay and next to them sat an open bottle on ice. Barbie was clad in a form-fitting Lycra dress, pale blue with silver zigzags running horizontally in an even pattern, except by her cleavage where they went a little haywire and mushed together. Antonia's mother would have described Barbie's friend as "rough." She was a bottle blonde with thin hair and dark roots. Her face was hollow with eyebrows plucked into obscurity and sallow skin despite her best efforts with a bronzer, blush and eye shadow. She had squeezed herself into a sequined top and skintight jeans that only illuminated the fact that she should not be wearing formfitting clothes. Antonia knew the type; everything about her screamed drinker and trouble.

They were talking loudly when Antonia approached, and seemed either oblivious or indifferent (most likely the latter) to the fact that they were the noisiest guests in the dining room. Antonia saw Barbie acknowledge her presence out of the corner of her eye, but she continued to drain her wineglass.

"Hello, Barbie," said Antonia.

Barbie turned and gave her a drunken smile. "Antonia! My successor. Come, I want you to meet my friend Lena. We're having a little 'girls night out.'" She made fake quotation marks with her fingers to emphasize her point before continuing. "Thought we'd hit the inn to check out the scene but hey, it's not a really rocking place anymore. I feel like I'm in God's waiting room. I mean, the average age is like, dead, you know?"

"This place used to be a blast!" Lena said accusatorily. She then hiccupped loudly. This caused a series of hysterical giggles on both her and Barbie's part.

"Come join us!" said Barbie, motioning to the stool next to her, which was currently occupied by an elder gentleman in his fifties, sipping a glass of scotch. "You don't mind moving, do ya?"

The man looked perplexed but before he could respond, Antonia jumped in. "That's okay, no need. I'll stand over here."

"Suit yourself!" said Barbie. She then glared at the man and leaned in to Lena and said in a loud theatrical whisper "That man is so rude! He should give up his seat to a lady."

The man made a motion to rise, but Antonia stopped him, apologized profusely and asked the bartender to buy him a drink. She then went to the other side of Barbie and Lena and leaned in. "Ladies, I have to ask you to keep it down. I'm very glad you came here tonight to have a drink, but as you can see it's a quiet crowd, so I would appreciate it if you could respect that and just keep it down a bit."

"What?" asked Barbie.

Now that she was closer, Antonia could see that Barbie's eyes were filmy with that glazed look of someone who has had too much to drink.

"I'm just asking if you could keep it down a little."

Barbie threw her arm around Antonia. "Aw, come on now. Loosen up a bit, will you? This place is so stuffy now! No fun at all. When I was Lady of the Manor, this place was booming! We'd rock out all night!"

"Wasted Wednesdays were the best," concurred Lena.

Antonia extracted herself from Barbie's arm. "I'm sure it was, but we have a different approach now. We're focusing more on fine dining."

"Boo!" said Barbie. She banged her wineglass down on the bar with a thud. Antonia saw Barbie had left about half of her lipstick on the rim.

"Where are all the hotties? I mean, what's up with the cheesy maitre d'? How are you going to get ladies to come hang out at the bar with a guy like that?"

Antonia turned around and saw that Glen had hovered close enough to hear, a fact that was confirmed by the color his face turned. He glared at Barbie and stomped away.

"Barbie, please use discretion. That was really rude."

"But true," interjected Lena.

Antonia sighed. This would not be easy. "Look, ladies, I appreciate your business, but I have to say that I'm not hoping the restaurant will eventually turn into a pick-up scene. That's not my goal."

"Clearly!" said Barbie. "All the hard work I put into making this place a smash success has now gone out the window. I've had so many of our old customers say that the place has changed, and not for the better, mind you."

This enraged Antonia. "Barbie, I think you're being awfully rude."

Barbie swiveled around in her chair and gave Antonia a fake smile.

"Rude is nothing compared to the way I've been treated. I devoted my life to this stupid inn—toiled away for the past five years, and then I get nothing, nothing in return! I have to move out. I don't get any money for all my hard work. Did you know that? Today, it was official. I get nada. That bitch Naomi gets it all."

"She's so ugly too," added Lena.

"Ugh, why did that fat bastard Gordon have to die? My life sucks now!"

"You seemed pretty happy with your boyfriend the other day," muttered Antonia.

"Excuse me?" said Barbie in a loud voice. Other patrons at the bar glanced up.

Antonia gave her a defiant look. "I saw you with your boyfriend at the IGA. The one I heard you were seeing before Gordon died. So you can shed those crocodile tears all you want, but I'm not buying it."

"How dare you?" said Barbie, she started to lunge for Antonia but instead lost her balance and fell off her barstool. She fell hard on her butt, her legs splayed open. Antonia took a step back while Lena reached down and tried to give Barbie a hand. She was also too drunk to help. Antonia motioned for the busboys to come and assist her. They hoisted Barbie up. Barbie dusted off herself and glanced around the room at the stupefied guests.

"I'm fine, I'm fine. These chairs are too damn rickety! You better watch out, Antonia or you will have a lawsuit on your hands."

"Follow me, please," said Antonia.

"I'm not done with my bottle."

"Yes, you are."

Barbie appeared about to refuse, but then ran her eyes from Antonia to the two busboys next to her, who were ready to spring into action to defend their boss, if need be.

"Forget it, we're leaving," Barbie said to Lena. She grabbed her purse from the bar, pulled out a fifty and threw it next to her glass.

"I'm ready," said Lena. "Let's go somewhere fun."

"I'll escort you out," said Antonia. "We ordered you a taxi."

"No need," said Barbie.

"Yes, need," replied Antonia.

Most of the guests averted their eyes as the group filed out of the dining room in single file, although some customers made a point to give Barbie and Lena disapproving looks. The two ladies wobbled their way out, with a drunken gait, with Antonia and the busboys holding up the rear. Antonia followed them as far as the front door, which she opened firmly. Barbie took a step to leave before abruptly turning around and pointing at Antonia.

"You are not one to judge me, do you understand?"

"I'm not judging you," protested Antonia calmly, "I am merely asking you to not make a scene at my inn."

The look Barbie gave Antonia was nasty. "Oh, really? Then what was that 'boyfriend' comment all about? You don't know anything about my relationship with Gordon! How dare you say that I wasn't sorry he died? You don't know anything. Gordon was no angel either, but that was between us. So go mind your own business and keep your righteous nose out of mine!"

Antonia was shaken when she returned to the kitchen. She had decided to bypass the dining room to avoid extending the drama with questions and glances. She abhorred it when she felt like she had lost her temper, and she definitely had when she mentioned Barbie's boyfriend. There had been no need to sink to Barbie's level and engage with the drunken woman. She should have stuck on topic and just gotten her out of there. But it did piss her off hearing all of Barbie's little jabs about the inn. The place was low-rent and shabby when Antonia bought it. She had made it a spectacular inn and restaurant. Barbie should shut her trap, as far as she was concerned. Antonia could hear her mother's voice in her head. "Why do you let her bother you?" And it was true; she shouldn't care. From this day forward, she would attempt to have thicker skin.

A situation like this called for knife work. Antonia grabbed her sharpest knife and and a bunch of scallions and started chopping them as furiously as she could. It was almost the end of dinner service and lord knew they didn't need chopped scallions, but Antonia needed to cut something and better to attack the onions than a person. She could always bag them and save them for scallion pancakes in the morning. Or perhaps make a nice beef stew. She'd recently come across a recipe that she wanted to try that included dark beer, Dijon mustard, chunks of potatoes, carrots and parsnips. It sounded delicious. She let her mind wander over flavor combinations.

The staff knew enough to leave Antonia alone until she calmed down. They were also busy with their dessert orders, and Marty finally had a chance to take a break. Antonia chopped and thought through what Barbie had said. So according to her, Gordon had at least one—or maybe many—lovers. That was interesting. And yet it made sense. Antonia had heard rumors, confirmed by Barbie tonight, that the restaurant at the inn used to be a big party scene. There had even been murmurs that there was a small population of "swingers" in East Hampton, so maybe Gordon and Barbie ran with that crowd?

"Antonia, here are the numbers for tonight," said Glen, interrupting her reverie.

Antonia put down her knife, removed her onion-cutting gloves (no tears for her) and took his paper. She glanced up, a smile on her face. "Wow, this is incredible."

"Yes, I know. We did well tonight," beamed Glen. "If not for the little tiff with that hussy, it would have been a perfect evening."

"I'll say," said Antonia. "And did it work out with the Felds?"

"Yeah, I gave them Joseph Fowler's table. He didn't show up tonight."

"Really?"

"Yes. Didn't call either."

"Hmmm, that's odd."

"A lot of people went to Guild Hall tonight. Maybe he did too."

"Could be."

"But come on, Antonia, turn that frown upside down! Let's not focus on the negative, this was a fantastic night," said Glen.

"You're right," agreed Antonia. "Maybe time to open some Champagne? I think we all deserve a glass."

20

After shutting down the restaurant and returning home, Antonia could tell at once that someone had been in her apartment. Nothing was out of place, nothing was stolen and there was no rabbit boiling on the stove, but the air was thick with someone else's scent. It wasn't distinct enough that she could place it, but she could identify that the odor wasn't organic to her living quarters. And besides, the energy of her abode had shifted. Antonia would admit that that sounded weird and New Agey, but it was true. She believed you could definitely sense when other people had been in your space and this was one of those moments.

She'd returned to her apartment at about eleven-thirty and as was her norm, flung off her shoes into the coat closet (to be straightened up later) and walked over to the fridge to pull out a bottle of wine, before retrieving a glass from the cabinet. (On weekdays she usually put on the kettle for a cup of herbal tea, but as it had been a tough week she deserved a glass or two of Cabernet Sauvignon—always from California.) Antonia indulged herself with a steep pour, took a large gulp and leaned back against the counter to savor the fruity flavor. It was a robust red that contained hints of blackberries, licorice and cherries, and it was tasty. After a second swig she paused and that was when it hit her. Her home had been violated.

Antonia stood still, the only movement were her eyes gliding along all of her possessions, taking inventory. Her television, laptop and iPod were all accounted for in their place, and that pretty much was the extent of valuables that she possessed, although once she caught her breath she'd check in the jewelry box on her dresser. She didn't own any expensive jewelry, but she had her mother's diamond engagement ring and a few gold bands that had also belonged to her mother; both were of extreme sentimental importance to Antonia and she'd be distraught to lose them. Fortunately, her jewelry box was something of a tangled mess with all her beaded necklaces and costume jewelry all mashed together so it was possible that a thief could miss the important stuff, or else be totally repulsed and give up.

She continued her scrutiny of the apartment. The throw pillows on the sofa remained askew in the position she had left them in the previous evening—even the shape of her body was still firmly squashed into her favorite cushion (she was too nervous right now to be dismayed by how large the imprint was.) Stacks of magazines, the cluster of mail on the kitchenette counter, the dirty tea-stained mug in the sink were all where she left them. There was nothing she could pinpoint at this moment, but she was absolutely certain that someone had been in her apartment.

Suddenly a thought occurred to her. What if the person was still there? She could feel her heart beating through her shirt. What if this was it, she was about to be killed, and the murderer was ready to add another innkeeper to his or her scorecard? Should she call 911? She slid her body across the counter—never removing herself from its protective embrace as if that would somehow help her (absurd thoughts for a moment of terror)—and took hold of the phone receiver. She was about to dial, but then she stopped herself. What if it was nothing? What was she going to say to 911? *Hello, I think someone might be in my apartment even though nothing is missing. It just smells different.* It would be wonderful for business to have three squad cars come screeching into the inn's driveway and wake all of the guests because Antonia had a feeling. No, she had to investigate it herself.

She slid a knife out of the block of wood that held a variety of implements of all shapes and sizes and congratulated herself for maintaining their sharpness on a regular basis. A set of good knives is always a great investment for all sorts of purposes, especially if they are in perfect working condition. The one she withdrew could filet a cow in two minutes, so she was certain if she got the right angle on the intruder she could do major damage.

Summoning her courage, she took a deep breath and a

step. She stopped. Perhaps she should give a warning first? Maybe a little shout out, like, "hey, who's in here?" But that might give an intruder an unfair advantage. And what did she expect, that some voice would call out and say, "hey, it's just me?" No, surprise was the only thing Antonia had working in her favor right now. She glanced around the room. Fortunately, she had been naïve when she arrived home and had whipped open the coat closet, so now she knew for certain that no one was lurking there. She hadn't seen anyone at least, and it was a fairly narrow space, unless Flat Stanley was alive and well, she could check that off her list. Antonia's eyes moved down to the bottom of the sofa and armchairs. Even though they were skirted she knew the space between the floor and upholstered furniture was only about three inches and could only harbor a homicidal mouse. It would be embarrassing as all get out if that was the creature who ended up doing her in. That left the bedroom and bathroom.

Antonia clutched the knife close to her side and began gliding across her carpet stealthily. She felt as if she were crossing a river in a jungle, unsure of what would meet her on the other end. Truthfully, right now she would prefer lions and tigers and bears to a killer. She took such baby steps that it was at least a minute for her to cross the entire living room to the threshold of her bedroom. The door was open, as she had left it, and she had a clear view of the mirror that hung over her dresser. In the reflection she saw her bed, the pillows scattered across the headboard and the cashmere throw neatly folded at the foot. Fortunately, there was no killer lurking in it. Antonia slowly pushed the door so that it hit the wall, just to ensure no one was standing in the miniscule space behind it. She stopped and listened, expecting someone to protest that they were being smashed, but heard nothing.

At this point she decided to raise her arm to a forty-five degree angle, so that the knife was held aloft and all she had to do was start hacking if someone were to jump out at her. She'd seen all those horror movies where young, innocent women stabbed criminals like that. Although it dawned on her that pretty much every one of those women were overpowered and ended up dead anyway. She could still try to beat the odds.

Antonia took a few more steps into her room. She quickly scanned her belongings. At first blush, it appeared that everything was as she left it. Yesterday's clothes lay on the slipper chair in the corner; the shades were still drawn (why bother opening and closing when she was out of the house all day anyway?) and more crispy dead leaves had fallen off of the plant on the window ledge. If she had expected to see drawers left flung open and exploding lingerie from a burglar's hunt through her belongings she saw nothing of the type. In fact, there wasn't anything immediately obvious that identified the fact that someone had been there. And yet, she knew she was right. Her eyes grazed every surface until they landed on the pile of magazines on the side table next to her bed. They had definitely been disturbed. Antonia always worked on *New York* magazine's crossword puzzle before she drifted off to sleep, and she always put it back on the desk sideways before she clicked off the lamp. Now it was on an angle. It was so subtle that someone could argue with her that she was being insane, but she knew at once that it was not how she left it. You don't all of a sudden change habits thirty-five years into your life.

Antonia took a tentative step into the bedroom. She swallowed hard. She didn't like to think of herself as a scaredy cat, but she also didn't like to think of herself as dead, the latest on the list of murdered innkeepers. She took one more step and then immediately dropped to the floor and yanked up the bed skirt. She held her knife up high, ready to stab but fortunately, there was no one lurking underneath. Not wanting to waste time and stay in that compromising Twister position on the floor, she leapt up and ran over to her closet where she flung open the door. Summoning all her courage she used her knifeless hand to push the clothes from one end of the closet to the other, the hangers scratching out in protest, until she ascertained with confidence that no one was in there. That left only the bathroom.

Once again, Antonia took a deep breath and eyed the bathroom. The door was ajar. Could someone be standing in the tub, hovering behind the shower curtain waiting to reenact a scene from the movie *Psycho*? Possible. Better to find out now rather than later. Antonia walked briskly to the bathroom and flung open the door so that it banged into the toilet. She peered inside, first looking left and right. Nothing. But the pink floral shower curtain was drawn shut and there was still a possibility of someone there. Antonia said a silent "Hail, Mary" before marching over the chunky pink shag bathroom rug to the tub and ripping open the curtain. She curled her mouth, ready to scream. Her heart was thumping so badly it may has well have jumped out of her body onto the cold porcelain. But she was lucky. No one was there. Her wide array of bath salts and bubbles stood untouched.

Antonia didn't realize she was holding her breath until she exhaled for a solid thirty seconds. Phew. She was lucky she hadn't caught anyone. But now she had to find out who had been there and what they were after. Antonia opened every drawer and cabinet in the bathroom. Finding nothing awry, she retraced her steps into the bedroom. She spent some time going through the magazines next to her bed, searching for some clue. Had the intruder thought that Antonia put something in the magazines? Or had he or she been searching for something but decided to kick back and take a break reading a magazine on her bed before continuing on? Maybe the intruder had poisoned the magazine somehow? Perhaps by placing a giant tarantula in it? If this murderer worked with bees, there was no reason not to assume they worked with other killer insects. With her index finger and her thumb Antonia gently shook each magazine towards the floor. She was semi-expecting some lethal insect to fall out to the floor, but the only results were a floating ticker-tape parade of subscription renewal cards.

Antonia leafed through her jewelry box and was relieved to find all of her heirlooms intact, safely tangled with several Mardi Gras beads. She opened drawers, went back into her closet and even shook out the insides of her shoes, but found nothing. Then she hit the living room. Although she had adrenaline pumping in her veins it was now almost midnight and Antonia was getting tired. The day had been long, and plenty filled with drama. Exhausted, she took only a cursory look at her bookshelves, barely flicking open copies of her cooking magazines. She ran her hands through the cushions on all the chairs but found nothing.

Then she spotted it. The cardboard box that Barbie and Naomi had been fighting over! It was resting on the chair in the corner, pretending to look unassuming, but Antonia knew better. She walked over to it and peered inside. This was it! It had definitely been disturbed. Whereas Antonia had left all of the miscellaneous sheets of papers and notes scattered around in the mess she had found them, whoever had been in her house and organized them. It was subtle, very subtle. Everything wasn't exactly lined up evenly, but things were stacked now one on top of the other, and nothing was upside down or half-hazardly arranged. The intruder had been interested in this box for sure.

Antonia picked it up and walked over to the coffee table where she placed it next to the television remotes. She sat down on the sofa and peered in. The musty smell of old cardboard filled her nostrils. She began slowly sifting through the contents again. There was no doubt in her mind that Barbie or Naomi had been the one to break in to her apartment. They both had motive, and she even had proof that Barbie had been at the inn that night. In addition, Antonia had been too lazy to change the locks, so it was possible that both women had the key still, which is why there were no signs of a forced entry. So whoever was in the apartment had searched for something in the box and was disappointed not to find it. When they didn't find it, they thought perhaps Antonia had removed it, so they searched all the obvious places where she may have taken a seat to peruse it further. It all made sense. Now she just had to narrow it down.

Even though she had already dissected the contents of the box and read through everything with a fine-tooth comb, she began pulling things out. Her eyes once again scanned the catalogues and pamphlets, as well as the notebook, which she casually flipped through until the last page where Gordon had written to Lucy about firing Ronald Meter. Nothing jumped out at her as having been displaced. She removed everything from the box and placed it in a Leaning Tower of Pisa stack on her coffee table next to it. She glanced at it idly.

Then something dawned on her. She quickly unstacked the top layer, removing the jumble layer by layer until she was able to extricate the notebook safely. She felt like she was playing Jenga. She flipped open the notebook again to the last page. Nothing was there. She opened the book and shook it, but nothing fell out. She was positive she had put the other note that she had discovered in her office—the one that Gordon had scribbled that he thought "that B" is trying to kill him—next to the note to Lucy about firing Ronald, "that beast." But it wasn't there. Antonia went through the notebook again but didn't find it. Then she started once again, sifting through the contents one by one, opening every page, every catalogue. It wasn't there. The intruder must have discovered it and taken it with them. But why?

Antonia leaned back on the sofa to think. Did it mean that Ronald Meter had been in her apartment? It was possible that he had a key; he had been the manager after all. Was he so worried about this note? It didn't really mean anything. Or was it Barbie? Barbie had been upset that her quest to get part of Gordon's estate was definitely over and she lost. Maybe she knew that it was the end of the road once she had snuck into Antonia's apartment to see the will really wasn't in the box? Man, Antonia realized, it could even have been Biddy if she weren't dead. She probably had a key. Ugh, everything was confusing. Antonia felt her eyelids become heavy with sleep. She didn't want to think anymore. She wanted to curl up in her bed and forget about this entire, wretched day. She'd definitely put the chain on her front door tonight, and make sure that she had a locksmith come in the morning.

She trudged to the door feeling violated and dirty. Someone had been leafing around her things. Granted, the box wasn't hers and that's what they were after, presumably, but it still felt awful to have someone come into her apartment uninvited. In fact, Antonia realized, the only person who had ever even been into her apartment was Genevieve. It was weird to think that she had never entertained there. Why would she? She had the inn. And who besides Genevieve would she invite inside? With a sigh, Antonia clicked the top lock and began to pull the chain across the loop when she suddenly stopped, and a wave of worry came over her. Something had just resurfaced in her mind, but she was so tired it had slipped away. Something else had been off about tonight, something other than being "robbed." What was it?

Then it dawned on Antonia: Joseph.

21

Joseph's house was not even half a mile away from the inn. In a city, it was walk-able. But at midnight in the country, Antonia was going to drive. It was basically two lefts, no stop signs, and voila. She hoped it was a futile trip, but there was a little nagging voice inside her that told her it wasn't.

When Glen had told Antonia that Joseph had failed to arrive for his dinner reservation, she had been so preoccupied with Barbie and her trashy friend wreaking havoc in the dining room that this news hadn't really registered. And the fact that the Felds took his table and solved the problem of the occupied barstools had seemed like a happy and fortuitous solution to the problem. But now that Antonia had time to dwell on it, she realized that it was highly unusual that Joseph hadn't shown up. First off, no matter what, she was certain Joseph would call to cancel if he couldn't make it. She knew that from the bottom of her bones. It wasn't like him to forget. He wasn't disorganized or absent-minded. He was aware that Antonia was busting her butt to fill those tables, so no way would he ignore his reserved table. Although Glen had thought that Joseph had possibly attended the Guild Hall performance and it ran too late or he forgot dinner, Antonia was positive that wasn't true. They had specifically discussed this performance and Joseph had said he had seen a recent revival of the play in Manhattan and was not going to attend the Guild Hall production. No, it didn't make sense. Antonia hoped she was wrong, but she had a bad feeling that something had happened to Joseph.

She had never been to his house but he had told her where it was, in the middle of Buell Lane, near Most Holy Trinity's parking lot. She prayed he had a name sign because there were a cluster of houses right there, but if not, she would just glide down the block on the hunt for his car, which was an old Volvo station wagon.

The night was very black, with a murky layer of filmy clouds that obscured virtually all the stars. The moon seemed to be half-assing it as well, burning on low-wattage, just kind of hanging out in the sky waiting until his shift was over. The air was cold, and Antonia was cranking up the heat as much as possible, but it still took her old Saab several minutes to warm up. In fact, she usually arrived at her destination before the heat actually went on.

A few cars glided along Route 27, mostly going west, but there was no activity whatsoever when she turned on to Buell Lane. She tapped her fingers impatiently on the cracked leather that covered the steering wheel. It was so wrinkled, it felt like chapped lips. The leaves fluttered in the wind, but the houses were mostly shrouded in darkness, except for the outdoor lights that hung over a majority of the front doors. On her left, the whiteness of the catholic church cut a decisively sharp impression into the inky blackness. Its floodlights made it it gleam as brightly as a Broadway theater. Antonia turned her head to the right when she passed the empty parking lot that was across from the church. She slowed her car down considerably.

There were no lights on at the first house past the parking lot and no car in the driveway. Antonia drove slowly to the next driveway, carefully checking the entrances for name signs. She saw only numbers. She peered into the property of the second house and knew at once it was Joseph's, even without spying the Volvo parked deep in the driveway. It just reminded her of him. It was a 19th century traditional Victorian; two stories, shingled, with white trim. The tall and narrow windows were flanked by long black shutters, and there was a wrap-around porch with white wicker rocking chairs and tables. Dozens of neatly cut-back hydrangea bushes bordered the house, and through the darkness Antonia could see that the rest of the property featured ancient trees and andromeda bushes.

Antonia pulled in and put her car in park. Although the front rooms were dark, there was a light on in the back that allowed her to see the shadowy furniture through the window. Was Joseph awake? She glanced at her watch. It was late, past midnight. He did say he was a night owl, though. For a second, she wondered if she was being crazy, driving to his house to check on him. But something told her, in absolute terms, that she was not. She exited her car with determination. She crunched over the driveway pebbles and walked up the creaky porch steps to the front door. It was the sort that had a window on top so she peered inside, cupping her hands around her eyes for a better look. In the faint light she could make out a large grandfather clock and a fruitwood table that held a dish of keys and some mail. Antonia took a deep breath and debated whether she should knock or ring the doorbell. She chose the former.

She pounded gently, but then grew bolder and knocked harder. She waited, her breath curling in the cool air. She took a moment to glance behind her, but her view didn't go past the thick hedge that lined Joseph's front yard. There was no response. Emboldened, Antonia pressed the doorbell and was greeted by the sound of an old-fashioned "ding dong" that was popular in sitcoms. She waited, her eyes glued to the window, expecting to see Joseph glide towards the door in his scooter.

The wind rustled through the trees. In the distance she heard the cars passing along Route 27, but other than that, it was dead quiet. Antonia debated her next move. Was Joseph asleep and she was a nuisance? She was about to leave but she pressed the doorbell again. She waited. But nothing. No movement. Discouraged, Antonia turned and stepped down the porch steps. She stared up at the house. The weather-beaten shingles collected into a wavy pattern at the very top by the roof, with a beautiful diamond paned window centered in the middle. She wondered if Joseph even managed to get up stairs these days. He probably didn't need such a large space.

Undeterred by the lack of response, Antonia decided to walk along the side of the house. She went right, moving along the driveway that ultimately dead-ended into a garage. The side windows of the house were high and obscured by thick green bushes that hadn't surrendered their leaves to fall. As she rounded the corner, she found the source of light, in a back room, presumably the kitchen. There was a metal ramp leading up to the back door, which Antonia walked up. She opened the screen door and peered into the window. She was correct; it was a kitchen, painted custard yellow with red trim along the cabinets. Her eyes scanned the old fashioned GE refrigerator, past the stove and the sink. All of the appliances were a cherry red, as well as the dishtowels that hung neatly on the oven door. Antonia felt a pang for Joseph. She imagined that his late wife, Margaret had put so much effort into making the kitchen sweet and cute. It was so sad that she had died. Antonia moved her eyes to the left and then suddenly jerked them right. By the door to the kitchen, she could swear she saw Joseph's crutch on the edge of the linoleum floor.

Antonia tried the door. It was open. She walked in the kitchen.

"Joseph?"

"Here!" came his voice, weakly.

Antonia ran through the kitchen and found Joseph on the floor in a narrow hallway that ran off of it. He had obviously fallen. Dried blood was on his head, and his crutches were askew and out of his reach. He attempted to sit up with difficulty.

"Oh my gosh, Joseph, what happened? Are you okay?" Antonia rushed to help him.

Joseph smiled weakly, but instead of sitting up, lay back down. His glasses were smashed on the floor next to him. His bowtie was crooked, but other than that he still appeared unrumpled and dandy in his blazer and cords.

"I'm afraid I took a spill," replied Joseph. "I'm not sure what happened, I was using my crutches and I must have slipped. The floorboards are old and uneven, I often catch myself. I should have been more careful."

"Joseph, how long have you been here?" said Antonia. She took off her scarf and wrapped it up in a ball and gently lifted Joseph's head to put it on.

"I don't quite know," said Joseph. "I think I passed out. What time is it now?"

"After midnight."

"Oh dear, I've been here quite some time. I tried to shout a bit, but I knew that was futile. There's no one about."

"Oh, Joseph. That's horrible. Listen, I think you need to get checked out. I'm not sure you should sit up yourself. I'm going to call an ambulance."

"I don't want to make a scene. But maybe you are right."

Antonia smiled and glanced into Joseph's watery blue eyes. "It would break my heart if something happened to you, so we need to get you fixed up."

Joseph smiled. "Okay."

22

FRIDAY

Antonia did not return home until four-thirty in the morning. She accompanied Joseph to Southampton Hospital and waited until his son William arrived from New York. Fortunately, Joseph was fine and had only suffered minor bruising on his back and a contusion on his head that was fixed by two stitches, but the doctors chose to keep him overnight for observation. Joseph had tried to make Antonia leave, insisting he would be fine, but Antonia would have none of that. She hadn't realized until now how important he had become to her in the short time she had known him.

Instead of going to bed, Antonia decided to head to the kitchen at the inn and start preparation for breakfast service. She was tired to the core, and grateful that baking had become so rote that she could practically do it with her eyes closed. Today she experienced none of the usual joy that sustained her as she measured and stirred. It was all about getting through it, her bed beckoning her. She waited until her morning team arrived at six, and then headed to her apartment to collapse. She was disappointed that there would be no walk on the beach for her, because she had been collecting amusing anecdotes to share with Nick Darrow as they walked along the coast. Now she'd have to wait another day to see him. She allowed herself to wonder if he had brought her coffee this time. She could almost taste the Dreesen's donuts they had shared as she drifted off to sleep on her puffy down pillows.

The alarm interrupted her deep sleep at noon. Antonia was disoriented with the confusion that comes when you nap at odd hours. She couldn't even imagine what it would be like to have a night job. There was something so inherently wrong with sleeping during daylight hours. Her body moved slowly today, with reluctance and confusion. She took a long hot shower, lathering herself with the new shea butter soap that she had picked up at White's Pharmacy, and washing her hair with a lavender shampoo that usually perked her up. Today, it did nothing.

After dressing slowly, as if sleep deprivation were an injury, she padded into her kitchenette and made herself a giant pot of coffee. She fortunately had the wherewithal this morning to tuck two freshly baked scones into a paper napkin and bring them back to her apartment and now she bit into the crumbly confections with gusto. This would only temporarily sate her. She felt as if she had a hangover, and that usually called for one thing: grease. She'd have to download some eggs and bacon into her system and maybe even get her hands on some sausage. Her stomach rumbled loudly at the prospect.

Antonia had a lot on her mind, but she was worried about Joseph first and foremost. When she talked to his son William, he mentioned that he and his brother had agreed that it was time to force their father's hand. Antonia wasn't sure what that meant and the question was on the tip of her tongue but for once, she kept her mouth shut. She knew better than to meddle in people's family business. That never worked well. Although she hoped that Joseph's sons wouldn't bully him into an arrangement that he wouldn't like. Joseph may be physically weak but he was sharp as a tack and had a very independent disposition.

Of course, she was also concerned about the inn. She was working her butt off and it was getting to her. It had been the right move to hire Soyla. Perhaps if Antonia trained her well enough, she could assume more of the breakfast baking and at least give Antonia some time off to focus on other things. But the money issues were frightening, and made her feel out of control. She'd have to make cutbacks, and that made her stomach turn.

Antonia was also worried about the intruder. As she glanced around her apartment in the daylight, she wondered if there was anything else that had gone missing that she didn't notice. It still made her shudder to think that someone had sifted through her personal belongings. She felt violated. Who had been there? What did they want? Had they been searching for something, or hoping to find her there to kill her?

And last but not least, the murders were haunting Antonia. She had sniffed around, snooped here and there, and yet she had basically come up with nothing. Everyone was a suspect. Although the police did think Biddy had been murdered, that could be entirely unrelated to Gordon's death. So then she was looking at two separate murders. And she had no more answers now than she did three days ago. She was so weary from the tension that she almost believed she should just let the police handle it and forget everything. But that was easier said than done. Especially if she was possibly the next target.

Suddenly, Antonia glanced at her watch, remembering that she had agreed to accompany Liz to meet the Mastersons, the couple looking for a caretaker. She had only fifteen minutes to get ready. She banged down her coffee mug on the counter and rushed to dress. With dismay she realized that there just wasn't enough time in the day.

*   *   *   *   *

"The houses around here are gorgeous," said Antonia to Liz, as she steered her old Saab down Ocean Avenue. They were in the estate section of town, referred to in recent years by brokers as "Georgica area" because of Georgica Beach, which was on one end of it. Antonia drove down this street every morning when she went to Main Beach, but she never got enough of this view. Now that the leaves were dropping, the thick bushes were becoming more penetrable and she could actually see inside the properties and catch a glimpse of the previously hidden houses.

The houses that are "south of the highway" in the Hamptons are amongst the most coveted in the world. Old Montauk Highway cut through these villages, slicing the property values into two distinct camps: southern properties could run in the multi-millions per acre for property value alone, and northern properties went from the hundreds of thousands to the lower millions, depending on size. Southampton had a much larger "south of the highway" area relative to East Hampton so although still very expensive, it was more accommodating to demand. And in addition, unlike East Hampton, the golf clubs in Southampton were north of the highway so they did not eat into the residential availability. East Hampton had a golf club as well as the large Hook Pond eating up much of its 'south of the highway' acreage.

"I know, East Hampton is the prettiest town in the world," agreed Liz.

"I mean, look at this house," said Antonia. She pointed to a large white three story Georgian Revival, with black shutters and columns. It was set in the middle of a meticulously landscaped yard, the grass that shade of neon green that it becomes in the fall—morphing from the emerald hue it wears in summer. "I always think of the Great Gatsby when I see that house. It is so impressive."

"Yeah," said Liz quietly.

"You don't agree?" asked Antonia.

"I do, but . . ."

"But?"

"That's actually my house. I mean um, my parents'," admitted Liz sheepishly.

Antonia turned and stared at her intern, her jaw dropping in surprise. "Really?"

"Yes," said Liz, embarrassed. "I mean, they bought it a long time ago, before East Hampton became all trendy. It was a total wreck, they had to fix it up a lot."

"Wow. It's amazing. Smart buy."

"Yes," said Liz.

Antonia could see Liz squirm out of the corner of her eye so she dropped the subject. When Liz came and asked for a job Antonia had no idea that she was from a fancy background. She was so low-key and quiet and unassuming. Also, there was no pretension or attitude that gave her away. And now it turned out that Liz's country house was worth about twenty million dollars? It was crazy. Here she was with all that money, and yet the girl showed up for work early every day. Not to mention that she didn't parade around in expensive clothes. Antonia had never seen her wear anything with a logo, or carrying a trendy handbag. She was mostly clad in jeans or cords and wore turtlenecks or long sleeved shirts. Her brown hair had a simple cut—hanging straight to her shoulders with bangs across the top. She wore no visible makeup—not that she needed it, she had that creamy un-blemished skin that young women are blessed with. She was pretty but in that wholesome all-American way. *It just goes to show you,* thought Antonia in amazement. *You never know who's working for you!*

Antonia made a right on Lily Pond Lane.

"This is my favorite street," said Liz, clearly relishing a change of topic.

"I agree. It's spectacular. I love that no two houses are alike.

It's the juxtaposition that appeals to me. If it was just all those shingled mansions it would be monotonous."

"I know. I'm not that into modern houses, but when there is only one or two of them, they definitely jazz up the landscape."

"My antiques would never fit in there, but they are certainly more low-maintenance."

"Agreed," said Liz, before pointing to the right. "It's this one here."

Antonia put on her blinker and turned into the gravel driveway. The Mastersons' house was beautiful. It was a sprawling shingled mansion that appeared to keep unfolding like a hundred year old piece of origami. The house was replete with blue shutters, a wrap-around porch, a gambrel roof, brick chimneys, and a large solarium attached on the north side. It loomed in the center of what must be at least two sprawling acres, shaded by ancient trees. A gracious circular driveway cut a discreet motor path through the pristine grass, with every pebble restrained by a two-inch metal border. It didn't look unlike most of the traditional houses in East Hampton except that everything was on a giant scale; rendering it larger and grander than any Antonia had been in before.

"Lovely," said Antonia as they exited the car.

"I know," concurred Liz.

23

To her tremendous relief, Joan and Robert Masterson were also lovely. In retrospect, Antonia had to admit she had been nervous. This was her first job interview since she was a teen; she had always been her own boss. She wasn't quite sure how she would handle being questioned about her ability to do anything, and had even prepared defensive answers for the imaginary interrogation that she thought she might face. Fortunately, Joan and Robert abstained from the Spanish inquisition. They were able to have a very nice chat and reach an agreement quite faster than Antonia had expected.

Antonia did not know many people who came from old money, but the ones that she had met all shared similar qualities. They tended to dance around questions rather than ask them outright, suggest things rather than insist upon them, and there was always a very subtle subtext that Antonia didn't realize until after the conversation had ended. Everything was shrouded in a politeness and an openness that was genuine, and yet she realized that despite the reserved tone, they were always able to get their point across.

The Mastersons had ushered Antonia and Liz into the cavernous living room that was big enough to accommodate three separate seating areas. The décor was tasteful but a bit tired—faded chintz chairs and sofas, skirted round tables covered in enamel framed pictures of their children on the beach, antique consoles with drawers that were a bit warped from the damp, and large plants set in Chinese pots. The color scheme was pastels—periwinkle, rose, sunshine and lime. The wallpaper was a bleached out blue and white stripe. The walls were dotted with colorful impressionist style oil paintings that hung in thick brushed-gold frames. The beamed ceiling was low enough to make the room feel cozier than it would have with a double-height roof. Antonia felt comfortable at once, and could imagine retiring there after a huge Thanksgiving meal to drink Cognac and dazedly watch the flames flicker in the fireplace.

They offered Antonia and Liz hot apple cider accompanied by ginger snaps, which Liz declined but Antonia accepted. After the perfunctory "getting to know you," which was basically where Antonia spoke her business resume out loud, the Mastersons explained their needs. Their caretaker of dozens of years had retired and they were seeking someone to check on the house twice a week, and be available to open it up to any servicemen or deliveries on a needed basis. It was fairly straightforward and Antonia knew she was up for the task. Pretty much a monkey with a lobotomy could do it, Antonia thought, but of course, didn't say out loud. There was no talk of money, for which Antonia was grateful. It would have been a little awkward to discuss it in front of Liz and besides, she had no idea what a caretaker would make. She'd been dreading that they might ask her to throw out a ballpark figure of what she thought she would deserve, in which case she would be struck dumb. Thankfully, the Mastersons said early on that all of the formalities are run through Robert's office, and it would be a woman named Cindy who she would deal with for all official transactions.

When the business was out of the way, Joan Masterson appeared to visibly relax. She was an attractive woman in her mid-to-late fifties with fluttery bird-like energy that caused her to constantly move. She'd pop up and down to pass the cookies, retrieve more cider, open the window, and, it seemed to Antonia, seize any excuse to be in motion. Joan wore her wavy brown hair in a stylish short cut, and was chicly dressed in a button down pale blue shantung silk shirt with the collar starched up, and camel colored cigarette pants that accentuated her thin frame. Her demeanor was perky, her eyes a dancing hazel, and Antonia had a clear image of her standing across the tennis court in ready position, smiling while awaiting a serve, only to hammer back a killer drive.

Robert was tall and lanky and looked every bit the WASP he was. His dark hair was thinning but he still wore it in a cut that would deny the growing presence of a bald spot. He had on tortoise-shell glasses over a face that still held echoes of youth. Antonia knew the type: he was one of those men that had always been handsome and turned heads but then one day suddenly looks old and it's as if not only can he not believe it, but his body can't either. He was a self-described athlete who played golf, tennis and sailed, and Antonia could imagine him years before on the lacrosse and soccer fields at Yale. He chuckled often, sometimes irrelevantly, and there was an air about him as if he had no idea why he was meeting with Antonia, and was perhaps slightly bored by the proceedings, but overall, appeared to be a decent guy.

"Did Liz tell you that Joan and I celebrated the Millennium at the Windmill Inn?" asked Robert. He had completely interrupted his wife who was discussing the potential deliveries that Antonia might intercept.

Antonia turned towards Robert, who was sitting on the far right of the sofa across from her, his body touching the edge. "No, she didn't."

He nodded. "Yes, we went to . . ."

Before he could finish Joan interrupted. "It was such fun! They had a costume party! Now we were all a wreck that day, I mean, weren't you? Well, Liz, you were too young, but of course you must have been nervous, Antonia."

Without waiting for a response she turned to Liz. "They were predicting that all the computers would go off when it hit the year 2000 and that would set off explosions and rockets. It was very doomsday-end-of-the-world. I was in a panic, as were most people . . ."

"Not most people, just conspiracy theorists and you," said Robert, adding a chuckle at the end.

"Not true. CNN was predicting the worst."

"CNN!" guffawed Robert. "A great source of news," he added sarcastically.

Joan ignored him and continued. "I was very stressed. I thought, this is it! People were storing things in their basements, and ordering gas masks on the Internet. Well, finally, we decided, if we were going to go out, we'd go out with a bang! The club was being renovated that winter so we said, what will we do? No one wanted to host; it's too difficult to get a staff to work on New Years Eve, so we all decided to go to the Windmill Inn. They were having a champagne and caviar costume party and we thought, such fun!"

"That does sound like fun," agreed Antonia. "I would have liked to have seen that."

"You know what?" said Joan, popping up. "I have pictures of the night! Sandy Donaldson had gotten a new camera for Christmas, it was fancy for the time, not a telephone that is also a camera, just a one off, and she was happy to take pictures. She gave me a whole packet of them, which I put in a book. It might be fun for you to see how it looked back then!"

"Joan, no need . . ." began Robert before fading off. Antonia supposed after so many years of knowledge, a spouse knows when another one is not going to listen.

Joan went over to the large cabinet that was flanked by the two windows that looked out to the back yard and opened it. On the top shelf Antonia could see stacks and stacks of CDs and an ancient stereo system that would probably bring twenty dollars at a garage sale. The second shelf held rows of thick leather-bound maroon colored photo albums, with the date monogrammed on the spine in a gold font. Joan ran her finger along the row until she found 1999 and pulled it out. She flipped through the pages as she walked towards Antonia, before settling on a section in the middle and handing it to her.

"Hmm. I guess you can't see much of the inn. It's mostly snaps of people, but you get the idea."

Antonia glanced at the pictures in front of her. A much younger looking Joan was elaborately dressed in a large jeweled ball gown complete with a corset. Next to her stood Robert who was wearing a Harvard football uniform. Just as Antonia suspected, he was ruggedly handsome.

"What were you dressed as, Joan?" asked Liz who had come around to stand behind Antonia and peer at the pictures.

"I'm Madame de Pompadour. I was going to be Marie Antoinette but Sandy was Marie Antoinette. I know it was a mix-up, but I clearly remember that I told her way in advance I was going to be Marie Antoinette. Oh well, what can you do. Madame de Pompadour is just as dramatic, and actually I had a better costume. Not to be competitive, but she waited until the last minute and I ordered ahead. You'll see her on the next few pages when she finally had Hal take some snaps."

Antonia slowly turned through the pages as Joan pointed out her friends and explained all of their costumes to her, most of which were self-explanatory. Robert took the opportunity to go make a phone call. Antonia moved over to the sofa so that Liz and Joan could sit on either side of her to see the album without leaning in. Joan had been correct; little of the inn was visible. If Antonia didn't know it so well, and hadn't spent so much time studying every single window, she was sure she would not have been able to tell that it was her inn. But it was still fascinating for her to see pictures of it. Almost like one of those magazine 'before and after' collages. Now that it was so ingrained in her and she was so invested in it, Antonia felt as if it were a new boyfriend where she wanted to greedily sop up all of the information about life before her.

"Oh look, there's Len and Sylvia Powers," said Antonia, pointing to a picture of her friends. They were dressed as Darth Vader and Princess Leia. They appeared much younger, and thinner, but their faces were flushed either by the heat or the free-flowing booze.

"Look at the cute little Yoda with them," said Liz, pointing to the corner of the picture.

"I didn't even notice him!" said Antonia. "That's their son Matt. Wow, he looks so little there. He just celebrated his twenty-fifth birthday at the restaurant."

"Right, I remember there were a few children there," said Joan. "It was difficult for most people to find a babysitter that night. We were lucky, our nanny Sita came with us from the city. She watched the kids."

Antonia turned the page and scanned the pictures.

"Wait," said Antonia. She pointed to a picture on the lower corner of the right page. "Is that Gordon Haslett?"

"Who?" asked Joan.

"The former owner of the inn?"

Joan squinted. "Yes, yes, it is. I didn't remember his name,

I'm sorry to say, but that's him. He was the host that evening. A very exuberant man. That was actually a good thing for the occasion, he made it more festive. Almost made me forget that the end of the world was at hand."

Antonia carefully studied the photograph, which was close cropped so that it only featured the subjects from the waist up. Gordon was dressed as a gladiator. His helmet was open so you could see his face, and he wore printed armor over a red tunic. In one hand he held a sword and shield, and the other arm was draped over a woman in a mascot bunny costume. At least Antonia assumed it was a woman, judging from size and frame. She was about a foot shorter than Gordon, who Antonia knew had been over six feet, and the bunny was slight like a woman. But her face was totally hidden by her mask. On the other side of Gordon was Joan's friend Sandy, with Joan next to her.

"Who's the bunny?" asked Antonia.

Joan squinted at the picture. "Good lord, I can't remember. I must confess I had a lot of champagne that night. The next day was a total blur. But in my defense, I didn't think there would be a next day. But here, keep flipping through and maybe the bunny ultimately took her mask off."

"Oh my Gosh," said Antonia when she turned the page. "There's Larry Lipper."

"Who?" asked Liz.

"He works at the *Star*. And of course he's dressed as a cop. The guy covers the crime beat, fancies himself as a law enforcement adjunct. But I bet the real reason is he wants to carry a gun."

"He's pretty short," said Liz. "Or are the two mermaids next to him giants?"

"No, he's tiny."

Antonia squinted. Larry looked like a pig in you-know-what. His head was approximately the same height as the girls' breasts and he wore a giant Cheshire cat grin on his face. *Probably the closest he ever got to a woman,* thought Antonia.

On another page, there was a group shot with Naomi peeking out of the background. It was impossible to see her costume because someone dressed as a pirate was standing in front of her, but her distinctive black bob set her out against the crowd. She appeared younger, but still just as severe.

Antonia turned the page and found more pictures of Gordon. It appeared he enjoyed mugging for the camera and wasn't shy. There were pictures of him with other guests, more of him with Joan and Sandy, as well as pictures of him with a glass of champagne and a microphone, no doubt ushering in the New Year, Antonia assumed. Antonia continued casually flipping through the pages as Joan gave a running commentary about every detail she remembered about the night. She was half listening and half staring at the photos, leaving Liz to make interjections on her behalf. As Antonia flipped further along she realized something: the bunny was in every picture that Gordon was in.

"Sorry, do you mind if I go back a page or two? I went too quickly." Antonia asked.

"Of course," said Joan.

Antonia turned back the pages and once again studied the

pictures of Gordon. Sure enough, even in the pictures where Gordon was in the forefront, the bunny was off on the side or in the corner, her body turned towards his. It was as if she didn't want to lose sight of him. *There was something creepy about the bunny stalking the gladiator,* thought Antonia with a shudder. Was it Barbie, she wondered? She didn't think so. First off, Barbie said that she had been with Gordon for five years, and this was over a decade ago. In addition, Barbie was tall and busty. That would come through even in a bunny suit. And Antonia was certain that Barbie would never wear what was basically a mascot outfit for a costume party. Barbie was the type who would shop in the "sexy" costume department. She'd show up as a "sexy witch" or "sexy vampire" or "sexy kitty," and so on. That was a woman who loved her body and her looks; no way would she conceal herself.

Was there a reason that the bunny was hiding in her costume, Antonia wondered? Because when Antonia reached the end of the album, there were still no pictures of the bunny without the top of her costume.

"Was it hot at the party?" asked Antonia.

"Hot?" repeated Joan.

"Yes. There were so many people in there, and Gordon looks a bit sweaty in some of the later pictures. I was wondering if you could recall if it was hot in there."

Joan folded her hands on her lap. She shrugged. "I'm not really sure. I suppose it was. I just don't remember. Sorry. The old brain is not what it used to be. My memory is mush."

"That's okay, not important," said Antonia.

Liz eyed her carefully. "There's that picture of the two girls dressed as mermaids in the front. They're only wearing bikinis so probably it was fairly warm."

"Good point," said Antonia.

Antonia wanted to ask Joan if she could borrow one of the pictures but she decided against it. First off, she'd have to explain why and what would she say? That she was hoping to track down a possible murderer and the bunny might have a clue? Also, judging from the stacks of neatly arranged photo albums in the cabinet, it was evident that Joan took particular pride in her scrapbooking efforts and Antonia didn't want to appall her by suggesting she take one apart. No, better not ask.

Antonia and Liz remained at Joan's for another ten minutes before taking their leave. Joan gave Antonia a warm handshake and said they'd be in touch with specifics shortly and Robert re-emerged to bid them goodbye. Antonia felt good about the Mastersons. They were nice people. If the money were worthwhile (and it probably would be; her standards were low), then she would definitely work for them. And Liz seemed to like them, so that was a good recommendation. Antonia trusted her.

"Were you wondering why the bunny didn't take off her bunny head?" asked Liz, after they had finished all of their chit-chat regarding the Mastersons.

Antonia turned to her in astonishment. "How did you know?"

Liz shrugged. "Just a guess. I thought it was weird too."

"Yes," said Antonia. "It was weird."

24

Antonia made a beeline to her office to make some phone calls. She could have done them from the privacy of her apartment as well, but she wanted to avoid it after yesterday's intruder. It was silly, she'd have to figure out a way to get over it but right now, but she still felt violated. And she had to figure out what to do about it. Maybe a call to the locksmith should have been her first plan of attack. She added that to her list of things to do.

She checked in with Joseph to see how he was doing. His son William answered his cell and said Joseph was sleeping and resting comfortably. The doctors had not found anything to cause alarm, and the MRI had come back clear, so he would be home tomorrow at the latest. Antonia breathed a sigh of relief at Joseph's clean bill of health. It had been nagging at her all day and she was thrilled that he was okay. The phone call was an overall success, until the conclusion when William announced his news.

"I think the only good news to come out of this is that dad agrees with me he can't stay at the house anymore alone. It's just too much," said William. He had a deep baritone voice. Antonia knew he was a lawyer and could imagine that it worked well on his clients.

"I could get you the name of some home care workers to help him. In fact, Rosalie, our cleaner has a sister . . ."

Before she could finish William interrupted her. "That's very nice of you, but I think we've convinced dad to move into the city."

"What?"

"My brother and I are both there and actually the timing is perfect because there's a studio apartment that's come up for rent in our building. It's great; my wife went to look at it. It's on the fortieth floor and looks out at the river. We have all the amenities in our building, pool, gym, and concierge service. It's brand new, so everything is in fantastic shape."

Antonia swallowed hard. It was wrong on so many levels. Take away the part that she would be devastated if Joseph moved in the first place, the concept of Joseph in a brand new high rise building in New York City was repugnant to her. She couldn't imagine him in his bowtie and glasses zipping along the carpeted halls of a Trump Tower. All those soulless, cookie cutter apartments that were interchangeable and lacked character were so not Joseph.

"Oh? What does your dad think about this?" Antonia finally asked when she could speak again.

She could sense William's hesitation on the other end of

the phone. "Well, it's still new to him. But he understands the situation has to change. It's just not safe for him to be alone anymore."

"Right," said Antonia.

"This wasn't the first time he fell, you know."

"It wasn't?"

"No, just a few nights ago he was on his way out to dinner and took a spill. Fortunately, he was near the phone and we were able to send a friend over to help him."

Antonia remembered she had asked Joseph where he had been a few nights prior and he said he couldn't make it. He didn't have a reservation that time so she wasn't worried, but he had become such a regular fixture that his absence was noticeable. She should have known then that he was in trouble.

"Is there anything I can do?" asked Antonia.

"You've been great so far. My family and I really appreciate your help."

"Please, anytime. I stand ready, willing and able. I adore your father."

She hung up feeling anxious. There was something about Joseph moving to New York that upset the universe. Why do we have to get old, she wondered? But then again, the alternative was worse.

Since Antonia knew the next phone call would no doubt elicit the same sensation, she quickly dialed to get it over with. She waited as the phone rang, before it immediately went to Larry Lipper's voice mail.

"Hi Larry, it's Antonia Bingham. I'd love to talk with you

when you have a chance. You can call me back at the inn, or if you are in the neighborhood pop by . . ."

She let her voice trail off. Larry was so hard to take, but she wanted to find out more about that New Year's Eve party. Since it seemed impossible for Larry to exist without hitting on women, he must have tried his luck with the bunny. Maybe he would be able to give Antonia an idea of who she was.

Antonia returned a few more calls, and also arranged for the locksmith to come by that afternoon and change the locks to her apartment. She was about to return to the kitchen when Lucy knocked on her door. She held some papers pressed against her chest.

"Hi," said Antonia. "I thought you were off today."

Lucy smiled wanly. "I decided to come in and slog through some paperwork. Also, my office was a mess, so I had to tidy it up."

Antonia glanced around at her mess and swallowed. Lucy must be repelled by it. "Well, feel free to tidy up mine if you want . . . just kidding."

Lucy actually laughed, if you could call it that. It was absent any mirth. "I wouldn't know where to start!"

"I know, pretty grim."

"I mean, I'm sure you have your own system of organization."

"Not really."

"Oh," said Lucy.

"Have a seat. I was just about to crack open my mini fridge and indulge in some Cracker Barrel and Triscuits, any interest?"

"No thanks," said Lucy, declining the food, but taking the seat. As Antonia reached open the door of her fridge and removed the bright orange cheese (not the most appetizing color), she noticed that Lucy was wearing her "day off" outfit—one that Antonia had seen before. It consisted of a red and white check shirt (with a matching checked scarf that she wore around her ponytail) and crisp blue overalls. As was her norm, it had a retro fifties feeling to it, and Antonia felt at once that she was sitting with Maryanne from Gilligan's Island. Antonia took a plastic knife out of her drawer and sliced off several thick wedges of the cheese. She took crackers out of the box that was perched on her window ledge and placed them on each one. She again offered Lucy one, but she recoiled.

"I just saw all these pictures of the Millennium party that Gordon hosted at the inn," said Antonia, popping a cracker in her mouth.

"Where'd you find those?" asked Lucy with surprise. "In that box Naomi and Barbie were fighting over?"

"No, these friends of Liz's had them. It was interesting."

"In what sense?"

"Well, you know. Seeing Gordon in action. Old pictures of the inn."

"Right."

"And looking at all the costumes. People went all out. There was this one . . ."

Lucy cut her off. "I'm not a big fan of costume parties myself."

"Oh. I guess I know what you mean. They're kind of a hassle."

"Agreed. I did dress up one Halloween as Jayne Mansfield. I like that old Hollywood glamour look."

"Jayne Mansfield?" asked Antonia, inadvertently glancing at Lucy's chest. "No offense, but how'd you pull that off? She was known for her rather, well, large attributes."

"There is such a thing as a padded bra, Antonia!"

"You're right. I just can't imagine you as Jayne Mansfield."

Lucy looked offended. Antonia immediately backtracked. "I mean, she was just sort of cheap. I think of you as a little more elegant. Maybe Lana Turner."

Lucy shrugged, probably still offended. "I wanted to make a statement. Anyway, the reason I came in was after you came in the other day and asked for the employee forms well, that's when I noticed I needed to clean out my files A.S.A.P."

Their brief banter had been broken and Lucy returned to being all business.

"Yeah, I hate that," said Antonia.

"I went through everything, moved some boxes downstairs into the basement. But then I saw these and thought you might be interested."

She handed Antonia the papers.

"What's this?"

"It's the corporate credit card statements from when Gordon owned the inn. It's from the last two years only, because my system is to shred everything after two years of safe-keeping. I thought it might be of interest to you."

Antonia glanced at the MasterCard spreadsheet. A quick scan revealed charges to True Value Hardware, Warren's Garden

Center, King Kullen, and Riverhead Lumber. There were various other costs mixed in as well, but those were the ones that appeared regularly. "Thanks, Lucy. Were there any red flags that stood out to you?"

"Not when I originally did the payments. But look how many charges there are to Warren's Garden Center."

"Why is that strange? I feel like I spend most of my money on landscaping costs."

Lucy gave her a small smile. "But Warren's wasn't handling our landscaping. Hector did most of it. So these were not purchases for the inn."

"Are you sure?"

"Fairly sure. It's something I should have caught earlier, but I'd only just become the bookkeeper and it was all new to me."

"Who had access to the corporate card?"

"Gordon, of course, and Ronald Meter. He was the manager at the time."

"And you think Ronald was buying something at Warren's?"

Lucy nodded. "Horticulture is his passion. As you know, Gordon fired him when he suspected him of siphoning money. These credit card receipts could prove that."

Antonia's mind raced. Of course she knew that there was a cloud of suspicion regarding Ronald's dismissal, but would he have been so stupid as to blatantly charge things to the corporate card? "Wouldn't Gordon have been hip to these expenses? I can't imagine they would go unnoticed."

"You would think so, but the bulk of the charges are from

January to May. That's when Gordon was in one of his dark moods, not really focused on anything. I think it's possible they could have passed him by."

Something didn't seem right to Antonia. It all felt very sloppy and unbelievable that Ronald would do something like that. There must be an explanation.

As if reading her skepticism, Lucy stood up. "Anyway, just thought you might like to see them. Not sure if they can help you at all."

"Thanks," said Antonia, who was already scanning the pages. Lucy stood up to make her exit.

"No problem."

Antonia studied the row of charges. The fees to the garden center were substantial. "So it was just Ronald and Gordon who had these cards?"

Lucy paused on her way out. "Yes. Gordon and Ronald . . . and of course, Barbie."

Antonia looked up. "Barbie?"

"Well, yes, she was Gordon's girlfriend. She had access to that as well," said Lucy in a tone that conveyed her perception that the question was inane.

"Interesting," said Antonia.

When Lucy had left, Antonia went through the expenses line by line. She almost missed it. On the last page, there was a charge on November 29th to South Fork Farm for $20. That was the honey farm where Soyla worked. And where they had the beehives. It was worth taking a visit.

25

Although it was the last thing that Antonia should be doing on a Friday night when she was needed in the kitchen to start dinner service, Antonia decided to take a ride out the farm stand. She promised herself it would be a quick trip; it would just be half an hour of her time and then she'd be back in her apron, grilling entrees. The farm was located on Town Lane, a long road in Amagansett that ran parallel to Route 27 and cut through farmland into the woods, before running into Old Stone Highway which led to the bay. It still amazed Antonia how East Hampton had such a disparate number of neighborhoods that all felt worlds apart. One could live by the beach or by the woods, by farmland or in town. And every locale had its own rhythm and vibes, quite different from the others. Many neighborhoods that had once been unfashionable were now being cannibalized by weekend folk, due to the demand, and the fact that people were priced out of the traditional second home area—which would be "south of the highway." Now, it was trendy to live in the un-trendy parts of town, like this.

The South Fork Farm was only about twelve minutes from the inn. Antonia often visited the collective farm down the road, but mostly in the summer, and hadn't been out this way in a few months. The sun was beginning to cast its shadow across the rippling grass and as dusk was approaching, Antonia slowed her car. Late afternoon and early evening was the time when deer chose to run in a pack into the middle of the street and get hit by oncoming traffic. Antonia wanted to avoid that.

When she paused at a stop sign, she glanced at the houses to her right. They were modest and close together, shaded by thick trees. She glanced into the driveway in one and saw Ronald Meter standing next to his Mini talking to a guy, gesticulating wildly as if they were in a heated discussion. She squinted. The guy looked familiar, where had she seen him before? She craned her neck to get a better look and then suddenly the car behind her honked. She jolted. Ronald and the guy turned their heads in her direction. As soon as she locked eyes with Ronald, fear flashed across his face and he quickly turned away from her. *That was odd*, thought Antonia. *Was he trying to hide from me?*

After cruising some time, she saw South Fork's Farm stand up ahead and turned on her blinker. There were three cars parked in the makeshift lot; weekenders, no doubt, stocking up on produce on their way out from the city. Antonia pulled in next to a dusty Lexus SUV and turned off her ignition. She glanced at her reflection in the mirror and saw that the lack of sleep and stress were definitely catching up with her. There were light red rims on her eyelids and puffy bags gathering under her eyes. Lovely. She whipped out a lip gloss from her bag and spread some on, plumping up her lips with a shade that L'Oreal called "Luscious" before exiting her car.

A man and woman in their late thirties, dressed head to toe in black athletic gear (her tiny frame coated in spandex Lululemon; his wiry body clad in Prada, judging by the abundant logos) were frantically heaping bunches of kale into their basket while their two young children haggled for their attention. Antonia watched them as they squeezed, sniffed and scrutinized every vegetable in the various bins. The intensity they displayed making their selections instantly gave her anxiety, but she found herself fascinated by their exchange.

("Bruce, these eggplants are good. Not too much bruising," said the woman.

Her husband came and held up the eggplant to the light.

"Right here, there's a dent," he said, dumping it back into the bin.

"What about this one?" asked the wife, holding up another.

The man looked at it, then shrugged. "What are you going to make with it?"

"Caponata?"

"Too much sugar."

"I can puree it. I saw an eggplant puree recipe in the *Times.*"

He nodded. "Okay, but I'm doing a butternut squash puree also."

"We can puree them both. Maybe do a puree cleanse this week instead of a juicing?" she asked.

"I'm juicing this week. You can puree. I need to juice. It's all about the cleanse."

And so on. . . .)

Antonia realized she was staring and moved towards the counter. New Yorkers were a funny breed, in her opinion. They were so tightly wound and usually in a rush. She admired their energy but sometimes found it too much to take. East Hampton was "the country" to them, and yet many were unable to shake their city attitude when they came out here. You'd see them zipping around the curvy roads in their SUV's, clamoring to get to wherever they needed to go *as fast as possible*. This bothered many of her local friends. She'd heard that one of the latest "tricks" the locals were pulling on the weekenders/ summer people was to drive the speed limit, which was 25. This (pardon the pun) drove the summer people crazy. They'd start flashing lights and honking, desperate to force the cars in front of them to speed up to no avail.

The farm stand was so charming and quintessential that it could be the set of a movie, thought Antonia. On a long wooden table shielded by a roof overhang were various baskets of glistening (and yes, some bruised) produce, "spilling" out of bins. As it was October, that consisted of many root vegetables and squashes—shiny purple onions, dusty beets, butternut squash, waxy yellow and blue fingerling potatoes. Along side them were rows of apples in every varietal—Macoun, Granny Smith, Macintosh, Gala and Fuji. On the far end of the table were bunches of wild flowers in rich colors arranged in vases, already carefully assembled in a manner that made it appear as if they had just been picked. The owners of farm stands had long become hip to the fact that it was all about marketing, so they also repackaged berries and imported plums and other fruits that were unavailable and blended them in with local wares by putting them in their own rustic packaging. (Most people didn't even realize that strawberries were no longer in season here after mid-June.) Artisanal maple syrups, jams and chocolates lined the shelves behind the counter, and off to the side of the stand was an entire wheelbarrow filled with pumpkins and gourds of various sizes.

And where would a farm stand be without baked goods? Many farmers didn't bake their own; instead they offered pies from the Blue Duck Bakery and Tate's chocolate chip cookies. But at South Fork they had a stack of lemon and poppy seed bread tied up in white parchment paper with a blue ribbon and bags of homemade oatmeal raisin cookies and cinnamon drops in cute gingham wrapping.

A middle-aged woman stood behind the counter ringing up an older man. Black roots were bleeding into her yellow blonde hair and Antonia sensed it had been quite some time since she had visited a beauty parlor, judging by the color and her frayed ends, which splayed out across the edge of her ears in a jagged cut. She wore thick black eyeliner under her pale blue eyes, and most of her face was freckled and blotchy from sun damage. She wore a heavy Irish sweater under a puffy vest, and shapeless Lee jeans. Her manner was perfunctory and she emitted that 'end of the day' vibe when all you want to do is get home and take a hot bath. Antonia waited for the man to collect his change and goods before she approached. Another quick scan of the premises revealed the jars of honey next to the register.

"Can I help you?" asked the woman after the man in front of Antonia had paid. She had a strong Long Island accent.

"Yes, I'd love two jars of honey, please."

"What size?"

"Oh, let's go for the big ones," said Antonia with a smile.

While not rude, the woman was definitely all business. Antonia watched as she scooped up two jars with her rough, callused hands and put them in a brown paper bag. She punched numbers into the ancient register before glancing up at Antonia.

"Twenty-two dollars."

Antonia gulped. "Wow, who knew honey was so expensive?"

The woman's expression didn't change as she took Antonia's money. "It's organic."

"Now what does that mean, organic? I keep hearing that, but I would assume all honey is organic, right?"

"Not so. A lot goes through China and they add sugar to it. We have our own bees here so we make it ourselves."

Antonia's heart sung with the opening. "You have your own hives?" she asked, playing dumb.

"Yup," said the woman. She handed Antonia her bag, and gave her a farewell expression. But this was Antonia's chance.

"So, where do you keep your hives?"

"By the farm, down there."

She motioned behind her, and Antonia glanced through

the field to the farmhouse in the distance. A tractor stood idle next to it.

"Interesting. I've never seen a beehive."

Before the woman could respond, a young woman, wearing tight jeans tucked into camel boots and a long gray sweater over a concert t-shirt came from the back and stood behind the counter.

"Mom, do we need more turnips?" asked the young woman.

Even if she hadn't addressed the woman as mom, Antonia could see the family resemblance at once. The girl was still young and fresh and carried that rosiness that youth possess, but she was a carbon copy of her mother. The skin on her face was gently freckled and had none of her mother's sun damage, and her blue eyes were animated, her features still sharp and not slackened. She wore her flaxen hair straight to her shoulders, and had on a striped hat like the one Antonia had recently seen on the cover of a J. Crew catalogue, and couldn't believe it was back in fashion.

"No, but we do need more carrots," said the woman.

"Alright, I'll go in a minute," said the daughter.

Antonia wanted to return the topic to the beehives but at that moment the New York couple came up with their multiple baskets and placed them with a thump on the counter.

"All ready?" asked the woman behind the counter.

"We think so," said the New York woman. "Although give us some of that honey, also."

The woman turned her attention to them and Antonia was left standing idle with her brown bag of honey. She waited a minute, but the New Yorkers were firing a million questions at the woman so she knew it would be awhile. Instead, she walked over the dirt path to the edge of the field and stared at the farm, which was about three hundred yards away. The farmhouse was white, clapboard, shutterless and definitely due for a paint job. Smoke was trickling out of the red brick chimney and lights were on in the downstairs rooms. Next to the house was a large barn, unpainted and sagging, with the big doors flung open. A tractor and other farm equipment scattered around the entrance. Antonia could see beyond there was a low building that almost looked like a greenhouse. Maybe that's where the hives were? She'd have to ask Soyla to give her more details on what went on there.

Antonia was at a loss now as to what she should do. Just as she was debating her next move, she saw the daughter leave the shed and start to walk in the direction of the farmhouse. This was Antonia's chance.

"Excuse me?" asked Antonia.

The girl stopped and turned. "Yes?"

"Um, I just bought some of your honey, I heard it's delicious, and I was wondering if there was anything I should know about it?" She was grasping.

The girl looked confused. She sunk her hands into the deep pockets of her long cardigan. "What do you mean?"

"I mean, um, well, it's organic, right?"

"Yeah."

"So, anything special about the methods in which you make it?"

"I wouldn't really know about that. My uncle, Frank, is the beekeeper but he's not here now."

"Does he ever have seminars? Or you know, classes on how to make them?"

The girl smiled at the ridiculousness of Antonia's question. "No, not really."

"Oh. You see, I had a friend who was trying to buy a beehive. Do you ever sell yours?"

She shook her head. "Naw. In fact, my uncle buys beehives. It's a good business these days. Then he rents them to some of the other farms and lets his bees pollinate their fields."

Antonia could tell the girl was being polite but really trying to get on with her carrot errand but Antonia didn't want her to go.

"I guess honey is more popular than ever. Must be a demand."

"Yeah, you're not the first to ask."

"I'm not?"

"No," said the girl. She gave Antonia a look as if to say, can I go now, but Antonia pressed forward.

"Who has asked?"

"I don't know, other farmers."

"Oh, anyone else?"

She shook her head. "I don't really know. We don't keep track."

"Oh," said Antonia. "Sorry, I'm really nosy, I know. I just had a friend who had a bee and I thought she bought it here."

"Bought one bee? No, we don't do that."

"Okay, alright. Sorry to waste your time."

The girl turned away, but then seemingly remembering something, turned back to Antonia.

"You know, there was one thing . . ." she began.

"What?"

"Well, and this was like last year, or maybe longer, this one woman came and asked if she could buy a bee. She was really weird. We said no, so she just bought some honey."

"Do you remember at all when this was? Could it have been December of last year?"

The girl pulled out her bottom lip and began chewing on it. She tapped her chin with her fingers as she did so. Antonia supposed this was her way of thinking hard. Finally, she spoke.

"Yeah could be. We shut down the stand after Thanksgiving so I remember it was closed and she came to the door of the house. Yeah, now that I think of it, I remember she kind of commented on our lawn decorations. We go all out at Christmas. We have one of those blow up nativity scenes, really cool."

"Oh that's awesome," said Antonia, trying to humor the girl. "And she liked it?"

"Um, actually no. I think she was kind of snotty or whatever, because she sort of mentioned it without saying she liked it."

"Maybe she's the Grinch."

The girl laughed. "Yeah."

"So, then what happened?"

"So, I let her buy the honey . . ."

"She paid with a credit card?"

"Yeah, she did. We used to take cash only but these days cash is like an endangered species. We had to switch over; my uncle was pretty steamed about that. All the taxes etc."

"I know. Killer. So then what?"

"I rang her up and then like, way later, I went to the farmhouse to get more of something, and she was like, there, hanging around the beehives. She said she was just looking, and I told her she couldn't be there. But then like, the next day, my uncle said he could swear one of his girls was missing—he calls them his girls. The bees I mean. I don't know if they're girls or not, but that's what he calls them."

Antonia felt her heart fill with excitement. "Do you think she stole it?"

The girls shrugged. "Dunno. But it was weird."

"What did she look like?"

"Kind of average."

"Blonde? Brunette?"

"Blonde I think . . ."

"Thin? Fat?"

The girl looked at the sky as if there was a picture of the bee thief in it. "She wasn't fat. But she wasn't thin . . . you know, she was kind of stacked."

"You mean big boobs?" said Antonia with a smile.

The girl giggled and held the back of her hand to cover her mouth. "Yeah. I only noticed because my brother was there and he was like, "wow, that woman has huge you-know-whats." They were so big, they looked kinda fake."

"That's funny," said Antonia, feigning laughter. "Very funny."

But Antonia didn't think it was funny at all. Humor was not what she was feeling. Antonia's alarm bells were going off big time. Because the girl's description matched Barbie to a tee.

"Do you think you have a copy of her credit card receipt?"

The girl looked suddenly suspicious. "Wait, why do you want it again? I thought you were asking about your friend . . ."

"I was, I was. Just want to make sure it's her."

The girl had lost all confidence in Antonia. She glanced worriedly at the barn then back at the farm stand. "I should go."

"Right, right. I'm just trying to get the honey for my friend who was here. I'm not crazy, but she's very particular and I wanted to make sure it's the right place. Here's my card, please take it. If you find her receipt, please let me know. I think she paid with a credit card from the Windmill Inn. I own it now. I just want to make sure."

Antonia pushed her card into the girl's face. She stared at it, before shoving it into her back pocket. "Okay," she said. "Gotta run."

"Thanks, you've been really helpful!" said Antonia.

The girl scurried away. With sadness, Antonia realized she'd never hear from her. Antonia needed to tighten up her cover stories in advance. There was no way she'd make a good under-cover spy at this point.

26

Despite the conversation ending in failure Antonia was buzzing over the fact that Barbie had most likely taken the bee from the farm stand. This girl was basically an eyewitness placing her there. So now all Antonia had to do was prove that Barbie stolen the bee and used it to kill Gordon. Ha! Easier said than done. Even if Barbie was at the farm stand that day, it was so long ago that it was unlikely the girl or her Uncle Frank, the beekeeper, would be able to say for sure that Barbie had stolen a bee. Antonia had to think. There had to be a better way. Another problem was that if it were Barbie who killed Gordon, why would she kill Biddy, too? There was no motive between those two.

The sky had already gathered into darkness by the time Antonia returned to the inn and the lights were twinkling inside in an inviting manner. The outside air was fresh and brimming with an autumn medley that consisted of fireplace smoke, grilled steak, apple cider and ocean mist. Antonia stopped by her office to collect any messages before rushing to change for dinner service. There was a small scribbled note in Lucy's handwriting on top of her desk.

Antonia-

Turns out we were using Warren's Garden Center back then. We purchased all of our trees and bushes from them. I was wrong to think the charges were frivolous. Sorry about the false alarm.

Lucy.

Antonia crumpled it up and pitched it in her trashcan. So Ronald hadn't been siphoning money from the inn. *That confirmation doesn't really change anything because Ronald as the main suspect was so three hours ago*, thought Antonia with a smile.

Marty and Kendra were buzzing about the kitchen and Antonia felt a tinge of joy and dismay that everything had proceeded smoothly without her. Here it was Friday night and they didn't miss a beat. Oh well, she supposed that was a good thing, and she joined in the kitchen rhythm. As she plated a gorgonzola-stuffed hamburger on a brioche bun, Glen popped into the kitchen to tell her (with an eye roll) that Larry Lipper was asking for her. She scooped some pickle chips onto the plate before heading out to meet him.

The restaurant was noisy and loud, and the crowd at the bar was two people deep. None of that seemed to bother Larry, though. His tiny body was perched on a barstool and he was tapping away on his laptop, ignoring the women who were standing next to him ogling his stool. A tumbler of bourbon was in front of him. He wore brown corduroys and a blue fleece over a blue checked button down. He was totally absorbed in his work and didn't notice Antonia at first. He was so much more pleasant this way, she thought, when he was focused and not trying to be a wise guy.

"Hey," said Antonia.

Larry glanced up. He had about a day or two's worth of beard growth on his chin and his eyes were tired, with little wrinkles creasing around the sides. He snapped down the cover of his laptop.

"Bingham."

"Lipper."

He gave her a smile and for the first time she noticed that he actually had nice teeth. Very white, very straight. *Oh well, you win some you lose some*, thought Antonia.

"You beckoned me here?" he said finally. "Just can't stay away, huh?"

He still had his playful tone but he sounded wearier than usual.

"I did?" asked Antonia with confusion.

"Yes, you left me a message?"

"Oh right! Wow, that seems like it was so long ago."

"What did you want?"

"What's wrong, Larry. You have a late night last night? You look half dead."

"Ha, well, yes, I did have a late night last night. Hot date. But that's not the reason I'm tired."

"What is then?"

"You're not going to believe what happened, Bingham," he said. "This is so up your alley."

Antonia tried to get closer to Larry but couldn't elbow her way through the crowd. "You know what? Let's go into the sunroom and talk. Much quieter."

"I want to eat, though," whined Larry. "You promised."

"I'll tell Glen to send a waiter in to take our order."

"Fine."

Larry packed up his laptop and followed Antonia out through the front door. She greeted some customers along the way and grabbed two menus from the maître d' stand. Glen was busy chatting with the guests at table four, so she mouthed *sunroom* and pointed and hoped that he would get that she wanted a waiter to find her there.

The sunroom was occupied by a couple having drinks. They were leaning closely together in an intimate conversation. As soon as Antonia entered they abruptly pulled apart.

"Sorry to interrupt," said Antonia.

The man rose quickly. "It's okay, we were just leaving."

"We can go somewhere else," Antonia protested.

"That's okay. We're done here," said the man with finality.

Antonia glanced at the woman who winced at his words. She put down her glass and stood up reluctantly. Antonia could discern the slightest remnants of tears in her eyes and wondered if she had just stumbled upon a break up. Both of them left wordlessly.

Larry plopped down on the sofa. "Thank God we got rid of them."

"You are too kind, Larry," said Antonia. She sat in the armchair next to him.

"Yeah, yeah. I'm just happy to sit in a comfortable sofa. I've had a long day."

"Yes, please tell me all about it. I'm dying of curiosity," said Antonia with sarcasm.

"Ha ha, I know you are putting on airs, but do you know where I've been all day?"

"Larry, I really have no idea."

He gave her a wicked smile. "I was at the police station. They brought Naomi Haslett in for questioning in the murder of Biddy Robertson."

Antonia was stunned. "You're kidding me."

He shook his head. "I kid you not. It's big news. They think she offed her."

"Why would she kill her?"

"Oh, Bingham, you know the ways of women! You're all crazy!"

"Ha ha. Seriously."

"Cat fight gone bad. Apparently, the two gals were friends way back when, neighbors, bosom buddies, thick as thieves, probably having slumber parties in their PJs, topless pillow fights, the works."

Antonia rolled her eyes. Larry was clearly enjoying this. He continued with relish.

"Then the inevitable falling out, who knows why—maybe

Biddy stole Naomi's lipstick and she got her panties in a bunch. So when Biddy confided that she was having financial issues and facing foreclosure, Naomi joined with Gordon to screw her out of the inn. After that, it was *on*. And I mean capital ON. Remember that item in the paper about the dead animal?"

Antonia nodded. "But why now? Why wait all those years to kill her?"

Larry took a large gulp, nearly finishing the bourbon he had brought in with him. The ice cubes clanked down in the glass when he replaced it on the table. He wiped his mouth with the back of his hand and gave Antonia a mischievous look.

"You'll have to read it in my column."

"Larry, not this again!" snapped Antonia in frustration. She was about to grab him by the collar and shake it out of him but he put his hands up to surrender.

"Now, now, Bingham, don't get all wild. Of course I'm kidding. I just wanted to see your face. I love how it gets all puckered up when you are pissed off."

"Stop jerking me around and tell me."

"Okay," said Larry, pausing to take another chug of his drink, finishing it off.

Antonia waited with impatience. She folded her arms like a school marm and tapped her foot. "Larry, just be normal for once," she commanded.

"I'm offended!" he began to protest, but then sensing Antonia's acute aggravation, he backed down. "How about another drink first?"

Antonia remained silent. All this back and forth banter made Antonia feel like she was on a sitcom.

"Okay, Okay. Wow, lady, you drive a hard bargain. Biddy Robertson told her son she thought that Gordon Haslett had been killed. She actually even implied that she knew who did it. She didn't tell him, but she did refer to the killer as a 'she.'"

Antonia's pulse raced. "And the police think the 'she' in question is Naomi?"

Larry nodded. "Yes."

"But why Naomi? What about Barbie?"

"Okay, this has to be kept on the down-low," said Larry, for once serious.

"Obviously."

Larry leaned in closer. "When the police searched Biddy's house they found a letter that Naomi had written Gordon. It was full of nasty stuff like, 'I hate you', 'I hate your girlfriend', 'You're screwing me' . . ."

"Why would she put that in writing?"

"It was on the back of some bill for a party that Gordon had. He had rented all these tables and chairs and linens from Bermuda Party Rentals. He expensed it all to the hotel, but the police confirmed it was a birthday party he had for Barbie. Naomi owned half of the hotel, so he was essentially taking money away from her. And I think the kicker was she wasn't even invited."

"How did Biddy get the letter?"

"They think she was investigating Naomi. Trying to find anything she could to get back at her. Somehow got a hold of the letter. I dunno, maybe went through her garbage?"

Antonia had never met Biddy but she wondered at the idea of her going through Gordon and Barbie's garbage to find incriminating evidence. Biddy was in her sixties, would she really go dumpster diving? Something didn't seem right, but probably the police knew more than they were telling Larry.

"Why would she be investigating Naomi *now?* They 'stole the inn out from under' Biddy twelve years ago."

"The son said that his mother never got over it and always hated Naomi. She had finally stopped talking about until recently when she was passed over for a position in the Garden Club. She felt Naomi was the one responsible because she trashed her to another member. And Biddy really, really wanted that job. Don't quite know why, because it was voluntary, not even paid, but supposedly prestigious for some reason or other. Not sure why weeding local public gardens is prestigious."

Antonia gave Larry a look. "They do more than that."

"Whatever. I hear the words 'women's' and 'club' in the same sentence and I run for the hills."

"We can talk about your mother issues later," said Antonia. "In the meantime, what about Gordon? Now do the police believe he was murdered?"

"They didn't tell me if they do or not but I get the impression they're not exactly trying to add any more murders to their load. Not good for the local economy."

"Good for you and your paper though," said Antonia.

"You're getting it now."

"Is there anything else? Any other details that you are 'forgetting' that I might read about in your newspaper this week?"

"Hey, come on. I told you everything I know."

"How did they get to Naomi in the first place? They must have had some cause to search her house. Don't you need a warrant for that?"

Larry scorned. "I'm working on that angle. No one is talking. Yet. It's very frustrating, but I'll wait. I'm like a cat stalking my prey. Now you gotta buy me dinner. Isn't that why you called?"

"I actually had another question, but yes, I will buy you dinner," said Antonia. "And I may actually do you the honor of joining you. I haven't eaten either."

Larry gave her a long leering look. "I know you want me."

"Larry, please."

"Don't deny it."

The waiter entered the room and Larry and Antonia put in orders for dinner. They both wanted the burger, and Larry made a big show out of asking for whole grain mustard to accompany his burger, insisted that his fries should be extra crispy. He made a big deal about excluding tomatoes and lettuce on his bun as if they were toxic. Antonia gave the waiter an eye roll as he patiently took down Larry's requests. Antonia added a glass of Cabernet, another drink for Larry, and an order of fried calamari, as well as a small mixed green salad that she planned to take at least one bite of in an effort to balance out all of the grease and carbs. It really wasn't easy for a carnivore to incorporate leafy green vegetables into her diet. When the waiter left, Antonia returned her attention to Larry, who had grabbed a handful of mixed nuts from the dish the waiter had brought in and was picking out all of the peanuts and throwing them back into the dish.

"Don't do that please, it's gross," Antonia admonished.

"I don't like peanuts."

"So don't eat the nuts. It's disgusting that you touch every single one and then put them back in."

"Everyone does it. Did you know they did a study and found that there is a ton of urine on bar nuts?"

"Larry. Oh my God, stop."

"It's true. People drink beer, go to the bathroom, and 'forget' to wash their hands then come back and dig into the nuts. They're like the foulest things on the planet."

"And you're contributing to it."

"I would hope that you would throw out the dish after each person eats some. If you don't, that's a major health code violation. I should write an article on this place."

"Okay, now you are bugging me," said Antonia with exasperation.

"Babe, I don't like to see you upset. Forget the health code thing and talk to me. What made you call in Double L tonight if not for some loving?"

"You refer to yourself as 'Double L'?"

"I do."

Antonia sighed deeply. This man needed help, he was so confused. But that wasn't her problem right now. She decided to drop the subject and move on.

"I wanted to ask you about the Millennium New Year's Eve party that was here at the inn. I met a woman, Joan Masterson, who showed me some photos from that night."

"Man, that was some night! We partied like it was 1999."

"I can imagine. I saw pictures of you ogling ladies. But what I want to know is if you remember who was dressed as a bunny that night."

"A bunny? A Playboy bunny?"

"No, just like a real bunny. An Easter bunny."

"Geez, Antonia, I have no idea! I was out of my mind that night. The booze was flowing, everyone was giddy, it was like the sixties, or what I imagine the sixties were like. I wasn't alive then."

"Well do you remember who Gordon was dating at the time?"

"No, I didn't even know the guy."

Antonia was dismayed. "You're a reporter, Larry. Come on, did you take notes on the evening? Could you remember any of the people who were there? You seem have to have some capacity for observation."

"Now, now," said Larry. "No need to be nasty. It's true; I wasn't paying much attention that evening. But I can find out."

"That would be great."

"What do I get in return?"

"Larry, I am so tired of this."

"Come on, I'm just kidding you," said Larry. He punched her arm. "Have a sense of humor."

"I'll try."

Antonia and Larry were deep into their burgers when Genevieve arrived in a dramatic flurry, stomping her way into the sunroom like an angry child. Her outfit was a bit more subdued today, Antonia noted. She wore black leggings tucked into black leather motorcycle boots, and a long green gray asymmetrical wool top with sleeves that flared at her elbows. Her hair was pulled back into a messy bun by a black elastic band, and the only makeup she had on was lip gloss.

"I've been looking for you everywhere!" she said accusatorily.

"And now you found me," said Antonia brightly.

"You're not going to believe this," Genevieve said, flinging her leather satchel purse down onto the coffee table and plopping in an armchair. "Ty has a girlfriend."

She said it was if she had just announced the Academy Award for Best Actor or the winner of the Nobel Peace Prize. She waited for Antonia's reaction, but when she didn't comment she continued.

"It's just bizarre that he wouldn't mention it. There were plenty of opportunities. And do you know how I found out? We're watching TV, he's sitting on the couch and I'm lying down, my head on his lap. He picks up his phone and starts texting. I don't really pay attention but then he's like, laughing, so I say, 'Who are you texting?' and he says Sarah. And I'm like, 'Who's Sarah?' and he says, 'My girlfriend.' Can you believe it? Does he have no respect?"

Antonia barely had time to react before Larry Lipper jumped in.

"Sounds like a loser."

Genevieve turned, noticing Larry for the first time, despite the fact that he was seated directly next to Antonia. "Yes, he is a loser. You're right."

"Men are jerks," added Larry.

Genevieve nodded. "I agree. Total jerks."

Her eyes went back and forth between Larry and Antonia but finally settled on the latter with a quizzical gaze.

"Sorry, do you two know each other?" Antonia said, making the introduction. "Larry, this is Genevieve."

A small smile crept across Genevieve's lips. She thrust out her hand. "Nice to meet you."

"You too. Not every night I meet a damsel in distress."

Genevieve gave Antonia a wide-eyed look and took a step back. "Well, I'm sorry to interrupt. I should go."

She stood up and began to retreat. Antonia belatedly realized that Genevieve erroneously thought she and Larry were on a date.

"Wait, don't go, it's not what you think," said Antonia.

Genevieve shook her head. "No, no, I gotta run. Just wanted to stop by."

"Larry and I are just talking murder. Don't you want to join us? Please don't go!"

But Genevieve was already out the door. Antonia stood up to go after her but Larry stopped her.

"Aw, let her go and lick her wounds."

"No, she wants to talk. She just probably thought we were on a date so she hightailed it out of here."

"Then she's very astute," said Larry. "No tits, though."

"Larry, you are really very irritating."

"Thank you," he said smugly.

27

SATURDAY

The weather report had promised temperatures would hit the mid-sixties and it was already warm and sunny by the time Antonia arrived at the beach at six-thirty in the morning. After living most of her life in Northern California where the weather was even and predictable, a steady hum of overcast and dry and never too cold, New York was a complete conundrum for Antonia. There was a schizophrenic element to the New York climate where one day would be frigid and cold and then the next positively balmy. Last year she'd made the mistake of putting away her summer clothes too early—for once, making a huge effort to be so clever and organized, she had meticulously folded everything in tissue paper and neatly packed it in a plastic under-the-bed container in late September only to reopen it again a few weeks later when the heat reemerged in full force. Nowadays, Antonia took her mother's old "layering is key" advice and piled on layers of soft fabrics, starting with cotton short-sleeved shirts and moving to loose cardigans, scarves, fleeces and so forth until she was in a cocoon of clothing that could be unwrapped one item at a time.

She wasn't sure if she should expect to run into Nick Darrow; after all she had skipped a few days, but she took extra care in her dress nonetheless. It was silly and overly optimistic, but thinking about Nick Darrow gave her a buzz. It was like being in a real life romantic comedy with someone who often starred in romantic comedies. Antonia had also brought with her two fresh out-of-the-oven banana chocolate chip muffins to present him with. She had tucked them into a white paper bag that was now smeared with grease stains, but if he didn't show she could always eat them herself.

Antonia headed west against the wind. Georgica Beach had suffered immense damage in recent years by two big hurricanes—first Irene then Sandy. Much of the beach was eroded and most of the jetty there was submerged under water. The dunes had been hit so hard it looked as if a digger had come in and tried to excavate them. They were cut open, raw like a wound, with darker sand spilling out like a burst bloodline and vine roots tangled in knots like veins.

Antonia glanced at the mansions teetering on the edge of the dunes, with their long wooden staircases that dead-ended into the sand. This expanse was mostly desolate as it was about a mile between public beach entrances. She spotted a few lone dog walkers in the distance, and strained to identify them, but unfortunately, there was no one who looked like Nick, which she supposed was just as well. It was silly of her to think about him or get excited over whether he may or may not appear. It made her feel young and immature, like a child. She decided to push thoughts of him out of her mind. Instead she busied herself examining the patches of shells that had washed up on the shore. Some days were better than others for finding sea glass, and this was one of the good ones. Antonia loved sifting through all the vacant mussel shells, shiny rocks, cracked seashells and discarded bunches of seaweed to catch that glimmer of light that was reflected in even the smallest piece of sea glass. There was always so much white glass to be found, seconded by brown, so finding a green or cobalt piece of glass was a bonanza. Antonia pocketed several pieces along her walk, rubbing their smooth surfaces between her fingers, and tried to make a mental note to remember to place them in the glass jar she had on her bookshelf. It displayed a year's worth of collecting and yet the jar was only filled half way so far.

Every time Antonia made it to the beach for her morning walk, she resolved to come every day. The smell of the salty ocean, the clean breeze, the vast expanse of openness—from the water to the sky, made her feel cleansed. It was like mental floss. It made everything in her life fall into place and gave her perspective. The fact that the previous innkeepers at her inn were being whacked off? No problem. With a sea this blue and a beach this vast what did it matter?

The foamy waves were slobbering along the shores, dragging more bounty with them. They would unfurl their rocks and shells then recoil lazily. Antonia was so engrossed in her hunt for a piece of sea glass by the break that she didn't notice that Nick Darrow had approached. It was only after one of his dogs came bounding over and put his wet paws on her knees that she glanced up.

"You made it today," said Nick with a smile. His hair was damp and neatly combed and he wore a black turtleneck sweater over khakis and brown boots.

"I made it," said Antonia, rising.

They stared at each other for a beat smiling. Antonia felt instantly awkward and remembered that she was clutching the white bag in her left hand. She thrust it towards him. "Here, I made you some muffins. But if you already ate, that's okay, we can just chuck them, it's no problem . . ."

"You made them for me? Thank you," said Nick. He took the bag from her and opened it, pulling out an oversized chunk. "They look delicious."

"No nuts, wasn't sure if you were allergic. . . ."

"I'm not."

"Banana chocolate chip."

"Great," he said, staring at the muffin. "I like the way all the sugar crystallized on top."

"Me too," said Antonia with perhaps too much enthusiasm.

Nick took a big bite. His eyes rolled back dramatically and he moaned loudly. "Oh my God, these are fabulous!"

Antonia flushed with excitement. "It's okay if you don't like them. Please don't feel the need to humor me."

"Stop it! They're great," he said through his full mouth.

Yes, he was an actor, and maybe he was just acting but

Antonia was thrilled by his reception of her food. There was no better high in her mind than feeding people well. Forget drugs, this was a better buzz.

They started walking along the beach, following the paw print path that Nick's dogs had etched in the sand. The conversation was mostly topical, about food and wine, new restaurants in town, and local politics. There were moments of silence where they watched the dogs or the surfers bobbing in the waves, but nothing felt awkward or stilted. Antonia was both relaxed and energized when she was with Nick. She felt frisson, as if two electrical wires were rubbing together to make a buzz. She was sure he viewed her platonically, but that was okay. Somehow it was enough for her alone to experience the jolt that he gave her, the little fluttering heartbeats that sustained her through the day.

When they had finished their walk and were leaning against the split-rail fence shaking the sand out of their shoes, Nick dropped a bomb.

"I'll miss this beach."

"Miss it?" asked Antonia, replacing her shoe. "What do you mean?"

Nick scanned the shoreline. In the distance a fishing boat was drifting along the water, miles away. "I'm leaving town tomorrow to go film a movie."

Antonia felt her stomach drop. "You are?"

"Yeah," he said, turning towards her. "It's always so hard to leave."

"I can imagine. How long are you going for?" she hoped

she sounded more casual than she felt and that there was no panic creeping into her voice.

"Four months."

"Four months?" asked Antonia. "Wow! That's a long time."

"I know. I hope I can get back for a break in between but it's not looking good. We're filming in Australia."

"Australia? Wow. You really couldn't go much farther than that."

"I know."

A thought suddenly occurred to Antonia. "What about your son? Doesn't he have school?"

Nick nodded. "He's coming. We'll put him in school there and have him tutored."

Antonia's stomach dropped again. She noticed he had said *we.* All her fears suddenly converged. It was clear that this son of his had a mother, and this mother was still in the picture. It was silly that she hadn't looked it up on one of those celebrity websites, but it was as if she had blocked it from her mind. She truly had not wanted to know for sure if he was married. She knew the confirmation would upset her, and now it did, but she had been wrong—it would have been better to be prepared. Because right now it would be very difficult to pretend that she was not upset. Disappointment was running wild all over her face.

Antonia took a deep breath. "Well, I think it sounds like an adventure . . ."

"Yes, it will be. We'll do some traveling, and I think it's a great experience for a kid to see the rest of the world."

Antonia placed a frozen smile on her face. "Absolutely. Australia's on my bucket list."

"It's great."

Before the conversation became protracted, Antonia had to take action. She needed to get away from Nick now, or she would definitely start looking like even more of an idiot. She started touching her pocket and pulled out her cell phone, glancing at the screen.

"Oh my, so sorry, I have a call from the inn. I should dash."

"Okay, well it's been great walking . . ."

But Antonia cut him off. She didn't want to hear his pleasantries. She smiled and spoke into the receiver. He had no idea that no one was there.

"Hold on one second," before turning to Nick and giving him her biggest grin. "Bon Voyage, have a terrific trip!"

And without waiting for his response, she walked away, forcing herself not to look back.

* * * * *

As soon as she pulled out of the parking lot, Antonia allowed herself to cry. Bitter tears came flooding out of her eyes, dripping down her cheeks and pooling around her chin. The nose lost it as well, and she could feel it running. She was a hot mess. The obvious and traditional path that Antonia's mind would take would be recriminations and "I told you so's." But today she didn't want to criticize herself for having a crush, for suffering from disappointment and heartache. Because somewhere deep down, she was actually happy that she felt this way.

However absurd it was, however much of a long shot, she was still glad that she had put her tiny little heart out there. She had cocooned it so well under all her layers of fat and fleece these past few years, insulating herself from any opportunity for romance. Every pound she gained was another layer to her shield, used to cover herself. It was as if she didn't want to be *seen* by men anymore. She couldn't bear it.

And yet she had inadvertently fallen for one of the biggest film stars on the planet. And they had formed a friendship. It was the stuff of movies, but then life was weirder than movies. Genevieve often told Antonia that she was too hard on herself, so here she was being indulgent. Now as she drove around the quiet streets of the estate section of East Hampton, she let the floodgates open. She heaved, she scream-cried, she blasted Alanis Morrisette on her car stereo (fortunately, she kept the CD handy). She was shedding tears for everything, wallowing in self-pity. And then just like a tropical storm that suddenly stops pounding its raindrops, so did Antonia. She felt better. The clouds cleared. She turned her car around and headed towards Joseph's house.

28

Joseph was seated on one of the pair of matching chintz armchairs in his living room with his feet resting on the accompanying ottoman. A blue blanket draped across his knees and was firmly tucked in at the sides. The fabric on the cushions was various shades of pink and blush and featured giant cabbage roses unfurling their petals across the linen tableau. Antonia sat across from Joseph on the slipcovered sofa, in front of the windows. The room was pleasant. As the house was very old, there was no distinction between the entrance hall and the living room; they folded into each other with a large banistered mahogany staircase running against the wall bisecting the formal area from the sun porch. A sizeable oval hook rug was beneath the seating area, and the walls were a cool blue. The furnishings had a woman's touch—consoles covered with an abundance of framed pictures; a corner cabinet displaying blue and white china; an antique quilt mounted on the wall;

a vase of dried flowers on the coffee table—and yet there was a masculine vibe as well. The oil paintings were of horses and hunters, the books on the small shelf under the side window were historical fiction and biographies of war heroes, and the bar cart in the alcove beneath the staircase exclusively featured hard liquor like scotch and bourbon.

Joseph had been pleased to see Antonia, immediately putting down his book on his lap and removing his glasses. It also appeared that his son William was even more pleased. As soon as Antonia arrived, the quite serious looking William begged off to go to the grocery store and Joseph barely bid him adieu.

"How's it going?" asked Antonia.

Joseph shrugged. "I despise being at the mercy of others."

"I hear you. But he is your son."

"And I love him. However, he's very highly strung. He's always been that way. Margaret and I never knew where that came from. I suppose it was good, in a way. He was always the one to put pressure on himself and push. He was a straight A student, a champion soccer and tennis player, captain of the debate team. We never had a bit of trouble with him."

"Sounds like a dream child."

"He was, he still is, and I don't mean to complain. But he was always so rigid. I just wished he would loosen up a bit. Everything is very black and white with him. And he's headstrong as hell!"

"Gee, I wonder where he gets that from."

"Oh no, I'm nothing like him. There is no reasoning with him. He has decided that I am to move to New York and that is that. No more discussion. Last I checked it was a free country."

Antonia smiled. "He's probably very worried about you and wants to make sure you're okay. Sounds like he's the type of guy that hates being out of control. Humor him for a while. I don't mean move to New York, but just let him think he's in control until he leaves. Then you can do what you want."

Joseph smiled. "Very good advice, my dear."

"I can sometimes brainstorm helpful nuggets," said Antonia with a grin.

"Now, I am way behind on everything. Please tell me what is going on with all the murders. I was thinking a lot about it in the hospital and it was the one thing that gave me energy. That sounds absurd and callous, and my sympathies go to the victims, but I do like a good puzzler."

Once again, Antonia filled him in on everything, the big news being that Naomi had been brought in for questioning in regards to Biddy's murder. After downloading everything she knew, Antonia waited as Joseph digested the information.

He finally spoke. "You know, I think it's time to take some notes here. Do you mind handing me my yellow legal pad? It's on the desk by the phone over there."

Antonia retrieved the pad and handed it to Joseph along with a pen. She watched as he wrote a headline in big bold letters: SUSPECTS IN GORDON'S MURDER: before she sat back down.

"You really think he was murdered?"

"Don't you?" asked Joseph. "And anyway, it doesn't matter. Even if it's just conjecture, let's look at it as a parlor game. We're playing Clue now. Barbie did it in the garden with the bee. . . ."

"Sounds good. Will we discuss each suspect one by one?"

"I think that's the best idea. All of this information is leading us somewhere, perhaps if we outline it we will see the connections."

"Good idea. Let's write down each suspect and list their possible motive."

"As well as their accessibility," added Joseph.

"Whom should we start with?"

"Let's start with Barbie. Don't they say that 80% of the time the wife did it? I suppose in this case, the 'common-law-wife'?"

"Right."

Antonia watched as Joseph wrote Barbie's names in large caps on the pad before underlining it. He looked up at her. "Motive?"

"I think we have to do bullet points on this one. She had the most motive. She had a boyfriend so she didn't need Gordon anymore."

"Then why not just dump him?" asked Joseph. "PS: I'll be playing devil's advocate to sharpen your theories. Actually, now I think it might be a pity William left. He is very good at cross-examination and making people second guess themselves."

"You're terrible."

"Go on."

"Okay. Barbie had a boyfriend. She had moved on. But she didn't break up with Gordon because she wanted money.

She believed he had written her into the will, and at the very least, legally, because she was his common-law-wife, she would get something and be his beneficiary. Maybe she had dreams of moving her boyfriend into the inn with her. And that's why she was frantically searching for the will and was so upset she couldn't find it."

"Don't you think she would have kept herself a copy of this supposed will before she killed him? Some sort of insurance?"

"You would think that, but maybe she's stupid. Killers can be dumb."

"Good point. What else?"

"Well, maybe she was getting desperate. She had accused other people of stealing, but it looks like she was the one who had been stealing. And, with Soyla and Ronald both fired, maybe her jig was up and she was about to get caught. Biddy confiscated the box of alleged stolen goods at the L.V.I.S. with intent to return it to the inn, maybe she implicated Barbie, and maybe Barbie killed her . . ."

Joseph cleared his throat. "Ahem. Let's get to Biddy's killer later. How do we think Barbie committed the crime?"

"Well, credit card receipts show that she was at South Fork Farms around the time of Gordon's death. Someone fitting her description inquired about purchasing a bee, and then stole a bee. Maybe."

Joseph glanced at Antonia over his glasses. "Seems flimsy. If she were planning on procuring a bee, why would she place herself at the farm stand by charging a purchase with her credit card? That's putting her directly in the line of fire, so to speak."

Antonia sighed with disappointment. "I agree. It's weak. It doesn't make sense why she would pay by credit card when she could have paid cash. And there are other ways to obtain a bee."

Joseph scribbled something down and circled it.

"What are you writing?" asked Antonia.

"I'm writing that the 'How' is unconvincing. As in the 'who, what, where, when and how?' It's very obvious, and there are other elements to this plan that appear very well thought out. Therefore, this bee from the farm doesn't make sense."

"Maybe she didn't have a plan at that point. Maybe that part was impulsive. And she didn't think that we would put two and two together."

"It's possible. We did decide the killer may be dumb."

Antonia thought back to her conversation with the girl at the farm stand. "Possibly, but what does bother me is that she was so obvious. I mean, I know that's Barbie's character, she's a little flashy, but to hunt down the owner at their farmhouse? The stand wasn't even open, and then to lurk around and steal a bee. It's as if she *wanted* to be seen. Wouldn't she have at least tried to go a little incognito?"

Antonia and Joseph both paused to contemplate that. After some moments, Joseph restored his line of questioning.

"Do we have any other evidence of past criminal behavior on Barbie's part?"

"Only that she was a thief. Possibly."

"What about anything violent?"

Antonia shook her head. "I would love to say yes, but I

don't think so. I know she and Gordon fought, but no one mentioned physical violence. There was no police report on her. I saw her when she was pretty much obliterated, and she wasn't throwing punches. So, no. Now where are we? Everything fits and yet doesn't."

"Let's move on for now. How about the gardener?"

"Hector? Well, yes, he had some motive, but I don't really think he did it. I mean, he was angry that his wife was fired, and Gordon sounds like a really annoying boss, but why would he kill him?"

"I'm writing down, 'weak motive.' But as a gardener, he probably knew something about bees."

"True."

"And Gordon was found in the garden. By Hector."

"Yes. And Hector's wife Soyla worked at the South Fork Farm, which has the beehives. He had access," acknowledged Antonia. "But then so does anyone."

"You really don't like the gardener for this one."

"I know," conceded Antonia. "I just don't see it."

"Alright. Who's next?"

"Ronald Meter. The manager. He was fired by Gordon and he keeps a beehive, which he at first hid from me, but then told me it was because he was ashamed he ate honey as he was diabetic."

"That's a bit bizarre."

"I agree. But the thing is, Ronald seemed angrier with Barbie than he was at Gordon. He felt she manipulated him."

"Perhaps he set her up?" asked Joseph.

"It all seems very elaborate. Why bother? Everyone thought Gordon had a heart attack. If he wanted to set her up, he could have framed her. Maybe snuck into their apartment and poisoned the toothpaste . . ."

Suddenly Antonia shivered. What if that's what the intruder in her home had done? Had she brushed her teeth since then? Of course. But what if it was in her shampoo? Ugh, was she going to have to throw out all of her beauty products? There was no way! She would risk death. Antonia desperately wanted to tell Joseph about the break in, but didn't want to upset him in his precarious state, so she bit her tongue. Joseph broke the silence.

"Maybe Ronald wanted it to be known that Gordon was stung?"

"The only problem is that I only heard that tangentially. The Powers were eating at the restaurant and their son was the first responder to the scene. If he hadn't mentioned it, it would have died with Gordon."

Joseph gazed off into the distance, deep in thought.

"What?" asked Antonia.

"I wonder if you should talk to him again."

"Ronald?"

"No, the Powers son."

"Matt?"

"Yes, Matt. Maybe you should find out a little more about what happened when he first arrived at the inn to try and revive Gordon. Who exactly was there? What transpired?"

"You know, that's not a bad idea. I'll try to follow up with him today."

"It might be worth it. Okay, let's move on to Naomi."

"I can't see her killing her own brother," Antonia confessed. "I mean, I know they fought, but at the end of the day, he's her *brother*."

"Wouldn't be the first. Re-read the bible."

"I know, but while they had their differences, from all accounts their relationship was always up and down and very volatile. Frankly, it seems that's how all of Gordon's relationships were. He was bi-polar. I just think that a sister, no matter how frustrated, would have empathy for that. Especially since they were apparently very close."

"Didn't you say that she was the one who brought up murder in the first place?" asked Joseph.

"Yes, she alluded to it, then denied it. But all the more reason to question why would she spotlight it if she had gotten away with it."

"True. But she wanted a quick burial, no autopsy, and she stood to inherit everything."

Joseph was right. There was something wrong with the whole scenario. "You have a point," Antonia conceded.

"Let's talk about the suspects in Biddy's murder," said Joseph, writing her name down in big letters and underlining it twice. "And let's go backwards because it seems like the police already believe Naomi had a hand in it."

"The motive is clear. Naomi and Biddy hated each other. They had a long-standing feud. There was enough acrimony to cause Naomi to move across town. She bought the inn out from under Biddy and Biddy never forgave her. Naomi threw a dead raccoon on her doormat. And the most recent blow-up was that Biddy wanted to become a bigwig at the Garden Club and Naomi was blocking her; Naomi did not want Biddy encroaching on her territory. I wonder actually, now that I think of it, why Naomi and Biddy hated each other so much? What was the genesis of their falling out?"

"Good question," said Joseph. "Either love or money is my supposition. It's usually one or the other with women, no offense."

"I agree. I've heard nothing about another man, so it must be money. Or they were just totally competitive."

"And why do you think Naomi killed her now?"

"That I don't know," sighed Antonia. "Why now after all these years? And why would she kill her and then steal Biddy's enamel box and drop it in the backyard of the inn so that it could be found?"

"How do you know Naomi did that?"

"Because she was lurking around the backyard one day. Acting all suspicious. And then the next day we found the box."

"Who found it?"

"Hector . . ."

Joseph shifted in his chair. "Hector seems to be quite the expert in finding things in the back yard."

"Well, he is the gardener," Antonia pointed out.

"Yes, it's just interesting. I'm putting that down under his name."

"Okay but I don't think it's unusual."

"Not unusual, maybe, but it needs to be noted."

"Okay."

"Anyone else have access to the backyard?"

"Everyone does, you know that. But I didn't see anyone else other than Naomi there . . ." suddenly Antonia trailed off. She remembered something.

"What is it?" prompted Joseph.

"I just remembered that Ronald Meter came to visit me at the inn the day before it was found. He came to apologize for his behavior, which in and of itself was a little strange, but then I toured him around. I left him in the sunroom and he said he was going to say hi to Hector in the backyard . . ."

Joseph raised his eyebrows. "The plot thickens."

"But again why?"

"Planting evidence, perhaps. We don't really know what goes on in a killer's mind. Did Ronald have any connection to Biddy?"

"He knew her through the L.V.I.S. And he didn't really react when I said she was dead, now that I think of it. . . ."

"Do you think the box of things Biddy put together from the inn contained things that Ronald stole? We've been assuming it was Barbie but it could have been him."

"You're right. But say he did, was that really motive to go kill Biddy? She could tell the inn that he stole some things and tried to donate it to get a tax write-off? Why would she tell anyone at the inn? It was all done before my time, when Gordon was in charge, and she hated Gordon and Naomi. This could actually work to her advantage, because she could bad mouth them to potential customers and guests."

"Indeed."

"What about Hector?"

"Hector is a frequent customer of the L.V.I.S. thrift shop. Their paths have crossed, but I'm not sure that matters. I don't see him having a strong motive to kill Biddy. Let's cross him off."

"If we are assuming the same person killed both Gordon and Biddy."

"Are you kidding? Of course we are assuming that! I'd hate to think there were two murderers out there!"

"Agreed. What about Barbie?"

"Again, maybe she dropped off the stolen items to the L.V.I.S. and Biddy called her out on it. Seems like a weak reason to kill Biddy. Although maybe it would unravel her whole plan."

"Possibly."

Joseph and Antonia became quiet and wallowed in their thoughts. Antonia felt dismay; they were no closer to an answer than when they had started. She sighed deeply.

"It all comes down to 'that B.' Who was the B in the note Gordon wrote, where he said that B is trying to kill me? Barbie? Biddy? That 'beast', Ronald Meter? That B could also be the word that rhymes with witch, maybe used to describe his sister? I don't know. . . ."

"It will come. We just have to keep thinking, my dear. It will come to us, I'm sure of it," said Joseph.

"I really hope you're right."

Gosh, Antonia was really going to miss Joseph if he moved away.

29

In addition to volunteering as an EMT, Matt Powers worked as a physical therapist for East Hampton Sports Medicine (EHSP), which was located on a cul de sac near the airport, just off Route 114 which led to Sag Harbor. Whereas vast farmland sprawled on one side of the road, dense trees, intermittent houses and small clusters of industrial one-story buildings muddled the other side. Antonia pulled into a designated parking spot in the lot in front of the large windowless aluminum-sided building. It looked more like a giant storage unit than a place of business or rehabilitation. The sign on the door alerted her that she was in the correct place and instructed her to enter rather than ring the bell. She pulled open the heavy steel door, a feat that took both hands and an extra dose of strength and nearly shocked all of her usually dormant muscles. She wondered if the door ever deterred patients suffering from arm or shoulder pain from proceeding with therapy at this location.

Immediately, the smell of feet, dry sweat and the sickly sweet air freshener used to conceal their stench smacked Antonia in the face, invading her nostrils like a hostile marching band. She glanced around the room. The center was set up on one side like a gym, with assorted sports equipment including a treadmill, two elliptical machines, a Stairmaster and a metal rack that held a panoply of weights and barbells of varying sizes. There was a stack of blue mats against the wall next to a basket of weighted balls, and pegs that held different colored bands and jump ropes. The entire wall on the gym side was mirrored, and currently there was a rather obese gray haired woman in spandex and a white collared shirt staring intently at her own reflection as she attempted to lift a five-pound weight aloft with her right arm. She was assisted in this endeavor by a peppy pony-tailed blonde in a Juicy Couture sweat suit who was murmuring encouraging words and prattling on endlessly about how the old lady could "do it." To Antonia's left, there were six different stations divided by curtains, mostly ajar, featuring long tables that one would find in a massage parlor or doctor's office. A rather large man was lying face down on one, moaning loudly, as Matt Powers leaned against his bent leg, pushing down his knee and attempting to get the man's foot as close to his buttock as possible.

Antonia felt a wave of nausea, which was always the case when she was confronted by anything that represented athletic endeavors. Gyms in particular made Antonia tense up because they reminded her of her P.E. classes in high school. Those were routinely the worst forty minutes of her day, exercises in humiliation and embarrassment. She was perhaps the least coordinated person she had ever met, and even jumping rope had been a display of ineptitude.

Matt glanced up at Antonia and she gave him a slight wave. He acknowledged her with a nod. Just as she did so, the receptionist seated at the desk that Antonia hadn't even noticed, spoke.

"Can I help you?" she asked. The girl was young, probably very early twenties, with light brown hair and a rash of acne on her forehead. She wore a blue hooded sweatshirt, lots of eye shadow, and was chewing her gum so aggressively Antonia thought it might pop out of her mouth. A worn copy of *Fifty Shades of Grey* was propped open next to her computer with a purple bookmark peeking out. Beside it was a movie theater concession stand sized bag of Skittles that was half full.

"Hi, I was wondering if Matt had a moment that I could ask him a question."

The girl glanced over at Matt. "He's with a patient now, but he should be done in about ten minutes. You want to wait?"

"Sure."

"You can sit there."

She pointed to two wooden chairs that were pressed closely together against the wall. On one, sat an older Asian man who was listening to something on his iPad. Antonia sat down next to him, taking care not to crowd him, which was difficult considering how tightly jammed the chairs were together. She stood and tried to move her chair away from his, but once she noticed that the chairs were entwined at the legs and the man would have to get up to facilitate extrication, she abandoned her effort. The man didn't seem to notice her; he was nodding along to whatever he was listening to, which Antonia couldn't make out despite their proximity. It sounded like someone speaking a foreign language but she couldn't be sure.

Antonia reached over and took one of the dog-eared copies of *Self Magazine* off the coffee table and began reading an article about the ten most fat burning foods. She ingested the information the way one might read about someone else's trip to Antarctica. All very interesting but she knew she would never attempt it.

The clock slowly ticked by and finally Matt's patient left and he approached Antonia.

"Hi, I hear you'd like to see me?"

"Yes, I was wondering if you had a minute?" asked Antonia.

"Sure, I got fifteen before my next patient. Let's go to my office."

Antonia walked through the gym, dodging the older lady who was now attempting to walk and lift weights at the same time, an exercise that was currently proving elusive and demoralizing despite her enthusiastic therapist who had kept up with chanting. "Yes, yes! You can do it!"

Matt closed the door to the office and motioned for Antonia to have a seat in the chair across from the desk. Antonia declined his offer of a Vitamin Water, but watched as he bent down and pulled one out of the mini-fridge. She noticed how well he fit into his tight sports pants and form-fitting t-shirt, his muscles rippling through like a male model in an advertisement for grooming products.

Matt popped the cap and downed practically the entire bottle before sitting in the leather swivel chair behind the desk.

"Sorry, it gets really hot in there. I get parched easily."

"No prob," said Antonia.

"So what can I do for you? Are you injured?"

"No, thankfully. I'm actually not here for that."

He nodded and she watched as his eyes scanned her body. Antonia felt a wave of self-consciousness and inadvertently wrapped herself further in her coat before rambling on.

"I'm here because I wanted to ask you again about when you found Gordon Haslett, the previous owner of the inn. I know you didn't want your mom to mention that you thought it was a bee sting, but I have reason to believe it was and I would just love to hear from you, blow-by-blow, what happened when you got there."

Matt's face didn't show any expression as he took another sip of his Vitamin Water, finishing off the bottle before pitching it in the trashcan next to him. He folded his hands neatly on the desk and leaned forward. Antonia noticed how perfectly his nails were filed and wondered if he was one of those guys who liked to get manicures.

"You get that I have to be careful with what I say. I don't want any lawsuits for libel coming out of this."

"No, I totally understand," said Antonia. "This is just for my purposes only. Let's just say that I became a little freaked out with all the stories about past innkeepers dying under mysterious circumstances, so I'm doing everything I can to prevent that."

He nodded. "Why don't you just move?"

"Move?"

"Yes."

"Well, it's not that easy."

He gave her a solemn look. "I get it. You have to make choices."

Antonia's face didn't register the surprise with the direction this conversation was taking. Instead she smiled sweetly. "Yes, choices. That's why I need your help. Could you tell me what happened?"

"Okay. Well, at approximately four-seventeen I received a distress call coming from 241 Main Street, the location of the inn. I happened to be nearby at Hampton Market buying my lunch. I was able to immediately respond to the scene, within approximately four minutes."

"Wow, I hope you paid for your lunch," said Antonia, jokingly.

"I did," said Matt.

Antonia could tell that all attempts at light-heartedness or humor would fall on deaf ears, so she decided to keep those comments to a minimum.

"Right, sorry. Please continue. I won't interrupt."

"When I arrived I found the victim lying on the ground in the back yard. He was unconscious, and his vitals were alarming . . ."

Antonia waited as Matt continued describing all of the technical features of Gordon's condition, as well as all of the efforts he made to attempt resuscitation. This part of the story was not the purpose of her visit, but she could tell that it gave Matt a certain amount of pleasure to pedantically delineate the procedural aspects of the case, so she patiently waited for him to finish. When he had done so, she proceeded with the line of questioning that interested her.

"Let's start with when you entered the inn. How did you know where to find Gordon?"

Matt furrowed his brow and didn't speak.

"Matt?"

"Yes, I just want to reconstruct the scene in my mind."

"Okay."

They sat in silence for what seemed like a minute while Matt reconstructed the scene in his mind. His forehead finally cleared, and he spoke at last.

"There was a woman at the front desk who told me he was out back."

"Can you describe this woman?"

Again, a lengthy pause. Antonia's patience was wearing thin.

"She had brown curly hair. Middle aged."

"Okay, you must mean Connie. Although she's only about thirty-eight, not really middle aged," laughed Antonia, attempting to lighten the mood.

Matt remained unmoved. "The average life expectancy for a woman in the United States is anywhere from 73.5-81 years of age. So technically she is middle-aged, assuming she lives to the median of the average."

"Really? I didn't know that. Good point but not fun to think about."

"As an EMT, I have to think about that all the time."

"Right, I'm sure. Okay, well, when you found Gordon in the yard, who was with him?"

Matt puckered his lips and squinted his eyes, again thinking hard. It was funny to Antonia because she knew that these looks must please the hoards of girls who found him attractive, and she could even hear them describing him as smart and impressive. But there was something so contrived and self-conscious about everything he did that put Antonia off. Sure, he was a nice guy, but a little too humorless. She found him to be nothing like his parents and again wondered if he was adopted.

"The gardener was there, the one who found him."

"Right. And how did he seem?"

"Upset. But not emotional."

"Guilty?"

"Why would he be guilty?" asked Matt.

"Sorry, wrong word choice. I meant concerned. Concerned that his boss died."

Matt shrugged. "I guess."

"Anyone else there?"

"Nope."

"So you only talked to the gardener and Connie the entire time you were there."

"Yes. But on the way out, when we were loading him into the wagon, his girlfriend showed up."

"His girlfriend was there?" asked Antonia, perking up.

He nodded. "Yes."

"Barbie?"

"I don't know that I ever heard her name."

"Are you sure it was his girlfriend?"

"I mean, I used to see them together all the time. I always assumed it was his girlfriend."

Antonia nodded. "And how was she reacting?"

He tilted his head as if it helped him to recall the scene. "I think kind of in shock, because she was keeping it together. She wasn't crying or anything. She just kept asking me if I thought he would make it, and what did I think happened."

Antonia perked up. "Did it sound like she was worried he wouldn't make it? Wait, I know that sounds absurd. I'm sure she was. I just mean, was she acting suspiciously?"

Again a long pause while Matt thought. "I don't think so, but then I wasn't focused on her. I did mention that I thought it was a bee sting . . ."

Antonia lunged forward to the edge of her chair. "And what did she say?"

"You know, this I remember. She said 'No, no, no.' Like really strong, as if I didn't know what I was talking about. She said it was December and there were no bees out in the garden. Then my colleague said 'Let's roll', so we left. She didn't come with us. En route we performed . . ."

His mouth kept moving but Antonia was no longer listening. So Barbie had wanted to shoot down the bee theory from the get-go. Very interesting.

* * * * *

When Antonia walked out to the parking lot she noticed that a thick layer of clouds had spread out against the sky, erasing any evidence of the sun. It had become a gray day that looked as if it would melt into a gloomy night, and the air was chilly and ripe with moisture and dampness. Antonia got in her car and turned it on to get the heat going. She put down Matt's business card on the seat next to her (Matthew Powers: Physical Therapy Expert, EMT, CPR Instruction, Notary, Life Coach, Motivational Speaker, it read) and dialed her cell phone.

Antonia's first choice would be to visit Barbie in person and confront her with this recent revelation, but she didn't know where she lived or even how to attain her address. She was certain that Barbie was too angry with her to agree to meet in person, so a phone call was her only option. Antonia scrolled through her phone for Barbie's contact info, which Barbie had given to her when they were on friendlier terms when Antonia first purchased the inn.

"Hello?"

"Barbie?"

"Yes?"

"Hi, it's Antonia Bingham. Please don't hang up," she added quickly.

There was silence on the other side and Antonia wasn't sure Barbie had adhered her advice.

"Hello?" asked Antonia again.

"Yeah, I'm here. What do you want?"

Antonia was uncertain how to phrase it. If she were accusatory or hostile, Barbie would just hang up. She had to make up something.

"I had a question for you. It's of a delicate nature, but it's important."

Antonia waited. Barbie didn't respond.

"Okay?" asked Antonia.

"Look, I don't have all day. I gotta get to work. Just spit it out," she commanded.

"Okay, when you found Gordon in the backyard, after his heart attack . . ."

"I didn't find Gordon," she interrupted.

"Right. I mean, I know Hector found him, but then when you came out to see him . . ."

"What are you talking about? I wasn't there."

"What do you mean?"

"I wasn't at the inn that day. I had . . . a meeting elsewhere."

Antonia was confused. "But Matt, the EMT worker, said you were there."

"He was mistaken. I wasn't there."

"Are you sure?"

"Are you friggin kidding me? I told you I wasn't there. Now is that all? Cause I have to go."

"Yes, that's all."

After her call Antonia exited her car again and went back inside the Physical Therapy center to confirm with Matt. He was working with a new patient but Antonia strode past the receptionist and approached him. He was massaging his female patient's thigh but answered Antonia's question.

"Sorry to bother you again, but I just want to confirm with you one last time. I just spoke to Gordon's girlfriend and she says she wasn't there when he collapsed, or anytime after that. Are you sure you saw her?"

Matt shrugged, as his fingers kept kneading the woman's muscle. "Some woman was there. I know I saw her at the inn a bunch of times. I remember she was at the New Year's Eve party I went to one year."

Antonia was utterly confused when she drove back to the inn. It wasn't until she pulled back into the parking lot that something dawned on her. Naomi had also been at the New Year's Eve party. Naomi was often seen with her brother. It was probably Naomi at Gordon's side when he died. And it was now possible once again that Naomi had killed him.

30

When Antonia entered the inn she discovered that all hell had broken loose. Both Glen and Lucy were waiting outside of her office, both vying to be the first to get her attention. They immediately spoke in unison, bombarding her with their urgent news. Antonia could only decipher the words 'accident,' 'hospital,' 'ghost' and 'haunted' before she threw the card down on her desk and threw up her hands in surrender.

"What's going on?"

Again they began to speak at the same time, and she silenced them.

"Lucy, you first."

Glen sniffed that he was not chosen and instantly began pouting, while Lucy began her story. Antonia noticed that the front of Lucy's beige dress was covered in a dark stain, almost the color of Hawaiian Punch.

"About an hour ago, I came to your office to go over some

of the latest bills. I knock on the door, of course, and I thought I heard you say to come in. When I open the door an entire bucket of red dye fell on top of me! Someone had propped it to the door so that when I opened it, it spilled. Nearly missed bonking me on the head!"

"Are you okay?"

"I'm fine, but my dress is destroyed."

"I'm so sorry."

"It's not your fault," said Lucy tersely. "Obviously you didn't rig your own door."

"Do we know who did?" asked Antonia.

Lucy shook her head. "No. Connie didn't see anyone come in, and neither did the cleaners."

"And no one fessed up? Thought it was a fun prank?"

"No," said Lucy. "But I think—"

Glen interrupted her. "Can I talk now? My situation is freakin' *urgent.*"

Lucy bristled and folded her arms with impatience. She refused to look at Glen while he spoke, instead focusing her eyes on Antonia's desk in an act of defiance as if to convey that whatever Glen had to say was of little meaning to her.

Glen's eyes moved from Lucy to Antonia with importance. He lifted his chin as if he was about to recite a church eulogy. "Kendra is in the *hospital,*" he announced dramatically. He paused to let the words sink in, before continuing. "The kitchen is a serious *disaster.* We have a full house booked tonight, and it's lookin' like nothing is going to get done."

He folded his arms and raised his eyebrow.

"What happened to Kendra?" asked Antonia.

"It went down like this: she went in the changing area to put on an apron, but she couldn't find any. She came back and started complaining that they were still missing. I admit at this point I just thought she was being a prima donna, especially when I found Rosita, who said she had put them all there. Kendra went back *again* and said there were none. So then we *all* went and looked, and sure as sugar she was right; there weren't any. Rosita started opening the lockers, like, where could they be? Then we all pitched in, and when Kendra opened your locker this giant hammer smashed her on the head."

"What? A *hammer*? Is she okay?"

"There was a lot of blood," said Glen, waiting for the words to sink in.

"Is she going to be okay?"

"I had Hector take her to the emergency room in Southampton. She's gonna be laid up for the night, but I think she'll be okay. But the big news is, someone is setting booby traps here at the inn. And I gotta say, I think they're trying to take *you* down."

Both Lucy and Glen stared at Antonia as she grasped what they were saying. Someone was playing mischief . . . or someone was playing murder. It was not good. No, not good at all.

"And we have no idea in either case who did it?"

They shook their heads. "No one saw anything," said Lucy.

"Let's call a spade a spade," said Glen. "Either someone is messing with you, or the joint is haunted."

"Haunted?" asked Antonia.

Glen shrugged. "Those are your two options. Take 'em or leave 'em."

"There must be a third," sighed Antonia. "What do you think, Lucy?"

Lucy's answer surprised her. "I don't usually proscribe to the belief that paranormal activity exists but . . . all these things are very, very strange. And with the coincidence of Biddy dying this week . . . maybe there's something to it."

"I didn't expect that from you."

"Well, regardless of what it is, we have decisions to make. Shall we cancel dinner service? I think we also need to consider shutting down the inn."

"Shut down the inn? Right now? Are you crazy?" asked Antonia.

"We can't do that . . ." agreed Glen.

"We need to seriously consider it," said Lucy sternly. "Think about the liability. It would cost the inn a ton of money if more of these things happened. What if a customer got hurt? Then we're to blame."

Antonia sighed deeply. Her head was spinning; it was all too much to absorb.

"No, we're not shutting down anything. Give me ten minutes to check my messages in my office then I'm heading to the kitchen STAT. Marty and I will get it under control. Dinner is on."

"But what about all these . . . accidents? What if they are some kind of warning?" asked Lucy.

Antonia grimaced, before nodding authoritatively. "Then

let them warn me. I'm not going anywhere. And I have Chubb insurance."

* * * * *

After they left, Antonia eyed the bills that Lucy had left for her on her desk, and did a quick flip through. There were the usual utility bills, which honestly seemed particularly high, and vendors' bills, which appeared to be growing with every install-ment. Wasn't Marty supposed to be haggling with those guys? It clearly wasn't working. The good news was a notice from the Town of East Hampton regarding her building inspection, which stated the inspector didn't think she had any violations. She smiled when she read the signature at the bottom, con-firming it. At least something was going her way.

Antonia had several voice mails, including one from a travel agent who wanted to book three rooms at the inn for the entire week of Christmas, which pleased Antonia to no end, and an-other from a woman inquiring about room rates for Martin Luther King Jr. weekend. A British man named Jonathan had called back to confirm that she had received his resume, which she had not, so she made note of that. There was a message from some bank that was clearly left in error, and one from the vendor who was still trying to entice Antonia into buying his beer. The last and most important message was from Larry Lipper, which she listened to twice.

"Hi Bingham, it's me, making your day yet again. I found out how they nailed Naomi. Anonymous call to the police. Apparently that missing carbon monoxide detector was found in Naomi's neighbor's garbage bin. Got that? Cops have been all over. They're fine-tuning the case against Naomi. She's going down for this."

Antonia leaned back in her chair and glanced out the window. Her mind drifted to the picture of Naomi standing in the backyard of the inn. She had been following a cardinal, she said. She was watching birds. Something clicked in Antonia's brain.

31

SUNDAY

Clarity strikes at the most peculiar times, but when it does, ah, the joy it brings. It's like a sudden pinprick in the brain that releases the juice of revelation that washes over the entire body. It's a cleansing bath of lucidity that transports the newly sober recipient to an alternate level of wisdom. It's the moment that you reprimand yourself for not seeing it earlier, but also experience the full euphoria at having reached your destination at last.

Saturday night had been challenging, frantic and exhausting for Antonia but she and Marty, with the help of Glen, Liz and Soyla (who she had called in for reinforcement and who had performed beautifully) had pulled it off. Antonia pushed aside all thoughts of murder and ghosts and poured every bit of passion she had into the kitchen, producing meal after meal and putting her whole self into it. She sustained this momentum from the second she entered the kitchen until she helped shut down the restaurant at eleven-thirty. The evening was busy, not without flaws, but overall a success. The rib eye with cauliflower gratin and caramelized carrots as well as the fettuccini with lamb ragout sold particularly well.

Afterwards, Antonia had carefully entered her apartment, slowly opening the door to ascertain if there were any hammers or buckets of ink waiting to clock her. When she was certain that the coast was clear, she congratulated herself on having changed her locks. She was pretty sure that's why she was still okay. Despite that fact, she still crept around her apartment in the dark; slyly checking under every piece of furniture and behind every door and curtain to make sure that nothing awaited her. She basically did a full cavity search of her apartment, which took about ten minutes, before she allowed herself to collapse into bed and sink into slumber.

She slept deeply but had strange dreams. Flashes of everything and everyone that she had come into contact with over the past week appeared in odd places. But what was even more bizarre was that the secondary players seemed to take prominence in her sleep. Gordon and Biddy hovered in the background of her mind, limiting themselves to the shadows, but random people like the girl from the farmstand, and Biddy's neighbor, Sharon Getz, and the Winslows—the couple who had just stayed at the inn—were center stage. Antonia's dreams were like a kaleidoscope where she would turn her head and everything and everyone in her mind would shake out in a different way, tumbling forward in different directions, but all somehow inextricably linked.

Antonia woke rested, despite the chaos of her dreams. She preceded her alarm, and rose to find a glint of light streaming through her shades, curling its way around the room. The day would be bright and sunny. A soft breeze slid through the open window, ripe with freshness and the salty lick of the ocean. Birds were chirping, their song an optimistic soundtrack to the morning. The day held promise. (The only bummer was that she wished she could go see Nick Darrow at the beach, but he would definitely be gone by now.) And as soon as Antonia sat up in bed, she experienced the moment of clarity that had eluded her.

"Of course," she said aloud, running her burgeoning theory through her mind. "It all makes sense."

She knew what she had to do. She gently unfolded herself from her thick comforter and padded across the carpet to her bathroom to wash her face. With each splash of cool water that hit her cheeks, her plan began to form. After quickly dressing, she went to the kitchen and began mixing scones and muffins, pouring in streams of chocolate chips and raisins depending on which baked item she was making. With each swirl of her wooden spoon, her plan further took shape. After closing the oven door and wiping her hands on her apron, she walked out into the cloudless day and across the bouncy green lawn to the back corner of the yard. She used her foot to slide through the leaves until her toe knocked into a rock. She had found what she was looking for.

At nine o'clock, Antonia made her phone calls. A few didn't answer, and she assumed they were at church or still sleeping, but she left enticing messages that would ensure they did as she instructed. The rest of the day was spent planning. Joseph came over in the afternoon to help her. There were still a few kinks but they both agreed that the plan could work.

"Humans are weak," Joseph had reminded her. "They can be broken."

Antonia had to hope that was true. It was the only way she could prove that Gordon Haslett and Biddy Robertson were murdered and that she had solved the crimes.

* * * * *

"What's all this?" asked Lucy.

She glanced at the round table that Antonia had erected in the parlor and covered with a blue and white floral tablecloth that was hemmed with a green fringe. Atop the cloth matching napkins were folded in a pile next to a box of antique silverware—the heavy kind, actual silver and not plated—and a stack of blue and white Herend china dinner plates. The centerpiece was a discreet low bowl of chrysanthemums and white hydrangeas.

"I'm setting the table," said Antonia. "You're just in time, do you mind helping?"

"Of course not," said Lucy, still wearing a quizzical look on her face. "But why are we doing it in here?"

Antonia smiled conspiratorially. She glanced around the room to make sure no one was lurking around to overhear. The room was quiet and still, an almost foreboding hush hanging over it.

"I'm sort of freaking out a bit, so I'm glad you're here."

"What's going on?" asked Lucy with concern. "Did something else happen?"

"No, it's not that," Antonia leaned in. "I'm shutting down the parlor for the evening. Regular dinner service will take place in the dining room as usual, but I'm having a special dinner party in here tonight. I've invited all of the suspects in Gordon and Biddy's murder over to dinner. I think I have an idea of who did it, I mean, I'm pretty sure, and I think if I get them all here the truth will come out."

Lucy's eyebrows shot up. "Who do you think did it?"

Antonia smiled. "I don't want to say yet. Sorry, its just that I think the element of surprise will be a real shock and I want to make sure I keep that effect. Hey, do you want to stay? I think it will be very entertaining."

"Do I want to stay? Of course I do," said Lucy eagerly. "I was supposed to go to an independent film in Sag Harbor, but I'll cancel that. This seems way more interesting."

"Great. Actually, I think it will be good to have more people rather than less, especially in case the accused gets aggressive."

Lucy looked worried. "Why haven't you called the police? I mean, what if this murderer goes crazy and decides to attack one of us? I'm not sure that's safe."

"I did think about that, but that may tip the murderer off. I need to make it look like this is a casual dinner to a certain extent. A parlor game, if you will."

"Why don't you just go to the police directly?" questioned Lucy. "Wouldn't that make more sense? I'm sure this will be more entertaining, but if you know for certain, perhaps it's best to put it into the hands of the professionals."

"I would, but I'm waiting on one more thing . . . I sort of need it to prove the case."

"What's that?"

Antonia pulled out two silver candelabras from the hutch on the side wall and placed them on the table.

"You'll see! Patience, Lucy, patience. And trust me, it will be worth the wait."

Lucy gave her a skeptical look and shook her head. "Okay . . ."

* * * * *

An informal white-skirted bar had been set up at one end of the parlor and a young dark-haired waiter was standing behind, slicing lemons and limes. A wide array of alcohol was offered this evening, everything from Stolichnaya vodka to Maker's Mark to Bailey's. Several bottles of California Cabernet had been uncorked as well as a nice 2006 Italian Pinot Grigio. An open bottle of Champagne was chilling in the ice bucket on the edge of the bar.

Antonia decided not to use the overhead lights and instead chose 'mood lighting'. She illuminated several lamps on the side tables and scattered dozens of candles around the room. She wanted the parlor to appear cozier and more intimate than usual. A fire was already crackling in the fireplace and a young waiter had been assigned the task of feeding it logs for the entire evening. Ambience, Antonia felt, was the key.

Joseph had been the first to arrive after a quick jaunt home to change for dinner. He had on a crisp white shirt and a blue bowtie and his eyes were twinkling with expectation. Antonia had already plied him with a sherry, and she stood next to him awaiting the assemblage of invited guests. They were both experiencing nervous anticipation coupled with healthy doses of adrenaline. Antonia was twisting her pearl stud earring distractedly, as she always did when she was tense. Her mother had always tried to get her to stop fidgeting when she was uncomfortable, but it had been a futile endeavor. She smoothed down her suede camel skirt and flattened the edges of her black turtleneck. When she ran out of items to perfect on her own body she had to restrain herself from adjusting Joseph's tie. A passing waiter offered her a breadstick and she took it eagerly, grateful to munch on something crunchy to calm her nerves.

Lucy hadn't gone home to change, and was still wearing a blue dress with a white Peter Pan color. She had spent the past few hours by Antonia's side, assisting her in setting up the entire room and overseeing the wait-staff. She had disdainfully removed Antonia's handwritten sign that had indicated that the parlor would be closed for a private event and absconded to her office to print out a neater version, which she had accurately taped on the door in alignment with the wood paneling. She was currently placing coasters on all of the surfaces so that there would be no watermarks left on the antiques from sweating glasses.

"Who do you think will be first?" Antonia inquired.

"I think the guilty party will arrive first," said Joseph with confidence. "How could they contain themselves?"

"Touché," agreed Antonia with a sly grin. "A very tense moment for the killer."

Joseph smiled back.

Suddenly the door slid open and Ronald Meter strode into the parlor. His eyes flickered around the room quickly, his unease apparent. Once he settled on Antonia he strode towards her slowly, his gait awkward. Faint dots of perspiration were breaking out across his forehead like a teenager suffering from an acne blowout. He had worn a corduroy jacket and a plaid tie for the occasion. Once again, his pants appeared to be about three sizes too large and were constrained by the leather belt that had been working overtime since his weight loss.

"Antonia, so nice of you to have me," he said in a halting tone as if he was unsure if that was the truth.

Antonia clasped his hands. "I'm very grateful you came. Do you know Joseph Fowler?"

Ronald glanced down at Joseph quizzically before remembering his manners and smiling. "I don't believe I do, nice to meet you."

"Likewise."

"Joseph here pointed out that perhaps my invitation could have been misinterpreted . . ."

"I'll admit it was sort of a head scratcher. I'm happy to be at the dinner but it did feel like a command performance."

"I think performance is the key word," said Antonia. "And you won't be disappointed."

Ronald gave her a quizzical look, before shaking his head slowly. "I'm not quite sure what this is all about."

"You'll find out in due time."

"You're being terribly cryptic. Shall I be nervous here?" asked Ronald, his voice breaking slightly.

Antonia patted him on the shoulder. "Of course not, Ronald. What do you have to be nervous about?"

They locked eyes and Antonia deciphered the tiniest hint of fear in his. He paused but then broke into a wide grin. "Why, nothing of course."

"Wonderful. Why don't you get a drink at the bar? We have sodas and mineral water."

"Thank you."

Ronald glanced over at the bar. He appeared to be about to say something but instead set off towards it. When he was out of earshot, Joseph spoke.

"He's uneasy."

"I'll say."

"How did you lure him here?"

"Told him that we had some things to discuss before he left town and he shouldn't leave without finding them out."

"You didn't leave him much choice."

"That was the point." Antonia took a small sip from the champagne flute that she had picked up from another passing waiter. She was tempted to drink more but knew she had to be completely sober in order to pull this off.

"I must say, I thought Barbie would be first," confessed Joseph.

"I actually staggered the times. I knew if Barbie arrived early and realized that I lured her under false pretenses she would stomp out of here. So I told her to come at seven-thirty. I want to make sure everyone else is in place so that her curiosity overrides her anger."

"Very savvy."

Hector and Soyla entered the parlor. It was clear to Antonia that they were wearing their 'Sunday best'—for Hector, that was a coat and tie and for Soyla, a forest green dress. Antonia had never seen Hector in anything but his work clothes and he cleaned up very nicely. His hair was neatly brushed, parted on the side and held in place with hair gel. Soyla wore her hair down and curled at the ends. Both looked very ill at ease, and apprehensively glanced around the parlor. Antonia strode up to them.

"Hector, Soyla, thanks so much for coming."

"Yes, miss. You sure you don't want us to help you?" asked Hector. Soyla clung to his arm, her eyes darting around the room like a hunted animal.

"I'm sure. I want you both to go get a glass of wine or champagne and get comfortable. It may be a long evening for you."

"Thank you," they agreed.

"You were a wonderful help last night," said Antonia to Soyla, warmly putting her hand over Soyla's. "Thank you. I could not have done dinner service without you."

Soyla looked down with embarrassment. "Thank you for the opportunity."

"You're wife is a natural," Antonia told Hector. "She'll be running the place before I know it."

"Thank you," said Hector, beaming.

"Now go make yourselves comfortable," admonished Antonia.

They scurried to the bar. Antonia eyed them as they placed a drink order. She watched the waiter pour them each a Coca-Cola, which they clasped with paper napkins before heading to the farthest corner of the room to huddle in conversation. Ronald floated over to them. They smiled at him with relief and began a conversation. Antonia walked back to Joseph.

"It's all going beautifully, my dear."

"So far so good."

Naomi Haslett was next. She entered suspiciously, a scowl on her face and her dark bangs cut shorter than usual, slashing her forehead in half. Instead of her usual white sneakers she wore brown boots over her black pants and a black blouse on top. She marched straight towards Antonia.

"What is all this?"

"Hello, Naomi, how are you?"

"Cut it, Antonia. I want to know what this so-called party is all about? Why the mysterious invitation?"

"I thought you might enjoy a dinner at the inn."

Naomi frowned. "Don't jerk me around."

"Naomi, I realize you are under a tremendous amount of stress right now because of everything with Biddy."

"That's none of your business."

"I agree," concurred Antonia. "But Gordon's murder is my business."

Naomi's eyes shrunk into slits. "This again?"

"We're not done, Naomi. It's time for the guilty to be held accountable."

Naomi rolled her eyes. "And I suppose you have appointed yourself the person to do this?"

Antonia smiled. "It has to be me. *I'm* the innkeeper."

They stared at each other for what seemed like minutes. Finally, Naomi broke her gaze and glanced around the room. "If you're looking for who killed Gordon, how come Barbie's not here?"

"Oh, she'll be here."

Naomi scoffed. "I think I'm going to need a drink."

When Naomi firmly had a glass of vodka in her hand, she studied the other guests with disdain, while punching the lime in her drink with a stirrer. Naomi's very being emitted hostility, her mouth curled into a permanent scowl. Antonia wondered if she had always been unhappy or if something had transpired in her life to render her miserable.

Joseph raised an eyebrow at Antonia. "She's tough."

"You think?"

Sylvia and Len Powers entered the parlor excitedly, bursting with energy and enthusiasm and wearing giant smiles on their faces. Antonia went over to greet them.

"Welcome!"

"Thank you for having us, Antonia. This is such a treat. A private party! We are so excited," boomed Sylvia.

Antonia could smell her heavy perfume and noticed that she had taken particular care in her outfit. She wore a formal pale pink silk dress with a lace bodice, and had pearls draped around her throat.

"Twice in a month to dine at the inn, very special," agreed Len.

"I'm so glad you can come," said Antonia. She glanced behind them. "How about Matt?"

"Oh he apologizes, Antonia, he is so upset to miss it. But he got called into work. Apparently, there's a six alarm fire in Quogue and they needed extra hands. He'll try and make it, of course, but it isn't looking good."

Antonia was momentarily deflated. She had wanted Matt there to help with her plan. Now she would have to bluff her way through some elements of her theory. Oh well, she told herself. Nothing she could do about it.

"Let's hope he can make it. But in the meantime, why don't you two get yourselves a drink? Also, we have some hors d'oeu-vres set up on a table over there and no one is touching them, I'm about to take it personally. Please help yourself."

"Oh, honey, you don't have to say it twice! We are there in a flash."

Antonia watched as they made their way first to the buffet, seguing past the bar. It was nice to have at least some people who were more focused on the food then the chain of events that were about to transpire. She watched as they selected small plates and filled them with glazed mini-meatballs, plump figs wrapped in prosciutto, and seared pepper-crusted tuna skewers.

Suddenly, Antonia felt someone approach her from behind and wrap his arms around her. The stranger's hands darted under her armpits and as Antonia gasped, they tickled her furiously. Her heart began pounding. She shrieked and whipped around.

"Larry!"

"Got ya!" he giggled mirthfully. He bent over, erupting in laughter. "You should have seen your face! God, priceless."

Antonia's blood began to boil. She looked around the room. Her shriek had unnerved everyone and they all stood staring at her, their mouths agape.

"Sorry, everyone. Larry startled me."

"She loved it!" he boomed.

They continued to stare uneasily, before slowly returning to what they had been doing before. Len and Sylvia had their mouths full of food and were hovering over their plates, additional bites already between their fingers ready to be hoisted once they had swallowed what was in their mouths. Naomi had taken another lime from the bar and was squeezing it carefully into her drink. Ronald was sitting alone on the window seat, staring outside and anxiously twisting the signet ring he wore on his right hand. Hector and Soyla were huddled in the corner like hunted animals, talking quietly, their eyes darting around the room defensively. Lucy was giving a waiter instruction about dinner service. Joseph was tentatively watching Antonia.

"Larry, don't do that again. It's really inappropriate," warned Antonia.

"Come on, you love it."

"I *do not* love it." Blood started to rise to Antonia's pale cheeks and she realized she had to relax. No use getting worked up. She needed to save her energy for later. "Let's just drop it. Do you have everything?"

"Of course I do, hot stuff. For you, anything."

"Great, thank you."

"Are you really certain you're going to get the fireworks you want? I mean, I've been in the crime biz a long time. Remember, Nicky Darrow modeled his character after me. It's not easy to solve a crime."

"We'll manage, I'm fairly sure."

"Alright. But I'm heading over to the bar. I'm just here for the booze." He gave the room one more glance. "Any hotties here?"

"Larry, really."

"Yeah, I didn't think so. But if any come, I've got dibs on sitting next to them."

He swaggered away.

Joseph rolled his scooter up to Antonia. "Odious man," said Joseph simply. "I don't like him one bit."

Antonia laughed. "I agree. He's so annoying. Not to mention juvenile."

"Let's just hope he can assist us. Aha, look who has arrived."

Barbie stood on the threshold of the door, a hostile and confounded expression on her face. Her distaste was palpable, and when she locked eyes with Antonia she immediately stormed towards her. Antonia's gaze couldn't help but be drawn to her ample bosom, which was attempting to jiggle its way out of Barbie's tight shirt.

"What the hell is this?" she demanded.

"This is a party, Barbie. Have a drink, dinner will be solved shortly. I mean served."

Barbie peered around the room, taking in each of the other guests with her eyes. "Unbelievable. You are one piece of work, Antonia."

"What do you mean?"

"Don't play that innocent game with me. You told me you found the missing will. Was that all a lie to get me here?"

"Everything will be explained, Barbie . . ."

"Oh no you don't. I can't believe I fell for it! Do you or don't you have the will?"

Antonia took a deep breath. She knew Barbie was going to be the toughest guest to convince to stay. And the most important. "Barbie, I don't have it at this moment . . ."

"I'm out of here," said Barbie.

She turned and began thundering towards the door. Antonia trotted after her.

"Please, Barbie. It will be worth your time to stay."

Barbie scoffed. "Yeah, right."

"Trust me," said Antonia with desperation.

Barbie stopped abruptly and turned around. Antonia practically walked right into her.

"Trust you? Tell me why I should trust you."

Antonia's mind raced. "Didn't you care about Gordon at all?"

"What's that got to do with it?"

"Well, tonight all of the outstanding events surrounding his death will be answered."

"I think we all know how Gordon died."

"True, true. But remember, you say you were supposed to inherit everything. What if we can prove that is true?"

"If you can prove that, tell me now."

An elderly couple entered the front door, bringing a gust of wind with them. Antonia paused to greet them and directed them towards the dining room. Connie was at her post and Antonia could tell she was eavesdropping, even though she kept her eyes averted and was pretending to write something down in the message book. The grandfather clock in the front hall ticked softly and the din from the dining room was floating down the hall.

Antonia was stalling. She had to keep Barbie there. She spoke in a hushed tone. "I can't right now, but—"

Barbie rolled her eyes. "Geez, this gets better and better. I am out of here."

Barbie put her hand on the front door knob and slowly pulled it open. Antonia pressed against it and slammed it shut.

"What the?" asked Barbie.

"You're not leaving," said Antonia sternly.

"Oh really?"

"If you leave now, you will be arrested and thrown in prison. You should stay and at least try and defend yourself."

Barbie glared at Antonia, who in turn glared back.

"You're bluffing," she said finally.

"Am I?" asked Antonia. "When you walk back into that parlor, and you will, look at every waiter in the room. Every single one of them is an undercover officer, carrying a concealed weapon. If you leave now, they'll just come and arrest you. So why not listen to what I have to say, have a wonderful dinner, and give yourself a chance to explain your side of the story."

Barbie hesitated. It was all Antonia needed. She turned and began walking back towards the parlor.

"Let's go," she commanded.

Barbie followed.

Antonia glanced at the expectant faces when she entered the parlor. She was met with a full range of expressions ranging from worried to angry to excited.

"Ladies and gentlemen, dinner is served."

32

The guests were just settling into their chairs when an attractive young woman in her early twenties appeared on the threshold of door. She wore a diaphanous dress that didn't leave much to the imagination. She scanned the crowd indifferently, her eyes dancing from one person to the next without any sense of recognition or emotion. Antonia immediately rushed over to her and began whispering something. The girl nodded in concurrence, before following Antonia to the table.

"I'm not sure if you all know Jennifer, but she will be dining with us tonight," announced Antonia.

"She sits next to me," said Larry, rising and pulling out the empty chair next to him. "Hi, I'm Larry."

Lucy gave Antonia a quizzical look, but she just smiled in return. There were sure to be surprises tonight. Even Joseph didn't know everything. There were some murmured hellos to Jennifer, but mostly curious looks as she slid into a seat between Larry and Antonia. Larry immediately began bending her ear, explaining that he was a hot shot reporter for *The East Hampton Star* and that Nick Darrow was a personal fan who had followed him around for a week to understand the ins and outs of the newspaper industry.

Close up, Jennifer was less pretty than she had appeared at a distance. Her long thin hair was very blonde, but overly processed, which rendered the ends brittle and uneven, as if they died on her shoulders and dissolved into a mass of split ends. She had blue eyes and clear skin but her face was slightly puckered as if she had just eaten something sour, and her dainty features were all slightly smashed together in the center of her face. She overcompensated for her small eyes by applying ample makeup in bright blues and pinks, which cheapened her slightly. But she was thin, had youth on her side, and sizeable cleavage.

"Hey, I know you," said Naomi, who had carefully watched Jennifer's progression into the room. She was across the table, unfolding her napkin onto her lap.

Jennifer turned from Larry and gave her a wan smile. "Nice to see you."

Naomi appeared to be about to say something but then stopped herself. Her eyes remained on Jennifer's face and she squinted slightly, before looking down. Antonia and Joseph exchanged glances.

A waiter came and began pouring the water, followed by another waiter who was offering white or red wine. Antonia watched as Barbie studied each waiter suspiciously, her eyes tracing their dinner jackets for any bulging weapons.

"Well, this is just so nice," prattled Sylvia. "I am so happy to be here tonight. Len and I were thrilled to receive an invitation. What is your connection to Antonia?"

She had addressed Hector, who was seated to her right. His look was pained.

"I work here at the inn," he replied.

"Oh, how wonderful! And what is it you do?"

"I'm the gardener."

"I love flowers!" and with that, Sylvia was off on a tangent listing her favorite blooms, describing her beloved rose bushes, and asking questions to Hector which she did not pause to wait for the responses to. Antonia congratulated herself on the seating arrangement. Sylvia would do all the talking, which she adored, and Hector wouldn't have to say a word, which she was certain was preferable to him. Ronald also couldn't resist conversing about horticulture, so he chimed in on the conversation, which appeared to momentarily relax him.

The waiters returned with trays that they rested on the nearby stands. After removing the silver lids, they carefully placed bowls in front of each diner.

"What's this?" asked Naomi with disdain.

She was staring at the small portion of fricassee of mushrooms and chives in front of her.

"It's butternut squash soup," replied Antonia.

"Where's the soup?" sniffed Naomi.

"It's here, Madam," said a waiter. He poured a fragrant stream of creamy butternut squash puree on top of the mushrooms out of a small silver pitcher.

"How wonderful!" said Sylvia, clapping her hands together.

"Hmm, I smell truffle oil," said Ronald.

"Fancy stuff," commented Len, who was sitting next to Antonia.

"I hope you like it."

"Can't wait to dig in."

The servers had placed two baskets of bread on the table and Lucy took one basket and began circling it clockwise. Joseph took the other basket and circled it as well. Guests selected from pretzel, olive and sourdough rolls. There were dishes of butter dappled with sea salt spread out around the table, which the diners also passed to each other. Soon everyone was busy chewing their bread or slurping up their soup and a temporary hush fell across the table.

Guests began sneaking looks at each other across the table, with some intentionally sending others nasty glances. At one point, Antonia saw Ronald glaring at Barbie, who gave him a defiant look in return. Later, Barbie was seen shooting Naomi a disdainful look. Soyla kept her head down, staring into her soup bowl. Larry continued to monopolize Jennifer with anecdotes about his career, and to Antonia's eye, she didn't appear to mind. She listened attentively as she ate her soup, her face unexpressive. She was a hard one to read, Antonia thought. She had a poker face. It had probably served her well.

Joseph began a languid conversation with Barbie about the full moon. He had purposely chosen a neutral topic to coax her out of her fury. Antonia watched as Barbie's body language relaxed, and she became less defensive. Joseph moved on to astrology and it was as if he had hit the conversation jackpot because suddenly Barbie came alive and began chattering away. Joseph gave Antonia a wink from across the table.

Sylvia was winning the award for group cheerleader. She moaned with pleasure with every bite she took and kept prompting Len to confirm her belief that the food was "out of this world." They both were working their way through the bread baskets at a furious pace.

Lucy snuck peeks at Antonia and raised her eyebrows as if wondering when the accusations would begin. She was experiencing the same impatient anticipation that Antonia and Joseph were feeling. But everything would happen in due time.

"May I?" a waiter asked Barbie, motioning the wine bottle in his hand to her glass.

"Yes, thanks," she said, before returning to Joseph and continuing to lay out why she was a "true Scorpio."

Antonia had made certain to tell the waiters to continuously fill the wine glasses and make sure the diners were fully lubricated. Ronald, Hector and Soyla were not drinking, but every one else was imbibing. It was ticking along as planned.

The second course was an option of New York Strip steak with fried buttermilk onion rings and creamed spinach or sunchoke risotto with bordelaise sauce and black truffles. Most guests opted for the former, with the exception of Jennifer and Lucy.

"I've chosen a wonderful California Cabernet to accompany these dishes, so everyone please have a taste," said Antonia.

Everyone obediently brought their glasses to their lips and took a sip.

Dinner service continued, with the guests warming up a bit more due to alcohol consumption and their lessening fear that something bad was about to happen. It was all warm and snug in the room, with the fire raging and the candles flickering. A perfect autumn evening in East Hampton. Antonia had purposely chosen a particularly rich menu in order to make the guests sleepy and off their guard. Then she would strike.

When the dinner plates were cleared, the waiters brought dessert. Each guest was given a hefty portion of sticky toffee pudding with a rich caramel sauce, accompanied by dulce de leche ice cream. In addition, silver trays with pyramids of petit fours and homemade almond madeleines were placed in the center for guests to select from.

"Antonia, you have outdone yourself!" said Sylvia, raising her glass. "Cheers to a wonderful hostess!"

Everyone raised their glass in Antonia's honor. She took the moment to run her gaze across every face in the room. Eleven sets of eyes stared back at her, and at least one of those eyes had planned murder. She knew it for certain now. She was in the presence of a killer. It was time to begin.

"Thank you all so much for coming. I am so happy to assemble this particular group tonight. It may seem very arbitrary, but there is a reason you are all here."

"Aw, we thought it was because you liked us," joked Len.

"I do like you, Len, and I'm glad you came. But I'm afraid there is a more serious reason that I have assembled this particular group."

Antonia stood up. All of the heads swung in her direction.

She began to walk around the table slowly, before pausing behind Joseph.

"We are here tonight because I have solved the murders of Gordon Haslett and Biddy Robertson. Not all of you are going home tonight. Justice will be rendered."

There was a collective gasp.

Then, in a dramatic bold gesture, two waiters shut the parlor doors with a bang and stood in front of them, folding their arms. They looked like soldiers guarding a crypt. No one could escape.

33

"What are you talking about?" asked Sylvia. Her mouth was full of sticky toffee pudding but she couldn't resist blurting out her question.

"Antonia, I'm not sure I follow. Why are *we* here?" asked Len. "And if this is murder, what about the police?"

"If you will all bear with me, everything will be explained in due time."

"This is absurd," snorted Naomi.

"Yeah, just tell us," shouted out Barbie. "Why do we have to listen to this fairy tale?"

All at once, the guests started shouting and talking loudly. The crowd was excited and angry. Antonia brought her fingers to her lips and whistled. Everyone froze. Joseph spoke.

"Now, now, let's all calm down. We can eat these wonderful desserts and listen to what Antonia has to say. We at least owe her that after this delicious meal," said Joseph.

"But this is ridiculous!" snapped Barbie. "Antonia is no detective, so why should we listen to her lies?"

"You have no reason not to," said Joseph sternly. "And if you believe that she will tell you lies and fairy tales, then what do you have to worry about? Just sit down and enjoy the show. All of you."

The guests murmured their agreement. This was it. Antonia had to start. She was nervous, but she had no choice. It was time to bring justice to the dead. She cleared her throat, and put her hands on the back of her chair.

"I'll start at the beginning. A year and a half ago I was living in California and my life was, well, not going anywhere. Then my friend Genevieve told me about this beautiful inn located in East Hampton, New York. It was a historic inn that was over a hundred and fifty years old. It was beloved in the town. But in recent years, it had become a little run down . . ."

"Hey, not true," interjected Barbie. "This place was fine."

"There will be time for rebuttals after I speak. Please refrain from commenting until I am finished," Antonia admonished.

Barbie was not pleased. Lucy shot her a hostile look. "Antonia's just being honest and calling a spade a spade."

"Shut up, Lucy," said Barbie. "No one wants your opinion."

"You shut up."

"Ladies, may I continue?" asked Antonia. "As you know, I purchased the inn. And things were off to a wonderful start. I was sad to hear about the death of the previous owner Gordon Haslett, but I had been told he wasn't the fittest man and had battled some health issues, so I thought nothing of his death in his early fifties. It was a sad footnote. But then last week things began to change . . ."

"Oh, I see why we're here, sweetie," said Sylvia in what she thought was a whisper but was more like a stage whisper. "It's because we told her the place was cursed."

"Shhhhhh!" commanded Lucy. She was sitting up stick straight, giving her complete attention to Antonia, like a nerdy teacher's pet trying to incur points.

"Sorry," said Sylvia meekly. She took several petit fours off the tray and put them on her plate, tucking into a cream puff.

"It's true, you and Len were the ones to alert me to the history of the inn," said Antonia. "Then I began my journey to investigate what really happened. And I came across some wildly disturbing revelations. Gordon Haslett did not die of a heart attack. He died from a bee sting. But this was no accidental death. How many bees are out there, braving a frigid December day in Long Island? No, this was a perfectly executed plan. This was a murder, contrived by a cunning killer who had meticulously planned and organized for years. A killer who knew Gordon was allergic to bees, and knew it would bring on sudden death. And this killer is in this room."

Again, the guests gasped. They looked at one another suspiciously. Antonia allowed the words to sink in. Then she continued.

"Biddy Robertson's murder will be solved tonight as well."

"Didn't Naomi kill her?" asked Barbie.

"Hey, watch it," said Naomi.

"But it's true. Naomi's been arrested for it," said Barbie.

"I was questioned, not arrested. Big difference, moron," sneered Naomi.

"Whatever. Antonia, I think you can just stop right now. The killer has been found," said Barbie, pointing at Naomi.

Naomi appeared ready to jump across the table and throttle her.

"Let me run this show, Barbie," said Antonia. "All will be revealed."

Barbie frowned and took a sip of her coffee.

"Len and Sylvia Powers," Antonia said, walking over and standing behind their chairs. They both glanced up, their mouths full of custard cream.

"Yes?" Len asked. But it came out more like "yef."

"You were amongst my first guests at the inn, and I have been so grateful how appreciative you've been."

"Thank you," said Sylvia.

Antonia hesitated. "You were also the first people to tell me just over a week ago about the history of the inn. I think, and I quote, you said, 'The story about the Windmill Inn is that the owners die under suspicious circumstances.' Isn't that right, Len?"

"Yes," he said, his wary eyes trained on her.

"Yes, it is. At first you were both reluctant to tell me about the inn's history of deceased innkeepers, but then it all came spilling out. The curse, the ghost story, whatever it was. You had your son Matt with you. He was, conveniently, the first responder to the scene of Gordon Haslett's death, was he not?"

"Yes, Matty is an EMT," said Sylvia, explaining to the

group. "He was supposed to be here tonight, but he had a fire to put out. Literally. He's a good boy."

"He is. A dutiful son, wouldn't you say?" asked Antonia.

Before Sylvia could answer Len interrupted. "What is that supposed to mean? I'm not sure I'm following here . . ."

"I'm just saying that Matt adores you and would do anything for you."

"What son wouldn't?" asked Len.

"I agree. Now Len and Sylvia, I'm thinking back to that dinner a week ago. You were so complimentary, and I continue to be so gratified by your support."

"Thank you," said Sylvia.

"I think you said that you had stopped coming to the Windmill Inn when Gordon Haslett ran it because the food was terrible."

"Dog food," concurred Len.

"Hey . . ." interjected Barbie.

"You'll have your turn," murmured Joseph, temporarily placating her.

"The interesting thing is that you said that you had stopped coming to the inn. But Matt corrected you. He said, and I quote, 'You didn't really have a choice.' I thought nothing of it at the time . . ."

"What are you suggesting?" asked Len.

Antonia walked around the table so that she was now facing them. She put her arms on the backs of the chairs in front of her and leaned across the table towards Len and Sylvia.

"Len, isn't it true that in addition to being the Head of

Security at the Dune Club, you are also a building inspector in the village of East Hampton?"

"I am . . ."

"I didn't remember that until the other day when I received my certificate from the town, signed by you. And thank you, you gave me a clear pass."

"You're welcome."

"But you didn't give Gordon a clear pass, did you? You cited him for many expensive violations, and in return he banned you from the restaurant? Barbie told me at tea that Gordon had fought with the building inspector, aka you, and that you hated him."

Everyone turned and gave Len an accusatory look. Len, in turn, appeared incredulous. "Are you suggesting that I *murdered* Gordon Haslett because I was *banned* from his crap restaurant? That's absurd."

"He didn't just ban you. He made a huge stink. Brought it to the town board and demanded an investigation. He said that you had given him a bad citation because he wouldn't comp your meals."

"And he lost that claim."

"But it dragged on for months. You were surrounded by a cloud of suspicion. The town started to crack down on allowing inspectors to frequent the restaurants they were auditing. Other inspectors were angry."

Len reddened. "There was absolutely no impropriety . . ."

"But with Gordon dead, it all ended. The case was thrown out. He was gone and all that fuss was brushed under the table."

"*I* suffered from all this . . ."

"So you had motive."

The room was so quiet that you could hear a pin drop. Everyone waited on the edge of their seats. Antonia paused. "And your son was the first responder, so he could have covered up . . ."

Len bolted up and threw down his napkin. "This is garbage. Sylvia, let's go!"

Sylvia was mid-forkful, dishing raspberry parfait into her mouth. For a split second, she debated putting it down, but instead crammed it into her mouth, before making a feeble effort to stand.

"Stop, stop. Len, Sylvia, please sit down."

"I will not."

Antonia went over to them, and put her hands on their shoulders. "Don't worry, Len. No one really thinks you killed Gordon. You may have had motive, but you are not a killer. Everyone knows that."

Len twisted his tie and glanced around the room. The eyes that met his were tentative, and some looked away.

"Then why did you make me out to be one?" he asked accusatorily.

"I'm just proving a point. I'm sorry."

"I'm outraged!" blustered Len.

"I understand, but it was necessary. Everything will be explained. Please stay."

"Yes, please do sit down, Len. Coffee and tea are on their way," offered Joseph. "And, if you do, I think you will be amused."

Len glanced around like a defeated man. "Amused? You mean all of this is a joke?"

Sylvia smacked her hand on the table. The china teacups rattled. "I know what this is! It's one of those murder mystery games where people all get dressed up and come in character. How fun! Len, this is a game. Don't worry. This will be a hoot! Let's see who did it."

Everyone began talking at once.

Len turned to Antonia. "I didn't even know Biddy Robertson."

"I know," said Antonia.

"I did nothing wrong. The place *was* a dump. I had no choice but to cite him. Not to mention, when I saw how disgusting the kitchen was, we stopped coming."

"I understand. I saw that kitchen, too. It was gross."

The waiters came around and began filling coffee and teacups, setting out pitchers of milk and cream. The conversations were now swirling in a collective buzz, adding a low hum to the room. There was excitement in the air, but also a sense of relief. But then just as suddenly a voice louder than the others spoke.

"This isn't just a game."

34

It was Ronald Meter who spoke. Every head swung in his direction. He sat gloomily in his chair, twiddling his teaspoon between his thumb and index finger. He was agitated, and sweating profusely, with his cheeks appearing more sunken than usual. His heavy lids looked up and he studied the crowd in front of him.

"I mean, right, Antonia? You've got something on all of us. So you may as well start with me now. I want to get it over with."

Antonia met his stare. She hadn't wanted to select Ronald Meter for the next moment in the spotlight, but now she had no choice. Her hand was forced. She couldn't let this happen again. It was to her benefit to be in control and running the inquisition.

"Yes, Ronald. I do have something on you."

Ronald nodded slowly. "Alright. Then go. What do you

want to say about me? Because I think in terms of Gordon, I'm a pretty easy target. In fact, let me lay it out for you."

He took a sip of water. Antonia noticed his hand was shaking.

"I have the motive. We all know that. Gordon fired me, and a prosecutor will say because of that, I wanted him dead. I had opportunity. I know the in's and out's of this inn like the back of my hand, having worked here for years. It wouldn't be hard for me to hide in a discreet place to find the right moment to kill Gordon. I had the weapon. I keep a beehive in my backyard. So I clearly killed Gordon with a bee because I wanted revenge."

"Is that a confession?" asked Sylvia, her voice shrill.

Ronald gave her a contemptuous look. Before he could answer Antonia interrupted.

"What about Biddy?"

"Biddy? Well, I knew her from the L.V.I.S. and I had actually briefly worked at the inn under her. Of course, I was not the biggest fan. She was a small-minded woman who had no clue as to how to run an inn."

"So you killed her for that?" asked Larry. "Come on," he said to Antonia. "Get real. This guy didn't do it."

"But he's saying he did . . ." said Jennifer.

"Plus, he's a thief and a liar," said Barbie. "He stole from the inn . . ."

"Correction, *you* stole from the inn," boomed Ronald.

Barbie shot up. "I did not, and I don't have to take this. I'm out of here."

"Barbie!" said Antonia. She motioned towards the two waiters at the door. Barbie saw them, hesitated, and sat back down.

"You may search my house, but never did I take anything from the inn," said Ronald. "As God is my witness, and you know I would never betray him or the promises I made to my pastor."

Antonia's eyebrows shot up. "Is that true?"

Ronald's expression momentarily wavered. "Yes."

Antonia nodded. "I've heard a few people call on God to be their witness lately."

"What's that supposed to mean?" asked Ronald.

"Well, take Hector and Soyla," said Antonia.

She motioned to the startled couple, whose eyes widened as soon as their names were mentioned.

"But we'll get to them in a second," said Antonia. "I want to finish with you. You have motive, it's true. And access. But what really got me is that you act suspiciously, as if you are hiding something. It was that skittish behavior that made me think it was murder, but now I know it was something else."

Ronald sat very still, waiting.

"What is it?" asked Sylvia.

"The other day I was driving by a house and I saw Ronald and a man talking in the driveway. I recognized the man but couldn't place him. And then I remembered. He's a vendor who is producing a local brew of honey beer. He's been by the restaurant several times to try and entice us into selling it. And Ronald is his partner. That's what the hives are for, are they not?"

Ronald looked stricken. He didn't speak.

"Why would he hide that?" asked Larry. "That's not a crime."

"It's not. Prohibition ended decades ago. But Ronald Meter has a pastor who preaches sobriety. In his mind, producing alcohol is a sin, am I right?"

Ronald slumped in his chair. Sweat was seeping out of his every pore. He spoke in a defeated tone, so quietly that everyone had to strain to hear him.

"Yes."

Antonia nodded. "I thought so. Ronald Meter may have a guilty conscience, but it's because he's betraying his faith, not because he is a murderer."

Antonia couldn't be sure, but she thought she detected a bit of relief in Ronald's posture at letting the secret go.

"Speaking of God," Antonia said, "I'd like to return to Hector and Soyla."

Again the couple recoiled at the sound of their names.

"They both said they were God-fearing people who would never commit murder. They are a couple who have come here to East Hampton to make a better life for their family. They work hard, long hours, and do whatever they can to provide for their kids. And then next thing you know, Soyla has been accused of theft and Gordon has fired her. That's a huge shame. A blemish. They have given this man nothing but blood, sweat and tears and this is how he repays them, by not trusting them. This makes them angry. Very angry."

Hector and Soyla shrunk so far back into their chairs that

they had virtually disappeared. If they could have pressed a button to make themselves evaporate, Antonia was certain they would have. She was about to continue but was interrupted.

"Let's get to the point here, Bingham. I'm guessing that everyone here had a motive for killing Gordon," said Larry, before turning to Jennifer. "Except maybe you, but I don't know. Maybe you're just eye candy."

Jennifer giggled.

"Yes, who are you?" asked Lucy. She looked at Antonia. "Why is she here?"

"No doubt some other woman who Gordon betrayed," said Len.

"It's true, when I look around this room I see so many people who hated Gordon," said Barbie.

Everyone began talking at once about how loathsome Gordon was and how reviled he had been. Suddenly Naomi stood up and shouted.

"STOP! Will you please stop! You are talking about my baby brother here!"

The group fell silent. They all stared at Naomi. Larry sing-songed under his breath.

"Awk-ward . . ."

Naomi gave him a withering look. "Antonia, you're right. Everyone here could have killed my brother. But we all know it was Barbie."

Barbie began to stand up and protest but Joseph put out his arm to stop her. "Just wait," he whispered. "Your turn will come."

"Yes, Barbie," said Naomi. "Shocker, right? She was his girl-friend. She's had me in court for months insisting she should inherit part of the inn, that Gordon left it to her. She killed him to get it. Everyone knows she was running around on him, shacking up with some other guy. She's a slut."

Barbie's face was purple and she was shaking with rage. Antonia glanced at her.

"Barbie did have motive."

"Everyone had motive!" screamed Barbie.

"True. But not everyone had access to the corporate credit card," Antonia said firmly.

All heads turns towards Barbie.

"What's that supposed to mean?" asked Barbie.

"During my research, I scanned through past credit state-ments. There was a corporate card that you had access to. Upon further research, I learned that the card was used to buy honey at a farm stand the same day a blonde buxom woman attempted to buy bees, and when denied, purloined a bee from the hive."

"You're kidding, right?"

"A worker at the farm stand saw the woman lurking around the hives. The beekeeper later confirmed that he thought a bee had been taken."

"This is absurd!" protested Barbie.

"Is it?" asked Antonia. "You have told me a number of times that you *deserved* the inn. That you put up with Gordon for years, so you were *due* a share of the inn. You were cheating on Gordon, and yet although you were not legally married, you didn't leave him. Why? Because you felt that you earned something after years of helping him make the inn somewhat successful. If you left him, you'd get nothing. So you had to stay. But maybe you got tired of waiting?"

Everyone stared at Barbie. She gazed evenly at Antonia. "This is nonsense. I didn't get anything from Gordon's death other than an eviction notice."

Antonia walked over to the side of the room and removed a piece of paper from a manila envelope. She held it in her fingers and returned to the table. Everyone in the room stared at the paper.

"You were searching for his will. You claimed it existed, and gave you half of the inn."

Antonia held up the paper. There were audible gasps in the room.

Barbie shot up. "Let me see that!"

Naomi also stood. "This is absurd! I don't believe it."

Antonia pressed the paper to her chest. "All in good time."

"Stop saying that and give me the will!" yelled Barbie, lunging at Antonia.

She reached across the table and knocked over a glass of wine, which began trickling down the table towards Jennifer. Soyla immediately grabbed her napkin and began blotting it out. Other people popped up to help, and another glass was inadvertently tipped over. It was momentary chaos with the crowd talking and giving orders and tossing napkins back and forth.

The two waiters from the door walked over and stood

beside Antonia. The crowd glanced at them, and as if sensing something, quieted at once and sat back down. They returned their full attention to Antonia.

"Where did you find that, Antonia?" asked Lucy.

"In one of the old boxes."

"Are you sure it's Gordon's?"

"I'm sure this document is valid," said Antonia.

"It sounds like you got her," said Len. "Maybe you should call the police now."

"What are you talking about?" said Barbie. "This means nothing. There is no proof whatsoever."

"Sounds pretty solid to me," said Sylvia. "And did she kill Biddy too?"

"Oh my God!" said Barbie, rolling her eyes. "Next you'll say I killed John F. Kennedy."

Antonia stared at her. "Biddy Robertson had put aside a box of items that were dropped off at the L.V.I.S. thrift shop. She recognized some of the items from the inn, ashtrays and such. Those items were later confirmed by Soyla to have been stolen. Perhaps you stole them?"

"Antonia, don't quit your day job," advised Barbie. "I'm not a murderer or a thief."

"What about the fact that gold earrings went missing by a guest at the inn? Soyla was fired for that. Then a week later you wear earrings to a meeting with the exact description."

"I got them for my birthday!"

"From who?"

Barbie glanced around the room, nervously. "A friend."

"Your boyfriend?" asked Antonia. "Which one, Gordon or the other guy?"

Barbie gulped. "I'm not sure. There was a box on my desk and it just said 'I love you'. I didn't want to ask Gordon if he gave them to me, because he would find out I was cheating. And I felt weird asking my new guy . . ."

"So you just wore them."

"Yes."

"And you didn't steal them?"

"No!" said Barbie emphatically. "They were a gift. And I didn't steal any of those things from the inn and drop them off at the thrift shop. Why the hell would I do that? I never go into places like that. I had no contact with Biddy."

"Biddy probably had something on her," said Naomi.

"Really, Naomi? Like what?" asked Barbie.

"That you're a thief and a hussy."

"Enough with that," said Barbie. "And enough about me. What about Naomi? I mean, really. She's the one the police think did it!"

"They're wrong," protested Naomi.

Antonia walked around the table again towards Naomi. She gave her a small smile.

"You are the one who has the most evidence against her."

"I'm not even going to engage," said Naomi, shaking her head.

"You inherited the inn when Gordon died. You had a long-term fight with Biddy, going back years where she accused you of taking the inn out from under her then leaving a dead animal on her porch."

"I'm tired of hearing about it."

"And you were lurking around the backyard of the inn the other day. I couldn't figure out what you were doing there. The next day Hector found this."

Antonia reached atop the bookshelf next to her and pulled down Biddy's monogrammed box. She placed it in front of Naomi.

"I've never seen that in my life," Naomi stated with such derision, it was as if the hotly-contested dead raccoon had reappeared in place of the box.

The other guests leaned in. "Whose is it?" asked Larry.

"It was Biddy's. And Hector found it in the backyard."

"Maybe Hector killed her and put it there," said Naomi, folding her arms.

Hector looked like he wanted to throw up.

"I thought of that, but he didn't put it there. The killer did."

"Oh me? Right," said Naomi.

"Actually, Naomi. I know why you were in the backyard."

"This will be good," she sniffed.

"Why *was* she there?" asked Lucy.

Antonia locked eyes with Naomi. "The other day when I was out there I stumbled on a rock. Didn't think much of it. But then something occurred to me and I went back out to check it out. The rock is a tombstone inscribed with the name "Teddy." That was your dog, was it not, Naomi? Your dog is buried there."

Naomi stared at Antonia and her face softened slightly. "Yes," she said flatly.

"It was something you said that gave me pause. You said 'there will always be part of my heart buried' at the inn."

"He was a wonderful dog," whispered Naomi, her eyes filling with tears.

Antonia was amazed to see Naomi become so emotional. It was as if she had cracked her shell. A tear slid down her cheek and Soyla handed her a cocktail napkin.

"So does that mean she didn't put the box there?" asked Len. "I'm confused."

"Me too," said Sylvia. She motioned for the waiter to refill her wine glass.

"I don't follow at all," said Ronald. "What's the point of all this? Do we know who the killer is?"

Once again the crowd began to argue, debating who the actual murderer was. Antonia watched them, all animated and riled up. She walked over and stood behind Jennifer's chair.

"There's one more thing," Antonia said loudly.

Everyone stopped and turned towards her with expectant faces. Some were shiny with perspiration; others had contented looks after the large dinner and large doses of alcohol, some nervous. But all ready for answers.

Antonia smiled. "I think we are forgetting Gordon's other girlfriend. She is the killer. She killed both Gordon Haslett and Biddy Robertson. And she thought she'd get away with it."

The crowd froze, their eyes moving from down from Antonia's face to Jennifer's. They all squinted, attempting to place her, desperately searching their brain to remember her. Jennifer sat solemnly, unmoving. She didn't even glance back at Antonia to confront her. A slow grin slid across her face.

35

"Who is she?" asked Naomi. "I've never seen her before."

Barbie shook her head. "I don't get it. She doesn't look familiar. What's her last name?"

"Jennifer, say it ain't so," said Larry, punching her playfully. "If you're a murderer, you're a sexy one."

Jennifer didn't speak. A sly smile was pursed on her lips.

"Why did she do it?" asked Naomi.

"Yeah, Jennifer, tell us why?" asked Len.

Antonia broke the silence.

"I'm not talking about Jennifer," she said firmly. "I'm talking about Lucy."

Every head in the room whipped towards Lucy in astonishment.

Lucy sat up straighter. "Me?"

Antonia slowly walked around the entire table until she was behind Lucy, the latter of whom now had to twist her neck to glance up at Antonia.

"Yes, you, Lucy. I can't believe it was in front of me all along and it took me so long to see it. It's actually amazing that no one ever considered it, but then Lucy, you have an amazing ability to hover in the background."

"This is ridiculous," she said, before adding in a whisper, "is this part of the plan? To accuse me to shake out the real killer?"

"No, Lucy. It's not part of any plan. In fact, *you* are the master of plans. Not me."

"This is crazy. I should go," said Lucy, standing up.

Antonia firmly pressed her down back into her seat. "You're not going anywhere."

"Lucy did it . . . it makes sense," said Ronald.

Barbie nodded. "Of course."

Even Naomi added reluctantly. "It does. . . ."

Lucy folded her arms. "This is insane. You have no proof."

"That's where you're wrong, my friend."

"Let's hear the evidence," said Joseph.

Antonia cleared her throat.

"When I first bought the inn a year and a half ago, it was Lucy Corning who assisted me in getting up and running. She had been the bookkeeper for the past several years, and she knew everything about the inn. She was so informative, that I promoted her from bookkeeper to manager. I thought here was a diligent employee. Savvy, too, which was amazing because she had really only worked at the inn for three years. But what I didn't realize is that Lucy had actually been around the inn before that. When she was dating Gordon Haslett."

Lucy shook her head firmly. "That is just not true . . ."

"It's not? Because if you look at the pictures of the Millennium party that Gordon held at the inn, there you are in the background of every picture with Gordon, dressed as a bunny."

Antonia dumped out the contents of the envelope that Larry had brought in front of Lucy. There were snapshots of her and Gordon, and in most, like in Joan Masterson's pictures, she had her mask on. But in the last one she held her bunny head in her arms and stared up adoringly at Gordon.

Lucy refused to look at the pictures so Antonia scooped them up and began passing them around the table.

"I don't quite understand why you hung in there with Gordon after he dumped you, but there is a certain tenacity in you. As Barbie said last week, 'I'm just wondering when that woman will disappear forever. She's like a tick that keeps hanging on.'"

"Ouch!" said Larry.

Lucy gave him a hostile look. "Fine. We dated briefly years ago, but so what?"

"I don't think it was brief. We had guests staying with us last week, the Winslows, who told me they were so happy to see Gordon's girlfriend still working at the inn. Barbie had been there that morning, so I assumed they thought she was still working here. But now I know they meant you. And they said that it had always been your dream to own an inn."

"There's the motive," said Ronald.

"That means nothing," said Lucy. "None of this proves anything."

"I think you wanted the inn for yourself. You told me you

got into vintage clothes when you worked at a vintage store, and which I realized was the L.V.I.S. thrift shop. You worked there when Biddy was a volunteer. She told you the inn was going into foreclosure. You alerted Gordon and he swooped in to buy it. You thought you would have your dream come true. But Gordon was volatile, unpredictable. He threw you over for Barbie. But you got your revenge. You began siphoning off money from the accounts. You were the bookkeeper; you had access. You put the money into Naomi's accounts or Barbie's accounts to make it look like they were stealing, but *you* are the thief. You also stole from people at the inn. The Winslows said you were so helpful in assisting them in finding something, but that's because you took it! And then you planted those earrings on Barbie's desk, pretending it was from her lover, hoping that she would tell Gordon and he would know she was cheating and throw her out."

"That's not true."

"But it backfired with Gordon. He still stuck by Barbie for some reason. And that enraged you, so you planned his murder. But somehow Gordon knew it. And it is his words from the dead that seized me."

Antonia paused. Everyone was on the edge of their seats.

"I found his note. It said, *I swear to God that B is trying to kill me.* That B. For the longest time I thought it was Ronald Meter, who he called the beast. Or Barbie. Or Biddy. But it was you. That bookkeeper. You were trying to kill him."

"You said yourself the girl at the farm stand saw Barbie!"

Antonia nodded. "You were the one who led me to the

farm stand. I was such a dupe. I thought I had discovered it on my own, but you planted the card statements on me, under a false pretense, knowing I would see that purchase. And yes, the girl at the farm stand said that it was a busty blonde woman."

"See? Not me."

"Did you forget you told me you went as Jayne Mansfield one Halloween? That meant you had the padded bra and the big shoes and blonde wig. I believe you wore that outfit to the farmstand when you stole the bee."

Lucy looked deflated. "I couldn't have. . . ."

"Matt, the first responder, told me he had spoken to Gordon's girlfriend at the scene. I thought it was Barbie, but of course it was you. Matt was at that Millennium party years ago, so of course he could identify you. And by the way, I'm pretty sure you called in that alarm in Quogue just to ensure that he wasn't here tonight."

"Please," she sniffed.

"Just like I'm sure you were the anonymous caller who alerted the police to the carbon monoxide alarm that you threw in Naomi's neighbor's garbage. By the way, Jennifer is here because she is Naomi's neighbor. Her brother Ty dated my friend Genevieve. Albeit briefly."

"So, that's why you're here," said Larry turning to Jennifer. "I'm so happy you're not going to jail so we can go out again."

"I saw a red Mini outside my house one night. I think that's when they put the alarm in my trash," said Jennifer.

"Lucy drives a red Mini!" said Hector, suddenly animated. It was the first time he participated in the conversation.

"So did she kill Biddy too?" asked Len.

"Yes," said Antonia. "Recently, Biddy told her neighbor Sharon that she was going to lunch with an old colleague and it would be interesting. She meant Lucy. I think they had originally schemed together on something to get back at Gordon but then Lucy changed her mind. Maybe Biddy knew she killed him and was blackmailing her."

"This is absurd," said Lucy under her breath.

"Is it? You've spent the last week playing tricks on me, locking me in closets, taking away step ladders, planting booby traps, all so I would think the inn was haunted and take off. And then you could buy the inn from me at a cheap price. The bank mistakenly called me with your mortgage application— the one you tried to hide from me the other day. I thought it was a wrong number, but something made me call the banker back to make sure. You want the inn and you will do anything to get it. Embezzlement, blackmail, murder."

"But why *this* inn? There are so many," asked Barbie. "It's not *that* special. No offense."

Antonia took a deep breath and let it out slowly. She turned and stared at Lucy, who gazed at her defiantly.

"Because this is her home."

"Okay, sure. But it was my home too, and I moved on," said Barbie.

"You don't understand. Before Lucy was adopted by her stepfather Walter Corning she was Lucy McKenna. Her parents Greg and Charmaine owned the inn. Sylvia, didn't you recognize her? Lucy was your student."

Sylvia squinted until a slow smile appeared. "Oh, heavens! Now I remember. So long ago."

"This is the place where Lucy's mother killed her father, shattering her idyllic life. And Lucy wanted it back. Wanted to erase the past, and reclaim it as her future."

There was complete silence. Everyone kept shifting their gaze between Lucy and Antonia, who were staring at each other intently. Slowly Lucy slid back her chair and stood up. She began clapping. Softly at first, but then louder and louder. Tears were running down her face but she was smiling like a madwoman. Her hands began banging against each other so hard it was as if her blood vessels would burst.

"Bravo! Bravo!" she said.

She continued to furiously clap. It became alarming, but she wouldn't stop, or maybe she simply couldn't. Her body started convulsing, and she began some sort of fit, her hands flailing, her eyes rolling. The other diners rushed to her.

"Call an ambulance!" Antonia yelled to the waiters.

"Call the police," said Joseph firmly.

"Aren't those waiters cops?" asked Barbie.

Antonia shook her head. "They're just waiters. I had to tell some little white lies as means to an end."

Barbie scowled. "You tricked me."

"But you got a happy ending, didn't you?"

Hector dialed 911.

36

EARLY MORNING MONDAY

The inn was quiet. The diners had left. The paramedics had left. The police had left. Lucy had left with them. The black night had spread out against the sky, licking its way into the edges of the horizon. There was no breeze, just a stillness in the brisk air. A comforting hush curled inside the corners of the inn. The dying fire was still doing its best to hang on, its burning embers emitting low flickers. Antonia and Joseph sat in the two armchairs in front of it, glasses of cognac in hand. They were weary and emotionally spent, but had that charge of adrenaline coursing through their veins that would not allow them to sleep.

"Well done, my dear," congratulated Joseph.

"Thank you. Couldn't have done it without you."

"That's not true, but I was happy to help."

"I'm so glad it's all over. I mean, it was surreal, but now things can return to normal. I don't need any more drama."

"I hear you. By the way, what was that skirmish with Barbie when she was on her way out?"

"Oh," said Antonia, pausing to take a sip. "She wanted the will. I had to break it to her that I was bluffing. It was a blank sheet of paper. She kind of freaked out when I told her."

Joseph chuckled. "I can imagine."

"I do think there was a will, actually. I think Lucy destroyed it. Why wouldn't she? Barbie was her rival."

"Maybe she'll confess."

"I doubt it," said Antonia. "I doubt she'll confess to any of it. At the end of the day, it's all circumstantial evidence. Not sure it's enough to convict."

"The police will dig up more. You did your part, now you can retire."

"Agreed. I will need a new manager, though."

"You'll find one."

"I'm sure."

Suddenly the front door burst open and Genevieve came rushing in. She was wearing a long black cape, and her hair was done up in a dramatic bun.

"I came as soon as I heard. Is everything okay?" she asked anxiously.

"Everything is fine now. Don't worry."

She walked over to Antonia, bent over her and gave her a big hug. "I was so worried. Listen, I'm on a date but I can stay if you need me . . ."

"I'm fine."

Genevieve cocked an eyebrow. "Are you sure?"

"Completely."

"Okay, well, I see you're in good hands. And this guy is hot! He's waiting in the car. He's in a band! They're playing next week at the Talkhouse. Promise you'll come with me."

"Done."

Genevieve went over to the bar and poured herself a shot of vodka, which she downed quickly. "Thanks for the lubricant," she said with a wink. "And now that I know you haven't been murdered or anything, I'm gonna head out."

"She's quite alive," remarked Joseph.

"Take good care of her!" she said to Joseph, flinging the cape over her shoulder and heading for the door. "She's my bestie!"

"I will."

Genevieve left leaving a trail of perfume in her wake. Antonia and Joseph smiled at each other.

"She's a little silly, but she's a good friend," said Antonia.

"I'm grateful to her, knowing she's the reason you're here in East Hampton."

Conversation paused while they sat and simply enjoyed the peace that silence brought. Finally, Joseph spoke.

"Well, my dear, I should call it a night. As much as I'd love to stay, time for me to get home."

Antonia looked at Joseph pensively. "You know, I was thinking something."

"Oh? What's that?"

"Upstairs we have these three little connecting rooms, designed like a mini-apartment. There's a bedroom, a sitting room, and a small, really tiny room that could fit a desk. No one has booked it yet, not even for a night. And I was just thinking, maybe you wanted to move into the inn? I mean, instead of moving to New York City. I would love it if you were here. You've become such a wonderful friend, I don't want you to leave town. And there's the elevator so you wouldn't have to use the stairs. Would you think about it?"

Tears welled in Joseph's eyes. He took out his handkerchief and wiped them away.

"Are you okay? Oh, please don't cry!" She leaned over and patted him on the back.

"That's the nicest offer anyone has given me. I'd love to move in here. Of course, I will pay you market rate. . . ."

"Joseph . . ."

"I insist. But yes, I would love to, my dear. I was dreading a move into one of those God awful buildings my son wants to stuff me into."

"Then this is the perfect solution," beamed Antonia.

Joseph clasped her hands and they sat there for a minute, enjoying the moment. Antonia was thrilled she had found someone like Joseph. He was a wonderful friend, and a surrogate father figure. She didn't know why she didn't think of asking him to move in sooner. It had all just dawned on her. Maybe she had been too distracted by murder, but now she was glad to be done with that.

"That's it for me," Antonia said. She was glad to be officially out of the crime solving business. "Now I won't ever have to deal with any more ghost stories or murders."

"Pity," Joseph said. He sat back in his chair and evaluated her.

Antonia raised an eyebrow.

"It's just that we made such a great team."

THE END

ALSO BY CARRIE DOYLE (WRITING AS CARRIE KARASYOV):

The Infidelity Pact

WRITING AS CARRIE KARASYOV WITH JILL KARGMAN:

The Right Address

Wolves in Chic Clothing

Bittersweet Sixteen

Summer Intern

Jet Set

ABOUT THE AUTHOR

Carrie Doyle is a best-selling author who lives in New York City and East Hampton with her husband and two sons.

Visit Carrie's author site at **WWW.CARRIEKARASYOV.COM** or learn more about Carrie (and Antonia and the Hamptons!) on **WWW.DUNEMEREBOOKS.COM**.

CHECK OUT THESE OTHER THRILLING HAMPTONS MURDER MYSTERY BOOKS:

Coming Soon!

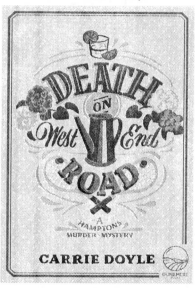

Please visit

WWW.DUNEMEREBOOKS.COM

to order your next great read or just to
hang out with Antonia and hear what
she says about the Hamptons!

DUNEMERE
Books